No Going Back

DS Pete Gayle crime thrillers, Book 4

By

Jack Slater

No Going Back by Jack Slater

No Going Back by Jack Slater

DS Pete Gayle's family problems are still unresolved and about to get worse when circumstances thrust him into another murder case. A woman's body has been found in woods outside the city. The frenzied killing and the way she was left, naked and posed, send conflicting signals. Was she known to her attacker or is a potential serial killer operating in South Devon? With no clues at the scene, Pete and his team must first identify the victim before they can even start looking for a suspect.

Also by Jack Slater

Nowhere to Run (DS Peter Gayle crime thrillers, Book 1)

No Place to Hide (DS Peter Gayle crime thrillers, Book 2)

No Way Home (DS Peter Gayle crime thrillers, Book 3)

Nowhere to Run – The Dark Side

The Venus Flaw

Copyright © 2018 by Jack Slater.

Jack Slater asserts the moral right to be identified as the author of this work.

This novel is entirely a work of fiction. The names, characters and incidents portrayed in it are the work of the author's imagination. Any resemblance to actual persons, living or dead, events or localities is entirely coincidental.

All rights reserved under International and Pan-American Copyright Conventions. By payment of the required fees, you have been granted the non-exclusive, non-transferable right to access and read the text of this e-book on-screen. No part of this text may be reproduced, transmitted, downloaded, decompiled, reverse engineered, or stored in or introduced into any information storage and retrieval system, in any form or by any means, whether electronic or mechanical, now known or hereinafter invented, without the express written permission of the author.

No Going Back by Jack Slater

No Going Back by Jack Slater

This book is dedicated to the boys – and girls – in blue: the men and women of not just the Devon & Cornwall Police, but of police forces throughout the United Kingdom, who work so tirelessly to ensure that we remain safe in our beds and on our streets, in spite of burgeoning bureaucracy, red-tape and a CPS that often seems resolutely counter-productive.

CHAPTER ONE

The night sky was heavy with dense, pregnant clouds as Detective Sergeant Peter Gayle drove along the narrow lane that led up into the hills from the small village of Budlake, north of Exeter. Despite himself, the countryside he was driving through reminded him of the brief conversation that had sent him out here. What he'd said to his wife, Louise, was true: he was surprised that more people in the station had not reacted badly to former DC Frank Benton's conviction and the four-and-a-half-year sentence he'd been given last week for stealing and selling the eggs and chicks of protected species of birds of prey. Pete and his team had proved he had been doing it for several years, dating back to well before he retired from the force.

He had yet to face the charges of police corruption which had led to Pete's investigation. That would be a matter for Headquarters to deal with.

Pete's only real regret was the devastation it had wrought on Benton's wife, Sylvia, who had clearly had no idea what he'd been up to all these years. She didn't deserve the consequences of Frank's actions, which would include the loss of his police pension and all the other benefits that went with it, as well as his prison sentence. The big house they'd bought out near Ashburton would have to go, he imagined. And they'd barely finished doing it up.

Ahead, the tall hedges to either side of the road gave way to woodland. He saw the flicker of blue lights through the trees and slowed his unmarked Ford. Splashes of blue showed at the roadsides in the beams of his headlights as he entered the woodland. It was the height of the bluebell season, despite still being April. He rounded a bend and was faced with a uniformed man standing in the middle of the narrow road, one hand raised. Beyond him, the road was blocked by several stationary vehicles. An ambulance, three police patrol cars, an expensive looking four by four that Pete was not familiar with and a black VW estate car.

The pathologist was here.

He stopped and rolled down his window, lifting his warrant card to the unfamiliar constable. 'DS Gayle.'

'Evening, sir. The scene's about forty yards in, to the left.' He raised a hand to point.

'Thanks.' Pete found a gap between the ambulance and the pathologist's car. He parked the car and stepped out. Blue and white police tape lined the edge of the road and lights had been set up around the scene amongst the trees. He could smell faint traces of wood-smoke in the air. He frowned. This was the last place to be building a fire.

Ducking under the tape, he walked up a long-established dirt path into the woods.

There was a clearing, the uneven ground packed hard and bare of vegetation for five or six yards around a rope and plank swing that was suspended from a thick branch. People were standing idly around the perimeter, dark blue uniforms marked out by the silver highlights of buttons, zips, insignia and equipment. The ambulance crew to his left as he stepped into the clearing were in green.

The pathologist, the only person there who stood out from the surrounding shadows and vegetation in his white overall, cap and mask, was crouched with his back to Pete. To either side of him, Pete could see the victim's feet, clad in high-heeled shoes, their black soles almost clean, and behind him were the extinguished traces of the fire Pete had smelled.

He stopped, pulling on a pair of gloves and accepting thin plastic shoe covers from an officer to his right and donning them before moving closer. He crouched at the fire, sniffing. There was no hint of accelerant. Someone clearly knew how to build a fire properly and had taken the time to do so. He stood up, moving slightly to one side so that he could see over the pathologist's shoulder.

'Hello, Doc. What have we got?'

'Peter. Good to see you.' Dr Tony Chambers glanced up as he withdrew his steel temperature probe and wiped it before replacing it in his bag. In front of him, the victim lay on the ground, arms and legs splayed. She was wearing a smart mid-length coat, which was laid open beneath her, and nothing else. Her hair, Pete could see under the bright lights that had been set up around her to illuminate the pathologist's work, was matted with blood, her face all but destroyed though the rest of her body appeared, at a glance, untouched except by a degree of blood spatter.

There was no blood on the ground around her.

'Female. Thirties, at a guess. Killed elsewhere, then brought here. Dead approximately eight to ten hours.'

Pete checked his watch. 'About lunchtime, then.'

'Or just after.'

'Any signs of a struggle?'

'No. Fingernails are clean. No injuries apart from those to her head.'

'So, a blitz attack. An angry outburst that got out of hand, perhaps.'

He saw the doctor's lips purse. 'Except, there are indications that she was initially incapacitated and killed a short time later.'

Pete grimaced. 'Raped?'

'To be confirmed. No obvious external signs.' Chambers turned back to what he was doing as Pete examined the scene carefully.

'Was she carried here or dragged?' he asked.

'No indications of the latter. Shoes and feet are clean.'

'Carried, then. So, a big fellow. She's what?' He assessed the body. 'Five-eight? Maybe ten stones?'

'Roughly,' Chambers agreed.

'Is the fire related?' Pete asked next.

'Yes. It's how she was found, apparently. The first responder can tell you more, but I gather he put the fire out with a CO_2 extinguisher.'

Pete glanced up and around. There were a lot of bodies attending, but there didn't seem to be much activity going on. 'Who is the first responder?'

'Here, Sarge.' A man stepped forward from Pete's left. A couple of inches shorter than Pete, he was shaven-headed and bulky, not all of it with the kit he wore, attached to his uniform. 'PC Carberry.'

'You put the fire out?'

He shrugged and glanced around at their surroundings. 'For safety, Sarge. And the CO_2 wouldn't destroy any evidence.'

Pete tipped his head. 'Who found her?'

'The chap with the Audi down there.' He nodded towards the road. 'He's sitting in the back of my car with my partner. Said he saw the light from the fire and stopped to see what was going on.'

As if the fire was set for the purpose, Pete thought. *The killer wanted her found.*

'OK. I'd best have a word in a minute then. The rest of you, let's see if we can find anything around here, shall we? The victim was clearly brought here and placed. How was she brought? We need signs of a vehicle. Footprints. Dropped cigarette butts, chewing gum or whatever. Anything and everything, before the scene gets contaminated any more than it already is. Torches and evidence bags. Someone between here and the road with a low-level torch although, if he used the path, any prints will be long gone, I expect. Let's comb the area, please.'

As the officers dispersed, Pete turned back to the pathologist and the body. He looked from one to the other and back. 'When you say she was incapacitated and killed later, what are you basing that on, Doc?'

Chambers' grey eyes met his briefly. 'If you look here...' he pointed at the body.

'I'd been trying not to.'

Chambers was pointing at the victim's groin. 'You see the blood here and here? The way it's run? It isn't spatter from the head wounds. She was shaved not long before she was killed.'

Pete let his gaze slide away from the victim's most intimate area, losing focus as his brain worked. Was this a humiliation thing, then? A personal killing, in every sense of the word? Or was it a ritualistic thing?

He refocused his gaze on Doc Chambers. 'Have you seen anything like this before?'

A slight tilt of the head. 'No. If it's a serial killer, either this is their first or they've moved into the area from somewhere else. Worth checking your database, though, perhaps.'

Pete nodded. When he got back to the station he would do exactly that. The police national database would quickly flag up any similar crimes that might have occurred anywhere else in the country. 'No way to identify her, I suppose?'

'Fingerprints. Dental records. DNA. Otherwise, it's down to you, Peter. The coat won't help. It's from a department store.'

'Right. No distinguishing marks? Tattoos, birth marks...?'

'Not that I've seen yet.'

He'd have to check the constantly updated lists of missing persons held by both police and charities, then. 'OK. Thanks, Doc.' He looked around. The surrounding darkness was intensified by the lights that were concentrated on the area he was standing in. He could see occasional flashes of torchlight from the surroundings, but little else beyond the clearing.

He stepped back towards the road, peering into the night. Took out his torch to check for any other paths in and out of the small clearing. From the road, the one he'd taken was the only option. He went slowly along it, checking both sides with his torch but, by the time he reached the roadside, he'd found nothing but more signs that Spring was upon them, new life burgeoning all around, throwing the death behind him into even more stark contrast.

Back at the road, he checked the patrol cars more carefully than before and saw the pale glow of skin in the back of one. He headed across. As he approached, the window buzzed down. A female officer was inside with a dark-haired man in his thirties, Pete guessed. He crouched at the side of the car to be on a level with its occupants.

'DS Gayle. You found the body?'

The man swallowed and nodded.

'And you are...?'

'Will Metcalfe.'

'OK, Will, tell me what happened.'

He swallowed again and coughed. 'I was on my way home from a party. A friend's place in Clyst Hydon. He's got engaged. I stayed off the booze. Most of us did, what with driving.' He closed his eyes briefly. Shook his head. 'I was coming up here and saw light flickering over there, in the woods. It looked like a fire and there were no vehicles around, so I thought I'd better stop and check it out. Call the fire brigade if necessary.' He paused, sucking in a deep breath. 'I went up there and... There she was.' He grimaced, eyes closing again. 'All that blood! She was obviously dead, so I called you guys. The operator said to wait here, so...' He spread his hands with a shrug.

'Did you see any other vehicles on the road?'

Metcalfe shook his head. 'Nothing.'

'OK. Were you first to leave the party?'

'About third or fourth, I think. Spread over a quarter of an hour or so.'

Pete nodded. 'Do you know who the others were, that left before you?'

'Yes, the first was...'

Pete held up a hand. 'Hold on.' He took out his notebook and flipped it open to a fresh page. 'Right. Carry on.'

'Yes. The first to leave were Terry and Carol Griffiths. Then Dan Shaw. And Kevin Philpot left just a couple of minutes before me with his girlfriend.' He paused, frowning. 'Sally, I think her name is.'

'Whose party was it?'

'Dom Foggarty. I've known him for years. We work together.'

'And where's that?'

'The Met.'

He would mean the Meteorological Office, as opposed to the London police, Pete knew. It was based in the outskirts of Exeter.

'Do you happen to know Mr Foggarty's number?'

'It's in my phone, in my car.'

'OK.' Pete beckoned him out with a tilt of the head and stood up, stepping back to give him room.

The black four by four was unlocked. Metcalfe reached in for his phone, which was lying in a shallow well in the central console. Swiping the screen to bring it to life, he tapped his way into the contacts list and passed it across. 'There.'

'Thanks.' Pete made a note of the number and the address that went with it, then handed back the phone. 'Are any of the others you mentioned in there?'

'Yes.' He tapped at the screen again. 'Here we go.'

Pete noted down all the information he could, then put away his notebook and pen. 'Right. Thanks for all that. I'll let you get on your way. I'll be in touch if anything else comes up.'

Back in his car, he used the hand-free system to make the first of several calls.

It took five rings before it was picked up.

'Hello?' The voice that answered was foggy with sleep.

'Hello. This is DS Gayle, Exeter CID. I gather you were at a party this evening. Can you tell me what time you left and which road you took?'

CHAPTER TWO

The car's Sat Nav told Pete he didn't need to turn around in the narrow, crowded lane. He could go straight on, re-joining the B-road back towards the city just outside Broadclyst and cutting across a large angle in the process. He headed through the National Trust forest with his headlights on full beam, as much to deter any deer or other wildlife as to see where he was going on the narrow, twisting lane. The trees thinned across the top of the hill but grew denser again as he started down the far side, crowding in on either side of the road. The route got narrower, twisting this way and that, almost as if following a game trail through the woods. He passed a side-track with a car park sign, slowing as the road got even steeper. Headlights showed from behind him in the mirror. Close together and circular, Pete recognised those of an old-fashioned Land Rover. Then he cursed as they suddenly flared brighter, the driver hitting high beam.

Pete rounded a curve and blinked in relief. But seconds later, they were back, still as bright and a lot closer.

'Damn it, what's your game?' Pete muttered. He tried tapping the brake lights, but it made no difference.

Another tight bend and the woodland dropped away on the right. A hedge replaced it, a steep field beyond. Seconds later, the Land Rover was right up behind him.

'What the hell?' Pete glanced at the mirror, already aware that the road bent sharply to the right ahead of him.

Spotlights suddenly blazed from the top of the Land Rover's cab, blinding him as its engine roared, the horn blared and it pulled out to pass him.

'Jesus!' Pete hit the brake, gripping the steering wheel tightly as the old Land Rover passed within inches of his shoulder. Then a metallic crunch jarred the wheel in his hand as the Land Rover's back end clipped his front wing, trying to force him off the road. He dropped the clutch and swung the wheel across, grabbing the handbrake to force the car into a sliding spin, leaving the Land Rover to surge on ahead.

The car bucked violently as one wheel mounted the grass verge. Vegetation scraped the underside. A tree loomed terrifyingly in the headlights, seeming to leap towards him out of nowhere. Then the other wheel hit the raised edge of the road. Pete turned further into the spin, right foot jabbing at the brake pedal and, instead of mounting the verge, the off-side wheel seemed to kick the car around further and faster, pulling the back end around with a squeal of tyres on tarmac.

An image flashed into his mind of himself stranded sideways across the narrow road, the Land Rover coming fast and furious, straight towards him, headlights filling his vision, no time to escape. Fear surged through him like a jolt of electricity. He pulled the steering wheel as far round as he could, holding onto the handbrake for all he was worth, his body rigid as he pressed down on the clutch. The car passed the perpendicular across the road and he hit the accelerator and let go of the clutch, handbrake still fully on. The near-side front wheel came down off the narrow verge, the engine roaring, then stalling.

Silence.

The car sat at a sharp angle across the road, almost filling it. The Land Rover had gone from sight around a bend further down the steep slope. The fear of those lights bearing inexorably down on him – or of another vehicle coming from the other direction, hitting the other side of the car and driving it through the hedge behind him and down that vertiginous slope – made him grab for the key and snatch it around, foot down on the clutch again. The engine turned over but refused to fire.

'Come on.'

He released the key and tried again. Again, the engine refused to start.

'Jesus! Will you do as you're told?'

He turned the key once more. This time, it fired. He put the car into first gear and, despite the urgency of fear, eased it forward. The front wheel hit the verge and slipped on the wet vegetation. He tried to force it onward, but it refused. After a moment's trying, he gave up and let it roll back, forcing the steering wheel around the other way to head back the way he'd come. The back of the car scraped the other verge and he braked again, fighting the vehicle into the direction he wanted, all the time aware of the possibility of the Land Rover coming back at him.

Finally, with more back and forth shunting, he got the car pointed in the direction he wanted and started back the way he'd come. Immediately, he noticed there was something off with the steering. He had to hold it steady all the time, the wheel fighting with him, determined to veer off to one side. Breathing hard, heart still hammering in his chest, he pushed on towards the top of the hill, where the woods opened out.

Rain started to spatter the windscreen, growing quickly heavier until he had to switch the wipers on.

'That's all I bloody need,' he muttered as the wipers thumped from side to side.

For his own safety, he was going to have to get out of the car.

Reaching the open, moor-like top of the hill, the short, fern-dotted grass level with the tarmac on either side, he pulled over, took out his mobile phone and dialled.

*

'Damn.'

Pete slumped back in the driver's seat.

Although he hadn't had a chance to see the registration plate on the Land Rover, his dash-cam had caught it. He had just run it through the DVLA, but it had come back to a sixteen-year-old Nissan Primera, registered to an owner in Weston-Super-Mare. One eye on his door mirror, he picked up his mobile phone and got a connection to the station in the Somerset estuary town.

'Police. How can I help?'

'This is DS Gayle, Devon and Cornwall police. I've just run a check on a registration plate that's come back to a blue Nissan registered to an address in Weston. The problem being, it was attached to a Land Rover down here in Exeter. Could you send a car past the address and check it out?'

'What's the address?'

Pete read it out from his notebook.

'OK. I'll call you back.'

'Thanks.' Pete ended the call, staring at the windscreen and the rain that was beading it, running down the glass in little rivulets as it pelted ever more heavily on the roof of the car.

Whether the Nissan's plates had been stolen or not, the attack on him had clearly been premeditated. The Land Rover driver had lain in wait, no doubt in a carpark off to the side of the road, watching for his victim to pass. The question was, had the attack been targeted specifically at Pete or completely random?

He was in an unmarked car, so it wasn't an attack on the police in general.

He picked up his smartphone again and accessed the database, searching for similar attacks on drivers reported in the area.

Nothing.

Was he the first victim or had the others simply not reported it, on the assumption that nothing could, or would, be done about it?

It was dark. There were hundreds, if not thousands of those old Landys in the county, never mind the country, and he had only got the registration due to the fact he had the dash-cam fitted. They were standard issue for police, but still relatively uncommon among the civilian population.

He was staring blankly at the little screen when he blinked suddenly and looked up with a jolt. Concentrating on what he was doing, he had completely forgotten to keep a look out for the Land Rover's return. He gave a sigh of relief when he saw no headlights in the door mirror.

He glanced back at the phone in his hand. The only other thing he could do for now was put a call out on the vehicle. He set the phone aside, took out his radio and keyed the mike. 'All units, all units. Be on the lookout for a dark green Land Rover with false registration plates.' He read out the plate details. 'Driver wanted for reckless driving and endangerment. Last seen heading south from Ashclyst Forest five minutes ago.'

*

He picked up the mug at his elbow and drank the last of the strong, sugar-rich coffee, letting his eyes close briefly as he swallowed. He'd been in the squad room for a little over half an hour, having been lent a replacement car from the workshop at Middlemoor HQ on the edge of the city and come back to the station to do what he could before heading home. He was alone in the big room, just one of the four sets of ceiling lights on so that the illumination was soft and relaxing.

He'd searched the missing persons databases but didn't really have enough data yet to reach any firm conclusions as to the victim's identity and the Avon and Somerset force had got back to him before he'd even got back to HQ with his damaged car, to say that the Nissan in Weston-super-Mare was still wearing its number plates. So those on the Land Rover that had run him off the road had been falsies. He remembered vaguely that one of the other detectives here in the station had dealt with a case of false number plate production down on the Marsh Barton industrial estate last year, but they'd closed the place down so was there another or had the driver made his own? Until they found the vehicle, there was no way of knowing and he'd heard nothing back on it yet.

He clicked into the police national database to search for crimes with a similar MO to that displayed by tonight's victim. He was still keying in the details when the phone on his desk rang, loud in the night-time silence of the big office.

He snatched it up. 'DS Gayle.'

'Peter. It's Tony.' Pete recognised the pathologist's voice. 'I've started the autopsy on our victim. You were right. On closer examination, there was a sexual assault. A very unpleasant one.'

'In what way?'

There had been no external signs of whatever had been done to her.

'A foreign object was used, rather than rape as such. A handle, perhaps. I can't be more specific, I'm afraid. But the significant thing is what was used as a lubricant.'

Pete frowned but said nothing.

'A particularly coarse variety of Swarfega-type cleanser.'

Pete sucked air, grimacing. The sandy scouring grains in that kind of cleaner were hardly what he'd have called a lubricant. 'Ouch. And she was alive at the time, I take it?'

'Indeed.'

'Christ. He really wanted to hurt her, didn't he?'

'It would appear to have been a particularly vicious attack.'

'Have you found anything else of any use?' Pete asked, not wanting to dwell on the victim's suffering.

'No more than I had at the scene, I'm afraid. There's a tiny smear of white gloss paint on her coat, fairly fresh, but she could have picked that up anywhere, of course. I've taken finger-nail scrapings, fingerprints, dental X-rays and DNA. There were some brown carpet fibres in her hair which I've also sampled. They've all gone to forensics, along with the DNA swabs from the buttons, belt and outside of her coat. As you suggested, I made sure they swabbed the likely points of contact if she'd been carried in it. So, we await the results.'

'Yeah. I haven't found any likely candidates on the missing persons lists, so I was just about to start searching for similar MO's from elsewhere. I'm surprised you've carried on and done the PM at this time of night.'

He glanced at the time in the bottom corner of his computer screen. It was just gone one a.m.

'If I hadn't, I'd have only been thinking about it so I thought I might as well. At least now I can go home and sleep without it being on my mind.'

'Point taken.' Pete knew exactly what he meant. Which was why he was sitting here now, instead of at home with Louise. 'All right, I'll talk to you later, Doc. Goodnight.'

'Night, Peter. I'll let you know the rest of the findings in the morning.'

Pete put the phone down with the vicious and deliberate cruelty of the attack still playing on his mind. It didn't tell him whether the perpetrator knew his victim but it did emphasise the need to catch the guy and lock him up so he couldn't do anything similar to anyone else.

He took a deep breath and focused on the computer in front of him, unsure if the extra details the pathologist had provided would help his search or not.

It didn't take him long to discover that there were no similar cases outstanding in the UK. Murder was a lot less common than many people imagined, he knew, with less than six hundred a year, according to the latest published figures. And most of those were either drug-related or domestic. There were aspects of this one that pointed in either direction. It could be highly personal or it could be the work of a potential serial killer. He could draw no conclusions yet. All he knew for sure was he had a victim who needed justice and a killer he needed to get off the streets before they could strike again.

He pulled up a whiteboard and started writing up the details of the case, ready for morning.

*

Sometime later, he let himself into the house as quietly as he could. The place was in darkness. He went through to the kitchen, closing the door behind him before switching on the light.

The write-on wipe-off pad that he and Louise used for quick notes to each other when their shifts didn't gel lay on the table. He stepped across to see what she had written.

Gone to bed. 11.43.

Unusually, they were both supposed to be working day shifts this week. She would need to be up by seven to be in the hospital for eight. Pete wiped the board clean and was putting it away when his mobile phone buzzed in his pocket.

He took it out and glanced at the number before touching the green icon. 'Hello?'

'Service and Maintenance at Middlemoor. DS Gayle?'

'That's right. What can I do for you?'

'Just wanted to let you know, we're going to need to keep your car for a few days. The steering rack's completely had it and the wheel rim's bent, plus there's damage to both front wings, the under-sill and the bumper.'

'So, how long do you reckon?'

The mechanic sucked his teeth. 'I should think, with the spraying and such... Give us a week. You've got a replacement, haven't you?'

'Yes.'

'OK, then. We'll let you know when it's ready.'

'Right. Thanks.' Pete ended the call and headed for bed. No matter what the time was now, he needed to make an early start in the morning.

At the top of the stairs, he could not resist looking in on Annie. As always, her door was not quite closed. He pushed on it gently and it swung just far enough that he could see into her room. She was sleeping on her side, facing the door, one small hand tucked under her head. Her little face looked so innocent in repose it brought a lump to his throat.

Two more years and she would be a teen, on the way to being a woman. But for now, the child in front of him was still pure and so incredibly wonderful in every way imaginable, he couldn't even think that anything bad might ever happen to her, despite the close call she'd had just a couple of weeks before.

As he watched her, two little vertical lines appeared, creasing the skin between her eyebrows – something she'd inherited from her mother. Was she dreaming? Or was her sleep being troubled by something more tangible? His breath caught in his throat as he waited for more outward signs from her, but none came. After a while, he eased her door shut and moved quietly away.

CHAPTER THREE

Pete was not the first of his team into the squad room in the morning. Two of his detective constables, Jane Bennett and Dick Feeney, were already at their desks when he walked in. The light from the windows behind her glowed in Jane's short red hair when she looked up.

'Morning. Anybody would think you were keen,' she said, nodding to the whiteboard he'd set up at the end of their desks.

'Yeah, how come we've got this one?' Dick asked from the desk next to Pete's then quickly raised his hands, palms out. 'Not that I'm complaining. Just curious, seeing as Simple Simon was on call last night.'

Pete looked at the older man with his grey suit that matched his hair and even his smoker's skin. 'Apparently, he'd already picked up a case.'

Dick grunted. 'What, that break-in on Smith Street?' His voice was louder than it needed to be with Pete now standing just two feet away. 'I'd have thought any real copper would have set that aside and taken a murder as a priority case.'

Pete had seen when he stepped into the big open-plan room that Simon Phillips was not yet at his desk but three of his team were in place and working. 'I didn't see the need to make an issue out of it,' he said as he sat down. 'Better to just get it solved.'

'Yeah, that way, we get the Brownie points and DS Phillips looks like the plonker he is,' Jane agreed from across the desks. 'So, do you think the Landy belonged to the perp or what?'

Pete tilted his head. She'd clearly been paying attention to what he'd put up on the case board. 'It's possible. Or it might just be a coincidence. A nutter with a grudge against coppers. Or maybe just a nutter, seeing as I was in an unmarked car.'

The brief silence that greeted his comment told Pete that both Jane and Dick were aware of the possibility that he'd left unsaid.

'So, how are we going to find him?' Jane asked. 'I've already started putting feelers out to the body-shops around the city, but an old heap like that - chances are the driver will do the work himself and not bring it out on the road again until it's done.'

'Which, in itself, might get noticed,' Dick pointed out. 'We could put it out there as if it's linked to the murder. "Any short wheel-base Land Rover pickup that's suffered damage consistent with a vehicle impact within the last twenty-four hours is being sought for elimination," kind of thing.'

Pete was nodding. 'Any sign of His Lordship yet?'

'No, but he doesn't exactly announce his presence,' Jane said. 'He could have been in his office since before we got here. How bad was the damage?' she asked, changing the subject.

'Bad enough. They'll be keeping it for a week or so.'

The door opened to his right, Ben Myers holding it for Jill Evans.

'Morning, boss.'

The two PCs hung their coats on the rack inside the door and approached their desks. Pete's team was almost complete.

The spiky-haired Myers sat down at the far side of Dick Feeney and looked across at the whiteboard. 'Blimey, no rest for the wicked. Another one already?'

'All the better for your continuing education, son,' Dick told him.

'Thanks, Gramps.'

The door to the squad room opened again. Pete heard several sets of footsteps entering then Dave Miles' voice behind him. 'Hello, hello, hello. I see a white-board out again. Morning, peeps. What have we got?'

He took his seat between Jane and Jill. The tall, dark and handsome contingent of the team, he was dressed this morning in a dark blue shirt with black trousers, tie and waistcoat.

'Christ, who's died?' asked Dick.

'We can't all wear the same thing every day,' Dave told him. 'Life would get boring if we did.'

'That's not for a funeral,' Ben said. 'He's going undercover. The Mafia's moving in to take over the drugs trade in the city.'

Jill clapped her hands together. 'I knew he reminded me of somebody!'

'Well, it ain't Robert De Niro,' Jane said from Dave's other side.

'Ooh, you know how to hurt a man, Red,' Dave retorted. 'I pity that husband of yours. So, what's going on, boss?'

'Now we're all here, I'll go through it,' Pete said. 'Our victim was found at ten thirty-seven last night by a passing motorist whose alibi is yet to be followed up on due to the time of the discovery. She was battered to death with what appears to have been a hammer, presumably after she was sexually assaulted. Then she was redressed in just her coat, taken out to Ashclyst Forest and posed with the coat spread open and a fire close to her feet so that she'd be found easily.'

'Very considerate of the perp,' Jill observed. 'Make sure she's found before any kids happen across her up there.'

Pete tipped his head, acknowledging the point.

'Any DNA?' Dave asked.

'Yes. We'll probably get results tomorrow.'

'And we don't yet know who the victim is,' Jill observed.

'No, but she was well-nourished, well-groomed, mid-thirties or thereabouts. I can't see it taking long for her to be missed.'

'I take it, as there isn't one on the board, we can't put a photo out to the media?'

'Like I said, the killer used a hammer,' Pete said. 'And he wasn't careful about it.'

Dave grimaced. 'So, a media request using height, weight and hair colour?'

'If nothing comes in today, yes. Meantime, I'd best see if the DCI's in, bring him up to date and set him on the press liaison folks about the Land Rover.'

Dave shook his head. 'I thought you'd have learned by now. You shouldn't pick fights with people who are bigger than you.'

*

Pete had barely regained his seat after speaking to the station chief when a deep, dry voice called from behind him. 'Peter.'

He turned around to see DI Colin Underhill standing in his office doorway at the far end of the squad room, his large frame clad in his usual woollen tweeds, looking like a farmer on market day. All he needed was a flat cap covering his steel-grey hair to complete the impression.

As their eyes met, Underhill stepped back, pushing the door wider to indicate he wanted Pete to join him.

Pete stood up. 'Back again shortly,' he said to his team.

Closing the DI's door behind him, he nodded. 'Guv.'

'I see you've got the case board out again. Sit down.' Underhill motioned to the seat opposite him.

Pete pulled it out and relaxed into it. 'A body was found up in Ashclyst Forest. Apparently, Simon had already caught another job when the call came in.'

'And Brian Chadwick was on duty.'

Chadwick was one of the sergeants who took charge of the control room. And an old friend of Frank Benton's.

Pete said nothing.

Colin let the silence hang for a beat. 'OK. Do you need anything?'

'Not at this stage,' Pete said. 'We're waiting on SOCO. We're also waiting for a missing persons report to come in to help identify the victim. She was pretty badly beat up, so we won't be able to put a photo out. We've got interviews to arrange in the meantime, to firm up the timeline and confirm the alibi of the chap that reported finding her. See if we can find any more witnesses. I've asked the DCI to arrange for signage to go up there on the road asking for witnesses to contact us.'

'And what's this about your car being in the workshop at Middlemoor?'

Pete frowned. He wondered sometimes how the DI heard about stuff like that. It was like he had some kind of sixth sense. That or spies in every corner of the force and of the city. But he knew better than to ask. 'A bloke in an old Landy tried to run me off the road on the way back from the scene. False plates on it. Don't know if there's a connection. We're not assuming anything but we're working as if there is for now. The DCI's putting out a request for information on any damaged Land Rovers through the press office.'

Colin nodded slowly and met Pete's gaze. 'And what about Tommy?'

'We don't know any more than we did yesterday. Louise is taking it personally. She's putting an ad in the papers today, asking for anyone with a problem with how the place is run to get in touch. She's already spoken to Letterman's colleagues at the hospital. They won't come out and say anything against him, but they haven't got anything to say *for* him either, which says a lot in itself.'

Colin tipped his head. 'You can't take silence to court, though. And getting him booted out without being able to replace him would effectively shut the place, which wouldn't go down well with a lot of people.'

'That's what I've said to Louise, but you know what she can be like when she gets the bit between her teeth. And, after the last twelve months, I'm not going to block her.'

It was almost a year now since their son, Tommy, had disappeared without warning one evening from outside the swimming pool in the city. DS Simon Phillips had been given the task of finding him or what had happened to him – a task in which he'd failed completely while Louise sank into a deep clinical depression that she'd only recently managed to climb out of.

Tommy had not resurfaced until late October, when he was implicated in the abduction of a young girl from outside her school and the deaths of at least two others. He had remained on the run until less than two weeks ago, when he had finally been tracked down and arrested in Plymouth and brought back to Archways secure children's home, here in Exeter, where Brian Letterman was one of the two qualified psychiatric staff.

Unable to handle Tommy, Letterman had decided that the only thing to do was to get him transferred elsewhere. Which meant out of not only the city, but the county. A move that Louise was determined to fight by any means necessary.

'I saw Tommy again yesterday,' Colin said. 'Had to explain why he hadn't had any visitors for a few days. He took some convincing, but I got there in the end, I think. I'm not sure what the consequences of that'll be for Brian Letterman.' He grinned briefly.

Colin had taken over the case that Tommy was involved in – the case against the man he had been with at the time of Rosie Whitlock's abduction, former teacher Malcolm Burton – and was in the process of trying to persuade Tommy to testify against him.

There were only three weeks remaining until the start of Burton's trial.

'Did you get anywhere with Tommy?' Pete asked.

Colin pursed his lips. 'Maybe. I think the situation with Letterman helped. But, if Burton's defence team call Letterman to the stand, that'll bugger things up.'

'Not if you call Louise to refute him. She'll testify to a grudge between Letterman and Tommy. So could I, for that matter. And probably some of the staff at Archways.'

Colin nodded slowly, thick fingers entwining on his stomach as he leaned back in his chair. 'I just need one more thing to bring to the table, to make sure of Tommy, and I think we'll be there.'

'The girl in Archways. The one he's friendly with. Comes from Crediton. Suicide risk.' He shook his head, struggling to recall her name. 'Use her as a character reference for him. It would give her a reason to stay with us, Tommy a reason to keep trying to help her and us another nail in Letterman's coffin.'

Colin was frowning, confused. 'What girl's this?'

'One of the inmates at Archways. Pupils, residents, whatever you want to call them. She's there because she's a suicide risk. Wouldn't have anything to do with anyone, apparently, until Tommy got through to her. They've got really pally. She's one of the excuses Letterman's using to try to get Tommy transferred out of there. Saying Tommy's unstable and if he was to turn on her, it would be the final straw for her.' He snapped his fingers and pointed at Colin triumphantly. 'Tabitha Grey. That's her name.'

Colin nodded. 'OK. I'll look into it. And if you need extra manpower or anything, let me know.'

'Right, Guv.' He stood up. 'I'd best get back. Don't want to leave the kids unattended too long. No telling what they'll get up to.'

'You're all right. I can see them from here.'

Pete turned to look through the half-glass door. He grunted. It was true: Colin could see the whole squad room from his desk. 'The all-knowing eye, eh?'

'Except for Tabitha Grey. Send Simon along on your way back.'

Pete looked round sharply, one hand on the door handle. Colin held his gaze but gave nothing away.

'OK,' Pete said finally.

*

'I spoke to Bill on the front desk while you were gone,' Dave told him as he sat down. 'Gave him the victim's details and told him we're expecting someone matching them to be reported missing.'

'Good.'

'So, what's that about?' Dave nodded towards the DI's office, over Pete's shoulder.

Pete shrugged. 'Just keeping up to date.'

Dave gave him a look. 'Not you, boss. Simple Simon.'

'I was just asked to send him along,' Pete said. 'I know no more than that.'

'Well, I do,' Dave said, looking past Pete towards Colin's office. 'I can't lip-read at this distance and I can't hear what's being said, but I don't need either to tell you the guvnor's giving him a good reaming. You can tell from the way he's standing.'

'I don't expect it'll make any difference,' Pete said, flipping open his notebook. He picked up his phone and dialled.

It was answered after several rings by a female voice. 'Hello?'

'Hello. Mrs Foggarty?'

'That's right.' She sounded almost reluctant to speak. Hung-over, maybe, Pete guessed.

'Hello. This is Detective Sergeant Gayle with Exeter police. I'm investigating an incident in Ashclyst Forest. I understand you were having a party last night.'

'Yes.'

'Would you mind confirming for me who was there and when they left?'

'Um... Yes, all right. There was Sally Taylor and Kevin Philpot. Carol and Terry Griffiths. Julie Worrall. Marie Batchelor. Dan Shaw. Will Metcalfe.'

Pete wrote quickly as she reeled off another half-dozen names. 'I see. And what time did things start to wind down?'

'The first people left around ten-fifteen, I suppose. There was a steady trickle from then, but the hard core didn't go until getting on for two. Why? Was there a complaint or something?'

Definitely a hang-over, Pete thought. 'No, nothing like that. As I said, I'm investigating an incident in the forest last night. I'm looking for possible witnesses, that's all.'

'Oh, I see. Well... Will would have gone that way. Carol and Terry might have. Marie could, though I doubt it. She likes to stick to main roads as much as possible. It was a job to get her to come here at all. She's not the most confident of drivers. Um... That's probably about it, that I can think of. All the rest live in different directions.'

'Right. Thanks for that...'

'How did you know about our party?' she blurted, cutting him off.

Ah, she's waking up at last, Pete thought. 'The person who reported the incident told me about it. Would you be able to confirm what times Mr Metcalfe, Mr and Mrs Griffiths and Miss Batchelor left the party?'

'Um... Carol and Terry were first to leave. They've got a little girl. They had to get back for the baby-sitter. So, around ten-fifteen. Will left a little while after them. Fifteen, twenty minutes, maybe. And Marie not until around midnight.'

Which confirmed what Metcalfe had told him last night.

'Could you tell me how I could reach them?'

'Yes, of course. Just a moment.' He heard her put the phone down. Moments later, she was back. 'Here we are.' She read out work and home numbers for the Griffiths, Marie Batchelor and Will Metcalfe.

Pete didn't need Metcalfe's, of course, but he didn't tell her that. He clicked his pen shut purely by habit and laid it across his notebook. 'OK. Thanks for all that, Mrs Foggarty.' He ended the call and looked up. Jane was grimacing while Dave was having difficulty suppressing a grin. 'What?'

'Don't know where the guvnor's gone off to, but it looks like before he went, he bored DS Phillips a brand-new arse hole,' Dave said.

'Slowly and painfully, with the toe of his size twelve,' Jane added. 'He won't be sitting comfortably for a while, that's for sure.'

Pete hadn't wanted it to happen – it wouldn't help the smooth running of the squad room – but he could understand why Colin had felt the need. He couldn't have people picking and choosing their cases or their caseloads. But this way could lead to bitterness and in-fighting. Pete had no problem standing up for himself with the likes of Simon Phillips, but this was a small office. They needed to work as a team.

Still, Colin knew what he was doing.

Pete picked up his phone again and dialled. He hadn't yet finished when it rang in his hand. He jabbed at the line button that had lit up. 'Gayle.'

'Pete. It's Bill, downstairs. I've got a call come in that might be of interest to you. Shall I put it through?'

'Yes. Thanks, Bill.'

There was a click on the line.

'DS Gayle, CID. How can I help?'

'Uh… Hello. This is… CID?' The woman sounded hesitant and confused.

'Yes. Our duty sergeant passed your call across to me. Can you tell me what the problem is?'

'Yes, of course. Our office manager, Claire Muir, is missing. She didn't turn up for work this morning so, when we couldn't get her on the phone, a colleague and I went to check on her. She's not at home, either. And nor is her car. It's not like her. Not at all. She's never… I've known her for five years and she's never done anything like this. Something's wrong, detective. I'm sure of it.'

CHAPTER FOUR

'You got a possible victim?' Dick asked as Pete put down the phone.

'Maybe. Jill, you're with me.' He stood up and slipped on his jacket. 'Jane, Dave and Dick, you can follow up on the names I got from our party hostess. See what they've got to say for themselves. Follow up on any leads they can give you. Ben, you can hold the fort. See what you can find on the computer about any of our potential witnesses and check on the possible victim – full background, known associates, home address, phone numbers and records, bank details, digital footprint, the works. And everyone remember; we're also looking for any links to anyone who owns an old Land Rover. Let's go.'

He led the way out of the squad room with the small, dark-haired and elfin-featured PC hurrying to keep up, heels clicking on the stairs behind him. They met Colin Underhill at the bottom, on his way back up. As usual, his expression gave nothing away.

'Guv.'

'You got something?'

'A potential victim. We're going to check it out.'

'Keep me informed.'

'Will do.' Pete strode on along the bland corridor towards the custody suite and the back entrance that led out to the car park behind the square concrete and glass 1960's built station.

The car fleet workshop at the Devon and Cornwall police HQ at Middlemoor had lent him a black Ford Focus. Pushing through the back door and out into the thin sunshine, he was thrown for an instant by the absence of his silver Mondeo. Then he spotted the smaller black car and stepped quickly forward.

He used the remote to unlock the car and indicate to Jill which one it was. They climbed in.

Jill pulled her seatbelt across and clipped it in. 'So, what do we know about her?'

'She's an office manager at Portside Insurance. Apparently well thought of. When she didn't turn up for work and they couldn't get hold of her on the phone, two of her staff took the trouble to go and check on her.'

Jill grimaced, nodding. 'And gave up time and commissions in the process.'

Pete stopped the car at the station entrance, checking for traffic. 'Exactly.' He pulled out, turning right towards the city centre.

Portside Insurance was located in a modern brick building off the ring road, down by the river. With the rush-hour over it took just minutes to get there. Pete parked in front of the small tower block and they went inside. A wide reception desk took up the whole of the left side of the large foyer, but there was only one person behind it. She looked up as they entered, noting Jill's uniform.

'How can I help?'

She was probably in her mid- to late-twenties, Pete guessed, her face soft and round, eyes large and serious.

He lifted his warrant card. 'I'm DS Gayle. This is PC Evans. We're here to see a Christine Thackeray.'

'Ah. Right. One moment.' She picked up a phone and dialled. 'Hello. It's reception. I've got a couple of police officers here to see you.' She paused. 'OK.' She put the phone down and looked up at Pete and Jill. 'She's on her way.'

'Thanks.'

Something about her manner told Pete that she was either worried or hiding something. 'Do you know Claire Muir?'

She frowned then met his gaze. 'There's a Miss Muir who works with Miss Thackeray. Is that her?'

Pete nodded. 'But you don't know her, as such?'

'She's pleasant enough. Says hello and such. But apart from that, no. Why? Has something happened to her?'

'Nothing I'm aware of. Why do you ask?'

'Well, the fact that you're asking about her. And you're here to see Miss Thackeray.'

'OK.'

A door opened at the back and a woman in a navy skirt suit stepped through. She had blonde hair tied back in a short ponytail. She hurried towards them. 'DS Gayle? I'm Christine Thackeray.'

Pete stepped forward and shook her hand. 'Pete Gayle. This is PC Evans. Have you got somewhere we can talk?'

'Yes, of course. This way.' She led them back through the door she had entered through into a corridor lined on one side with glass-walled offices, most of them unoccupied. She stepped into the first and offered them the two seats on one side of the desk while she took the one on the other side.

Pete settled himself, leaving his notebook in his pocket for now. 'So, what can you tell us about Claire Muir?'

'Well, as I said on the phone, she's completely reliable. I mean, I imagine that's part of the reason she got the supervisor's job, as well as her people skills. She's a good friend, a good motivator.'

'It sounds like that's a recent thing. The job.'

'A little under a year. Nathan left – Nathan Hollingsworth – and Claire went for the promotion and got it.' She shrugged as if it had been a foregone conclusion.

'Were there any other candidates?'

'Of course, but nobody minded when Claire got the job. We were all pleased for her. As I said, she's a great manager.'

'OK.' Pete nodded to Jill to make a note. 'So are you a friend of Claire's, a colleague, a relative or what? As you were the one who went to check on her.'

'I didn't go alone. Toby came with me. I suppose a friend. A bunch of us go out fairly regularly. Evenings, weekends. You know.'

'Sure. So, did you go inside her place this morning?'

'No, no. I don't have a key or anything. But we knocked. Rang the bell. Looked through the windows. The place was all locked up as normal, but there was no response and we couldn't see anything out of place inside. And her car wasn't there, as it would have been if she'd been in. She only went off yesterday to get a dental check-up and we haven't heard from her since. She didn't come back to work in the afternoon. I tried calling her, but there was no response then, either. So, when she didn't turn up this morning, I called her sister, Sally, to see if she knew what was going on with her. She didn't, so I called you guys.'

'What's her address?'

'Number 24 Anderson Road. It's off the Topsham Road, out past the school.'

'OK. Can you show us her desk or office while we're here?'

'Of course.' She stood up. 'This way.'

She led the way out of the little office and across to the lifts. Pressed the button to call one.

'How many people are in Claire's team?' Pete asked as they waited.

'Seventeen, plus her. We do customer queries rather than selling. We're one of four teams covering different aspects of the job.'

'Press one for this, two for that, three for something else and then listen to five minutes of interrupted lift music,' Pete said with a smile.

She tipped her head. 'That's us.'

'So, as a friend, I'm guessing you'd know if she's got a boyfriend.'

There was a ping as one of the two lifts arrived. Brushed steel doors slid open.

'Um... Yes.'

'Why the hesitation?' Pete asked as they stepped into the elevator.

She pressed the button for the third floor and turned to face the doors. 'They've... Well, they've had their ups and downs. They're together again now, but it's been a bit of an up and down relationship. Don't get me wrong,' she said as the doors slid closed. 'They love each other. Just... It's sometimes like he loves her a bit *too* much, you know?'

'A bit intense,' Pete suggested.

'Yes.'

'Possessive? Controlling?'

'Oh, Claire wouldn't let him control her.' She turned to meet Pete's gaze. 'She's too independent for that.'

'Does she stay over at his place sometimes?'

'Well, I suppose so, but that's not where she is. I phoned him to check.'

'OK. Have you phoned anyone else? Friends from outside work? Family?'

'Of course. I did all that before we went looking for her.' The lift stopped and she led the way out, turning left along a corridor that, this time, had solid walls on both sides.

'So, for two of you to go off out and look for her, you must have asked permission?' Pete suggested.

'Of course. We told Richard Dunne. He's the overall customer service manager. His office is that way.' She pointed back over her shoulder. 'Right at the front of the building on the left.' She stopped and opened a door. 'This is us.'

They entered a large open-plan office, the desks separated from each other by blue fabric-covered dividers about four feet tall. The carpet was thick underfoot, the suspended ceiling dotted with lighting panels. There was a constant hum of chatter, men and women talking into headsets.

'Claire's office is over here.' Christine pointed to a glassed-in corner at the far side of the room and led the way towards it.

'OK. Do you want to let Mr Dunne know we're here while we have a look in there?'

'Um... Yes, OK.'

She'd clearly expected to stay with them.

'Thanks for all your help, Christine. We'll come back to you with any other questions that come up.'

'Right.' She smiled briefly, mollified. 'That's OK. I just... Want to know she's safe, that's all. Here we are.' She opened the half-glass door for them and stood aside.

'The desk isn't locked or anything?' Pete checked, stepping into the small office.

'No. I left her address book there on the desk.'

'Excellent. Thanks. Oh, could you let me have a list of the other members of the group you said socialise regularly with you and Claire? And we'll need Claire's phone number too, to check the records.'

'Of course. No problem.'

When she'd gone, Pete directed Jill around one side of the desk while he went the other. He picked up the black A5 address book, flipped it open to confirm what it was before checking the desk drawers for a diary. There wasn't one. The computer sat blankly in front of him. It could contain a digital one. He picked up the receiver of the desk phone, pressed zero and stepped around to the side so that Jill could get to the drawers.

He was shocked when it was picked up on the second ring. 'Reception. How can I help?'

He recognised the voice of the girl on the front desk. 'This is DS Gayle. Have you got an IT department here?'

'Yes. Hold on, I'll put you through, detective.'

'Thanks,' he said as a click sounded on the line, then it rang again.

This time it took longer to be answered. A male voice came on the line. 'IT.'

'This is Detective Sergeant Gayle of Exeter CID. I'm in Claire Muir's office in your customer service department. I need to know if you'd be able to override any password she may have on her desk computer.'

'Well...' He stopped, realising that his immediate answer wasn't going to be appropriate. 'Yes, I suppose we could. We'd need permission from Management.'

'Right. Thank you.' Pete put the phone down. Jill looked up from what she was doing, raising an eyebrow.

'They can,' he said as he noticed, at the edge of his vision, Christine Thackeray approaching again with a man in tow. Wearing a smart, well-cut suit and tie, he looked to be in his late forties, his neat dark hair beginning to grey at the temples. Pete stepped out of the office, leaving Jill to continue her search, and extended a hand to the man.

'DS Gayle, Exeter CID.'

'Richard Dunne.' His grip was firm and dry. 'What can I do to help?'

'Well, if we could find somewhere to sit and talk, the three of us...'

'Of course.' He held up a hand for Christine to lead the way.

'How well do you know Claire?' Pete asked as they started back towards the corridor.

'Fairly, I suppose. As a colleague. We don't socialise, apart from the usual office parties and so on.'

'OK. I know Christine can help us with that side of her life. One thing I do need from you, while I think of it, is for you to contact your IT department and get us into Claire's computer so we can see if she kept a diary on there and check her email and social media.'

Dunne's lips pressed together doubtfully as they stepped out into the corridor and turned left, towards the lifts.

'We're just trying everything we can to track down a colleague. We're really not interested in company stuff.'

Dunne nodded, stepping out briskly along the corridor. 'No. Yes. I'll... Make the call as soon as we're finished.'

Pete kept pace easily, but Christine was struggling to keep up in her tight skirt and heels. Did Dunne always walk this fast? It was almost like he was subconsciously trying to get away. He glanced at Christine and the expression on her face told him all he needed to know. 'Or they could be working on it while we talk. It would save time, which can be vital in cases like this.'

'Of course.' Dunne grimaced. 'I'm not sure I have the authority, though. I'll have to check with my director.'

*

'Anything?'

Jill looked up from Claire Muir's computer as Pete stepped back into the small, glazed office.

'Nothing of interest. There is a diary on here, but only a work one – appointments, meetings, annual leave and so on. Nothing in her company email. She doesn't use her private one from here and her Facebook account doesn't get used much, either. You?'

'She seems like a model employee, from what her boss said. Keeps her personal life personal. Leaves it at home. Which agrees with what you've just said. We'll have to check her home and talk to her boyfriend. With a bit of luck, he might have a key to her place. Did you find a contacts list on there?'

'No. She'd have it on her mobile, I expect. Wherever that is. I've looked and it's not here. We have got the address book, though. It seems to have a mixture of business and personal entries.'

'Well, she had yesterday afternoon off, so she'd have taken the phone with her, I suppose. It might be in her car, wherever that is.'

'First, we need to find out *what* it is, unless you've already done that?'

'A white Toyota IQ with a 64 plate. That should be enough for a check, with her name. And I've got her phone numbers, address and a partial for her boyfriend along with his number.' Pete picked up the address book from the desk. 'I'll see if he's in here while you get Ben to ping her phone, see if we can get a location on it.'

'Right, boss.' She reached for the radio on her uniform. 'PC Evans for PC Myers, over.'

Pete flicked through the pages of the address book. Static hissed from Jill's radio, then Ben's voice came through the speaker. 'PC Myers.'

'Ben, can you get Claire Muir's phone pinged?' She read out the number.

'Will do.'

'Here we go,' Pete said as he found the boyfriend's entry in the book. As he'd expected, it was simply a first name but it had his land line, mobile, work number and address. He picked up the desk phone, dialled nine and entered the mobile number. It was picked up almost as soon as it rang.

'Claire? Where've you been? I've been worried sick since Christine phoned.'

'This is DS Gayle with Exeter CID. Is this Stuart?'

'Yes. Sorry, I thought... The number came up as Claire's. Police? Is Claire OK?'

'I'm calling from her office. Can I ask where you are? I'd like a quick chat, if that's OK.'

'Yes, of course. I'm at work, but it'll be fine. But what about Claire? What's happened?'

'We don't know yet. So where's work?'

'Oh. I'm at Thomas and Elsfield on Upper Paul Street.'

Pete visualised the picturesque narrow, cobbled lane off Queen Street in the city centre. 'Who should I ask for? I've only got your first name.'

'I'm Stuart Elsfield, one of the partners. We're accountants.'

'Ah. Thank you. I'll be there soon.' He raised his eyebrows at Jill as he ended the call. 'An accountant, no less.'

'They ain't poor.' Jill logged out of the computer and shut it down.

'And, as a partner, he'd be able to come and go more or less as he pleases, which gives him opportunity, to go with the up-and-down relationship as motive.'

Jill tipped her head to one side as she began to smile. 'Her car provides means, even if he hasn't got one of his own. And most blokes own a hammer, don't they?'

CHAPTER FIVE

'So, how long have you known Claire?'

They were sitting in Stuart Elsfield's office on the first floor of one of the tall, old buildings on the west side of the narrow street. The high ceiling allowed for the window behind Elsfield, who was sitting at his antique mahogany desk, to be over six feet tall and still not reach the floor or ceiling.

'About six months. We've been going out for about four.'

Pete nodded. 'How would you describe your relationship?'

Elsfield pursed his lips briefly. 'Passionate,' he said after a second's thought. 'We're both strong-minded individuals and no two people see eye to eye all the time, do they? So things occasionally get heated, but making up afterwards is equally intense.' He smiled.

Pete smiled with him, keeping things friendly. 'When did you see her last?'

'Sunday. We spent the day together.'

'A good day?'

'Yes. We went down to Exmouth, spent the day on the beach and around the town, went to a restaurant on the front, then came home.'

Pete nodded. There weren't many restaurants on Exmouth seafront. It would be worth checking with them. 'Have you got a picture of her? There wasn't one in her office.'

'I'm not surprised. There aren't any in her house, either. Not up, at least. I've got some on my phone.' He took it out and started searching for them. 'Here we go.' He handed the phone across. Pete saw an attractive dark-haired young woman smiling into the camera. The colour and style of her hair matched the victim he'd seen in the woods last night. More than that, he couldn't say for sure.

'She's beautiful,' he said, handing the phone back. 'Could you send me a couple of shots?'

'Of course, if it'll help.'

Pete handed him a card. 'There's my number.'

He started tapping at the screen again. 'There we go. I've sent three, including the one you saw.'

'Thanks. Does Claire have family in the area?'

'No, she's from Birmingham. Moved down here for work. Her parents are still up there but I don't think she's particularly close to them. Especially her mum.' His mouth pulled briefly into something between a smile and a grimace. 'Mums and daughters – it can go either of two ways, can't it? They're either really close or they clash. I think Claire was more of a daddy's girl. Part of the reason she moved down here, I think.' He shrugged. 'She won't admit it, of course, but you know… Getting away from old memories and all that.'

'Yes.' Pete paused. 'I have to ask. Standard procedure. Where were you last night between about seven and eleven?'

He frowned. 'Am I…?'

'As I said: standard procedure. We always ask everyone connected to the victim.'

His lips pursed. 'Well, I was at home. Alone, I'm afraid.'

Pete nodded. It wasn't exactly helpful, but it wasn't unusual either. 'One other thing. I'll have to go and see her place. Have you got a key?'

Elsfield grimaced. 'I did have, at one stage. Not now, though. One of our spats: she asked for it back and it's just never come up since.' He shrugged. 'It's never been an issue.'

'No problem. Oh, what do you drive, by the way?'

Elsfield frowned at the sudden change of tack. 'A Rav 4, why?'

'A vehicle was seen that might have been relevant. Wasn't one of those, though.'

The accountant's expression shifted subtly. 'So... God. It's like it's just hit home. She's really gone. Until now it's felt like she'd just gone off without telling anyone. Maybe gone to see her family or something.' He shook his head. 'I know it makes no sense. She's not the type to leave people in the lurch like that. But you saying that – a suspicious vehicle was seen – it's suddenly like one of those things you see on TV. I'm suddenly involved in a real-life crime or something.' He blew the air out of his lungs in a long gust then met Pete's gaze with an intense stare. 'God, I hope she's all right.'

'You and a lot of other people, Mr Elsfield. Thanks for your time.'

*

Walking down the steep, narrow street back to his car, which he'd parked on Queen Street, Pete took out his phone and dialled.

'Ben,' he said when it was picked up. 'Get onto the locksmiths, get them to come out to the victim's place and open it up for us. I'll pick you and Jill up out the back of the station in ten minutes.'

'Right, boss.'

Pete put away his phone as he stepped around the corner. He nodded to an approaching traffic warden. 'George.'

'Sarge. That yours?' He tipped his head at Pete's car a few yards away.

'For now. Mine's in dock.'

'A good thing it's got the blues front and back or I might have given it a ticket,' he said, referring to the hidden lights in the front grille and on the parcel shelf.

Pete clapped him on the shoulder. 'I could always arrest you for interfering in an investigation, George.'

The older man laughed. 'You'd have to catch me first. I'm on my feet all day, remember.'

Pete laughed with him. George was closing in on retirement and his normal gait was a slow amble. 'They don't call you fleet-foot for nothing, eh?'

George's head bobbed lugubriously. 'That's me.' He'd never been called anything like it in his life, except perhaps in irony, and they both knew it. 'You know I'm in for the next local marathon, don't you?'

Pete's eyes widened in shock.

George laughed. 'Gotcha.'

He raised a hand and ambled away, still chuckling, as Pete unlocked the car and climbed in.

A few minutes later, having negotiated the city centre's circuitous road system, Pete drove up the side of the police station on Heavitree Road. Ben and Jill were waiting outside the back door. Pete circled the car park and stopped beside them.

'The locksmith will be there in half an hour,' Ben said as he sat in beside Pete while Jill got in the back.

'Right. We need to check her place and talk to the neighbours, see if they saw anything and what they've got to say about her. What did we get on her mobile phone?'

'Nothing. It must have been inactivated,' Ben replied. 'I put in a request for its history, but I haven't got anything back yet.'

With traffic queueing towards the city centre, he turned left out of the station then right to cut across towards the Topsham Road. He was just shifting into third gear along a hedge-lined road of large, detached houses when his phone rang. He hadn't had chance to connect it to the car's Bluetooth system, so he handed it to Ben. 'Put it on speaker.'

'DS Gayle,' he said when Ben complied, holding it out between them.

'Peter. Tony Chambers. I've completed the post-mortem on our victim from last night and there are some findings that I need to discuss with you.'

'I'm just on the way to her house with Ben Myers and Jill Evans. Can you give us the edited highlights and I'll pop round as soon as I can?'

'Uh... You sound like I'm on speaker.'

'That's right. New car. Had a bit of a bump in mine on the way back last night. Why?'

He heard Chambers draw a heavy breath. 'Well, apologies to PC Evans, but the main thing that I couldn't tell you last night at the scene was that the victim... Have you identified her, by the way?'

'It's not official yet, but she was probably Claire Muir, originally from Birmingham.'

'I see. Thank you. Well, she hadn't been raped, as such. However, her mouth and stomach contents showed semen, evidently from just before she was killed. And there are signs of strangulation, although the hammer was what killed her. And I can confirm it was a hammer.'

In the back seat, Jill made a noise in her throat.

'So, sexual humiliation.' Pete pictured the body in his mind. 'Like a spurned lover, maybe. Thanks, Doc. I'll see you soon.' He nodded to Ben to end the call.

Jill sucked in a breath. 'Combine all that with the fact that she'd been shaved, dressed in just a coat and heels and left on display like that... Are you sure you don't want to drop me off at the boyfriend's to have a quiet word with him?'

'Let's wait for the DNA, shall we? If it matches, it'll be me and you together, Jill.'

*

Claire Muir's house was a 1930s semi in a smartly maintained street near the edge of the city. The small open-fronted garden was brick-paved with just a narrow border of colourful but low maintenance shrubs down one side and a pair of hanging baskets either side of the front door. Her car was notable by its absence.

Pete pulled onto the paved garden area, leaving plenty of room for the locksmith to park alongside. 'Right, while we wait we'll knock up the neighbours, see what they have to say about Claire and the recent comings and goings here. I'll check around the back of the property then go right. Jill, you go left and Ben, take the far side of the road.'

They stepped out of the car and Pete locked it as he moved across towards the wooden fence that separated the front garden from the back at the side of the house. There was a simple latch on the gate. He stepped through, moving carefully to avoid ruining any forensic evidence that might be present. All the windows were closed and the door into the kitchen locked. He returned to the front of the house and crossed to the attached property. There was no doorbell so he knocked and waited.

Silence.

He tried again, but still got no response, so left a card and moved on. Here, he could tell that someone was in even before he rang the bell. He could see the flicker of the TV through the net curtains of the bay window.

The door was opened by a woman in her sixties; one of those women who look elegant even in jeans and a sweat-shirt. 'Yes?'

Pete held up his warrant card. 'DS Gayle, Exeter CID,' he said. 'We're looking into the disappearance of your neighbour, next door but one.' He nodded to his left.

'Disappearance? God! I only saw her yesterday.'

'What time was that?'

'When she went off to work. About half past eight. I was in the garden, pulling some weeds. She waved and said, "Good morning." Perfectly normal. And she's disappeared?'

'She's been reported missing, yes. What can you tell me about her?'

'She's a perfectly nice girl. Friendly, helpful... I don't know how long she's lived here. She was already here when I moved in last year. She came round and offered us tea or coffee at hers when we'd finished. We don't see all that much of her. She's busy with work and that boyfriend of hers.' Her nose wrinkled in distaste.

'You don't think much of him?'

Her mouth twitched. 'I don't know him. All I can say is what I've observed and that hasn't all been good. He can be rather... Aggressive at times. Not physical, as far as I know, but loud. Pushy. And I do know that, a couple of weeks ago, Claire suspected him of having someone else.'

'Really?'

'She said as much when she was throwing him out. I was unpacking the car from the supermarket.'

'I see.' *But he wasn't violent, she'd said.* 'Do you know if she had any problems with anyone else at all?'

She shook her head. 'Not that I'm aware of.'

'OK. Well, thank you. You've been very helpful, Mrs…?'

'Atherton. Margaret.'

'Thank you, Mrs Atherton.'

She waited until he'd stepped off her property before closing the door.

The next house was one of the few on the street where the owners hadn't opened up the front garden for parking. Instead, the small space was neatly manicured and colourful, a diamond-shaped flower bed in the centre, surrounded by grass, then narrow borders with more bedding plants.

Pete rang the bell. Faintly, he heard a shout from inside and waited for movement to follow. A figure appeared dimly through the stippled glass in the top section of the door and approached slowly. A lock was released. Then another. A third and the door finally cracked open a few inches, a chain holding it secure while an eye peered through the gap.

'Yes?'

'Morning, ma'am.' Pete held up his warrant card for her to see. 'I'm DS Gayle from Exeter police. Beautiful garden you've got. I was hoping to have a word about one of your neighbours, if that's all right.'

'May I?' A hand reached through for his badge and Pete allowed her to take it, noting the gleam of old gold on her ring finger. Moments passed then the door was pushed closed, the chain slid free and it opened again. The woman closed the small leather wallet and handed it back. Her steel-grey hair was neatly curled, her pale, almost translucent skin lined with age, but her brown eyes held a strength of character that Pete immediately liked. 'Which neighbour is it you want to ask about?'

Pete tipped his head to the left. 'Three doors up. Miss Muir.'

'Ah, yes. Claire. Lovely girl. What about her?'

'Well, she's been reported missing, so we're trying to find out all we can about her, so we can figure out what may have happened to her.'

'Missing?' She started to look over her shoulder then stopped herself. 'Missing? Claire? Since when? I only spoke to her a couple of days ago.' She shook her head as if denying the possibility.

'And how was she? How did she seem?'

'She was fine. Her normal happy self. Missing?' She shook her head again.

'Do you know if there was anything going on in her life that she wasn't happy about? Any problems or anything unusual that she'd mentioned?'

'No... But she's a feisty little madam. If there was, she'd just get on and deal with it. She's not one to moan about things.'

As she spoke a van turned into the end of the road.

'I see. Well, thank you for your time. If you or your husband do think of anything, give us a call, won't you?'

'Of course.' She shook her head. 'I can't believe she's missing.'

As Pete turned away, he glimpsed the side of the approaching van. He couldn't read the name printed on it at this angle, but there was no mistaking the large key drawn vertically towards its back end.

He met the locksmith at Claire Muir's door. He was a man in his fifties, small and wiry. He checked Pete's ID. 'Missing persons case?'

'That's right.'

Which meant there was no warrant required.

'Right-o.' He went to the back of his van and took a small case from inside. Checking the lock on Claire's front door, he opened the case and took out a bundle of skeleton keys. He rummaged through them, selected one and tried it in the lock without success. He tried another. Still no good. The third one slid in smoothly. He carefully twisted it and... *Click.* The door opened.

'There you go.'

'Thanks.' Pete signed the paperwork he proffered, took his copy and stepped inside. The house smelled fresh and clean. He pushed open the door to the front room. It was set up as a formal dining room. All was neat and tidy. Moving on, he checked the back room - the sitting room which he'd seen from outside. Again, nothing was out of place. The kitchen was similarly neat. A breakfast bowl and a mug sat in the sink with a spoon and a teaspoon, waiting to be washed up. Otherwise, everything looked as it should. Returning to the hallway, he checked upstairs. The bathroom was straight ahead off the landing. It smelled of shampoo and soap. The bath gleamed in the light from the window above it.

Pete moved on.

She clearly used the back bedroom. The bed was turned down to air. Pete checked the bedside cabinet but found no diary. The front box room was set up as a home office. A search again turned up no diary but he did find her latest phone bill and bank statement. He placed these in evidence envelopes and took them with him, along with the laptop computer from the desk.

The third room was the spare. The one untidy room in the house, it was cluttered and junky, but not in a way that denoted violence. The whole house was untouched. She had simply gone out to work as normal and not returned.

Jill was waiting for him by the front door when he stepped out and Ben was crossing the road towards them. He waited for the spiky-haired PC to join them before asking, 'Anything?'

Jill grimaced. 'Nope. Consensus is she's a nice girl, a good neighbour, but nobody's seen or heard anything out of the ordinary.'

'Except for the old boy over there,' said Ben, nodding towards a house almost opposite where they were standing. 'He said he'd seen her ex out here a couple of times in the past ten days or so.'

'Really?'

Ben nodded. 'The old boy's into cars and so's her ex, apparently. He's got a few, including a customised A40 van, whatever that is.'

Pete wondered if that collection included an old Land Rover. 'Did you learn anything else about this ex?'

'His name and the fact that he lives in Broad Clyst.'

A smile crept slowly across Pete's face. 'Does he, now?' He had driven through Broad Clyst last night, on the way to Ashclyst Forest, where what Pete was becoming increasingly sure was Claire Muir's body had been found. It was a small, rural village. The kind of place where an old Land Rover would not be out of place. 'I think we'd better track him down and have a word, then, Ben. Well done.'

CHAPTER SIX

Pete's phone rang as they were returning to the car. He took it out and checked the screen. Leaning on the roof of the car, he tapped the green icon and raised the phone to his ear. 'Guv?'

'Where are you?'

Unusually abrupt for Colin, Pete thought. 'The victim's house. We're just on the way back. Why?'

'When you get here, come and see me.'

'Why? What's up?'

'Never mind now. Just do it.' There was a click and the hum of a dead line. Pete grimaced, staring at the phone for a second before putting it away. What the hell had got into him?

He sat into the driver's seat.

'All right, boss?' Ben asked.

'Dunno, Ben.' He passed the laptop over to Jill in the back seat and started the engine.

'Not in trouble again, are you?' she asked with a smile.

'It's a tough life, stuck between the management and the kids,' Pete said. 'You're neither and both. Can't win, either way.' He turned the car around and started back down the road.

'Ah. Get the violins out, Ben, we'll play him a tune.'

'You stick to keyboards, Jill. See if you can get into that computer. And Ben, see what you can get from these.' He slipped the bank statement and phone bill out of his jacket and passed them across.

Back at the main road, he signalled right and waited for a break in the traffic, trying to figure out what Colin Underhill's problem could be. What had he or his team done that would make the DI so irritable? He was naturally gruff, but he wasn't normally as short as that. And he was a friend as well as a boss. He was Godfather to both of Pete's kids, had been a mentor to Pete when he came to Exeter. They'd barely got started on this case. They couldn't have done anything wrong yet, surely? He hadn't rubbed any of the witnesses up the wrong way, as far as he was aware.

Their last case had ended in a less than ideal fashion, by some standards, but they'd got the right person. He was sure of that. Had her family put in a complaint? An accusation of some sort? There were no independent witnesses to what had happened, of course, but they were decent, law-abiding folks. Surely not?

'Boss?' Ben's voice broke into his thoughts.

'What?'

'We going or what?'

Pete blinked and looked up and down the road. It was clear of traffic. 'Oh. Yes.' He pulled away. 'Miles away,' he admitted. 'Trying to figure out what's up with the guvnor.'

'He's management,' Ben said as if that was all the explanation that was needed.

Pete chose not to pursue the matter. He would find out soon enough.

*

'What the hell?'

Anger coursed through him like molten lead. The urge to stand up and pace was almost overwhelming, but he stayed still with a conscious effort.

'We're his parents, for Christ's sake. Don't they have to at least inform us first?'

'I suppose that's why he's not going until the day after tomorrow. So they've got time to do that.' Colin sat forward in his chair. 'I only found out because I went to talk to him again.'

'The day after tomorrow? That's ridiculous. How can they expect us – you – to conduct an enquiry from that distance?'

Not only had Dr Brian Letterman got his way in getting rid of Tommy from Archways secure children's home, it seemed like he'd managed to block his transfer to the nearest similar establishment in Bristol. Tommy would be going to Southampton, a two-and-a-half-hour drive away.

'Can't you stop it?'

Colin shrugged. 'I've tried. I spoke to DCI Silverstone, the prosecutor… There's nothing else I can do. If Archways was full, he'd have to go somewhere else.'

'Yes, but it's not, is it? It's just run by boneheads. I'd have thought the DCI would stick his oar in on your behalf, at least.'

Colin grimaced. 'Yeah. Turns out, he and the good doctor have a membership in common. One that you and I don't share.'

Adam Silverstone was a lot of things, but a golfer wasn't one of them. 'What?' Pete demanded. 'The funny handshake club?'

Colin didn't reply, but the look on his face said all that was needed. Pete's lips tightened. 'Well, if the bloody Masons are more important to him than the job, then he's not fit to wear the damn uniform, as far as I'm concerned. And I don't give a shit who knows it, him included,' he added when Colin gave him a warning look. 'So you're going to be traipsing back and forth from Southampton, wasting five hours a time, for the next three weeks, just so an incompetent fucking wanker like him can keep in with his mates and jeopardise a case against a damned child-molester and killer in the process? I hope you've already been onto Middlemoor about this?'

'Calm down, Pete. And keep your voice down if you don't want to be back in uniform tomorrow.'

Pete almost laughed. 'Let him try. I'll have him slung out of the force for corruption if he even thinks about it. There's no way this is happening without a fight. No way.' Again, Pete struggled to stay seated.

Colin's hands slapped on his desk. 'Shut up,' he snapped. 'I'm trying to save your career.'

'You think I give a damn about that, compared to my son? Sod the force, if that's the choice.'

'Damn it, be quiet. And don't interrupt me when I'm talking. You're a damn good copper. I don't want that going to waste for the sake of DCI Silverstone's convenience. Yes, I've raised the matter at Middlemoor. The divisional commander is aware of the situation and it's not going to do the DCI's promotional prospects any good. But he's asked that we tolerate it for now. As you say, the trial starts in three weeks. Tommy'll have to come back to Exeter then, if not before. But in the meantime…'

'So, we're stuck with the useless pillock?' Pete interrupted. 'That's going to go down like a lead balloon in the station.'

Colin sighed. 'In the meantime, we need to keep our noses to the grindstone and focus on what's important – putting criminals behind bars – while the DC does what he can about Tommy's situation.'

Pete's jaw was clamped tight, almost to the point of his teeth hurting, but he was beginning to calm down. He would stand by every word that he'd said, but it wasn't Colin's fault. 'Sorry, guv. I didn't mean to go off like that. But you wait until Louise hears about this. You won't need a phone to hear her from here to the hospital.'

'Break it to her gently. For the sake of her patients, if nobody else. How's the case going?'

Pete pulled in a deep breath and let it out. 'Early days. We've ID'd the victim. Got her home computer, looked at her work one, spoken to her boss and some colleagues as well as her boyfriend and several neighbours. She wasn't abducted forcibly from her house. I need to get uniform to look for her car. It's not at home or at work. But she had taken half a day's leave – we don't know what for – so it could be anywhere.'

'Suspects?'

'The boyfriend, of course. I've spoken to him, but I haven't had chance to check his alibi yet. And an ex. Apparently, he was seen in the vicinity of her house recently.'

'Right. I'll put the alert out on her car if you give me the details. You get on with the rest of it.'

'Thanks.' Pete took out his notebook and read off the details of Claire Muir's car while Colin wrote rapidly on the pad he kept permanently on his desk.

'You calmed down now?'

Pete met his level grey eyes. Inside, he was still seething and would be until the situation was resolved, but… 'I'm in control, if that's what you mean.'

Colin nodded, accepting that. 'Don't go doing anything stupid.'

Pete grunted. 'You know me, guv.'

'That's why I said it.'

Pete couldn't help a brief chuckle. 'Yeah, right. I'll be fine.'

'I know. But in the meantime – don't do anything stupid.'

*

Pete ignored the stares from members of the other three teams in the squad room as he walked back to his desk and plucked his jacket from the back of his chair.

'That glass really needs sound-proofing,' Dave said to no-one in particular.

'Is everything OK?' Jane asked.

'No, but it's not relevant to the case we're working so don't worry about it. I've got to go and see Doc Chambers. While I'm gone, I need her call logs – mobile and land line. I need her email accessed, her laptop checked for any form of diary or any other sign of a motive, and her boyfriend's alibi checked. And Ben, see what you can find on that ex that the guy across the road told you about. That should keep you all occupied for a few minutes.' He put his jacket on and checked his pockets for car keys and mobile phone. 'I shan't be long.'

He was still seething with anger and frustration as he headed out. He waited until he was in the car before calling Louise at the hospital. He'd have preferred to tell her in person, but he had too much to do on the case and she had the support of her colleagues there. She'd be OK, he was sure.

The call was picked up quickly for a change.

'CDU, Nurse Patterson. How can I help?'

He didn't recognise the voice or the name. 'Hello. I need to speak to nurse Gayle.'

'I'm afraid she's with a patient at the moment. Can I take a message?'

'No, sorry, this is a confidential matter. I'm calling from Exeter police station.'

'Um… Doesn't…? Couldn't…? Is everything OK? Is this about her husband?'

'No, no. It's about her son. If she could call back as soon as possible... In fact, if you get her to call her husband, that'd be perfect.'

'Right. OK.'

'Thank you.' He lowered the phone and was about to touch the red icon to end the call when her voice came hurriedly back.

'One second. Are you still there?'

'Hello, yes.'

'She's just come free. Hold on.'

'Thanks,' he said as the receiver on the other end clattered down and a distant voice called out.

Moments later, Louise was on the line. 'Hello? Nurse Gayle speaking.'

'Lou, it's me. Sorry, but I had to let you know as soon as possible. They're moving Tommy. To Southampton.'

'What?'

'Colin just told me. He tried to block it – even went to the divisional commander – but it's going ahead regardless.'

'Jesus! That fucking useless waste of oxygen. Just because he can't do his bloody job, he thinks he can play with people's lives to make his own easier? I'll have the incompetent bastard struck off before I'm finished. You see if I don't. He won't be able to get a job as a bloody dustman, never mind going anywhere near a hospital. And you wanted me to go easy? He's not going to know what's hit him.'

Pete couldn't help but smile. This was the old Louise: the strong-minded fighter for good and for what was right. There was no hint of the utter defeat and bottomless depression she'd been suffering until a few weeks ago. The relief that flooded through him at the sound of her anger felt wonderful. 'I never said go easy. I just said think about what you're doing before you do it. But I'm with you all the way. Always have been. Gloves off and anything goes. Just don't jeopardise yourself in the process, that's all I was trying to tell you.'

'Screw that. This is our son we're talking about. Never mind gloves, my claws are going to rip his guts out. What does Colin say about it?'

'He's no happier than we are. He's in the middle of building his case against Burton. The trial's in three weeks. But there's not much he can do about it for now.'

She snorted. 'What about Tommy? Does he know?'

'I'm not sure and *I* can't go there to tell him, but you could. Whether he knows or not, it'd be good if you went to see him.'

'If he'll see me.'

When she and Annie had last gone to Archways, Tommy had done all he could to get rid of them. Annie had been devastated and ran out of the place crying.

'Maybe if you don't take Annie…'

'Huh. Don't worry – I won't. Not after last time. And I'll tell him why, while I'm at it.'

Pete nodded. If the boy cared for his sister at all, that might well be a good thing. 'OK. I'd better get on. I just thought I ought to tell you as soon as possible.'

'Right. See you later.'

Pete told her he loved her and hung up, then started the car and headed for the mortuary.

*

'So, what did Doc Chambers have to add to the equation?' Dave asked as he shucked off his jacket on returning to his desk.

'Confirmation of the victim's time of death at between one and two pm yesterday, DNA from the semen found in the body and confirmation of prints and DNA being found on her coat. The DNA from her coat matches the semen, but no hits in the database. Nothing on the prints, either. What have you got for me?' Pete asked, his gaze taking in the whole team.

'Quite a bit, but no killer yet.' As usual, Dave acted as spokesman. 'There's nothing useful on her computer – no diary or anything like that. I've got her land line call log. Seems to be all friends, family and work colleagues. Ben got her mobile log and its tracking info. She didn't go home from work that lunchtime. Looks like she went into town instead. We've found her car, though.'

'Where?'

'Princesshay multi-storey.'

Pete pictured the concrete car park less than five minutes' walk from where they sat. She could have gone anywhere from there. 'What about her phone?'

'Looks like the battery died on her. It's in the car, attached to the charger.'

'Shit.'

'Yeah. I spoke to Graham in the CCTV room, though. He's finding the footage from round there at the relevant time to see if we can pick up which way she went and if she met anyone. Jill was going to head down there in a minute.'

'Was I?' Jill demanded.

'We all know how much you like being in dark places with older men,' Dave said, referring to the sixty-three-year-old flasher that she'd apprehended the previous year by tracking him through the dark, unlit alleyways west of Fore Street.

'You mind I don't have an accident with my truncheon,' she warned him.

'As the policeman said to the actress.'

'What happened to the bishop?' Dick asked.

'He got arrested. Inappropriate behaviour with an actress.'

'Yeah, and you'd know all about that, wouldn't you?' Jane elbowed him not too gently in the ribs.

'Oi! Assaulting a police officer. Did you see that, boss?'

'I thought she was just attracting your attention, Dave.'

'Oh, cheers. I reckon I'm going to have to change my name to Charlie Brown.'

'Why?' Ben asked.

Dick pursed his lips. 'The song,' he said. '"Why's everybody always picking on me?" And no, I'm not old enough to remember when it first came out.'

Pete sighed. 'Sit still, Jill. I haven't started anything yet so I'll go and see what Graham's found, if anything.'

CHAPTER SEVEN

'Gimme a chance. She only phoned ten minutes ago and I've been tied up helping uniform track a bag-snatcher since before that.' The stocky blond man returned his attention to the screens in front of him. 'You can sit there and look for yourself if you want.' He picked up his radio. 'He's turned into Castle Gardens.'

'Castle Gardens. Received.'

Graham put down the radio. 'Bugger,' he muttered. 'He could go any-bloody-where from there. Do you know what you're doing there?'

'Yes, thanks.'

Pete had settled himself into the spare chair in the dimly lit room and was selecting the cameras he needed to concentrate on. There was one on the short road that led between the council offices and the library into the multi-storey car park behind them and others on the High Street, overlooking the pedestrian entrance to the shopping mall the car park was attached to. He guessed there were others on the car park entrance itself and perhaps even inside the mall, but they were not controlled from here. If he needed them, he'd have to get onto the council or the company that ran the car park itself.

He started with the camera on the road entrance. Claire's little white Toyota would be easy to pick out. It was a distinctively shaped model and hadn't been on the market for all that long. There couldn't be that many around. He selected a start time of twelve noon on the day in question and hit play and fast forward. Cars began to speed up and down the short stretch of road. A few pedestrians hurried comically across the lower portion of the screen, looking like they were in an old black and white movie being played at the wrong speed. The time readout at the bottom of the screen wound steadily on. 12:10. 12:15. 12:20. He slowed the replay, anticipating her arrival at any moment. 12:25 came and went. 12:30. Where the hell was she? By the time 12:45 passed, he was wondering if the clock was correct, but he dismissed the thought. Of course it was. He stuck with it until 1:00 pm, before hitting the pause button.

'Anything?' Graham asked.

'No.'

'Maybe she didn't put the car there.'

Jill would have told him what they were looking for, when and why, Pete thought.

'Maybe.' *In which case, it won't be her but her killer on the footage. Wouldn't that be nice?* He pressed play again and sped up the replay. If the killer had dumped Claire's car, it could have been any time after about 1:30. He waited for the time readout to reach that point and slowed the replay from thirty times real speed to six times, focussing once more on the screen as the traffic hurried in and out of the car park.

Half an hour later, the timestamp had reached 4:00 pm, there had been no sign of Claire Muir's car on the screen, Graham's team of uniformed officers had found and arrested their man and Pete's concentration was waning when a thought popped into his head and he groaned.

'What's up?' Graham asked without shifting his gaze from the screens in front of him.

Pete hit the pause button and turned to face him. 'What if the killer didn't put the car there? What if she did, but earlier? If she was planning to do some shopping after work, she might have put it there first thing. It's not that far to walk and there isn't much parking where she works. Plus, it wouldn't make any difference to how much it cost if she got a day ticket.'

'Well, on the plus side, you'd have a fairly tight timeframe to check.'

Pete grunted. Now that he'd thought of it, it would be a distraction at the back of his mind until he checked. He reset the search time and hit play once more. Minutes later, he swore softly and paused the footage. 'There she is. 8:42 am.' He couldn't see the driver through the sun's glare across the windscreen and the image quality would never allow him to read the number plate, but the car was the right type and colour. He could check with the car park manager for gate footage to confirm it. Or Graham could. Knowing the people involved, dealing with them on a regular basis, the blond man would have a far better chance of getting an efficient response from them. Pete did a screen grab and turned back to Graham. 'Do me a favour? Call the company and get the entry footage.'

'Humph. Sometimes, I feel so used.'

'It's called being part of the team.'

'Yeah, when it suits you. The rest of the time, I'm just forgotten, down here in my little cubby-hole.'

'Which is just the way you like it.' Pete clapped him on the back.

'Beside the point,' Graham said, keeping up the pretence.

'All right. If you can prove it's her, I'll buy you a tub of glace cherries. How's that?'

'Done. Leave your screen as it is.' He picked up the phone and dialled. 'Hello, John. It's Graham, Heavitree Road. Can you do me a quick favour? Yeah. 8.42 am yesterday. A white Toyota. One of those little square ones. Cheers, mate. See you.' He put the phone down and looked up at Pete. 'On its way. He'll email it to me. I can send it on to you upstairs.'

'Perfect,' Pete said although he felt strangely deflated. It would have been good to see the killer rather than the victim dropping the car off. He needed an easy case right now, with all the other stuff going on in his life. 'I'll leave you to it, then.'

'Typical. Get what you want and clear off. Wham, bam, thank you man.'

'So that *was* you I spotted going into that gay bar on South Street the other night.'

'Oi! Don't go starting rumours like that. I've got a reputation to protect.'

Pete laughed and reached for the door handle. 'I'll see you later. With a tub of cherries if you've earned it.'

*

'Well, the car's a bust,' Pete announced, settling himself back at his desk. 'She put it there herself, on her way to work in the morning. Has anyone got any good news?'

'Maybe,' said Jane, putting a hand over the mouthpiece of the phone she was holding to her ear. 'I'm on hold. I phoned Claire's parents in Kings Heath to notify them. Spoke to her dad. He asked if Sally knew. Turns out Sally's her sister. Three years younger. Moved down here in January to take a job at the Met Office. They lived together for a few weeks until Sally got a place of her own.'

'So, she might know what's been going on in Claire's life.'

'Hopefully. I'm waiting for her to come to the phone. Hello?' She looked down, concentrating on the telephone. 'Yes, this is DC Jane Bennett with Exeter CID. Have you heard from…?' She paused as the person on the other end broke in. 'Yes, I'm really sorry. Could I or one of my colleagues come and speak to you…? Well, the sooner the better… OK, thank you. Bye.' She put the phone down. 'Boss?'

Pete nodded. 'You go. You'll get more from her, woman to woman. I need to go and talk to the ex.' He grabbed his jacket and they walked out together.

'How's things with Tommy?' she asked as they descended the stairs.

'Not good. The resident psychiatrist at Archways is a born-again arse hole. Tommy doesn't do himself any favours, winding him up, but he can't cope with the lad so he wants him gone. And it looks like he's going to get his way. Tommy's being transferred to Southampton.'

'Eh? That's crazy! How are we supposed to deal with him from there, with Burton's trial coming up? And his own won't be long, either. They don't normally hang around in the juvie court. You got a date for it yet?'

'No.'

They went through into the back corridor on the ground floor.

'Still… First offence, stable family; they won't exactly throw the book at him, will they? Especially if he's going to be helpful in the Burton trial.'

'That "if" is still there, though, from what Colin's told me. And the fact that I can't go and see him isn't helping.'

'Yeah, but surely he can see that's not your fault? I mean, it makes sense, doesn't it? And Louise and Annie have been.'

'Until he drove them away, the other day. Poor Annie was in a real state afterwards. She won't be going back there, that's for sure.'

'What the hell was that in aid of? She hasn't done him any harm. Jesus, if I could, I'd go round there myself and give him a right bloody talking to!'

Pete laughed. 'And if you'd got a legitimate reason to go there, I'd say do it. It might well be exactly what he needs. I know Colin's sorely tempted, but he's got to try and keep the lad on-side for now.'

Only direct family and relevant professionals like case officers, solicitors and so on could visit the children in secure homes, and Jane had no official reason to go there. As Tommy's father, Pete would normally have had access to him, but the fact that he was also SIO on the Malcolm Burton case prevented it. He did still have rights, however…

'I wonder…'

'What?'

'If I could demand a second opinion on Tommy before he's transferred.'

'I don't know. Might be worth finding out, though. Have you got someone in mind?'

'The police psychologist at Middlemoor.' He pictured Dr Abigail White in his mind; calm and graceful with dark hair cut in a long bob and brown eyes that inspired confidence. She took no crap from anyone, he recalled with a smile. 'She'd have Brian Letterman for breakfast.'

'It wouldn't hurt to give her a call. At least she'd know if she could intervene or not. Or maybe if anyone else could.'

'True.'

Jane hit the door release and Pete pushed the back door open, letting her step through ahead of him.

'See you later.'

'Yep.'

Her little green Vauxhall was in the second row of the car park while Pete's black Focus was near the back. Pete heard her engine start before he reached his car. He raised a hand without looking round.

By the time he'd reached the narrow drive down the side of the station, she had turned out onto Heavitree Road and gone from sight. It was late morning and traffic was yet to build to the lunchtime peak. Signalling right, he paused at the station entrance to let a box van and a couple of cars pass, heading towards the city centre, then checked to the right again, struggling to see past a filthy old van parked half on the narrow pavement a few yards down. As far as he could tell, the road was clear. He pulled out, checking left again. As he did so, an engine roared and tyres squealed. Pete's head snapped round. The van had pulled off the pavement and was surging towards him. He couldn't see the driver clearly through the dirt on the windscreen though they were just feet apart now. Instinct screamed at him to stop and reverse, but there wasn't time. Instead, he hit the accelerator.

A horn blared from somewhere.

'Shit.' Adrenaline shot through his veins like an electric shock. Had he missed a vehicle approaching behind the van?

The question hadn't even fully formed in his mind before he could see the answer. Then the car was slammed sideways in a jolting impact, metal crunching, glass smashing as the van hit just inches behind him.

Pete stood on the brake, rage erupting as the adrenaline surged. He slammed the car into reverse and hit the throttle again, hoping to force the van across towards the brick wall that fronted the station. Metal ground against metal as the car shot backward, the ruined front wing of the van scraping along the driver's door as Pete pulled the steering wheel around, trying to force the bigger vehicle in the direction he wanted.

The back of the Focus hit the wall, jarring him again in his seat, then the van impacted right on the angle of the solid, earth-banked brickwork.

'Gotcha.'

Pete killed the engine with one hand as the other yanked up the hand brake and unclipped his seat belt. He scrambled over the central console and out the passenger door, determined to haul the driver out of the van and into the nick but, even as he reached the front of the crumpled car, he heard the slap of feet on pavement and saw the door on the far side of the van was hanging open. He glimpsed movement to his left, beyond the back of the van. The man was off and running, already with several yards start.

Pete changed direction and set off after him, anger lending him a speed that he was unused to. The man's feet flashed pale as he ran down the narrow street. He was wearing trainers with his jeans and dark sweater.

Still, Pete was determined to catch him. Jacket flapping at his elbows, he ran as hard as he could.

The guy was forty yards in front. Almost as tall as Pete, he was solidly built. Pete couldn't see his hair colour for the black beanie or balaclava that covered it, but he glimpsed the white skin of his face as he stepped around an old lady dragging a shopping trolley slowly towards them and reached out a gloved hand to yank her violently towards the road. She screamed, staggering, hands going out to protect herself. The tartan trolley hit the ground, fruit spilling from it as she went down on her knees.

Again, Pete was forced to ignore his instinct. He leapt right, one foot pushing off the wall that bordered the pavement on that side, and hit the path again, still running.

A few yards further on, a group of people were filling the pavement outside the fish and chip shop, waiting for it to open in a few minutes' time. A lorry was lumbering up the hill past them, restricting the fleeing man's options.

'Move,' he roared.

Several faces snapped around to see what was happening. Some stepped back, others had nowhere to go. He ploughed into them. Shouts of fear and protest erupted as he barged through, at least two men and a woman falling back against the side of the moving lorry. A scream tore the air but, fortunately, no-one fell under the big wagon.

Pete saw a chance.

'Stop. Police,' he yelled over the commotion. Maybe the crowd would close in, blocking the man's headlong flight. But it was too late. An arm came up, the closed fist smashing into a man's face, knocking him back to bounce off the wall behind him. Another was caught with a barging shoulder and spun away, staggering as he struggled to stay clear of the lorry, hands going out defensively.

The fleeing man was through and clear.

But he'd cleared a path for Pete. As he charged through, he saw that he'd gained a good ten paces on his quarry. There were maybe twenty-five or thirty yards between them now. He caught a flash of pale skin as the man glanced over his shoulder. He seemed to redouble his effort, arms pumping hard as he put all he had into outrunning Pete.

He was fast approaching a narrow, Victorian side-street. It seemed like he was going to charge straight across, regardless until, at the last moment, he put out an arm and used a lamp post to swing himself around onto a new track, going up the red brick terraced street.

Pete's lungs were beginning to burn. He didn't know how fit the man in front of him was, but his heavier clothing wouldn't be helping him. His body would be heating up fast by now. Pete hoped he could out-last the man if not out-pace him. He used the same move as his quarry to swing around into the side-street and plunged onward, the other man now no more than twenty paces in front of him.

The front doors of the small houses opened directly onto the pavement, a line of parked cars just three feet or so from the house fronts. The sun was shining directly up the line of the street at this time of day. The two men's footsteps hammered on the concrete slabs, echoing off the walls that crowded in to either side. A door opened a few yards ahead. Pete saw the front of a pushchair emerge as if in slow motion.

Would the man keep going, barge past or jump over it, or would he dodge left between the parked cars? Whichever choice he made, it would slow him. Pete would gain more ground. Breathing hard, he nevertheless put on an extra spurt, aiming to make the most of the opportunity.

The pushchair emerged further across the pavement, blocking half its width now, the running man closing fast, now only a couple of house widths away from the growing restriction. Pete expected him to shout out again, telling the mother to pull it back, but he didn't.

Pete did it for him. 'Stop. Police,' he shouted again.

The man ignored him, but the pushchair stopped.

At the last second, the man jumped to the left. Pete thought he was going through a gap between parked cars and prepared to mirror the move, but then shock jolted through him.

The man's left foot slammed onto the metal doorpost in the side of a dark grey saloon car. Metal crunched and bent, but it gave him the angle he needed. His right foot came up, left pushing off the side of the car, driving him up and over.

A woman screamed.

His right foot hit the top of the pushchair, tipping it backwards as his arms came up, hands hitting the door jamb, pushing him downward. The baby wailed in protest as it was tipped violently up and back, the man disappearing from Pete's view into the house, somehow avoiding an impact with his head on the top of the doorframe.

'Shit,' Pete gasped.

The man now had a potential hostage and an upturned kid between them and his pursuer.

Pete's heart hammered. An instant of indecision made his legs falter, but two quotes flashed into his mind, in direct conflict with established procedure: "The best form of defence is attack," and "There is no defence against the unexpected." He didn't know where either came from, though he thought the first might be Confucian, but he either had to act on them or let the man escape.

At least the upturned pushchair was preventing the door from closing.

Then it was too late.

He'd run out of pavement.

CHAPTER EIGHT

'Eh?'

Tommy Gayle leaned back in his chair in Brian Letterman's cluttered office, shocked by what he'd just heard. 'Are you fucking serious?' He leaned forward again. The desk between them was just too far away to touch so his elbows settled on his knees. 'Did you ever do geography at school?'

'Geography has nothing to do with it.'

Tommy was sure Brian was trying to conceal a smug grin. It was there in his eyes and in the tiny twitches at the corners of his mouth.

'It's a question of availability,' the man continued. 'And there is nowhere closer.'

'So, while I'm on remand for a case in Plymouth – to the west – you want to send me to Southampton. To the east. And, me being the only person in this place – or anywhere else, as far as I can make out – to get through to Tabby, you now want to split us up just 'cause you can't cope with me taking the piss. Because that's all it is, isn't it? You want rid of me. I spoil your sense of authority in this little kingdom of yours so you're going to risk Tabby's life just to try and get your sense of self-importance back. Well, I'll tell you what: you say I've got three more days in this dump. Your smug little life here's over. And that's a promise.'

Tommy surged up out of his chair and had the satisfaction of seeing Brian lean back, a flash of fear crossing his bland features. Then he spun away and headed for the door.

'Sit down,' Brian shouted. 'I haven't finished with you yet.'

Tommy kept going until his hand was on the doorknob. Then he turned. 'You haven't just finished with me, Brian. You've finished, full stop. I'll see to that if nobody else will.'

'Gavin!' Brian called.

The door handle twisted under Tommy's hand and the door opened. He stepped back automatically as the towering, muscular figure in his white T-shirt and trousers entered, seeming to fill the room with his calm but immovable bulk.

'Thomas and I seem to be at odds,' Brian said. 'Perhaps you can help?'

'What's the problem?' Gavin asked.

'This arse hole can't cope with me,' Tommy said, cutting Brian off. 'He can't do his job, so he's frightened he might lose it unless he gets rid of me. I say he needs me. Or, at least, Tabby does because *he* certainly hasn't got a clue how to get through to her. What do you think?' He planted his fists on his hips, staring up at the big man. 'Do you think Brian's sense of self-importance is worth Tabby's life? 'cause I don't.'

With the risk of immediate physicality gone, Gavin folded his thick arms across his chest. 'I'm sure Brian knows what he's doing.'

'Hah!' Tommy laughed. 'Got you brain-washed, has he? Can't think for yourself? This place gets more of a joke by the minute.'

'I don't see anyone laughing,' Brian said.

'You wouldn't. Don't like people laughing at you, do you? Little man in a little world, that's what you are, mate.'

'I think Thomas needs to cool off for an hour or two, Gavin. Take him to his room, would you? I don't think he'd benefit from contact with anyone else at the moment.'

Now Tommy laughed outright. 'That's right, Brian. Give up. Again. Daren't let anyone else see what a failure you are. Well, I ain't gonna forget in a couple of hours.'

'Come on, you,' Gavin said, taking his arm in a large hand.

'I ain't gonna forget this and nor are you, Brian,' Tommy called over his shoulder as he allowed himself to be led out of the room. 'That's a promise.'

Gavin pulled the door closed behind them, cutting Tommy off from further comment to the Archways' resident psychiatrist. But Tommy wasn't done yet. Not by a long way.

'You know he's a closet abuser, don't you?' he said to the big man.

Gavin didn't deign to reply. He'd heard all kinds of baseless accusations made against staff in this place. It was something the inmates resorted to regularly when they didn't get their way.

'That's why he wants rid of me,' Tommy went on regardless. 'He knows I know. I spent months living with one. I can smell 'em. And he gets flunkies like you to aid and abet him. My dad's a copper, you know. I know about aiding and abetting.' Tommy chattered on in a matter-of-fact tone as Gavin led him down a corridor, through a secured door into reception and on, through another secured door into the residential section of the building. 'And if he thinks I'll forget about him, just 'cause I'm not here anymore, he's got another think coming, I'll tell you that. I'll stir all kinds of shit up once I'm out of here. They don't know him in Southampton, do they?'

'Tell me something,' Gavin said as they passed the wide archway that gave into the common room. 'What is it that you get out of being so deliberately nasty to others?'

'Eh?' Tommy stopped in his tracks, staring at Gavin, hands on hips. 'What the fuck's that supposed to mean? When have I ever been deliberately nasty to anyone here? The only thing I've ever done is defend myself when other folks have started stuff. What are you, a religious nut? Turn the other cheek and that? Not a chance.' He set off towards his room again without prompting.

'It's not a question of turning the other cheek, Thomas,' Gavin said, moving after him. 'It's about using reason rather than violence. Violence begets violence.'

'Exactly,' Tommy shot back. 'People leave me alone, I leave them alone. They're violent to me, I give it back to them. With knobs on.'

They reached Tommy's room and he went in. Gavin stopped in the doorway, his bulk all but filling the gap.

'So, what had your sister done to you, the other day, to make you send her running out of here in tears?'

Tommy glanced at him and looked away. 'Yeah, well, that was different. It was for her own good. For *their* own good – her and Mum,' he said quietly.

'Really? How?'

Awkwardness and embarrassment gave rise to a flare of anger that Tommy allowed to swell and take hold. 'Well, if you can't figure that out, you ain't much good at your job, are you? So, if I'm supposed to be in solitary for two hours, you'd best bugger off and leave me be.'

*

Pete's foot hit just above the point where the other man's had impacted on the side of the grey car. He used his thigh muscles to catapult himself into the dark interior of the little house, bunching himself up to go through the reduced gap between the upturned pushchair and the door lintel. The unseen woman screamed again but the contrast between the bright April sunshine and the darkness within meant he couldn't see what he was leaping into. He caught a flash of pale skin in the dimness, but that was all.

His raised hands touched the door jamb and he started to straighten his legs, ready for impact. He made out a face twisted in terror, a slim figure pressed against the wall to his right, a sofa to his left. Then his feet hit the floor and he let his knees absorb the impact.

He could see now that she was alone.

'Police. Where is he?'

She was young. Mid-twenties, maybe. Dark hair pulled back into a ponytail, eyes huge with terror and shock. She blinked. 'Th...' Her voice faltered as a door slammed somewhere behind her. Her hand came up, flapping vaguely towards the back of the house. There was a doorway in the opposite corner of the room. Pete reached out to touch her shoulder as he went half-over and half-around a sofa that was too big for the room, heading after the fleeing man.

The back room was laid out as a kitchen diner, a small circular table in the middle with four chairs around it. A door was once again in the opposite corner. Beyond it, he could see a quarry tiled floor, a few inches lower than the main one. Light showed from the left. A tall, narrow window was directly in front of him, giving a view out to a narrow side-return with the garden beyond.

No sign of life or movement.

Three steps and Pete was across the room, the back door half-open to his left. He went through, pushing off the brick wall that faced him to add momentum as he leapt past the single-storey bathroom extension. A blue brick path crossed the end of the side-return, a common route along the rear of the terrace. He glanced left, then right.

Nothing.

Using his own movements as a guide, he went left, cursing as he found himself slowed by the need to check each little side-return he passed. The first was empty but for some wooden planters, the walls painted white. The second and third were completely filled in with full-width extensions, the first one modern, glazed and open, revealing a big kitchen-diner. Next-door was more enclosed, brick built with patio doors in the end. Pete ran past both, then paused to check the next house. He popped his head around the corner of the side-return and the pale sole of a shoe came at his face from just inches away.

He jerked back, but not fast or far enough.

The rubber sole hit him directly on the side of the face, knocking him backwards. His arms went out, trying to save himself, but he hit the low fence behind him and began to tip, feet leaving the ground. Another kick to the back of his thigh finished the job and he landed on his head and shoulder in an ungainly heap.

Ignoring the pain, letting the anger and embarrassment drive him, he rolled quickly and scrambled to his feet, determined to catch his man despite the lead he'd regained. He leapt forward but the kick to his thigh had been well placed. The leg collapsed under him. Pete cursed as his hands went out again and this time managed to keep him upright, though his knee hit the brick path painfully.

It wasn't his leg that he was most pained by, though, as he knelt there, listening to the slap of running feet echoing from the narrow passage down the side of the next house in the row.

He took out his phone and hit a speed dial number.

'Police, how can I help?'

'Do not allow anyone near that bloody van out the front there until SOCO have gone over every inch of it. I want to know who it belongs to and who the hell was driving it.'

'Pete. I take it you lost him?'

'No, he got away. There's a difference and I've got the bruises to prove it.'

*

Back at the station, Pete met Dick Feeney in the car park. He'd phoned on the way back to ask him for a ride out to see Claire Muir's ex. There wasn't time to wait for the car-pool at Middlemoor.

The woman whose house he had bounded through in pursuit of the van driver was shaken and indignant but all right when he checked on her. He had found her seated on the sofa, the baby on her lap as she crooned softly to it. When he got back to Heavitree Road a uniformed constable was already standing guard over the accident scene. If he hadn't been, Pete would have got Jill to go down and wait for SOCO, but he was glad there was no need. There was more than enough to do without losing two members of the team.

'Bloody hell,' Dick said as he saw the car and van at the station entrance for the first time. 'You made a job of that. Have you heard of the three strikes rule?'

'Don't even think it,' Pete said as they pulled out onto the road.

'Psssh-up pup pup, psssh-up pup. Psssh-up pup pup, psssh-up pup.' Dick murmured the first bars of the Push Bike Song from the early 1970s. 'Riding along on…'

'Shut up and drive, Mungo.'

Dick laughed. 'Did you get a look at him, or at least hear him speak?'

'He's a white bloke but I never saw his face and the witness didn't get much more than a fleeting impression, either. And the only word I heard him say was, "Move," as he went through the fish and chip queue. But it's not going to be easy to track down whoever was there now, is it?'

'No. It's a shame there aren't any cameras down that end of the road. You could always go down there at the same time tomorrow, though - see if any of the same people are there.'

Pete grunted. It might come to that yet, bearing in mind that the man was wearing gloves and a hat. Pete's phone rang as Dick drove up the inner ring road. He took it out and checked the caller ID.

Silverstone.

He debated for a couple of rings whether to take it or not, but there was little point in putting off the inevitable. He hit the green button. 'Sir?'

'What the bloody hell's going on with you, DS Gayle? Two cars in two days? I will not have one of my officers showing that degree of carelessness, Detective Sergeant. The force can't afford it.'

It sounded like the bloody idiot was serious! Not that Pete had ever heard him joke. 'I was being targeted, sir. I don't yet know why or who by, but yes, I am OK. Thanks for asking. And I will get to the bottom of it.'

Silverstone ignored the jibe. 'As the target, I'm not sure you should be investigating it, Peter. In fact, I know you shouldn't.'

'Except that we haven't established yet whether it's related to the murder of Claire Muir, which I *am* investigating, sir.' Pete jumped in quickly, before Silverstone could take that line of argument any further.

'Yes,' the senior officer said dubiously.

Pete flipped a switch on the radio, creating a static crackle. 'Sorry, sir. We're going into a bad area. I'll have to call you back when I can.' He ended the call before Silverstone could respond and switched his phone off. There were more important things to focus on for now.

Dick looked from Pete to his phone and back again. His expression didn't need words to say, *Really? Are you sure that's a good idea?*

Pete dialled again and got through on the second ring. The voice on the other end of the line made him pause in surprise. 'Lou?'

'Pete? What's up?'

'There's been a bit of an issue this afternoon. I need you and Annie to be extra careful. Be aware of who and what's around you.'

She was silent for a moment. 'What kind of issue are we talking about?'

'Another attempt to get me. It didn't work,' he added quickly. 'I just need to know that the two of you are safe, that's all. In case he tries to get to me through you.'

'You think *we're* in danger now? Jesus! This is getting crazy.'

'I'm just being cautious, that's all. I don't think you or Annie are in any danger – I think he's got a specific target and that's it. But better safe, eh?'

'And how's Annie supposed to cope with this? She'll be terrified, poor kid.'

'We'll just have to put it to her carefully, that's all. We can't not tell her. Just keep your eyes peeled and your ears open, OK? Maybe we can tell her she's looking for anyone suspicious that might be coming after me rather than saying she's in any danger herself.'

'And that'll help, will it?'

'It would take the immediate danger off her. We can talk about it later and work something out.'

'Hmm. All right.'

'I'll see you later.'

'Yeah. Love you.'

'You too.' He ended the call and turned to Dick Feeney in the seat beside him. 'What have we got on the bloke we're going to see?'

'Steve Raymond? He and Claire went out for about eight months before she dumped him. He didn't take it well. And she wasn't the first one he got nasty with. He's got a record of violence against women, especially ex-girlfriends. A couple of years ago there was a girl called Heather Campbell that he'd been going out with for a while until he got pissed one night and gave her a bit more than a slap. Put her in the RDE with a broken cheekbone, broken arm and some bruised ribs. She took a restraining order out against him but he ignored it. Went back for a second go a couple of weeks later, which is when we arrested him. He did eighteen months for assault with intent. Is Louise all right?'

'She'll be fine. Nice fellow. Anything since then?'

'Nothing official apart from a drunk and disorderly a year last Christmas.'

'So what happened with Claire and him?'

'According to her sister, she got sick of his drinking and belligerence and threw him out. They were living in her place. He's renting where he is now. From his uncle, apparently. He came back a couple of times, yelling through the letterbox and stuff. Slashed her tyres once. Pissed in her front garden. A couple of other minor things, but he seems to have maybe learned his lesson as far as ABH and so on. Unless he just got more sneaky.'

He glanced at Pete as they joined Cowley Bridge Road on the way out of the city.

'Have we got a full list of his vehicles yet?'

'Yes. It doesn't include a Land Rover, though, if that was your next question.'

Pete nodded. 'Shame. What about a white Transit van?'

Dick laughed. 'No such luck.'

'Oh, well. I'm sure we'll find something on him.'

*

'So, what do you plan to do about it?' Tabitha asked, outrage fighting for dominance with the disappointment on her pretty face.

'I don't know. What *can* I do that'll be effective with all these cameras all over the place?'

Tommy had been allowed out of his room only fifteen minutes ago. It hadn't taken long for Tabitha to find him and ask what had happened.

'Cameras, yes, but do they have sound?'

Tommy frowned. 'Why? What are you thinking?' She clearly had something in mind and, from the look in her eyes, he was sure he was going to like it.

She stared up at the camera in the corner of the common room where they sat, separate from the rest of the occupants, leaning close so that they could talk without being overheard. Around them, some of the other kids were playing pool, table football or cards, watched by the staff member standing beside the door, arms folded across his chest. It was afternoon break time. Soon they would all be heading back to class but, for now, the common room was a cacophony of noise.

Tommy reached out to put his hand over hers on her knee. 'You don't need to drop yourself in it for me, you know. I probably deserve at least half of what they're going to throw at me anyway.'

'I know.' She sandwiched his hand between hers. 'But, like you said, he's…'

'Tabitha. Tommy. Sit back, please.'

Tommy looked up to see a staff member coming towards them from the doorway. He shared a glance with Tabby and sat back in his chair.

Tabitha stood up to face the man, hands planted firmly on her hips. 'Why? You worried we're going to start snogging in front of the other kids? Or are you jealous? You want some of this?' She shook her braless breasts at him provocatively.

He stopped. 'Sit down, Tabitha.'

'Really? If I ain't gonna snog Tommy I damn sure ain't gonna suck you off with an audience, mate.'

Almost as shocked as the man standing in front of them, Tommy saw the staff member's face begin to darken. Tabitha stood defiantly, waiting for a response. What was she playing at? She was like a different person. 'Tab?'

She ignored him.

'Well?' She demanded of the man in the white T-shirt. 'Cat got your tongue, has it? You want mine but you can't use yours? How's that fair?'

The staff member cleared his throat. 'Right, young lady. I think you'd better go and see Brian. Come on.'

Tabitha winked at Tommy then turned back to the man as Tommy relaxed in the knowledge that she had a plan and this was part of it. 'What? Can't you stand up for yourself?' she demanded. 'Got to take me to the headmaster's office? Thought that would be the manager, not the shrink.'

'It would be but, as you well know, Mr Forsyth isn't here so Brian's in charge in his absence.'

'Yeah, and I bet he's loving it. While the cat's away...' She laughed.

'Come,' the man said firmly. 'Now.'

Tabitha flounced forward, head held high as she threw a sarcastic salute. 'Yes, sir.'

She had to be playing a part. Acting a role. Tommy had seen her playful before, but not like this. This was so different to the normal Tabitha, it was unreal. Tommy wished fervently that he could see and hear what she was going to do when she got to Brian's office, but it wasn't going to happen. He would just have to settle for hearing about it afterward. He hoped she wasn't going to get herself into too much trouble on his behalf.

CHAPTER NINE

The farm was a quarter of a mile north of the village, up a long track with a hedge up one side that was bright with the new leaves of Spring while, to the other side, rough pasture was fenced off with a double strand of barbed wire and occupied by black and white Hereford cattle.

At the top of the long, rising track, the farmhouse was block-like, built of grey stone with a low-pitched roof of similarly coloured tiles, giving Pete the impression of an out-building of Dartmoor prison. It was accessed via a filthy yard surrounded by out-buildings, dominated by a big open-sided barn with a metal roof, under which stood a tractor, several farm implements including a muck-spreader and a baler, and all of the five vehicles that Dick had told him on the way here that their target, Steve Raymond, owned.

Behind the big Dutch barn stood a mobile home.

Raymond's home, Pete guessed.

Dick stopped the car as close as he could to the rickety, peeling gate of the small garden that was walled off from the yard in front of the house and Pete noticed that he took the key from the ignition as they stepped out. Pete switched his phone back on and dropped it on the car seat. Dick locked the car behind them and Pete grinned. Dick had got the same impression of the place as he had.

The front door had been painted white a long time ago, but it looked like it had never been cleaned since. There was no knocker or bell. Pete stepped forward and hammered on it with the side of his fist. They waited, the silence broken only by the occasional twitter of a bird. Finally, the door was snatched open, surprising both of them. Having seen the farm, the man standing before them was almost a cliché. Tanned and lined, grey hair covered, even indoors, with a cloth cap, he was four or five inches shorter than Pete, but stocky and strong, his stomach pushing out the front of his green overalls just as his belligerence pushed out his stubbled jaw and pinched in his thick eyebrows. He said nothing, waiting for them to speak.

Pete lifted his warrant card. 'DS Gayle, Exeter CID. And you are…?'

'Don Raymond.'

'Steve's uncle,' Pete concluded.

'So?'

'Where were you yesterday evening?' Pete matched bluntness with bluntness.

'Here.'

'Can anyone verify that?'

'Mrs left years ago.'

Pete took that as a no. 'What about Steve? Did you see him? Or hear him coming or going?'

A grimace and a shake of the head.

Pete was about to ask if Don knew the younger man's whereabouts now when he was distracted by the sound of an engine. He glanced down the hill to his left to see an old Land Rover coming up the track.

'Hello. Who's this, then?'

Raymond stuck his head out to take a look. 'That's Steve.'

Pete looked at Dick. 'I thought he hadn't got a Land Rover?'

'It's mine. I left him to finish up, came back in his. I keep the tools in mine.'

'So you've been working together this morning?'

Raymond grunted.

'Doing what?'

'Fencing in the bottom field.'

'All morning?'

'Yup.'

The Land Rover pulled into the yard, stopping behind Dick's unmarked car. Even from a distance, Pete had seen the spotlight on the roof above the driver's position. Now he could see that it looked like an adapted motorcycle headlamp. He could also see the numerous dents, scratches and chips in the dark green paintwork, bare metal showing through here and there despite the thick covering of mud, old and new.

Except for the passenger side front wing, he noticed as the driver opened the door and stepped down. That looked relatively clean and fresh, unlike the man who now approached them. Stocky and bullish, he was dressed in stained jeans, a black donkey jacket and black beanie hat.

'What happened to the front wing?' Pete asked as he opened the garden gate.

'Put it on last week. A beast kicked it.'

'Stephen Raymond?' Pete asked the approaching man.

He nodded slowly. 'Yes. What do you want?'

'We're police. Exeter CID.'

'I guessed.'

'We're here to speak to you, actually. When did you last see or speak to Claire Muir?'

'Dunno. Weeks ago since I seen her. Longer than that since we spoke. Why?'

Pete could see on the man's face that he felt nothing for her. 'We're investigating her death and we're wondering why your vehicle was seen at her address at least three times in as many weeks recently if you're no longer in touch with her.'

That stopped the younger Raymond in his tracks. 'Death? How? When?'

The reaction seemed genuine, if muted. 'She was attacked and killed yesterday. We're trying to trace her movements since she left work at lunchtime.'

'Well, she wouldn't have been here or at my place. Why ask us?'

'Your place?' Pete asked, ignoring the question. 'We were under the impression you lived here. Over there,' he added, nodding towards the mobile home, one end of which was just visible beyond the barn.

'For now, ah. Till the house is finished.'

'And where's that?'

'The yard in Stoke Canon.'

Dick had told Pete about Raymond's scrap yard on the edge of the nearby village. It would have been their next stop, had its owner not turned up here. Would be anyway, Pete decided. He would need to speak to whoever was in charge there in Steve Raymond's absence. He nodded. 'I see. So, you're planning to live on-site?'

'Saves petrol. And security.'

'True. So, where were you from noon onwards yesterday?'

'What? I didn't kill her. I told you, I ain't even seen her for weeks.'

'What you didn't tell me is why you've been seen at her house several times recently. It's not like it's on the way to anywhere, is it?'

'Who says I've been there?' He frowned belligerently.

'Neighbours. And I dare say CCTV cameras on Topsham Road will support them if I bother to check. So...?'

His frown darkened even further. 'I miss her, all right? I've been trying to figure out how to try and get her back.'

'Well, that wasn't going to happen, was it?' Dick said. 'Between the new boyfriend and the restraining order which you've just admitted to breaching.'

His gaze switched rapidly to Feeney. 'No, I ain't. It says I can't be close to her. Says nothing about her house. If she's not there, there's no problem.'

'Except that, now she's been attacked, it speaks of motive,' Pete said. 'And it still ignores the new boyfriend.'

Raymond's lip curled. 'Best thing to do with him. He's a waste of space. Bloody Nancy-boy.'

'You know him?' Dick asked.

'I've seen him. Poncing around in that stupid little motor, pretending it's a four by four.'

'It is,' Pete pointed out.

'Ah. Never been off-road, though, and never will. Not designed for it, is it? Bloody waste of tin, if you ask me. A fashion statement, that's all. They're the type of thing that gives real ones like that a bad name.' He jabbed a thumb at the Land Rover over his shoulder. 'Driven by ponces trying to make out they're country folk.' He snorted. 'No wonder they call 'em Chelsea tractors.'

'Did Mr Raymond ever tell us where he was yesterday?' Dick asked.

Pete pursed his lips. 'No. He seemed to avoid that question somehow.' He turned back to Steve Raymond. 'Where were you, Mr Raymond?'

'My dinner's getting cold.' He stepped forward, ready to push past them.

'So, we've got clear motive and no alibi.'

Raymond stopped, fixing Dick with a glittering eyed sneer. 'Got no evidence either, though, have you? Out the way, I'm busy.'

With nothing to hold him on, they had to let him go. The door slammed behind him and the two policemen looked at each other.

'What do you think?' Dick asked.

'I think that Land Rover would bear a closer look while it's standing there in the open.'

'It's on private land.'

'Yes, but they left it there knowing we were here and they didn't tell us not to look at it.'

They set off towards the garden gate and the battered old Land Rover beyond.

'Do you reckon he's good for it?'

'He's good for something, Dick. I just don't know what yet.' Pete was staring at the spotlight on top of the cab, its chrome back pitted, stained and peeling. Its size suggested it had come from a big old motorbike. It would certainly be bright enough to go lamping for deer or badgers at night. 'Have we looked for gun licences for either of these jokers?'

'Stephen hasn't got one. Don't know about his uncle.' Dick held the gate open for Pete and followed him through. They examined the front wing of the Land Rover while they had the opportunity.

'That's been replaced not repaired,' said Dick. He looked at Pete. 'Quicker that way.'

'They're built for it,' Pete said. 'The panels were bolted on instead of welded. And he has got a scrap yard.'

'I'm guessing that's our next stop while we're out this way?'

'Be a bit silly not to, wouldn't it?'

Pete's gaze was caught by the bright cleanliness of the Land Rover's number plate. He wandered around to the rear of the filthy old vehicle. That one was comparatively spotless, too. Taking out his note pad, he wrote down the registration. He would check the database while Dick drove over to Stoke Canon. Steve Raymond was a long way from innocent. It was just a question of exactly what he was guilty of.

*

Tommy was sitting alone at the far end of the common room from where the other kids were playing when he heard the fire door from reception being barged open. He maintained his relaxed pose in the easy chair, hands locked together behind his head, but his attention was snapped into focus by Tabitha's voice.

'Two hours! Wait a minute, I'm the victim here. How come I'm getting punished for what he made me do?'

The huge black staff member, Aloysius, marched along the corridor, past the open side of the common room, with Tabitha's small hand engulfed in his.

'It happens often enough in his office,' Tabby went on when Aloysius didn't respond. 'How come it's so different when he's in Mr Forsyth's? Ah, now I get it! He hasn't figured out where Forsyth keeps his security cameras, has he? He can…' The safety door leading towards the residential section closed behind them, muffling her words, although he could still hear her voice.

What the hell had she done? Tommy knew she'd been determined to spoil Brian's plans, but he'd had no idea how far she'd been willing to go to achieve that. Her mention of the security cameras suggested she'd done something drastic, but how had she engineered the opportunity? And what had she actually done? Whatever it was, it had to have been pretty dramatic to get her two hours' solitary. He struggled to suppress a smile at the thought that she was willing to take such action for him.

The thought gave him a warm glow deep in his chest that he was still basking in when Aloysius returned, stopping at the entrance to the common room to announce, 'Tabitha's in her room. She's to stay there for two hours without any interaction with anyone.'

Tommy turned his gaze towards the big man.

'What are you looking at me for?'

Aloysius held his gaze without replying.

'What?' Tommy sat up straight, arms falling to his sides. 'Come on, out with it.'

'Nobody else needs telling, Thomas. You stay away from her room. You do not speak to her until she comes out. Understood?'

'You might have a funny accent, mate, but you are speaking English. I'll tell you what, though. Whatever happened to her in the manager's office, it's no good you and Brian buggering about with the footage. There's a dozen witnesses here to what she said on the way past and coppers don't believe in co-incidences. I can tell you that for a fact.'

'I know all about you and the police, Thomas.'

Tommy stood up abruptly, fear and anger surging through him. Had he made a mistake? Gone too far? The last thing he needed here was the other kids knowing who and what his father was. But to back-pedal would be to show weakness. 'You never know,' he said. 'Maybe Malcolm Burton won't be the only paedo they'll want me to testify against.'

Aloysius' eyes glittered beneath clenched brows. 'Do not presume to threaten me, Thomas Gayle.'

'Did I mention your name? I don't think so. No.' He glanced across at the other kids, as if expecting support, although he wasn't. 'Look to your colleagues, mate. Have a think about which ones of them might be open to allegations like that.' *Ooh,* he thought, pleased with himself. *Let's stir up a bit of dissention in the ranks. I like it. I like it a lot.*

CHAPTER TEN

Pete and Dick were a mile out of Stoke Canon when Pete's phone rang in his pocket. He pulled it out and tapped the screen. 'DS Gayle.'

'Boss, its Ben. I've checked on the Transit out the front here. It looks like the number plates have been swapped, from the marks on the screws. And the VIN's been taken off with an angle grinder so that's no good either, unless SOCO or the workshop at Middlemoor can recover it. I'm guessing the driver was wearing gloves, was he?'

'He was,' Pete said heavily.

'Makes it sound sort of professional, doesn't it?'

'Yeah, thanks for that, Ben. That really brightens my day.' It was true, though. The man knew exactly what he was doing and, unlike the Land Rover up on the hill, it was broad daylight and it did appear that Pete had been specifically targeted. Jane had driven out just in front of him and been left alone, after all. And yet, the fact that he was in a different car meant that, if that were true, they must have been watching him. 'If you're right, you'd better figure out who it is pretty quick. Otherwise, you'll end up working for Simon Phillips. I'll put it in my will, to make sure.'

'Oh, cheers. No pressure, then.'

'As we said before, the timing's got to be significant. Check out previous convictions to see if anyone's been released recently and, if not, concentrate on the cases we've got in the works now. And we all know which of them is the likeliest.'

Dick took a left turn off the main road through the village onto a narrow lane, hemmed in tightly on either side by dark stone terraced cottages with small, infrequent windows and doors that opened straight onto the road.

'I thought we'd eliminated him?' Ben asked.

'You know what Sherlock said about the impossible and the improbable. Maybe we just need to dig deeper.'

'Right. I'll let you know if we find anything.'

The doors and windows disappeared as the houses gave way to what were probably out-buildings backing onto the road, making it even darker and more oppressive. Pete put his phone away. Beyond the stone walls, tall, densely packed trees hemmed the lane in almost as densely.

'I don't fancy meeting a tow-truck up here,' Dick observed.

They appeared to be going up a valley, the road so narrow that, if they met another vehicle of any size, one of them would have to reverse. A bend took the lane around to the right, presenting them will a wall of dark trees. Beyond it, a passing place opened up on the right side of the road.

'There you go,' Pete said. 'No problem.'

'Right.'

Another fifty yards or so and the road bent around to the left. They rounded the bend and saw, some way ahead, a break in the trees on the left with a high fence of dark grey corrugated iron. Getting closer, they could see rusting and broken old vehicles stacked up like discarded metal carcasses. A wide gateway led into the filthy, pot-holed dirt yard, a porta-cabin standing over to the right with a set of wooden steps leading up to the door, which was closed. Beyond it, a half-built house was surrounded by yet more mud, blue tarpaulin flapping around it within the framework of scaffolding. Rolling down the window as they splashed and bounced across the yard, Pete could hear no movement other than their own and that of the blue plastic sheeting.

He checked his watch.

Ten past three in the afternoon. Where had the day gone?

'Quiet, isn't it?' said Dick.

'Tea-break time?' Pete shrugged.

Dick nodded as he pulled up outside the cream-coloured porta-cabin. 'Let's see if we're offered one, eh?'

'You'll be lucky.'

They stepped out of the car and Pete noticed that Dick used the remote to lock it again as they mounted the wide steps up to the temporary building. He opened the door. 'Shop,' he called as he stuck his head inside.

The place was deserted. It was as filthy as he'd expected, but surprisingly tidy, the larger portion set out as an office with the right-hand end divided off, two doors leading through. Toilet and kitchen, Pete guessed. Another door led through the back wall, the dirt-stained carpet suggesting that it also led somewhere rather than being a redundant standard fitting. Like the others, though, it was closed. So where was everyone?

'Hello,' he called more loudly than before. 'Anyone about?'

He glanced back at Dick, who shrugged. 'The place is open so they've got to be somewhere.'

The back door of the cabin opened abruptly and Pete's head snapped around as a small, ferret-like man in jeans and a dark sweater stepped through. Small, shrewd eyes assessed Pete and Dick as they stepped inside and Dick closed the door.

'What can I do for you gents?'

'Nobody on the building today?' Pete asked. 'I'd have thought this weather would be ideal.'

'They're waiting on materials, apparently. So…?' He spread his hands, waiting for the answer to his earlier question.

'I see.' *More like waiting to get paid,* Pete thought as he reached for his warrant card. 'We're police. DS Gayle. This is DC Feeney. And you are…?'

'Chris Tucker.'

He gave Pete's badge no more than a cursory glance. He'd already guessed who they were, Pete imagined. As hard as they might try to blend in, there were some people who could tell a copper as soon as they saw them. Usually those who needed to avoid contact with law-enforcement as much as possible. Still, it wouldn't hurt to start off gently. Put the guy at ease if he could. 'We're here about Steve's ex, Claire. You know her?'

Ratty, shoulder-length brown hair swung as Tucker shook his head. 'She never come here. Why?'

Pete didn't imagine she had visited the yard. It wasn't the sort of place he could see her in. 'Steve not around?' he asked, avoiding the question.

'Said he'd be in later. Don't know what time, though.'

'You work here full-time, do you?'

He grimaced. 'Just help out now and then. I live local.'

'Still, he must trust you, to leave you in charge.'

A shrug. 'Yeah, well… I've known him a long time.'

'Have you had an old white Transit through here, this past week or so?' It had to have been somewhere for the last several days. This was as good a place as any. But the man shook his head.

'No.'

Pete nodded. 'Just a thought. What security do you have here? Cameras? Dogs?'

'There's a couple of Alsatians. We shut them up during the day.'

Pete noted the use of the word 'we.' Tucker was more than occasional help. Or at least he thought of himself that way. 'Right. OK, then. If Steve's not here...' He nodded to Dick to lead the way out then turned quickly back to the smaller man. 'Oh, have you got an old Land Rover Series model here? My brother-in-law needs a left front wing off one.'

'We have, but he's out of luck. Steve had it off last week for his uncle.'

'Yeah? Damn! Oh, well, thanks anyway. We'll let you get on.'

As they stepped down from the door of the cabin, Pete glanced across at the partly enclosed building. 'Wasn't there a trace of paint on her coat? I wonder how the new house is coming along.'

Dick paused, looking at the slippery puddled mud between them and the flapping tarpaulin. He gave a small shrug. 'Best have a look, then. He can't complain if he's not here, can he?'

'Not fenced off, is it? Which I'm sure it ought to be, being in a publicly accessible place like this. Health and Safety and all that.'

Dick grunted and they headed that way. They'd barely passed the end of the porta-cabin when the door opened behind them and Tucker called, 'Can I help you with something?'

The two policemen looked at each other. Pete tipped his head.

'We're fine,' Dick responded. 'Just wandering while we're here.'

'There's nothing over there but the site and there's no public access to that.'

'Of course. Just wondering how he's coming along with it, that's all. And talking of public access, it ought to be fenced off, seeing as the public has access to the rest of the site. Breach of safety regulations as it is. There's a bloody big fine that can be applied to that.'

'I wouldn't know about that. It's not my place, is it? But, what I do know is, you aren't allowed over there.'

'You only work here, right? One thing about Health and Safety regulations: they make it very clear that it's everyone's responsibility to see that they're adhered to. So, as an employee, albeit part time, being aware of the breach, you'll have reported it, won't you?'

Pete smiled as he stepped up to the scaffolding and reached out to give it a shake before stepping under it where a gap showed between two sheets of the blue plastic tarp. He didn't hear Tucker's response, but it was a lot more muted than his previous comments. Looking through, he could see that the construction was a long way from water-tight. Roof trusses stuck up into the grey sky like the wooden ribs of a huge carcass while the gable ends of the house were up to full height with the inner block work, but still to be finished on the outer skin of red brick, and temporary woodwork still framed the window and door openings.

There would be no fresh paint here for some time yet.

Shame, he thought. The idea of arresting Steve Raymond held a strong appeal.

He turned back towards the car. Dick was standing on the steps leading up to the now closed door of the cabin, a grin lighting his grey-shadowed features. 'Anything?'

Pete shook his head. 'What did you say to him to get him to back off?'

'Told him if he let us do our job, we'd let him keep his.'

Pete nodded. That was Dick: dry as an old bone and subtle as a brick.

*

'I'm not going to tell you, so give up asking, will you?' Her tone made it an order rather than a request, and one thing Tommy had learned in his short lifetime was exactly how far to push and when to quit.

Now seemed to be that time. 'OK. I just wanted to... Well, to let you know how much I appreciate what you did. Whatever it was.' He glanced around the dining room, glad that the rest of the kids were sitting well away and not taking any notice of them as they filled their afternoon break with idle chatter and raucous laughter.

'Don't worry about it.'

All she'd told him about what had passed between her and Brian in the manager's office was that what she'd done was easier for her than it would have been for anyone else here. And that left only one possibility he could think of. The idea astounded him. That anyone would go that far to help him.

'What's the matter now?' Tabitha asked.

'Nothing. Just... Thanks, that's all. It's not... Nobody's done anything like that for me before.'

She snorted. 'I bet they bloody haven't.'

A picture popped into his mind and he was far more familiar with the feelings it engendered. Yet, somehow, again, they were different when it came to Tabitha. In some ways like those he held for Rosie Whitlock, but more intense. He looked at her, wondering. Was this what it felt like to...? He held back from admitting the possibility even to himself, carefully rewording the thought in his mind. Was this what it felt like to care about someone? And for them to care about him?

A nearly overwhelming urge for physical contact swelled up inside him. He almost reached out to hug her but managed, with a powerful struggle, to hold himself still. Then another thought popped into his mind and he grinned. 'I'd have loved to see Brian's face.'

She sniggered. 'It was a picture. Like a real-life cartoon. Uh!' Her eyes went wide, her mouth dropping open as she mimicked the psychiatrist's expression. 'Between that and the panic, there was an instant when you could see the real Brian. The dirty old lech.'

A different feeling sparked in Tommy's chest. A feeling he didn't understand, but it included anger and at the same time reminded him of Annie. Christ, this girl was doing things to him that he'd never imagined were possible! And she hadn't even touched him, apart from maybe an accidental brush of hands.

'Don't tell me you're jealous now!'

Tommy blinked. 'Eh? Of...' He paused, a grin stretching his lips. 'Well, who wouldn't be? A view like that, I'd love to see.'

'Perv.' She gave him a shove that almost tipped him off his chair.

'Uh... No. I'm male. You're female. We're about the same age. How's that pervy?'

'Yeah, well. Not going to happen, is it? Not here.'

Tommy grinned again. 'But somewhere else, maybe.'

'Thomas.'

The door had opened and one of the staff members had stuck her head through to call his name.

'Yeah?'

'You've got a visitor. Come on.'

He frowned, staying where he was. 'Who is it?'

'Your solicitor.'

He stood up, relieved that it wasn't his mum and sister again. Although she had said, "a visitor." Singular. He should have picked up on that. Was surprised that he hadn't. But what did Clive Davis want now? 'OK. Lead on, Mrs McDuff.'

She paused, staring hard at him, then ducked back from the door as he neared it and led the way towards reception. Through into the far corridor, she stopped and opened the door to one of the interview rooms.

Clive was waiting inside. He half stood as the door opened and reached out to shake Tommy's hand. 'Mr Gayle.'

'Mr Davis. What's up?' Tommy asked as they sat across the table from each other.

A small man, no more than eight inches taller than Tommy, he was slender and ineffectual-looking, but Tommy had learned that, behind the smart suit, grey hair and glasses lurked a mind that was as sharp as a pin and didn't believe in wasting time. There would be a purpose to this visit.

'We have a date,' said Davis.

'Very kind of you, Mr Davis, but you're not really my type,' Tommy grinned.

Davis didn't return the smile. 'Friday of next week.'

'For?'

'Plymouth crown court in the matter of carrying an offensive weapon in a public place.'

'Bloody hell! They don't hang about over there, do they? Life in the big city, eh?'

Although Exeter was the county town, Plymouth was much larger and more urbanised.

'Juvenile court, Thomas. It's independent of the main court, one of its primary objectives being to facilitate the efficient processing of cases, thereby minimising delay and the possible pre-trial stresses and so forth of its defendants.'

'Well, good for them. But how's that going to work with me being transferred to Southampton the day after tomorrow and you being here in Exeter?'

Davis pursed his lips. 'It's less than ideal.'

'Huh! You're telling me, mate.'

Davis paused, his expression tightening even further. Tommy could imagine what he was thinking. *'I'm not your mate, Thomas. I'm your solicitor. Reluctantly.'* And that reluctance, which was plain to see every time he looked in the man's eyes, could be Tommy's downfall. But there wasn't much he could do about it from in here. Except…

'How about you get Colin Underhill back in here?'

Davis raised a grey eyebrow. 'Really? You've decided to…'

'It'd be another bit of pressure on Forsyth to overrule Brian and keep me here, wouldn't it?' Tommy said, cutting him off.

'Except that Mr Forsyth is currently out of the country.'

'Well, who's his boss, then? There's got to be someone in overall charge of these places.'

'Indeed. I'll look into it. And the Detective Inspector: you're sure you want to follow that path now? Once you're on it, there's no stepping off again. Not without harming your own case.'

'They haven't got a case against me. It's Mel Burton they're charging.'

'For the moment, yes. I gather a decision is yet to be made regarding yourself. There is conflicting evidence.'

'What? We've got Rosie's testimony. What else is there?'

'I don't know all the details at this point, but I gather there's some forensic evidence that points to your deeper involvement.'

Tommy frowned. Was he trying to be clever? Deeper involvement... 'Is that supposed to be some sort of euphemism?'

Davis sat back in his chair. 'I was simply trying to say that, if you mess them about, the Crown Prosecution Service will be far more likely to pursue a case against you as an accomplice rather than a victim.'

'Well, I know that. I ain't stupid. So are you going to get Uncle Colin back here or what?'

'If you're certain that's the route you want to take now.'

'I'm sure.' To be fair, Tommy thought, he had been stringing them along for a while. But it was in his own best interests now to admit what he'd known all along was going to be the path he'd take. There was nothing to be gained and a lot to be lost by delaying the decision any further.

'Very well. Now, with regard to next Friday...'

*

While Dick drove back into Exeter, Pete's mind drifted back to his conversation with Ben. It was a sad reflection that a life he'd spent trying to make Devon a better and safer place should have created so many potential enemies, but it was part of the job. People with the selfishness and arrogance to ignore the law were not likely to forgive or forget those who made them suffer the consequences of their actions, he supposed. Which was no help at all in narrowing down the list of possible suspects, but...

He pictured the Land Rover closing in on him last night, lights flaring.

He blinked.

Damn. His mind went to the vehicle standing outside the farmhouse earlier. The spotlight on the roof above the driver's seat.

A single spotlight while the one last night had had five: two large ones at either end and three slightly smaller ones between them. He released a sigh of frustration.

'What's up?' asked Dick.

'It was a different Land Rover. The one last night had five spotlights on the roof, not just one. And the roof of Raymond's one didn't show any signs of being altered.'

'Ssh... And I was quite enjoying the thought of Steve Raymond in hand cuffs.'

'Yeah. It'll have to go on the back-burner for now, though.'

Dick nodded. 'So we're back to square one.'

'One step forward.'

'I never was into dancing. Give me a straight-forward stroll, any day.'

'We haven't got time to stroll. This is a sprint to the finish. Otherwise, somebody else could get hurt or worse.'

'So what's the next step, do you reckon?'

'Well, if it wasn't Raymond, we need to have a closer look at the current boyfriend to start with. See if we can rule him in or out.'

'I thought he had an alibi?'

'He says so, but we need to confirm it. If Claire thought he was seeing someone else on the side, that would give him motive.'

'Or her, whoever she is,' Dick pointed out.

'Except the killer's male,' Pete said as they entered the outskirts of the city, passing the roundabout that led onto the Cowley Bridge.

'Hmm. Not a closet gay, is he, this boyfriend of hers? Swings both ways or whatever they call it these days? Girls for appearance's sake, boys for pleasure?'

'And you said you were too young to remember the fifties.'

'I am. What's that got to do with it?'

'Well, who gives that much of a damn about appearances anymore? Especially in that sense. No.' Pete shook his head. 'There's more to it than that. But you can do a full background on him when we get back, as you brought it up.'

'Oh, thanks.'

'The only thing we can be sure of is, it wasn't him in that Transit van, earlier.'

'So we're looking for two suspects. At least. Great.'

'Life's a bitch…'

'Yeah, I'm not going to answer that. Just in case.'

Pete laughed as Dick glanced across at the tyre and exhaust centre he'd visited more than once just days ago, on their previous case. 'It's good to know somebody cares.'

CHAPTER ELEVEN

'Where's Jane?' Pete asked as he and Dick reached their desks.

'Cape Canaveral.' Dave jabbed his pen at the floor. 'Seeing if life can survive in a black hole.'

'Well, I didn't hear any screams on the way past,' Pete said, getting the reference to the CCTV room. 'So either he's already dead or he hasn't tried anything on with her yet.'

Despite Graham's reputation for flirting with the women of the station, they were all aware that Jane was one who he knew better than to try anything with. He'd tried it once and been shot down in flames. They now had a cautious tolerance of each other like two cats with overlapping territories.

'What else is new?' he asked, reaching for the power button on his computer screen.

'Well, for one thing, the relationship with Stuart Elsfield wasn't all sweetness and light.'

'Really?'

'I took a call a few minutes ago from her next-door neighbour. You put a card through her letterbox earlier.'

'Yes. She wasn't in when we were out there. What did she have to say?'

'Well, she couldn't give much in the way of details – the walls aren't quite thin enough for that – but she did say that they had more than one ding-dong that she heard, especially in the last three or four weeks. The gist of what she did hear was that he was sometimes not where he was supposed to be. Claire thought he was playing around on her. He denied it, but she wasn't entirely convinced. She'd found a name,' he said as Jane entered the room and crossed towards them. 'Mrs Dawson presumed it was on his phone. He refused to tell her who it was but maintained it was nothing she needed to worry about.'

'I can see how that might not go down too well,' Pete admitted.

'Too bloody right,' Jill agreed. 'I'm with her.'

'You would be,' Dave retorted.

Pete caught the wink he aimed at Dick as he said it.

'What's that mean?'

'Suspicious mind. And female.'

'Boss, can I hit him? Please?' Jill asked.

'Hey! I don't even want to count the number of laws that would break,' Dave protested. 'Assaulting a police officer, violence in the workplace, sexual harassment... Ow!'

The small dark-haired PC had slammed a fist into the top of his arm.

'Ooh.' Dave rubbed his arm. 'That actually hurt, Titch. Have you been practicing?'

'You want me to try it again? See if it was a fluke?' She raised her fist again.

'Now, now, kids,' Pete said, raising his hands. 'That'll do.'

Jill lowered her fist and Pete wondered briefly at how easy it had been to regain control, until Colin Underhill's deep, dry voice came from close behind him. 'Pete. Have you got a sec?'

He turned quickly in his chair. The DI was standing just a couple of feet behind him. 'Of course, Guv. What's up?'

Colin tipped his head, beckoning Pete to join him in his office. 'How's it going?' he asked as Pete stood up.

'It's like running a crèche sometimes, but I think I'm still in charge.' He turned back to his team. 'Dave, give Dick a hand with the background on Elsfield, just to speed things up. Let's find out why Claire thought he was cheating on her. And see if we can confirm his whereabouts at the time she was killed.' Then he followed Underhill up the length of the squad room and stepped into the half-glazed office, closing the door behind him. 'Guv?'

Underhill sat down and motioned to the chair in front of his desk. 'I had a call from Tommy's solicitor a few minutes ago,' he said. 'His court date's been decided. It's next Friday.'

'What?'

'And Tommy wants to talk to me.'

'He's... decided to testify?'

Colin shook his head. 'I don't know yet. It would be the sensible thing to do, but that's been true from the get-go. Maybe the court date and the move, coming so close together, has pushed him into it. We'll see.'

'But… A court date in Plymouth, a move to Southampton days before it. How can that make sense? How can it be allowed to happen?'

Colin shrugged. 'Out of our hands, mate. We just have to deal with the consequences. But if he has decided to testify against Malcolm Burton, that'll help bring some pressure to bear in his favour.'

'I bloody hope so.' Pete felt exhausted by the emotional rollercoaster his son had dragged them all onto. 'I don't know how much more *I* can cope with, never mind Lou and Annie.'

Underhill stood up. 'I'll let you know what happens when I get back.'

'Right. Thanks.'

'Oh, and…' Colin caught his gaze and held it. 'Probably best to tread light around Simon for a day or so. You know what he's like for sulking.'

'Yeah.' Pete nodded. 'Cheers for that.'

He stood up and preceded the DI out to the squad room.

'We're going to have to get you some padded trousers,' Dave said as he regained his seat moments later. 'You're in and out of there like a fiddler's elbow, lately.'

'It's not my arse that needs padding, Dave.'

'Whose, then?'

'Can you get a waistcoat big enough to go over one of those American football outfits?' Jane pondered.

'Ben? Do you want to swap desks?' Dave asked.

Ben looked up from his screen. 'No, thanks. It's dangerous enough here. Ow! What was that for?' he demanded of Jill.

'Just keeping you in your place.'

'I wasn't moving.'

'Ah,' Dave crooned. 'I love you too, Jill.'

'Has anybody here got anything sensible to say?' Pete demanded.

'Why change the habits of a lifetime?' Jane asked.

Pete shook his head. 'You lot are enough to drive anybody to religion. Dick, tell me something useful.'

Dick looked up from the notebook he was writing in. 'Stuart Elsfield's Rav 4's not as clean as most of them.'

'And how's that useful?'

'Well, it usually is. Apparently.'

'So, he's taken an unusual trip out to the countryside? As of when?'

'As of two hours ago when his receptionist saw it.'

'So, where does he park it? Get onto Graham and see if he can pick up its last movements.'

'He's going to fall out with you,' Dave said. 'Keeping him awake all day like this. He's not used to it.'

Pete looked across the desks at him. 'I haven't heard your contribution yet, Dave.'

'That's because I haven't been able to get a word in. You might want to hold off on disturbing Graham again for a minute,' he continued over Jane's soft whistling of the end of Buddy Holly's *That'll Be The Day*. 'Elsfield was picked up on the ANPR camera on Cowley Bridge Road at twelve minutes past five yesterday afternoon, heading out of town.'

'Was he, now?' Cowley Bridge Road was the route Pete had taken out of the city last night to reach the Ashclyst Forest, where Claire Muir's body had been found. 'And when did he come back?'

'He didn't. At least, not that way.'

Pete raised an eyebrow, waiting for him to continue.

'I've checked as far as this side of midnight. There's nothing. From there or anywhere else.'

Pete was nodding slowly. 'I think perhaps we ought to go and have another word with Mr Elsfield. Can I trust you lot to work peacefully and productively if I leave you alone for more than two minutes?'

'Well, I wouldn't want to make promises.'

'Yeah. OK, you go, Dave.'

The surprise on Dave's face was a reward all its own, but he had no argument. 'Right,' he said, switching off his screen and standing up.

'It's all right,' Jane said. 'You'll be safe with him. It's only women that he's got an appetite for. I think.'

'What's that song about the big, bad troll, Ben?' Dick asked.

'Why ask me?'

'You're the youngest one here,' Jill pointed out. 'Most likely to remember.'

'Well, I don't.'

'Or you don't want to admit it,' she grinned.

'Whichever, it's not relevant,' Pete cut in. 'Jane, you spoke to her sister earlier. Get back to her and ask about Claire's previous boyfriends. Who's up for an evening's door-knocking? We need to finish the canvas of her neighbours.'

'The more of us doing it, the less time it'll take,' said Dick.

Jane picked up her phone. 'I'd best call my old man or he'll be reporting me as a missing person.'

'I'm in,' said Ben, drawing a nod of agreement from Jill.

'Meet you out there, shall we?' asked Dave. 'Time you've talked to the boyfriend, it won't be worth coming back here.'

Pete checked the time. It was almost four. 'Right. I need the colour and location of the Rav 4. I don't suppose she gave you the registration, did she?'

'No,' Dick replied. 'But I looked it up.'

'Good.' Pete slid his notebook across the desk. 'Here, write it all down while I...'

His desk phone rang, interrupting him. He picked it up. 'DS Gayle...'

'My office. Now,' DCI Silverstone barked. The line clicked dead before Pete could respond.

'OK,' Pete said to Dick. 'Hold that thought. Seems I've got another stop to make before I go and see the man about his car.' He stood up and headed out of the squad room.

Along the corridor, he knocked on DCI Silverstone's door.

'Come.'

For once, Silverstone was sitting back in his chair, waiting for Pete to enter rather than concentrating on paperwork, or at least pretending to. His fingers were intertwined on his lap. He looked relaxed as he gazed up at Pete.

'Sir?'

'Keeping you occupied, are we, Peter?'

'Sir.' Where the hell was this going? He didn't have time for bullshit. There was far too much to do.

'But presumably you enjoyed your time off last year.'

'Not exactly, sir. In the circumstances. I was grateful for it, but I'd have preferred not to need it.'

'And yet you seem bound and determined to get some more. Only without the prospect of coming back or drawing a police pension. Why is that, I wonder?'

Pete felt his brow crease into a frown. *Here it comes,* he thought. *We're getting to the crux of the matter at last.* 'Why would you think that, sir?'

He could guess the answer, of course, but he wasn't going to admit anything.

'What else am I to think when one of my officers hangs up the phone on me and refuses to take my calls for over an hour thereafter?' At last he sat forward, hands splayed on his desk, the relaxed exterior vanishing as his true feelings blazed through his dark eyes. 'I don't need to feel the love here, Sergeant, but I do demand the respect due to my rank. And don't give me that balderdash about going into a poor reception area. We both know there's no such thing in this city anymore.'

'I wasn't in the city, sir. I was heading out to interview a person of interest in the Claire Muir case. He lives on a farm outside one of the villages to the north of here. In the hills.'

'And I assume the details will be in your daily report?'

'Of course.'

'So I can check on the mobile reception in the area.'

'If you see fit, sir. Yes.' *You probably will, as well,* he thought. *You're petty enough.*

'Disrespect me or this uniform again, Detective Sergeant, and I'll have you on a disciplinary faster than you can blink. Is that clear?'

'Crystal, sir.'

Silverstone raised a hand to waggle the forefinger at Pete. 'One more breach of protocol, Gayle,' he warned. 'Just one more… Now get out of my sight.'

'Sir.' Pete turned and reached for the door.

There was no way he'd ever disrespect the uniform. The DCI, however, was another matter entirely. Respect for any individual, whatever their rank, was earned and Adam Silverstone had yet to do anything that Pete knew of to achieve that. But he did have the power in his hands to take away Pete's career, his livelihood and the only job he'd ever wanted to do. A job that he was, with no sense of arrogance, really good at and that allowed him to actually be of use to society. Much as Silverstone was a waste of space and oxygen, Pete wasn't going to give him any excuse to do that if he could possibly help it.

*

'You spoke to one of my DCs earlier about the condition of Mr Elsfield's car?' Pete leaned on the high-topped counter in front of the receptionist's desk. There was no-one else in the small room, but he noticed that she glanced around anyway before responding in a subdued voice.

'That's right. It's normally immaculate. Polished to within an inch of its life. But today, it's all filthy. I think someone mentioned that Miss Muir had been found in the woods somewhere, so I thought you ought to know.'

'Well, thank you. Can I have a word with Mr Elsfield?'

'Of course. His client left a couple of minutes ago, so he's free now.' She picked up the phone at her elbow and dialled a three-figure number. 'Mr Elsfield? Detective Gayle's here to see you again.' She listened. 'Yes, sir. I'll tell him.' She put the receiver down and looked up at Pete. 'He'll be down in a moment.'

Pete nodded his thanks. 'So you always park in the multi-storey, do you?'

'A lot of the shop-workers and so on do.'

'And Mr Elsfield?'

'Yes. Almost always.'

They were talking about the multi-level car park of the Guildhall Centre on Paul Street, just a few dozen yards from where they were. Pete had gone there before coming here, to check the condition of Stuart Elsfield's Toyota. As she'd said, the sides were splattered with dried mud, but the top looked clean and well-polished as if, as they suspected, he rarely took the vehicle out of the city. Pete knew he lived up near the cricket ground, but that didn't entail any rural roads.

'And it was clean yesterday, was it? The Rav 4?'

'Yes.'

The door to his right opened and Stuart Elsfield stepped through. 'DS Gayle. Have you got some news?' He extended a hand, which Pete shook.

Pete shook his head. 'Just a few more questions, I'm afraid.'

His hopeful expression faded. 'I see. Well, you'd best come through.' He held the door for Pete then led the way back to his office. He waited until they were seated with the door closed before asking, 'What can I do for you, Detective Sergeant?'

'You said you were at home all evening yesterday.'

'Yes.'

Pete sighed and leaned forward in his chair, elbows on his knees as he focussed on Elsfield's face. 'That leaves us with witnesses saying that Claire suspected you of being unfaithful and the need to explain why your car was picked up on a camera going out of town on the Cowley Bridge Road between five and a quarter past.'

'I wasn't...' He stopped, shoulders slumping slightly. Drew a breath. 'I was about to say I wasn't speeding, but you don't mean that sort of camera, do you? And I was certainly not being unfaithful to Claire. I'm not that kind of man, Detective Sergeant. Yes, I went out that way. Straight from here. I have every Thursday since the first week of January. I go to Thorverton. There's a dance teacher there. I've been trying to learn how to dance, so I could take Claire out and surprise her. Not that I got very far. And it's all wasted now, isn't it?'

'OK. I also gather you're fairly particular about your car. It's cleanliness and so on.'

'I like to keep it smart, yes.'

'So, how do you account for the state it's in now?'

'Have you been out to Thorverton lately, Detective?'

'Not for a few months, no.' Pete recalled the last time he'd been out that way, searching for possible dump sites for a body that had been found caught in the shrubbery at the edge of the river here in Exeter.

'If you had, you wouldn't need to ask. From the farm shop down to the weir, the road's a right mess, I can tell you. A bloody disgrace, in fact. How nobody's had an accident down there, I don't know.'

'I see,' Pete nodded. 'You didn't report it, though?'

'Report it? To whom?' he frowned.

'Us. The council. Road users such as farmers, quarries and so on are required by law to clean up any excessive mess that they leave on the highway, to maintain public safety.'

'I see. Well, that's news to me.'

'Fair enough. I will get it looked into. But that leaves us with the question of how you got home. Because it wasn't down the Cowley Bridge Road, was it?'

'No. I never do come back that way. I cut across Wreford's Lane and down Pennsylvania. It's a bit longer, but a lot less fiddly.'

'Right.' Pete could see what he meant. Although the alternative would probably be a little shorter in distance, there was a lot more twisting and turning and a lot more junctions to negotiate than there would be on the route he'd described. 'And you haven't thought of anything since we last spoke that might help? Anyone Claire might have been having a problem with?'

Elsfield shook his head. 'No, sorry.'

Pete stood up and shook his hand again. 'I'll leave you to it, then.' The younger man's attitude as he'd answered Pete's questions had said one thing, loud and clear. *Another dead end.*

CHAPTER TWELVE

By the time Pete had got back to the spare patrol car that he had had to borrow until his own car was back on the road – which he'd been told would not be until Monday – he had confirmed at least part of Stuart Elsfield's story. The accountant had been in Thorverton with the theatrically upper-crust sounding dance teacher from five-thirty to six-thirty last night, as usual. It didn't clear him of Claire's death. Only one thing other than finding the real killer would do that. But it was one more nail in the coffin of the theory.

He set off towards Pennsylvania Road, using the car's intricate comms system to contact the force headquarters as he drove.

When the call connected he asked for Dr Abigail White's office and was surprised when the police psychologist answered herself. 'Dr White. How can I help?'

'Hey, Doc. It's Pete Gayle. Cutbacks got your secretary?'

'Peter. How are you?'

'I'm OK. I was just calling for a bit of advice.'

'Yes?'

'My son, Tommy. He's currently in Archways Secure Children's Home. The head psychiatrist there, Brian Letterman – do you know him, or of him?'

'I've heard of him. Met him a couple of times professionally. Why?'

'Well, Tommy's not getting on so well with him. He's got a trial coming up soon in Plymouth, plus there's the issue of Malcolm Burton's trial in a few weeks now.' She was familiar with all this from their previous conversations, he knew. 'Letterman can't cope with him, though, so he's decided that he needs to get rid of him. To Southampton.'

'That's...' She stopped herself, but Pete had noted her instinctive response. 'What are you asking me, DS Gayle?'

'I'm asking if there's any way I can get an independent second opinion, psychologically speaking, about the impact of that kind of move on Tommy – or its necessity in the first place.'

'Well, I don't know all the circumstances, of course, but medically speaking, we all have the right to a second opinion. Obviously, Tommy's not in a position to exercise that but, as his parent, you are on his behalf.'

'So, I'd need to speak to a qualified professional such as yourself and ask them to interview him before he's transferred in three days.'

'Three days?' she demanded, shocked.

'That's right.'

She hesitated, her silence loud over the speakers. 'If I... Your wife works at the hospital, doesn't she?'

'Yes.'

'If I were you, I'd see if she can get someone from there to go and assess Tommy. If no-one's available, then get back to me. I'll see what I can do, but I can't make any promises.'

'That's fair enough.'

'Let me know as soon as you can.'

'Will do. Thanks, Doc.'

He ended the call and dialled Jane in the station.

'You lot will have to get on without me a bit longer,' he said when she picked up the phone. 'I've got another little job to do before I join you at Claire's.'

'OK. How did you get on with the boyfriend?'

'That's the extra job: confirming his story. At this stage, though, he looks doubtful for it.'

'Two down, then.'

'Yeah.' The phrase *three strikes and you're out* popped into his mind but that wasn't acceptable in this case. 'Which leaves us with a whole lot of legwork to do. Unless the sister had any little nuggets to share?'

'Sadly not. Claire had a couple of serious boyfriends back in Birmingham, but neither of them caused any problems after they broke up. Or before, come to that.'

'OK. I'll see what Elsfield's neighbours have to say, then join you at Claire's place.'

Pete parked at the end of the short, curving road and walked the few yards up to Stuart Elsfield's 1960s built house. A small green east-European hatchback stood on the driveway of the house next door. Pete went up the drive and rang the doorbell. It was answered by a woman in her fifties, he guessed, dark grey hair falling onto the shoulders of a white blouse which she wore with a dark skirt.

'Yes?'

He held up his warrant card. 'DS Gayle, Exeter CID. I'm investigating a case that involves one of your neighbours and I wondered if you'd seen or heard anything out of the ordinary along the street here yesterday evening.'

'No, I don't think so. Why? What's happened?'

'You'll no doubt see in the press tonight, there's been a death. It was a friend of someone who lives up here.'

'Oh, how awful.'

Pete nodded. 'Well, thanks for your time.' He heard the front door close behind him as he walked back past the little green car.

There was no vehicle on the drive of the next house down, but Pete rang the doorbell anyway, noting the sign on the door saying that the occupiers did not accept any cold-callers as he waited for a response. After a few moments, the door opened to reveal a grey-haired man in an open-necked shirt, cord trousers and slippers.

'Yes?'

'I'm DS Gayle, Exeter CID.' Pete again showed his warrant card.

The man studied it myopically, then returned his gaze to Pete.

'Were you in yesterday evening?'

'Yes.'

'Did you see or hear anything unusual? Vehicles coming or going? An argument, perhaps? Any other noises?'

'No. Why, what's up?'

'Just routine enquiries. Nothing to worry about, sir. Have a good evening.' Pete turned away and headed for the last house in the row.

'They won't be in for another half hour or more,' the man behind him called. 'Still at work.'

Pete turned to give him a nod. 'Thanks.' He crossed the road instead, towards the house opposite.

'Same there,' the old man called before shutting his door.

Pete checked his watch. It was a quarter to five. A bit early for people to be home from work, maybe, but he would speak to whoever he could, then go back around to those he'd missed. The house opposite the old man's had a small white Audi on the drive. He headed that way and was reaching for the doorbell when his phone rang in his pocket.

He checked the screen.

Colin.

He tapped the green icon as he turned back towards the street. 'Guv?'

'Tommy's finally agreed to testify against Malcolm Burton. I've just taken a statement from him.'

Pete stopped in his tracks, his free hand reaching for the roof of the white Audi for support. 'Thank Christ.'

'Yes. I don't know what we're going to do about him in the meantime, though. I'll call the CPS in a minute and see if they've made a decision yet on whether to charge him as an accessory or not but, either way, with his court date coming up in Plymouth next week, I can't see much chance of him coming out on bail. He's pretty much proved himself to be a flight risk over the past few months.'

Much as Pete wanted to, there was no arguing with that. 'Yes, but Southampton's hardly practical in the circumstances, is it?' He straightened up and continued out to the road, heading slowly back towards the patrol car.

'No, but he's too young for any other option apart from where he is now. It's not like we can keep him in the cells at the station for a week. They're not set up for that sort of thing. And especially not for kids.'

'Is there no way Letterman can be overruled? I mean, he's not actually the manager there, is he? He's only in temporary charge because the manager's on holiday.'

'True, but he's out of the country and unreachable and it's not like those places are government run anymore. They're independent. Just contracted by the local authorities.'

'Well then, they're answerable to the local authorities and Social Services, surely?' Pete crossed the road, still moving back towards the patrol car he had parked just around the corner.

'Yes.' Colin sounded unsure, almost cautious.

'So, if we got Social Services onside, they could intervene. We do plenty for them.' Pete stopped himself at that, but his mind ran on. *They wouldn't mind doing something for us in return, surely?* He checked his watch. 'If you're quick, you might even get hold of them before they clear off home. Especially on a Friday.'

Colin grunted.

Pete had no doubt the DI had seen straight through his comment, but it had been worth making anyway. They were both fully aware that Social Services had someone either working or on call twenty-four seven, but that was unlikely to be the person in charge.

Reaching the patrol car, he rested one hand on its roof.

'Best call them before I speak to the CPS then, hadn't I?'

Pete's eyes closed as he sagged with relief. 'Thanks, Guv.'

'Don't thank me yet. I haven't done it and I'm not guaranteeing a positive result when I do.'

'I know. But thanks anyway.' Pete felt a strong temptation to call Louise and tell her the news, but he resisted. There was no point getting her hopes up only to have them dashed in another half hour or so. He put the phone away and turned back to continue with the task he'd set himself until he heard from Colin again.

*

The next thirty-five minutes passed with agonising slowness. After twenty, he'd spoken to the occupants of all but one of the houses within three doors of Elsfield's and the ones opposite. None had seen or heard anything out of the ordinary last night and two confirmed that Elsfield's Toyota was on his drive at half past seven and at ten-fifteen in the evening. Which left more than enough of a gap, of course, but was nevertheless strongly suggestive of his innocence, Pete thought as he drove down towards the city centre and through onto the Topsham Road.

Where the hell was Colin? What was taking so damned long?

He was passing the school, almost at the turnoff to Claire Muir's address when his phone finally rang. He used the car's hands-free Bluetooth facility to answer it.

'Gayle.'

'Boss, its Jane. We're all done here. We're going to head off unless you've got something else you need us to do tonight.'

Tension stiffening his arms and neck, Pete held back the curse that popped into his mind when it wasn't Colin Underhill on the other end. 'No, that's fine, Jane. Thanks, all of you. Did you find anything useful?'

'No. Did you?'

'No. I think we can move Stuart Elsfield down towards the bottom of the suspect list.'

'Another one bites the dust, eh?'

'It looks that way. So we'll have to start fresh in the morning.'

Tomorrow might be Saturday, but this wasn't a nine-to-five job when there was a killer to track down before they potentially claimed another victim.

'See you then.'

'Night, Jane.' Pete turned around to head back towards the city centre and the station. He didn't know for sure, of course, but he guessed Colin was probably still in his office.

Rather than queueing down to the ring-road and around towards the station, he was working his way through the minor roads, not far from where Rosie Whitlock lived, when his phone finally rang again. He tapped the screen to take the call.

'Pete Gayle.'

'Its Colin. Where are you?'

'Davenport Road, heading back to the station. Why?'

'We'll talk when you get here. See you in a minute or two.'

'Wh…'

The dial tone cut off his question, humming out of the car's speakers.

'Dammit!'

As much as he liked and admired Colin Underhill, there were times when he could happily hit him over the head with a road-mender's mallet, he reflected as he drove along an almost deserted road between the high hedges and wide gateways of some of the most expensive houses in the city. While, most of the time, his dry taciturnity was ideally suited to his role, it could sometimes – like now – be incredibly frustrating.

CHAPTER THIRTEEN

He'd taken no more than three steps away from the car when he stopped in amazement, the front door opening in front of him.

'Daddy!' She reached out with both arms for a hug.

'Hello, Button.' Pete stepped forward into her embrace, lifting her off the front step into his arms and groaning. 'Either I'm getting too old for this or you're getting too big, kiddo.'

'I'm the same size as I was yesterday. And last week. I thought you had a black car?'

'It must be all those brains weighing you down then,' he retorted. 'I did. But now I've got this one until mine's ready, next week.'

'How come?'

'The black one got damaged. How was your day?' He stepped forward, carrying her over the threshold and kicking the door shut.

'No dramas.'

I wish I could say the same! Pete set her down on the second stair, but kept his arms closed around her. 'Tell me something,' he said.

'What?'

'Your bedroom's at the back of the house, so's the kitchen, and the sitting room curtains are drawn. So how do you know I've arrived before I even get to the front door?'

'Ah,' she said with an impish grin. 'I'm a detective's daughter.'

Pete laughed. 'You're a scamp, I know that.' He let her go and set his briefcase down on the floor, smacking her backside playfully as she ran past him towards the kitchen.

'Ow! Child abuse!'

'Don't even go there, Missy.'

'Somebody's got to if you want your tea.'

Pete shook his head, giving up. The girl was as sharp as a pin, her mind capable of switching direction in an instant or following a train of logic that he had no chance of keeping up with. He stepped through to the lounge where he found Louise in her usual place on the sofa. But, rather than watching TV, she was actually reading a booklet of some kind.

'Hello, love.' He sat down and leaned over to kiss her. 'How've you been?'

'Busy,' she said. 'The advert's in. Both of the local papers for the next week. And there's feelers going out gently for someone to take Letterman's place if he leaves Archways. Or to take the junior role if his colleague gets promoted.'

'Ooh.' He grimaced, hoping she wasn't stirring up a load of trouble for herself in the process. 'Talking of that, I spoke to Dr White at Middlemoor earlier. She's reluctant to get involved herself – time constraints, I suppose. She's the only one there so I suppose she must be pretty busy. But she did suggest you have a word at the hospital, see if you can arrange a second opinion on Tommy while he's still here. If you can't, she said get back to her and she'll try, but…' He shrugged.

'We can do that, can we?'

'It seems so.'

'Good. I'll see what I can do in the morning, then. I heard Annie saying you've got a different car again. What happened? You weren't…?'

'Somebody had another pop. I'm fine. Unfortunately, so's he. He got away.'

'Christ, I know your job's not the safest, but this is getting silly.'

'There is some good news,' he said, cutting her off before she could get started on a rant about his safety and its connection to hers and Annie's.

'Like what?'

'Tommy's agreed to testify against Burton. Colin went to see him again this afternoon. And it seems you're not the only one who's got it in for Brian Letterman. Tommy's friend. Tabitha something? Colin doesn't know exactly what happened and nor does Tommy, it seems, but there's been some sort of problem between her and Letterman that's meant his voluntary suspension while it's investigated.'

'So…' She sat forward quickly, hands reaching for his as her eyes widened hopefully.

'Decisions made up to now stand,' Pete said. 'For now, at least. But the other bit of good news is that Colin's spoken to the head of Social Services and they've agreed to talk to whoever takes over running Archways until the manager comes back. It'll probably be the deputy manager from Bristol or Southampton children's home, but we don't know for sure yet. It's only just happened.'

'So, he could stay put.'

'He could. But there's no guarantee of it.'

'He's staying where he is?' Annie demanded from the doorway.

'Maybe,' Pete cautioned.

'Maybe's better than nothing,' she said. 'I understand what he was trying to do the other day. Trying to make it not hurt so much when they sent him away.' Her large, serious eyes flicked from Pete to her mother and back again.

Pete shook his head slowly. 'It's completely beyond me,' he said.

'What is?'

'How your mum and me raised such a clever-beyond-her-years daughter.'

'You didn't. I got it all from school.' She turned, nose in the air, and flounced away towards the kitchen. 'Tea's nearly ready.'

Pete turned to meet Louise's gaze, his head full of wonder while his heart was bursting with pride and love.

'Well, she damn sure didn't get it from me,' she said softly.

Pete smiled. 'I think it might be about evens between us.'

She sighed. 'So, what happened with Tommy?'

Pete felt his lips pressing together as he shook his head slowly. He knew what she meant. It felt almost like all the good aspects of both of them had been saved for Annie while all the negatives had come together in Tommy. But then, if Annie's last comment had been right… And if Rosie Whitlock's assessment had been, too… 'Maybe I pushed him too hard.'

'Are you coming or what?' Annie demanded from the kitchen.

Pete winked at Louise. 'Nag, nag, nag,' he called back.

*

'This is pretty good, Button. You might just have found your calling here.' Pete forked up another mouthful of the tagliatelle carbonara that Annie had prepared with salad and crusty garlic bread. 'You made it all on your own?'

'Yes.'

He looked at Louise, who shrugged. 'She wanted to.'

'So what went into it?' The richness of the sauce, counteracted by the salty tang of the bacon was perfect with the slippery flat strips of pasta.

'Bacon, ham, mushrooms, cream, egg yolks, salt and pepper.'

'And where did you learn that combination?' Surely, at ten years old, they weren't doing cookery at school?

'Off the side of the jar, silly,' she said. 'I just heated it up in the microwave while the strips boiled and the bread was in the oven. I haven't got all night to be messing about in the kitchen, you know.'

They were all still laughing when Pete heard his mobile ringing on the hall table, where he'd left it with his keys. He got up and went through to check who was calling.

Forensics.

He picked it up and answered it. 'DS Gayle.'

'Good evening, Detective. Harold Pointer here. I've got some results for you.'

'Hello, Harold. What can you tell me?'

'The Transit van that you had an altercation with in front of your station was clean, I'm afraid. Completely clean. No prints, no DNA. Nothing but a few fibres. Black wool and green cotton. One would surmise that the van had been cleaned thoroughly before it was driven to the location and the driver wore hat and gloves along with generic, hard-wearing jeans and jacket or something of the sort.'

Supporting Ben's theory of a professional job, Pete thought.

'The damage to your Mondeo was caused by contact with an old-model Land Rover in its original livery. Other than that, the only thing we picked up were traces of mud and plant fibres consistent with the location of the incident.'

So, had that one been cleaned as well? Which suggested the same perpetrator. A determined bugger if nothing else.

'As far as your murder victim,' Harold continued, 'we have surprisingly little also. There were two small traces of paint on her coat. Both were white but, surprisingly, one was gloss and the other emulsion. And both were smears rather than specks, so new paint. There were a few grains found in her hair which appear to be gypsum plaster. And approximately the bottom third of the back of the coat had a profusion of beige carpet fibres clinging to it.'

'So, she'd been somewhere that was being decorated.'

'In quite a bland, modern style, yes.'

Pete's mind immediately conjured an image of the new-build construction at her ex's scrapyard, but it was nowhere near far enough along in the process for the evidence that Harold had found. It had to be from somewhere else. 'OK. Thanks, Harold. I'll see you soon.'

'I sincerely hope not, Detective Sergeant.'

Pete laughed. 'I meant in court. As a witness.'

As they ended the call, Pete realised that he had to circle back. He'd only eliminated one possible location. Well, two if you included Claire's own house. He put the phone back on the side table and returned to the kitchen.

Louise met his gaze as he sat down. 'Results?'

'Yes,' he said, picking up his fork. 'Nothing very helpful, though. I'm going to have to pop out again for a little while after this. I shan't be long, but it needs doing while there's someone in.'

*

'Detective Sergeant Gayle.'

Stuart Elsfield stood in his doorway, one hand on the half-open door, the other on the frame. He didn't look any more pleased to see Pete than he sounded.

'I don't want to be here anymore than you want me to be, Mr Elsfield. But you wouldn't want me to do anything less than a thorough job of finding your girlfriend's killer, would you?'

Elsfield stared at him flatly for a second. 'What can I help you with?'

'Could I come in for just a moment?'

His lips tightened but he stepped back, reluctantly allowing Pete to enter. 'What's this about? Am I a suspect here?'

Pete carefully wiped his feet and closed the door, letting the question hang for a few seconds before he met the younger man's gaze. 'Frankly, at this stage, Mr Elsfield... No, you're not. But I wouldn't be doing my job properly if I didn't do everything possible to eliminate you, would I? Our court system is based on reasonable doubt, so I can't afford to leave any if I'm going to secure a conviction on whoever did murder Claire.'

'Fair point. What do you want to know?'

'That you haven't been having any decorating done.'

'I could have answered that over the phone.'

'Yes, but that wouldn't let me check for myself, would it? Do you mind?' He lifted an arm, indicating his desire to go further into the house.

'Actually, yes.' Elsfield folded his arms across his chest. 'Very much so. But go on.'

'Thanks.' As Pete stepped through to the living room, his mind was already jumping ahead to the next task on the list. *Hold on,* he told himself. *One thing at a time. Concentrate on the here and now.* He checked the carpet, the walls, the skirting boards and the smell of the air in the room before moving on to the next one.

It didn't take long.

Back in the hallway a few minutes later, Pete reached out to put a hand on Elsfield's shoulder. 'Thank you,' he said. 'That gets us one step further on the road to a conviction.'

CHAPTER FOURTEEN

With no school and Louise not working, Pete was the first of his team into the squad room the next morning. He had typed up yesterday's case notes and was updating the white board when the door opened to his right and Dave strolled in, followed by Dick and Jill.

'Morning,' said Dave as they crossed towards their desks.

'Morning all.' Pete continued writing. When he finished he set down the marker pen and turned to face them. Three expectant faces met his gaze. 'Two things to say when you boil it down. First: it wasn't her boyfriend. And second: whoever killed Claire Muir seems to have done it in a place that was being, or had very recently been, decorated.'

As he moved back to his seat, the door opened behind him and Jane and Ben came in, both with their coats over their arms and coffee mugs in hand.

'Ah. Good.' Pete settled himself into his chair. 'Now you're here, Ben, you can go out again. I need you and Dave to go out to Don Raymond's farm, check out the mobile home behind the barn where Steve's been living and, also, the house if you can gain entry legally.'

Ben glanced fondly at his coffee. 'What are we looking for?'

'Signs of remodelling or redecoration. Plastering, painting, carpeting. Any or all of the above.'

'Trace evidence on her coat and in her hair, Spike,' Dave explained.

'Oh, right.'

'In the meantime, Jane, you could go and visit the sister. She hasn't been here long.'

'Yeah, but she's female, boss,' Ben pointed out. 'Even if she had a motive, she couldn't very well have left the victim with a mouthful of...' He shrugged. 'Well, she couldn't, could she?'

'No,' said Pete. 'But she might be connected to the bloke who did. Which means her place could still be the killing ground. It needs checking. Although first, she needs asking if she knows of anyone in Claire's life, or her own, who's been redecorating.'

'So, what are the rest of us doing?' Dick asked as chairs scraped back, coats were donned and half the team headed for the door.

'Well, I suspect Dave and Ben are on a hiding to nothing but it has to be done,' Pete told him. 'I can't see Steve Raymond bothering to do up the inside of that mobile home. There's a bit more of a chance of his uncle doing something to the house but again, it doesn't seem likely, judging from the outside. I think Jane's got more chance of finding something useful with the sister. But in the meantime, we also need to figure out who's behind that Transit yesterday and the Landy the night before. All I can say about the driver is he's white, heavily built and he knows what he's doing. But I didn't recognise him. So, who sent him? Did Ben find anything useful yesterday?'

'Not that I know of.'

'So we pick up where he left off. I don't want to have to send Louise and Annie to stay with her mum. The bloke's not trying to warn me off anything – there's been no message. And he's tried twice. If it's third time lucky I want that to be for me, not him. Let's have a look at Ben's daily notes and go from there.'

*

Tommy noticed the new face at the top table as soon as he sauntered into the dining room, among the last to arrive as usual. Dark curly hair cropped tight to the skull contrasted with the man's pale skin while his almost colourless lips seemed to match with the narrow, blade-like nose and his lack of interaction with the people around him displayed an arrogance that could only come with...

Tommy hid a faint jolt of surprise as he realised exactly where the new man was sitting.

The primary seat in the room. The head of the table.

Tommy glanced around. Tabitha was already in her usual place at the back of the room. He went to join her and was just taking his seat when the last student arrived. Inevitably, it was Sam Lockhart, still determined to be king of the hill despite his unsuccessful encounter with Tommy only a few days ago.

Tommy glanced across and thought he saw the glitter of the new man's eyes as Lockhart took his seat. *Hello,* he thought. *The new guy's not impressed.* He looked across at Tabby. 'Morning. Who's he?'

Cutlery rang on glass like a high-pitched boxer's bell and Tommy looked round at the sound of a chair scraping back.

The new man had stood up.

'Now that everyone's here, I'll introduce myself.' He had the thick, lilting accent of Wales. In most people it would have softened their tone. Not him. It sounded almost like a threat. 'I'm Dr Llewellyn. I usually work at Moorside Young Offenders Institute in Taunton, but I'm here to replace Dr Letterman for a while as he's had to take some time off unexpectedly.'

Tommy suppressed a snigger and glanced across at Tabitha.

'I don't know how long I'll be here but, while I am, there's going to be a few changes. For those who aren't familiar with Young Offenders Institutions, they've replaced what we used to call borstals. They're part of the prison service and that's how they're run. And that's how this place is going to run, as of this moment. Zero tolerance. No messing about, no second chances and no namby-pamby cow-towing to the do-gooders and protectionists. You're here to learn from your mistakes. You will do exactly that and the main thing you'll learn is the law of consequences. All actions have them, like a law of physics. Except here, the reaction won't be equal and opposite, it'll be dire and unpleasant. I believe in two things: the power of deterrence and the punishment fitting the crime. You do as you're told, when you're told, and you'll be fine. Don't, and you *will* regret it.'

He sat down abruptly, picked up his knife and fork and continued eating.

Tommy looked at Tabitha again and gave her a grimacing nod. 'Whatever you did to Brian, it worked.'

'Yeah, and backfired big-time, by the look of him.'

'For some, yes. All we've got to do is stay out of his way, though, and we'll be fine. And, on the plus side, I'm still here.' He gave her a quick grin then jumped as something hit him on the ear. He snapped his head around to see Lockhart grinning at him, expecting a response in kind. A small button mushroom lay on the table near Tommy's elbow. He picked it up, still staring back at the bigger boy, and popped it in his mouth. Bit down once and swallowed. Then, quite deliberately, he returned his attention to Tabitha.

'He don't give up, does he?' she observed.

'He don't learn easy,' Tommy agreed. 'He will learn, though. One way or another.'

'Hey, don't go getting into trouble 'cause of him after all the effort I went to, to keep you here.'

'I might be daft but I'm not stupid. He wants to stir up shit, he'll be the one dropped in it, not me.'

Tabitha looked dubious.

'Trust me. I know how to stay out of trouble when I need to. I've had years of practice.'

'Mr Gayle.' Llewellyn's voice rang out again across the room. Tommy's head snapped around to see the Welshman looking straight at him. 'You won't be going to your first class this morning. You'll go straight from here to the manager's office.'

A few soft sniggers sounded from around the room as Tommy turned back to Tabitha and said quietly, 'What have I done?'

*

Dick set down his pen and looked up from his notebook. 'Between Graham with the CCTV and Bob's mate at the prison with his records of visits and phone calls, we can say for sure that Achabaihan's habits haven't changed and Petrosyan isn't getting any more visitors now that he was a week ago.'

'So, unless they're talking Armenian or passing notes under the table that the guards aren't seeing, we can rule them out,' Pete said.

'I wouldn't go that far until we've spoken to the guard who oversaw their meeting, but it's certainly a working theory. So, who else can we rule out so far?'

'Well, Neil Sanderson's had no visitors at all – not even his wife. And it's not going to have been Kevin Haynes, is it?'

Sanderson was a paedophile who Pete and the team had discovered while investigating Malcolm Burton's case, a few months before, and Kevin Haynes was another who Pete had arrested after he'd attacked a young girl in that same period, but Haynes had been remorseful and more than willing to come into custody and receive whatever treatment was available for his obsession.

'It doesn't have to have been Sanderson, though,' Jill put in. 'It could be one of his mates, frightened that he might spill the beans.'

'Yeah, what was the name of that judo nut from Swindon that he was linked to?' asked Dick.

'He was already in prison, somewhere up north,' Pete argued.

'He could be out on parole by now, though,' Jill pointed out. 'How many cases do we come across where parolees and people out on bail have absconded?'

Pete grunted. 'Far too many.'

Jill tilted her head. 'Worth checking, then, I'd have thought.'

'Be my guest.'

'The trouble is, he's only one of a whole damn network,' Dick said.

'And aren't you a cheerful sod this morning.'

Dick shrugged. 'Just saying. If it were me, I don't think I'd put off sending Louise and Annie over to Okehampton for a bit.'

'Yes.' Jill glanced up from her computer screen. 'But you aren't happy unless you're miserable, are you?'

'Eh?' Dick looked from Jill to Pete and back again. 'How does that even make sense?'

Pete shrugged. 'You tell me. But in the meantime, you could dig out Sanderson's phone and Internet contacts and start checking them out while I go through Frank Benton's.'

Pete took out the former DC's case file and opened it, but his mind had not got past Dick's comment about sending Louise and Annie to his mother-in-law's. He hated the idea, but that was a purely selfish reaction. He didn't want to be without them. What he should be thinking about was their safety. This guy had tried twice and failed. If he switched tactics and put them in danger, Pete would never forgive himself. As much of a pain as it was – for all of them, not just him – he had to talk to Louise about it when he got home.

*

He was working his way through Frank Benton's known contacts, most of whom in the last year or so had been on the other side of the law, when his desk phone rang. An internal call. He picked it up.

'Pete Gayle.'

'It's Graham. I've just finished going through the footage for the hour following your little accident out the front here, trying to find where the driver popped up afterwards. There's nothing. No sign of him at all. I thought you'd want to know.'

Pete's eyes widened in surprise. The CCTV operator was being pro-active without even being asked. 'Cheers, mate. Thanks for trying.'

'No problem.'

Pete put down the phone. That was what teamwork was all about: people seeing the need and helping each other without even being asked. It felt good that he'd engendered that kind of reaction from someone in the station that he didn't even work with directly.

'What's that, then?'

Pete blinked and looked at Dick, who was watching him closely.

'You got something?'

'Nothing. But of itself, that means something.'

'Eh?'

'Our man in the van yesterday didn't pop up on CCTV after I chased him. So either he was picked up or he hopped on a bus somewhere. If he was picked up, that leaves two possibilities – either he's local and whoever picked him up knows him and will probably be aware of the incident with the van by now, if only from last night's news – or he's not local, in which case whoever he's working for must have picked him up because he wouldn't have any other contacts in the city. But if he used the busses, then we can find him on the footage from them. We've got the date, time and likely pick-up points.'

He turned around in his seat. Colin Underhill's office was in darkness. 'Anybody seen Fast-track this morning?'

'Not in person, but his car's here,' Jill said.

'OK. You get onto the bus company, see if you can get hold of the vehicle camera footage, I'll go see him and get a press announcement organised, asking for anybody who has any relevant info to come forward. If it was a friend or family member, they might not have linked him to the stolen van, but they'll recognise him from the CCTV out the front here and the time period when they picked him up.'

'A friend or family member's not likely to come forward, though,' Dick pointed out. 'And an employer certainly won't.'

'No, but they might well ask him what's going on or talk to another family member about it and that could get back to us. If nothing else, it could put the pressure on him a bit, make him back off.'

Dick lifted the sheaf of papers he was working through. 'Which could give us time to track him down the hard way.'

'Exactly. Especially if I can persuade Fast-track to get us some help with the paperwork.' Pete pushed his chair back and stood up, heading for the door.

He was still going to have to talk to Louise, but he would try anything that might increase her and Annie's safety.

CHAPTER FIFTEEN

'Gayle.'

Tommy had been standing in front of the manager's desk for several long seconds, the big coloured staff member Aloysius close behind him at the door, when Llewellyn finally put down his pen, looked up and spoke. Tommy knew the technique for what it was. Designed to intimidate, to show dominance, to make him feel small, insignificant, inferior. Whatever. He was small. He was used to that. But if he'd been that insignificant, he wouldn't be standing here, would he? And as for inferior... He held the Welshman's dark gaze boldly.

'Your dad's a copper. You think that gives you some sort of get out of jail free card, do you? Coming here must have been a bit of a shock to the system, then, eh?'

A pause that Tommy imagined he was supposed to fill, but he had no idea what with so he said nothing.

'Hasn't taught you anything yet, though, has it? You already know that your move to Southampton's off the cards. You think that's some kind of victory, do you?'

Another pause. Again, Tommy held his silence.

'Well, let me tell you something, Gayle. It's not. In fact, it's just the opposite. Because now that Brian's gone, I'm here instead. And the namby-pamby, softly-softly, be nice to the children approach is over. You step out of line, speak out of turn or break the rules in any way whatsoever, it won't be half an hour in your room: it'll be real punishment. Prison style.' He raised a hand to point at Tommy. 'I've got my eye on you and so's every other member of staff in this building. Cross me, Tommy boy, and you'll wish you had been transferred to Southampton. Is that clear?'

'Did you single me out for a reason or am I just the first on a list for this pep talk? Sir.'

'You're singled out all right, Gayle. I know exactly why I'm here and, for as long as I'm inconvenienced by your presence here, you're going to be equally inconvenienced by mine. Do we understand each other?'

Tommy squeezed his lips together. 'I understand you completely. Can't say if it's mutual.'

Llewellyn nodded. 'I understand arrogance when I see it, Gayle. And while I'm here, you will address all members of staff as Sir or Ma'am when you speak to them. I've already had a store cupboard or two cleared out for anyone who thinks the rules don't apply to them.'

Again, Tommy held his silence. If he said nothing, he could say nothing wrong. And apart from that, he didn't want to encourage the man in his sense of power and omnipotence.

Llewellyn lifted his gaze to the man at the door. 'Take him away, Aloysius, and fetch the girl. Tabitha. We'll deal with her next.'

Tommy almost reacted, the flare of anger almost overcoming his reason, but he stopped himself. Was the Taff trying to get a rise out of him? 'What, you can't cope with boys so you have to pick on girls now? Sir.'

Llewellyn smiled slowly. 'Why would you care? Little hard-nut like you, I'd have thought it was all about me, me, me with you.'

Tommy straightened his back again, confidence and control reasserting themselves. 'Well, there you go then. You've answered your own question, haven't you?'

The Welshman frowned. 'What question?'

'Do we understand each other? Obviously, you don't. Sir.'

Llewellyn nodded. 'And equally obviously, it's mutual. Nobody likes a smart-arse. And I don't tolerate what I don't like. So, to make sure you do understand me...' He switched his gaze back to the man behind Tommy. 'Broom cupboard.'

'How long for, Mr Llewellyn?' the big black man asked.

'I'll let you know. If I remember. And don't forget the girl.'

*

'Shit.' Pete stopped in the act of turning a page over in the file on his desk.

'What?' asked Dick.

'I've just realised: I'm wasting my time here.'

'What, you got somewhere better to be, boss?' asked Jill.

'No, but it's not going to be anything to do with Frank, is it? If it was meant as a warning to back off, the bloke had plenty of chance to say so and it's too late to have any effect on the case.'

'It could be simple revenge,' Dick pointed out.

'Yes, but who ever liked Frank enough to kill someone for putting him away for eighteen months? And if it was one of his customers – again, he had plenty of time to say something.' Pete slapped the file closed and set it aside. 'We haven't got time to waste on the improbable until we've exhausted the likely culprits.'

The door opened to his right and three uniformed PC's entered. Mike Douglas was followed by Sophie Clewes and Nikki French.

'Morning, Sarge. You want a hand with something?' Mike asked.

'Yeah. Nothing exciting. Not yet, at least. We've got a whole lot of paperwork to plough through, looking for possible suspects.'

'In what?'

'Two attempts on my life. A bloke tried to run me off the road in a Land Rover the other night, then tried to ram me with a stolen Transit van yesterday. I'm presuming it's the same guy.'

Mike laughed. 'You hope so, you mean.'

Pete waved a hand at the empty desks around them. 'The others are out and about so pick a pew, each of you.' He waited for them to seat themselves. 'Now, let's look at this with a bit of logic. Who are the most likely candidates, bearing in mind the guy's tried twice and made no contact or comment?'

'So, we're thinking it's not someone directly angry at you or he'd have said so when he had the chance,' Jill clarified. 'So, someone with an agenda or someone who's being paid to do a job. But, he's tried and failed twice so, as careful as we've seen he is in terms of leaving evidence behind, he's not likely to be a professional as such.'

'So your average heavy,' Mike put in from Ben's chair at the far side of Dick Feeney. 'Like one of The Armenian's enforcers, for instance.'

'Exactly.'

'But we've established that it's not. Or at least that Petrosyan hasn't ordered it,' Dick added. 'We've got his phone records and visitor log. His only visitor, apart from his brief, has been the taxi driver and the last time he went to see him was over a week ago, as part of their normal routine.'

'It would take a few days to set something like this up if you were doing it carefully,' Nikki pointed out.

'Who's his brief?' Sophie asked.

'A bloke from London. East European,' Dick told her. 'Don't even ask what his name is.'

'But he'll have gang connections,' Mike said. 'Bound to. Part of the job, especially in London.'

'I'll call the Met, see what they have on him,' Pete said. 'But, who else do we need to focus on?'

'Well, other than Petrosyan, the up-coming trials we've got are for Sanderson, Burton and the kids who attacked Annie. But Ben's already gone through the kids' parents and he didn't find anything untoward. Just a bunch of wealthy bankers and businessmen, a lord and a couple of foreigners.'

'What sort of foreigners?'

'An Arab who went to university here in Exeter and a Brazilian bloke who's got a horse-training facility just this side of Sidmouth.'

'Well, whoever the driver was, he was no jockey,' Pete said, recalling the fleeing man's size and build. 'But it's worth checking further on.'

'So we focus on the trainer and the paedophile links?' asked Sophie.

'Looks like it.' Pete nodded.

'Right.' Mike clapped his hands and rubbed them together. 'Hand out the files and let's get to it.'

Pete gave Sanderson's file to Sophie and Nikki, who had taken Jane and Dave's seats across from him, and passed Malcolm Burton's to Mike. 'Share that with Jill, Mike. Dick, you take this horse trainer and his employees. I'll see what I can find on Petrosyan's solicitor.' He took a small personal contacts book from the top drawer of his desk and picked up the phone to dial.

'Metropolitan Police Headquarters. How can I help?'

'This is DS Peter Gayle, Devon and Cornwall Police, based in Exeter. I'm looking for information on a foreign national who I gather is working as a solicitor based in London. I'll spell his name, rather than try and pronounce it.'

A short laugh greeted the comment. 'Go ahead.'

Referring carefully to Gagik Petrosyan's file, Pete spelled out the name of his solicitor.

'Right, let's see…' Pete was sure he heard the slap of a key over the line. 'So, he entered the country as a minor, along with his parents. Educated in Hackney. University of London. Passed the bar and he's been practicing as a solicitor, concentrating on his fellow countrymen and other East European clients for the most part, since then. Had some notable successes – or should I say notorious? A couple of work-gang cases up in Lincolnshire. A well-known people-trafficking case here in London, involving enforced prostitution of women brought in from Albania and the Ukraine. A couple of drug cases.'

'So, it's safe to say he's got connections with East European criminal elements,' Pete concluded.

'Oh, yes.'

'And has there ever been any suspicion of criminal activity on his part or on his behalf?'

'No, but he makes a very nice living legally. Why would he put that in jeopardy?'

'Fair enough. But I could do with a list of contacts, professional and otherwise.'

'OK. What's the interest from your neck of the woods?'

'He's defending a drug trafficker here in Exeter. There's been some activity that we need to exclude him from, if he's not involved. Intimidation type stuff.'

Another laugh came down the line. 'Trying to scare off the witnesses, is he? That's par for the course with them. Not known for being subtle.'

'Yeah, we're wondering if he's brought someone in from outside the area to do the dirty work.'

'Sounds plausible, knowing the way they operate. Give me your email address and I'll send over what we've got.'

'That'd be great. Thanks.' Pete reeled off his police email address.

'Got it. Gayle. Are you the one who rescued that girl last year? Something to do with a big paedophile ring?'

'The ring's a separate issue. The National Crime Agency took that over. But yes, that was us.'

'Nice one. How's she doing?'

'She's...' Pete pictured Rosie, the last time he'd seen her, three weeks ago. At home with her parents, she was quiet and subdued. She'd stopped going out with her friends. All out-of-school activities had ended for her. She was no longer swimming or playing tennis. She had to be dropped off in the school grounds and picked up every evening. Her personality had changed dramatically from the popular, out-going girl she had been. But she was fierce in her determination to see justice done, not just for herself but for the other girl who she had briefly been held with in the barn on Malcolm Burton's property a few miles from the city. 'She's not too bad, considering. Her physical injuries have healed. It's the psychological ones that'll take time. But she's a strong kid. I think she'll get there.'

'Good. Right, I'll get this stuff over to you.'

'Thanks again.' Pete ended the call and put the phone down. Looking up, he saw Jill staring at him. The look on her face did not bode well.

'Jill?'

'Steve Southam, the paedophile from Swindon, is no longer in Morpeth prison. In fact, he's no longer in prison at all. He absconded from a transport vehicle on the way to a hearing regarding the Alison Stretton case three weeks ago.'

'Jesus! Why weren't we told about this?' he demanded.

Jill shrugged. 'Not our case, boss. It was Avon and Somerset who charged him.'

'Who's Steve Southam?' Sophie asked.

'You remember Neil Sanderson?'

'Yes.'

She had helped significantly on the case, last year, when Sanderson had been charged with possession and distribution of illegal images of minors including his own daughter.

'Before he came down here, he lived in Bath. There was a young girl who was killed while he was there. Alison Stretton. Sanderson had been teaching her Judo. It came out during my interviews with Sanderson that Steven Southam was a likely suspect. He'd been at the club that night, seen the girl there. Sanderson suspected him but was too frightened to say anything.'

She nodded. 'And now he's in the wind. But…' She glanced across at Jill. 'You say Avon and Somerset charged him, why would he come after the Sarge?'

Jill shrugged. 'He's known to be a vicious bugger. It could be as basic as that. He can't get to Sanderson, so he's coming after the boss instead.'

Pete shook his head. 'He'd have bigger priorities than me. Sanderson's wife, for example. Or his daughter.'

'It could be worth checking with them,' Jill said.

'Yeah. I can't see her taking my calls,' Pete countered.

'I'll ring her.'

'OK.'

Pete's computer pinged. An email notification popped up in the bottom right of the screen. From the Metropolitan Police.

'Ah, here we go.' He clicked on it as Jill picked up her phone. His email opened up with a greeting from PC Gavin Overstone of the Metropolitan Police that had a zip file attachment. Pete sent Overstone a quick thanks and saved the file to his computer before opening it. The unpronounceable name was accompanied by a photographic portrait that he didn't recognise. The last known address was in Ruislip. Even having been to London only twice in his life, Pete recognised that as coming up in the world from Hackney. The man was not married and had no known children. A brief life-history included his family ties, which were still mostly in East London. Parents, three brothers and a sister. The sister, Gretchen, had married and was the licensee of a pub only a couple of miles from her parents' home. Two of the brothers were joint owners of an import business based in a place called Hayes in Middlesex. Pete took a map book from the bottom drawer of his desk and looked it up. He was not surprised to learn that it was not far from Heathrow airport.

The third brother – the youngest – had taken a less salubrious path in life. He was currently in Belmarsh prison, a third of the way through a nine year stretch for assault with a deadly weapon, attempted murder, and wounding with intent.

His contacts list might make interesting reading, Pete thought. *But one thing at a time.* He made a note on the pad at his elbow and moved on.

'Bye,' Jill said and put down her phone.

Pete glanced up from his screen. 'Anything?'

She shook her head. 'It took some doing to persuade her not to hang up on me. She's not exactly happy with us, but she's not had any worrying contacts from anyone. Not had any contacts much at all, apparently. So much for friends rallying round in times of need, she said.'

'Guilt,' Sophie Clewes said. 'You can't tell me she knew nothing about what was going on under her own roof with her own daughter. She had to have at least suspected.'

Sophie, Pete recalled, had been under said roof at least once, visiting the property with him while they were investigating Sanderson.

'Still, it's one thing having suspicions,' he said. 'It's quite another acting on them, especially when it's the person you love. The person you've lived with, built a life with for years. That can't be easy for anyone.'

'It's a question of priorities, though,' Nikki argued. 'When it's your kid potentially at risk, you'd do whatever it took, no matter the consequences, wouldn't you?'

Pete nodded. He could identify with that.

'Still,' Jill put in. 'I'm convinced she hasn't heard or seen anything from Steve Southam. And like you said, boss – he'd be more likely to go after her than you.'

So one line closes as a whole lot more open up, Pete thought. 'OK. Let's move on, then.'

CHAPTER SIXTEEN

He put it off for as long as he could but eventually, with Annie in bed and asleep, there was no more getting around it, especially when Louise asked him outright, 'What's up? You've been quiet all evening. You might have got away with it with Annie but I've known you a damn sight longer, so come on – spill.'

Pete knew from long experience that once she'd latched onto something like this she wouldn't let it go. She'd be like a dog with a bone. And, as reluctant as he felt to put the problem into words, it was the right thing to do. For her, for Annie and ultimately for himself.

But still he put it off a little longer. 'Did you manage to get anyone interested in a visit to Archways, to see Tommy?' he asked.

Louise's lips pursed. 'No. And don't change the subject.'

He smiled briefly, drew a long, slow breath and let it flow out as he turned to meet her gaze. 'OK. I'll call Dr White in the morning – see if she can do anything for us.' He paused. 'It's something Dick Feeney said this morning. I suppose I knew it already, but...' He took her hands in his. 'This bloke who's driven into my car twice in two days – he's not likely to give up. And he's not a kid, messing about with spray paint and ball bearings in my tyre valves. He means business. He's trying to put me in hospital at least. We haven't been able to identify him yet. He's still out there, cooking up his next move. And if that move...' He stopped, throat clogging. Squeezing her hands gently, he swallowed and carried on. 'If anything happened to you or Annie because of something I hadn't done or hadn't said, I'd never...'

'Whatever he does is his responsibility, not yours,' she said. 'We're a family. For better or worse, in good times and bad.'

'Yes, but if there's a truck coming down the road with the horn blaring, you don't just stand there, do you? You get out of the way. It's only sensible. And it'd be sensible for you and Annie to go and stay with your mum for a few days.'

Louise frowned. 'What about Annie's school? She can't just duck out. That's crazy. And I've still got to go to work. They're short enough already. So where's the benefit in going to Mum's? If he wants to find us he'll still do it.'

'Yes, but he's not coming after you, is he? He's coming after me. I don't want either of you caught up in anything, that's all. He's not worried about collateral damage as long as he can get to me. He proved that yesterday. And we've got no idea what he's got up his sleeve next. It's a pain, I know, but it's better to have a few long days to-ing and fro-ing than to do nothing and get hurt because of it.'

'I don't see you offering to go into hiding.'

'If I did, we'd never catch him, would we?'

'What, so you're the bait, are you? Sitting here like a worm on a hook, waiting for a bloody great fish to swoop in out of the murk.'

'It's not like that and you know it. I'm not just waiting for him. We're trying to identify him so we can track him down before he tries anything else. And if I'm around, he's likely to be, too. If I'm not, he'll vanish. It's as simple as that.'

'Then get on with it because I can't see putting Annie through that kind of upheaval and worry. She's got enough on her plate as it is without throwing the idea of potentially losing her dad into the mix. How's she going to cope with that, eh?'

Pete's lips pressed together, his head dropped, eyes closing as he fought against the images in his head. After the last year, it would be too much for any kid to bear. Even Annie's resilience would be broken.

'School would be a waste of time for her anyway,' Louise said. 'She wouldn't be able to think, never mind concentrate enough to learn anything. No. We're staying. You just catch the bugger before he does any more harm.'

Relief at her response fought with guilt at his selfishness and the worry that had sparked the conversation in the first place. Pete wasn't sure how he should feel or how he did feel. Reason said that they had to go, but Louise was right – what kind of effect would it have on Annie if they did? She'd be worrying for him just as much as he was now, for her. To send them away was the easy answer for him, but what about for them? His eyes closed again as his mind struggled with the problem, his hands latched onto Louise's all the while.

And in the end, that was the answer.

His body was telling him what his mind couldn't, he realised. His eyes opened and Louise was smiling at him.

Smiling!

'You know I'm right,' she said gently.

His eyebrows rose, head tilting in acknowledgement of the truth.

'There you go, then. Conscience appeased. Now, what do you know about him?'

'I know if he took you or Annie from me I'd tear his bloody arms off and feed them to him. But, more usefully, I know a few people who he isn't.' He withdrew his hands and turned to sit more comfortably on the sofa. This could turn into a long conversation.

*

'Dad.'

Annie's voice came from Pete's small upstairs office and she sounded serious.

'What's up, Button?' he called from the kitchen table, where he was eating a late breakfast of scrambled eggs on toast with bacon.

'I think you ought to see this.'

'What?' he frowned, picking up his coffee mug and draining it.

'On the video from last night.'

She'd taken to checking the recordings from the two tiny motion-activated security cameras he'd fitted to the front of the house several days ago, when they'd been having a problem with vandalism, looking for foxes, hedgehogs or other wildlife that wandered the streets after dark.

'I haven't got time, love. I've got a lot to do today and not a lot of time to do it in.'

One of the conclusions he and Louise had reached last night before they finally went to bed, sometime after 2.00 am, was that they would do their best not to add any further to Annie's worries. The kid had more than enough on her plate, especially after the last year or so.

Pete forked up the last of his bacon and put it in his mouth.

He heard her footsteps thundering fast and hard down the stairs and her little face popped into the kitchen, small fingers on the door jamb beneath. Her brow was pinched, two little lines showing vertically between her eyebrows. 'You're going to work?'

He swallowed. 'Yes. We've got a man to catch before he harms anyone else and we've got to figure out who he is first.'

'Well, you need to see this before you go.'

'Button, I…'

'Dad,' she cut in. 'Twenty seconds. I think it's important.'

That stopped him. She wasn't the type of girl to say that unless it was true. 'OK. What have you got?'

'A man. On the cameras last night. You need to see it.'

'All right.' He popped the last piece of egg on toast into his mouth and stood up to follow her. He'd converted the box room at the top of the stairs into an office which, over the years, had gradually been filling up with case files but, since the Spring of last year, had got stacked out with files on Tommy as Pete followed the case and pursued his own limited lines of enquiry. The desk against the back wall held his home computer, scanner and printer. The screen was filled with a grainy still image of a shadowy figure moving past the patrol car that sat on their drive outside. The time-stamp, he saw as he got closer, was four-seventeen.

'Hit return and it'll start playing,' Annie said from behind him.

He sat down and tapped the key.

The dark, street-lit image resolved and began to move. The man walking past the end of their drive suddenly stepped to the left and ducked down behind the big patrol car with its light bar and large black number 14 on the roof. Pete's eyes widened as he leaned forward in the chair, concentrating on the screen. A tiny, shadowy movement showed beyond the car, near the bottom of the windscreen, then vanished. Nothing happened for several seconds. Almost a minute dragged by. The screen flicked to black as the motion sensor timed out then re-triggered, the time readout jumping forward another minute as the screen showed the man – now visibly wearing a dark ski mask – stepping away from the car and heading back down the street, the way he'd come.

Pete hit the pause button and sat there, stunned.

'So,' Annie said. 'What was he doing for two whole minutes?'

Pete let go of the breath that he hadn't even realised he was holding. 'I don't know, Button, but I'd put odds on one thing: it was nothing good.'

'What's going on?' she asked as he turned his chair to face her. 'This is the third car you've had in as many days and somebody's out there tampering with it at stupid-o'clock in the morning. This isn't some kid from Risingbrook getting back at you for taking his toys away, is it? This is...'

He reached out and took her small hands in his. 'Not a problem, Button. Nothing for you to worry about. We're...'

She snatched her hands away and planted them on her hips. 'Don't patronise me. I'm not six.'

Pete struggled to resist the smile that threatened to creep across his face. 'And don't I know it. I'm not trying to patronise you. I'm just saying we've got it covered. We're already after the guy. That was a large part of what I was doing yesterday in the station.'

'Well, you haven't got him yet, have you? So it's not covered. Not properly. He was out there last night, on our drive, doing God knows what to the car you were about to go out there and drive if I hadn't watched this.' She reached out to point at the screen.

'You're right,' he admitted. 'Thank you. I expect I'd best go and see what he was up to, hadn't I?'

'Preferably before you get in the car.'

Pete paused, images of Northern Irish police checking the undersides of their cars with mirrors on sticks before getting into them back in the day popping into his mind. This girl was ten years old. How did she know about things like that? 'How do...?' He stopped himself before he said something that she might not have thought of. He didn't want to put anything into her head that wasn't already there. Not anything like that, at least. 'Never mind. I'll check it out, all right?'

She relaxed, hands dropping to her sides. 'Right. Be careful, Dad.'

Pete stood quickly and went to her, wrapping her in his arms. She returned the hug almost fiercely, her face buried in his chest. Stroking her hair, he realised exactly where her head was. *Christ, when did she get so tall?* It seemed like she'd grown three inches without him even noticing. Had he really been that wrapped up in work and Tommy and… God knows what else?

He clung to her a moment longer, then slid his hands out to her shoulders as he took a step back and looked down into her eyes. 'I'm going to be fine, all right? We will catch this bloke. And soon, we'll be a full family again.'

He had told her and Louise on the day it had happened that Tommy had agreed to testify.

'It's less than a week now until Tommy goes to court. They won't give him a custodial sentence on a first offence of that kind. So, once it's over, he'll be coming home. In fact, now that's happened and Colin's taken over the Burton case, I can even go and see him at Archways. And I will. Today. I'll take your mum with me this afternoon, while you're at Sonia's.

She had arranged to spend the afternoon with her friend, at her house a couple of streets away.

'You'll see him tomorrow, probably, after school.'

He and Louise had talked it through last night and agreed that it would be best if they saw Tommy and assessed his mental state before letting Annie go back there, after what had happened the last time she'd seen him. The first time Pete had seen him since his arrest was not likely to be easy. They didn't want to inflict that on Annie. Pete was aware that Tommy had been in punishment the day before. That's what Louise had been told when she phoned to arrange a visit with him, she'd said. She'd been understandably distressed by the news that she couldn't go yesterday, but the lad was not exactly known for staying out of trouble. And at least they had the good news that he was staying at Archways for now and Brian Letterman was gone, at least temporarily.

He squeezed her shoulders.

'We'll be fine,' he said. 'All of us.'

*

Five minutes later, he was less sure.

There was nothing outwardly wrong with the car. The tyres were all still inflated, there were no scratches or dents in the bodywork, no broken windows or puddles of fluid underneath it. But when he lay down on the concrete drive beside it and peered underneath with Louise's small illuminated make-up mirror, he saw exactly what the man had been doing for over two minutes.

The fact that they'd seen the man approaching the drive without any kind of bag or box had eased Pete's mind slightly as he stepped out of the house to see what had been done to the patrol car, but that only served to intensify the jolt of shock that he felt now as he glimpsed the results of the dark figure's two minutes' work. Cold fear gripped his skull and ran like a wave through his neck and upper body.

There was no mistaking the presence of the small, irregularly shaped object attached to the underside of the car, two thin wires leading away from it towards the engine compartment. A couple of pieces of black electrical tape held the wires in place. Pete traced them across with the tiny light from the mirror towards the front wheel, where they got lost amongst the levers, pipes and brackets at the end of the axle.

He'd seen all he needed to.

He stood up, closing the compact. His legs were trembling slightly as he took out his mobile phone and dialled the force headquarters at Middlemoor on the edge of the city.

'Devon and Cornwall police. How can I help?'

The prospect of putting what he'd just seen into words made the need to lean on something almost overwhelming. He reached out to the roof of the car then snatched his hand away again before making contact. 'This is DS Peter Gayle from Heavitree Road station.' He gave his badge number. 'I need bomb disposal dispatched to my home address ASAP. I've just checked my car and there's a suspicious device attached to its undercarriage.' He took a couple of steps backwards and leaned against the garage door.

'Right, Sarge. If you could give me some details to pass onto them…'

'It's small – maybe eight inches long by four by two – with a pair of wires coming from it across to the inside of a front wheel. Probably the triggering device, I expect. The charge is placed under the driver's position. We've got the perpetrator placing it on CCTV, but we can't make an ID from it. What we can say is it took less than three minutes to fit the device.'

'OK. I'll get a team mobilised. I'll call you back on this number with an ETA as soon as I've got one.'

'Thanks.'

Pete ended the call and let his legs slump beneath him to sit on the concrete drive, his back to the garage. Who the hell was this guy? And what was he going to tell Lou and Annie? An RTA was one thing – even a couple of attempts at it – but this was something else entirely. The perpetrator clearly didn't care about collateral damage or innocent bystanders as long as he got his target. Pete's wife and daughter were in significant danger until this bastard was caught. Much as he hated the idea, and notwithstanding the conclusions he'd reached with Louise last night, they couldn't stay here. Not now. Not until this was over and done with. But how was he going to tell them?

'Pete?'

Louise's voice came from the front door, just a few feet away around the side of the garage.

'Pete?'

He got quickly to his feet and stepped around the corner. 'Hello, love.'

'What's going on?'

'There's… A bit of an issue with the car. I've got someone coming out to look at it.' He held a finger across his lips then beckoned to her. She frowned, but stepped out, closing the door behind her.

'What?'

'The bloke Annie saw on the camera. He put something under the car.'

'Jesus! A bomb?'

He nodded. 'Possibly. The disposal team are on the way, but I don't want Annie seeing them. Can you make sure she doesn't? Give her something to do in the kitchen or out the back? You got any cookie dough? She loves baking.'

'No, but I've got recipes from scratch. A bomb? This is crazy! Who the hell can be that pissed off at you?'

'Pissed off or desperate.'

'Eh?'

'To keep me quiet. Put an end to a case.'

'Whatever, this takes things to a whole new level.'

'And when it doesn't work, that leaves the question of what the hell he's going to try next unless we can track him down today.'

She let go a deep sigh. 'Which takes us back to what we were talking about last night, doesn't it?'

'Yeah.'

Her face pinched as she struggled with the thoughts in her head. 'I don't want to leave you to face this on your own.'

'I don't want you to, either. But your safety's the main concern here, along with Annie's. And it'd be stupid to take risks that you don't need to. Especially when we know how severe those risks are now.'

'I know, but…'

'Nothing. Facts are facts, like them or not. And the facts here are that staying at home puts the two of you in danger that's both severe and avoidable. There's no sense in that and we both know it.'

There was a click from the front door and Annie was standing there in her pyjamas. 'Mum? Dad?'

'Hey, Button.' He glanced at Louise. She nodded, squeezed his hand and headed back to the house.

'What's going on?' Annie asked.

'There's a problem with the car, love. Your dad's called someone to come and see to it. They'll be here soon, I expect.' Louise ushered her back inside and glanced back at Pete as she closed the door behind them. The expression on her face was a tragic mixture of love, desperation and hope.

CHAPTER SEVENTEEN

The Royal Navy explosive ordnance disposal team took forty-three minutes to reach Pete's address from their base in Plymouth. They had to have been blue-lighting it all the way, he guessed, but there was no fanfare as the dark blue box van turned quietly into the end of the road.

He raised a hand to the uniformed driver and the van stopped just beyond the end of his drive. Driver, passenger and two more men climbed out and approached as Pete stepped past the car to join them at the end of the drive.

'Pete Gayle.' He showed his badge.

'Captain Mark Cunningham, EODT.' The man who stuck out his hand was as tall as Pete, in his late thirties with short dark hair and a neat, dense beard. His dark gaze was direct, his grip firm and quick.

'We've got a package attached under the driver's seat with two wires crossing to the back of the front wheel here on the passenger side. It was placed at four-fourteen this morning: took him just over two minutes to do.'

'How do you know that?' Cunningham frowned.

'CCTV cameras. I fitted them recently because of another issue. Can't make out any ID from it, though, unfortunately, and we can't see what he was doing because he was on the wrong side of the car. He wasn't visibly carrying anything, though. Must have had it under his jacket.'

'OK. We'll see what we've got initially and take it from there.' Cunningham raised a hand. 'If you'd like to join me round by the front door there, Jeff will suit up and have a look.' He nodded to a smaller blond guy in his mid-twenties who nodded in return and headed back to the van. Opening the back doors, he climbed in, the other two members of the team returning to the cab for now as Pete stepped around the corner of the garage to the front door with Cunningham.

'So, I take it you're not one for entering popularity contests, then?' Cunningham asked. 'Another issue recently that needed cameras installing, now this…'

'Oh, you've missed the two attempts to kill me in the car,' Pete said in a similar tone. 'Hence this one, I expect. I normally drive an unmarked but it got wrecked a couple of nights ago. Then its replacement did, the following day. But the cameras were put up to catch some kids who were playing silly buggers with spray cans and screw drivers out here. That's not related.'

'I see,' Cunningham nodded. 'So they're queueing up for a pop at you then, are they?' he asked with a grin.

'Price of being a good copper.'

The navy man grunted. 'It never used to be.'

Pete nodded as Jeff stepped around the front of the car and briefly into view, now clad in full dark-green armour, helmet, Perspex mask and shield, a small bundle of equipment in one hand and what looked like a selfie-stick in the other.

'Sign of the times,' Pete said as he caught the glint of light from the mirror fitted to the far end of the stick in Jeff's right hand.

The man in the armoured suit went from sight briefly, returning moments later as he knelt to place a small light on a bendy-legged compact tripod, aiming it at the underside of the car. He switched it on and stood up to look under the vehicle with the mirror. After a long moment, he stepped to one side, angling the mirror to follow his line of sight. Then he took a step back, nodded to Cunningham and went around to the other side of the car, where he went down onto his knees to look behind the front wheel before standing back up and beckoning to his commander.

Cunningham grunted. 'Give us a moment,' he said to Pete and headed over to talk to his subordinate.

They conversed briefly then headed for the back of the blue van with its Royal Navy logo on the side. The doors opened and the two other members of the crew handed Jeff a number of items that Pete couldn't see. Cunningham climbed in and Jeff turned back to the car. Approaching it, he dropped to his knees and went from sight behind it.

Pete waited, tension clamping his jaw and stiffening his limbs.

What had taken the dark figure two minutes to install in the small hours of the night seemed to take ten times that to deal with, every second feeling like a minute as Pete waited, hoping and praying that Annie wouldn't open the door behind him and step out to ask what was going on.

Seeing a bomb-disposal team on her driveway would scare the crap out of the girl. And rightly so, he admitted to himself. It wasn't doing him a whole lot of good, either. But finally, the armour-clad figure came upright, one hand raised in victory while the other clutched the dismantled components of the device he'd been working on.

He turned back to the van. The doors opened before he reached it and he handed over what he held. Pete watched Cunningham examine the components carefully as Jeff climbed in past him and disappeared into the shadowy interior. Then Cunningham looked up and waved Pete across.

With a deep sigh, he stepped forward.

'Whoever your man is, he knows what he's doing,' the leader of the bomb disposal squad told Pete six minutes later. 'It's not a design I've ever seen before, but it does come up on our database. It's been used twice before here in the UK – in London and Manchester. It also comes up internationally. There are similarities with devices from Turkey and Lebanon.'

Pete nodded. His suspicions were correct then. It was just a matter of proving it.

'Entirely home-made, but very clever,' the man continued. 'Even the detonator's not a manufactured one. The wires led to the brake pad and the wheel so that, when you put your foot on the brake at the point of starting the car, the circuit would have completed and… Lift-off. The charge was shaped to create an ejector-seat effect, only without the removable roof. The driver would have been killed instantly and the car flipped over in the process.

'A home-made detonator?' Pete said.

'All it needs to do is create a spark or a bang, depending on the nature of the main charge. In this case, a spark. Perfectly simple to do, especially with an electrical circuit like this one.'

'And a shaped charge, yet it was small enough and safe enough for him to carry in his jacket.'

'It's all perfectly safe until it's assembled. The charge won't go off without the detonator, the detonator won't go off without the circuit. If you put it all together in the right order, there's no risk to the installer at all.'

Pete wasn't sure if that was reassuring or even more chilling. 'OK, well thanks for all you've done, guys,' he said, including the rest of the team. 'I hope we'll catch the bastard before you get to see any more of his handywork.'

Cunningham insisted on making sure the car started safely before they left. Once the van had turned out of the end of the road and gone from sight, Pete went back indoors. Louise and Annie were in the kitchen at the back of the house. They were baking. The smell from the oven was wonderful.

'Ooh! Do I get to lick the spoon?' he asked.

Annie was subdued as she looked up from what she was doing.

'All sorted,' he said before she could ask any questions. 'I need to pop into the station for a while, but I won't be gone all day.'

Annie put down the wooden spoon she was using to stir the mix and, without speaking, ran to him and wrapped her arms tightly around him, squeezing hard.

Pete hugged her back, looking up at Louise. 'Are you sure this girl's got no Italian in her? The way she talks with her arms, I'd swear she has.' He ruffled her hair. 'I love you too, Button. And it's all sorted and safe out there.'

'You'd best go and put a stop to this crap, then, once and for all,' Louise said firmly.

Pete tipped his head. 'That's the plan.'

She stepped forward and all three embraced.

Inside, he was all too aware that he could still have weeks or even months of work ahead before he could catch the perpetrator but he couldn't say so. Not here, not now. His arms tightened around the two most important females in his life and he felt Louise respond. Then her arms slid back, her hands resting on his sides.

'This isn't getting it done.'

'No,' he said. 'But it's what I'm doing it for.'

*

Back upstairs in his office, he used a more sophisticated program than the usual one to go through the camera footage again, checking it frame by frame, searching for anything that would give a clue as to the masked figure's identity. But finally, he had to admit defeat. There was nothing, except the man's build and movements, proving – to Pete's mind, at least – that it was the same man he'd chased away from the station entrance after the impact with the Transit.

At some point he heard Louise enter Annie's room, next door. The low sound of voices came through the wall, but he couldn't make out what was being said and, by the time he finished, Louise was back downstairs in the kitchen. He followed her down. She was in the process of tidying up from their baking session.

'Annie?'

'Still in her room. She needs a bit of time.'

He nodded.

On top of everything that had happened in their lives over the past year – and the past couple of days – she was reaching the age when her hormone balance would be starting to shift in preparation for up-coming puberty, making things even more difficult for her to cope with.

'I need to make a move,' he said. 'I can't do any more from here.'

'Did you find anything?'

'Not yet, but I will.'

Her lips pressed together, her gaze falling away for a moment. Then she looked up at him again. 'I don't want to put any more pressure on you, but... Find the bugger and catch him, yes? ASAP.'

Pete grunted. 'That is the plan.'

CHAPTER EIGHTEEN

Tabitha was sitting alone at breakfast when Tommy walked in. She had picked the table furthest from everyone else and was concentrating on what she was eating, ignoring the chatter and noise from the rest of the room. He grabbed his food from the counter and went to sit across the corner of the table from her.

'Morning,' he said.

She continued eating in silence.

He kicked her playfully under the table and she looked up, her eyes fierce. 'Fuck off.'

Tommy's eyes widened in surprise, but he'd faced worse. 'I was in solitary all day yesterday. What's your excuse?'

'I toe the line, to the letter, or they'll send me home. Which includes not mixing with you. You're a bad influence. So, like I said – fuck off.'

He shook his head, confused. 'Send you home? But...' Knowing her history, the reasons she was here – the fact that, unlike every other kid in this place, she would prefer to stay here than go home – he could see that, for her, it was the ultimate threat. 'Bastard! Well, I wasn't to know that, was I? I'm sorry. I really am. I'll do what I can, but...'

'Don't. You'll only make it worse.'

'Why the hell would they send you home? That's crazy. I'm only going to be here for another few days. My trial's on Friday and they won't send me back here. It's a first offence, and a minor one at that.'

'Not everything's about you,' she snapped.

'You said I'd be the reason you'd be sent home. I'm just saying, there isn't any reason.'

'Well, that won't stop that shit-head.' She sent a venomous glance towards the head table, where Llewellyn sat facing them, Aloysius and several of the other staff grouped around him.

Not for the first time, Tommy wondered exactly what she'd done to get rid of Brian. It had to have been something pretty drastic.

Even from the far end of the room, Tommy saw Llewellyn's gaze lock onto his and a tiny, almost imperceptible grin light the man's face.

Smug bastard.

He was in control and he knew it.

Tommy let his gaze fall away and, for the first time since he'd sat down, remembered his food. He picked up his cutlery and cut a piece of his scrambled egg on toast.

It tasted of nothing. Like eating rubber on cardboard.

Sending Tabitha home was like a death sentence. She'd commit suicide. Tommy knew it with a certainty that gripped his chest and lit a simmering rage inside him. She was fifteen. Legally, she could leave home in another year. But practically, where would she go? Without her parents' support, she wouldn't be able to go to university.

'What are you aiming to do for a job when you leave school?' he asked quietly.

She gave a grunt of laughter. 'I'm here because I'm a suicide risk. You think I've bothered making plans for the future?'

'Dunno.' He shrugged. 'You might have, before you got to that stage.'

'Well, I didn't, OK?'

'So you just moped? Poor me, all day, every day?'

'What the fuck do you care? Just piss off and leave me alone, will you?'

He ran his knife through his scrambled egg and toast. 'You're not the only one who's had it tough, you know. I'm just trying to get you to see you could do something useful for the others, that's all.' Cutting a portion, he stabbed it with his fork and lifted it up.

'What do you know about having it tough? You've got family that love you. I've seen your mum and sister here.'

Tommy suddenly saw red. 'Yeah, not my dad, though, have you,' he spat. 'He hasn't been anywhere near here.' He swallowed. 'Hasn't had any more to do with me than he could help ever since…' He stopped, mouth clamping shut, blocking the words that he'd never spoken. His throat clogged, stomach lurching as if it might throw his breakfast back up at him. He swallowed.

He glanced up from his plate and saw Tabitha staring at him.

'What?' she asked quietly. 'Ever since what?'

His lips pressed together. He'd never told anyone about that. It was too shameful, even now, six years later. But as he stared into her brown eyes with their little sparks of yellow, the black irises wide, he heard a voice, a low murmur, saying, 'I was attacked. I was eight years old. Some kids were picking on me. I hid in the reeds at the bottom of the playing field. Teacher found me, I don't know how long after. Sat me on his knee and told me it would be OK. Next thing I knew, his hand wasn't on my leg anymore. It was on my crotch. I didn't take any notice at first. It seemed like an accident.'

At some point, he figured out that the voice was his. That he was telling her this. But once he'd started, he didn't even think of stopping. The flow of words continued and it felt so natural, so right, that he couldn't have stopped if he'd wanted to. 'At eight, you don't think of things like that, do you? Sexual things. Especially with someone of the same sex. Someone you're supposed to be able to trust and rely on. Who's telling you what you want to hear. That everything's going to be OK and all that. Anyway, I realised he was fondling me through my shorts and I reacted. Got up and turned on him. But as I got up, he'd got hold of my shorts so they came down. I was exposed. I knew that was wrong so I made a grab for them but his hands were so much bigger than mine. So much stronger. My pants came down and there I was, bare-arsed in a school playing field, just me and a full-grown man. He... He... Well, he didn't rape me that time but he used his hands in ways that... He said it had to be our secret. That he knew where I lived. He could hurt my sister, my parents.' He swallowed. The big, slow tears that were running down Tabitha's face were the most moving thing he'd ever seen. 'It went on until I left the school. And I've never told a soul before now.'

'Oh, my God,' she breathed. 'That's awful!'

Tommy blinked. 'Yeah. So, like I said – you can get through just about anything if you really want to. It's a matter of motivation. In my case, revenge. I will see the fucker in jail at some point. Or castrated and bleeding to death on the floor. Trouble is, he's six-foot-three and what am I?' He spread his hands.

'Half his size?' she said with a quick grin.

'Yeah, well - half a pint of rum's got more punch than a full pint of lager.'

'You've got the fire in your belly, I'll give you that. But you've got to be practical.'

'That's why he's still breathing and out of prison. Probably abusing other little kids as we speak.'

'At this time of day? It's a bit early, isn't it?'

Tommy was about to snap back at her for taking the piss when he saw the look in her eyes and realised what she was doing.

The flare of anger evaporated, replaced by a deep and intense gratitude.

'You see?' he said. 'I told you you'd got talents and value in this life.'

*

'Jesus! Are you OK?' Jane demanded when Pete finished explaining where he'd been.

'I'm fine.'

What about Louise and Annie? They must be terrified.'

'Yeah. It was Annie that spotted the problem. If she hadn't, I wouldn't be standing here now. I'd be in a couple of million pieces sprayed across the front of our house.'

'Ew,' Jill grimaced. 'She'll have that playing on her mind for months, if not years, I should think. How did she spot it?'

'She's taken to looking at the footage from those two cameras we put in the other day, seeing what's wandering about out there overnight. Foxes, hedgehogs and so on.'

'Good thing she has, then,' Jill said.

'Yeah. Anyway, it proves a connection to Petrosyan. I don't know what the link is yet, but it's there.'

'How can it be?' Ben demanded. 'We've got his communications constantly monitored. The only visitors he has are his brief and the taxi driver – and he only goes in once a fortnight. And I checked with the prison staff: they speak English throughout. They insist on it to stop him organising anything he shouldn't from in there.'

'So, either they're having coded conversations, or it's the brief rather than the cabbie,' Dick added. 'And it's a bit James Bond to be talking in code, isn't it? Something like that would take some organising, in itself. And is either of them clever enough?'

'Petrosyan's been running a major drugs operation for several years,' Pete said. 'He might look like a thug, but he's not stupid. We can't afford to underestimate him. I agree it's more likely to be the solicitor passing messages for him, though. He's got a privileged position. Private conversations. He's in and out more often than Achabaihan. We need to concentrate on running down all his connections. His brothers. His sister. His cousins, colleagues, former clients. It's going to be a big job and it's urgent. And at the same time, we need to close in on whoever killed Claire Muir.'

'Who the hell was it that said Sunday was a day of rest?' asked Dave.

'Dunno,' Dick replied. 'But it wasn't a copper, that's for sure.'

Pete ignored them. 'Jane, you said Sally Muir's boyfriend's been doing some redecorating?'

'So she said. Re-working his front hall, I think it was.'

'Right. Come on, then, let's go and see him. While we're gone, what I picked up from the Met's in the case file. Ben, maybe you could follow up on the two brothers who've got an import-export business based near Heathrow. And Jill, his sister's a pub landlady. Check on her husband and anything that might be known about their contacts or clientele. Dick and Dave can share the other members of his family. When we get back we'll broaden it out from there.'

He grabbed his jacket and headed out, Jane at his heels.

'How are Louise and Annie coping?' she asked as they went down the stairs.

Pete's feet didn't slow, but his face twisted into a grimace. 'Lou's doing better than I thought she might after the last year or so but Annie... I don't know, to be honest. She got a bit emotional this morning but she's just a kid. What can you expect?' He led the way through into the back corridor. 'She's been a gem, but I don't know how much more she can take. She really needs a break, poor kid.'

'Well, Tommy should be home soon. That ought to help, surely.'

'Yeah. I need to make a call in that regard while we're driving. There's going to be some major readjustments going on there, though, isn't there? I mean, after the way he treated her last time they saw each other. She says she understands, but...' He shook his head. 'You might understand something like that on an intellectual level but it's still going to leave a scar of some kind, isn't it?'

'Easier to say you forgive than actually do it.'

'Oh, I don't doubt she forgives him,' he said as they passed the custody suite. 'But it's bound to change the way she reacts to him, isn't it? Make her a bit more cautious around him and so on. And he's going to sense that, which won't help anything.'

They reached the back door and Pete hit the button to release it. The weather had turned chilly and grey. The cold hit them as he pushed the door open.

'Bugger, it's like winter again out here,' he said as the cold seemed to penetrate all the way to his core.

'He'll understand the difference in her, though,' Jane said as they started across the half-empty car park. 'He caused it, after all. The important thing will be how you and Louise treat him.'

Pete unlocked the patrol car, then paused.

Jane noticed his hesitation. 'Worried, boss?'

'Wouldn't you be?'

She gave a dry chuckle. 'I reckon I'd go back to the push-bike for a while if it was me.'

He drew a breath. 'Well, you know what they say about falling off a horse.'

'Yeah. It hurts.'

Pete laughed and reached for the car door. If it wasn't safe here, where would it be?

CHAPTER NINETEEN

Hot air blasting over his hands from the drier in the boys' toilets along the corridor from the canteen, Tommy barely registered the opening of the door and certainly wasn't aware of how long it stood open.

The first he was aware of a problem was when he was shoved hard from behind by a hand between his shoulder blades.

The curved chromed tube coming out of the front of the drier unit hit him hard in the chest and he turned fast, hands balling into fists.

There were five of them, led by Sam Lockhart, whose nose was still red and scabbed from their last encounter.

'Thought you'd have learned from last time,' Tommy said.

'Yeah. Not to get interrupted by the staff.' Lockhart shoved him hard in the chest with both hands.

With nowhere to go, Tommy caught the undersides of Lockhart's sleeves with both hands and dragged him in close then wrapped his arms tight around the bigger lad's neck. 'You want me to finish what I started, do you?' He snapped his teeth together, *click click.*

'You wish.' Lockhart used his superior size to lift Tommy bodily off the ground and turn towards the others. 'Grab him, lads.'

Tommy saw the danger and twisted his body, but Lockhart had got hold of his waistband. All he could do was writhe so, instead, with Lockhart supporting his weight, he kicked out wildly with both feet at the other kids, legs flailing. They backed off briefly until Lockhart saw what was happening and set him down. Then

Tommy took the opportunity to stamp hard on one of his feet. Lockhart gave a weird, strangled gurgling sound as he fought not to yell out. Tommy stamped again, aiming for the same foot, but missed. One of the others took the chance to dart in, grabbing his other foot and lifting it. Tommy let him, then kicked him as hard as he could with his free foot, aiming for the crotch but catching him in the lower stomach instead.

The kid doubled over, retching, a thin trail of bile drooling from his lip as he backed off.

'Come on,' Lockhart gasped. 'Get hold of him.'

Two of them darted in. Tommy lifted a knee that hit one of them directly in the face as they bent to grab his legs, knocking him back with blood pouring from his nose. But the second boy had got both hands around his left leg. As Tommy's right returned to the floor, the boy lifted, using the muscles of his back to raise Tommy bodily off the floor again. Tommy tried stamping down again, but he was too small. It didn't work. He was raised up almost horizontally.

With one angle of attack failing, he went for another. One arm clamped around Lockhart's neck, his hand reached for the bigger boy's face. His nose. Lockhart tried to shake him off, twisting his head, but Tommy's hand found what it was aiming for and grabbed, squeezing.

Lockhart struggled not to bellow, trying to pull his head back from Tommy's grasp but, with the arm locked tight around his neck, he had no escape.

Tommy felt himself being lifted up again, the grip on his leg moving down to his ankle as the limb was pulled out straight. He jerked it back, trying to pull downwards to aim his knee at the face of the boy holding him, but he had no leverage. Instead, he simply lifted himself higher, suspended between Lockhart and his other tormentor. He twisted, kicking across with his free leg, aiming for the boy who was holding him. The boy ducked, Tommy's foot sliding across his scalp. Then someone else reached out, grabbing his free ankle. He snatched it back and the grasping hands hit the back of the other boy's head and let go.

Tommy could feel Lockhart straining to support him.

Another of the boys came in from the side, taking the chance to drive a fist at Tommy's face. He saw it coming but could not avoid it completely. He turned his head so it caught him on the cheek, but the last of the boys was on his other side. He swung too and the turn of Tommy's head took his face directly into the line of the kid's fist. It hit him in the eye, one knuckle impacting his nose, just below the bridge. Pain exploded in his skull. Then Lockhart started punching him hard in the ribs and back.

Tommy jerked his still captive leg back and slammed the heel of the other foot downwards, hitting the boy holding his leg directly on the top of his head. He staggered under the blow and went down to his knees, letting go of Tommy so that his hands could go to the floor. Tommy writhed, twisting his whole body as his feet hit the floor. Lockhart, hard against the sinks behind them, bent at the waist. Tommy kicked backwards, his foot going between Lockhart's legs to hit the wall beneath the sink.

But that was fine.

Tommy used the wall as a push-off point and ran forward. The boys bunched around him parted instinctively. The far wall loomed, more handwashing basins lined along it at waist height, but Tommy didn't stop. The room wasn't that big. Five paces across at the most. Holding tight to Lockhart's head, he surged forward. There was a crack of impact and Tommy doubled over the curved gap between two sinks as Lockhart's head hit the white china and, unable to avoid it, Tommy ducked to head-butt the wall. It hurt like hell, but as he bounced off, turning to face the others, he saw that the move had worked.

Lockhart was lying in a heap on the floor.

Tommy didn't stop to allow the others to take stock. With adrenaline coursing through his veins and blood smeared across his lower face, he leapt forward, aiming a punch at the throat of a lanky kid with greasy dark hair and an angrily spotty face. The kid stepped back. The punch missed its target, hitting him high on the sternum instead, the force reduced by his backward step but still enough to hurt Tommy's fingers.

It was too high to wind the kid, though.

Tommy grabbed his shirt and used him for leverage to kick out at another one of his attackers, a high judo kick that caught him low in the ribs and slammed him back into the side of the end stall. He hit the thin wall with a crash and bounced off into another kid, who staggered forward as Tommy straightened up. Tommy saw him coming and aimed a punch at his face but the kid he was holding onto jerked sideways so that the punch missed and Tommy had to focus his attention in front of him once more as a fist hit him in the stomach. Tommy coughed but used his existing grip to, instead of bending at the waist, lift one knee hard and fast into the kid's crotch.

The kid choked and doubled over his pain, hitting the floor on his side and curling into a foetal position as Tommy spun towards the remaining two, one of whom already had a bloody nose.

They raised their hands in surrender but Tommy shook his head, immediately regretting it as pain flashed through his skull. 'No, you don't,' he grunted.

With one of them standing directly in front of the space in front of the stalls that led to the doorway, the other blocked from it by his friend and backed up against the side of the end stall, Tommy went for the one with the easier escape route. As he turned to flee, Tommy dropped heavily onto one of the others, who was curled up on the floor, and shot his legs out to tangle the fleeing boy's feet, bringing him crashing to the floor. With the softer landing of a body beneath him, Tommy was up again almost instantly as the last remaining attacker yelped, 'No,' and took a step back.

This was the kid who'd punched Tommy in the eye.

His back hit the side of the stall behind him and Tommy lunged, feigning a blow to the stomach with his left and following it through with an upper-cut to the face with his right. The kid's feet went out from under him and he sat down hard. Tommy aimed a kick at his face which he dodged, though not completely, Tommy's foot glancing off his cheekbone to slam into the thick board behind him with a loud bang. The boy in front of the stalls was beginning to get up. Tommy took a step to the side then leapt high, coming down with his full weight and momentum, both feet on his back. The air grunted out of him and Tommy stepped forward, kicking back hard to slam his heel into the prone kid's skull. Then he spun around, arms up in defence, just in case, but the floor was littered with the bodies of his would-be attackers and smeared with their blood. One of them groaned and looked up blearily at him.

'Last warning,' Tommy told him. 'Any of you try anything like this again, one of you's going to the hospital. And you won't be coming out of there in one piece if you come out at all.'

*

'Will Grayson?' Jane held up her warrant card for him to see. 'Devon and Cornwall CID. Can we have a word?'

He frowned. 'What's up?' A big man, over six feet, he was standing in the doorway, one hand raised to the frame, T-shirt clinging to the muscles of his chest and shoulders while a pair of shorts revealed powerful calves. He was barefoot. 'What's this about?'

'You're intimately involved with Sally Muir, yes?'

'If you want to put it that way. Is she OK? I only spoke to her a couple of hours ago.'

'She's fine. Her sister isn't, though. She may have told you?'

'Yes.'

'How well did you know Claire?'

'We met a few times. A couple at her place when Sally was staying with her. A few times on the town with workmates and so on. Why?'

'And that was it, was it?' Jane ignored his question again. 'You were just passing acquaintances?'

He was frowning again, not liking her responses. 'Yes.'

'I gather you've been doing some decorating recently.'

He let his hand fall away from the door frame, folding his thick arms across his chest as he set his feet squarely apart, filling the space. 'Yes.'

'What have you been doing?' Jane asked.

'What's that got to do with anything?'

'We're in the process of trying to narrow the suspect field. Eliminate people from the enquiry so we can focus down on who attacked Claire. Did you do the work yourself or get someone in?'

'Can't do electrics but the rest, I did.'

Jane nodded. 'Must be handy being able to. A lot cheaper as well.'

'More satisfying, too,' he agreed.

'So, what have you been doing to the place?'

'Re-doing the hall, stairs and landing. Making it a bit more welcoming.'

Jane raised an eyebrow. 'May I?'

He grunted. Stepping back, he held out a hand. 'I suppose.'

She stepped forward, followed by Pete.

Inside, the entrance of the 1960's house had been thoroughly redecorated, the stairs either stripped or replaced, the walls and ceiling freshly painted. New doors led off with silver handles rather than the brass ones in Pete's own place.

'Nice job,' he said, speaking for the first time as he noted the fresh, pale colours. 'Did you do the plastering?'

The big man shook his head. 'That's one of the few things I don't do and there wasn't any need for it, thankfully.'

Pete nodded. 'What colour is that? It's not white, is it?'

'One of those hint type things. Orchid white, they call it. I tried white but it was a bit harsh. That just takes the edge off a bit.'

'It works well. When did you finish it?'

'Last weekend.'

Pete was nodding again. 'And you don't know of anyone who had it in for Claire? Anyone she'd had a problem with?'

He shook his head with a grimace. 'The only problem I know of that she had was with her computer. She thought someone had hacked it. But that was two or three months ago.'

Pete tipped his head. 'Why would you know about that? It's the first we've heard of it.'

'I work with them. She asked me to have a look at it.'

'So you went to her place.'

'It's a laptop. She brought it to me.'

'And had it been hacked?' Jane asked.

'There was some malware on it but I don't know about hacked as such.'

'And you dealt with that for her?' Pete made it a question rather than a statement.

'There are programs that you can download off the Internet. I cleaned it up for her and installed an up-to-date anti-virus program.'

'And that was three months ago?' Jane checked.

'Something like that, yes.'

She glanced at Pete.

'Is that the only time she's been here, as far as you recall?' he asked.

'Yes.' Grayson shifted defensively.

Pete lifted his hands, palms out. 'We're not here to judge. Or to pass anything on to Claire's sister.'

'There's nothing to pass on. I'm seeing Sally, not Claire. I helped her out that once because she asked me, knowing what I do for a living. Sally doesn't know about it, but that's because Claire didn't want to worry her. She's a bit on the nervous side. Panics easily.'

'OK,' Pete said. 'Well, I think we've taken up enough of your time for now, Mr Grayson. We'll be in touch again if we need to.'

'I hope you find him quick, if only for Sally's benefit.'

'Thanks.'

Pete led the way out and down the short drive. When he glanced back at Jane on reaching the footpath, he saw that Grayson was still standing in his doorway. He nodded to the big man and unlocked the car.

Grayson didn't go back inside until they were both sitting in the car, pulling their seatbelts on.

'What do you reckon?'

'There was no smell from the gloss in the hall so that's been done a few days at least. Not sure if he was telling us the whole truth, but we can check. For one thing, there'll be details on her laptop of when the anti-virus was uploaded. And for another, we can talk to the neighbours here, see if anyone recognises Claire, and

Claire's neighbours to see if they recognise him. Have you got her picture on you?'

'Only on my phone, but we can go and fetch paper copies and come back.'

Pete pursed his lips. 'I'd rather not waste the time. It doesn't look like an area full of old folk. We'll chance it with the phones. I've got her on mine, too.'

He had the phone half out of his pocket when it rang in his hand.

He checked the screen and lifted it to his ear. 'Ben?'

'We've just got some news in from Middlemoor, boss. They've managed to recover a VIN from the Transit van. Running it through the system, it comes back to one that was nicked out by the airport three days ago.'

'Ah. When you say, "out by the airport"…?'

'From outside an industrial unit a few doors away from the antique place.'

Pete pictured the big, grey metal building in his mind. Surrounded by other, smaller units, it was the biggest and best known of several businesses that occupied the site.

'What time was it taken?'

'Overnight is all the owners can say for sure.'

'Get onto the antique place, then. They've got a camera covering the gate. Also, there's one at the airport parking area just along the road from there.'

'I remember.'

They'd made use of footage from both cameras last year during the investigation that led to Neil Sanderson's current incarceration.

'Didn't the bloke from the antique place take a bit of a shine to Jane, boss?'

Pete could almost hear the grin on Ben's face as he said it. 'Maybe, but she's out here with me so you'll have to do for now.'

'Any news your end?'

'Investigations are still on-going out here, Ben. Keep me updated, OK? And Ben... Someone needs to check the anti-virus software on Claire's laptop. When was it installed or upgraded last?'

'I'll get onto that when I've made these two phone calls.'

'See you later.' Pete ended the call but kept his phone in his hand. 'Right. Let's see what the neighbours know.'

CHAPTER TWENTY

'Thomas James Gayle.' Llewellyn looked up at him from behind the manager's desk. 'What happened to your face?'

'Ran into something.' Tommy shrugged. 'Not paying enough attention, I suppose.'

'And whose "something" would that have been?'

'Eh?'

'Whose bony little something did you run so carelessly into?'

Tommy frowned. 'Don't know what you mean, guv.'

'Of course.' The Welshman nodded. 'Not wanting to be known as a grass is as old as mankind, Tommy. It's perfectly understandable in some ways. Completely illogical in others,' he shrugged. 'But there we are, eh? I thought you were brighter than that, though, to be fair.'

'Eh?' Tommy repeated.

'Well, you're only here for a few more days, probably. What do you care what the other kids think of you?'

'I don't.'

'Exactly. So why defend them? They clearly don't deserve it.'

Tommy didn't respond except a quick grimace.

'Show me your hands.'

Tommy frowned at the sudden change of tack but held up his hands, palms up.

Llewellyn's head tipped to one side. 'The other sides.'

Tommy paused just for the sake of it then turned his hands over.

'Knuckles are a bit swollen there. Was that the same something you ran into or another one?'

'Don't know. I suppose you put your hands up automatically when that sort of thing happens, don't you? Self-defence.'

Llewellyn smiled briefly at his use of the term. 'Yes. I thought it might be. So, you know nothing about five boys including Sam Lockhart getting into a fight a little while ago?'

'I know Lockhart's a bit inclined that way. But you know that already. I wouldn't be stood here else. You also know I haven't got five friends in this place who'd get into a scrap for me.'

The Welshman nodded deeply. 'Touche, Mr Gayle. I was told you were a bright one. Oh, well. If you're determined to stand alone there's not a lot I can do about it. Except to say that, whatever the odds, any permanent damage will be paid for. Do you understand, boyo?'

'I don't see a problem. All I want's to be left alone.'

'But, being small, people see an easy target, right?'

Tommy grunted agreement.

Llewellyn leaned back in his chair, relaxed, fingers interlaced across his stomach. 'Well, much as I can't prove it. This time. I suspect that won't be the case here anymore. But *five*?'

Tommy shook his head, suspicious of a possible trap. 'I don't know what you're on about.'

'Don't play dumb, Gayle. I know you're not. I'm just wondering how one small boy can take on five larger ones and win, that's all.'

'I thought you said they'd fought amongst themselves.'

'Ah. Good thinking.' He nodded, sitting forward again, hands on the desk. 'I didn't say that and you know it. But it's a good excuse. A very good one. Doesn't account for your knuckles or that black eye that's coming up, but it's good, I'll give you that. Very good. Just not quite good enough.' He stood up, leaning over the desk. 'One thing I will not tolerate is being lied to, Gayle, however cleverly. And you are lying to me. The proof is there on your face. And on your hand. So, for that, you'll have another day's isolation. No interaction. No visitors. And all privileges revoked.'

Didn't have any of them in the first place, Tommy thought. And neither Colin Underhill nor his solicitor would be coming on a Sunday.

'Which means, from now on, you sit where you're told to. Front of the class – every class – and with the staff at mealtimes.'

Tommy pictured Tabitha in his mind, laughing over their meal trays. *No more.* Anger flared deep inside him. He almost lashed out in verbal response but managed to keep himself in check. Just.

The grin that twitched at the corners of the Welshman's mouth showed that the reaction had been noted, though. 'Don't like that, do you?'

'I'll survive. I hope Tabby does, too. If not, there'll be a major fuss. Police enquiry. All sorts of shit would come out, wouldn't it?'

All traces of humour vanished from Llewellyn's face. His eyes glittered. 'Do not presume to threaten me, Gayle. Whoever your father is. In here, I'm in charge and don't ever forget it. I can allow your life to be tolerable or I can make it hell on earth.'

Six days, Tommy thought, but kept to himself. He'd lived through a lot worse than Llewellyn could ever manage, and for a whole lot longer, but there was no point in saying so.

*

'Any good?'

Pete stopped, one arm resting on the top of the patrol car they had been about to get into as he met Jane's gaze across the large number painted in black on the white panel. 'No. You?'

She shook her head. 'It occurred to me, though – what if she was seeing someone else, apart from Elsfield? We've been working on the assumption that she was suspicious of him, but what if it was the other way round? Might not have been Lover-boy over there.' She thrust her chin towards Grayson's house behind Pete. 'But you never know.'

'Not the type, though, was she?'

'Not that we know of, but we've only got Elsfield's word for the state of their relationship. It might have been over and done with in her mind, hence the arguments – him trying to cling on, maybe. I mean, you've got to admit, it's going a bit far to get secret dancing lessons, isn't it? There's not many blokes would do that – for a wife, never mind a girlfriend.'

Pete grinned. 'Spoken like a true cynic. So who could she have been seeing, if she was seeing anyone?'

'Don't know,' Jane shrugged. 'But a check of her mobile, home phone and email records would tell us, surely?'

'It should do.' Pete tapped the car roof and ducked inside. 'We'll have a look when we get back. Other than that, we'll need to speak to her sister again and the woman who reported her missing – Christine Thackeray.'

'Right.'

She let Pete start the car and move away from the kerb before taking out her phone and dialling.

'Dave?' she said when it was answered. 'Save us a few minutes, would you? Look out the vic's phone records – mobile and land line – and her email account. I need to go through them when we get back.'

She paused, listening.

'OK, if you want to. We're looking for a possible bit on the side.'

Pete heard Dave's laugh over her phone. Then he said something.

'I meant for the victim,' Jane scolded.

'Stop digging for Christ's sake,' he said. 'You're getting worse by the second.'

She glanced across at him. 'I get enough shit from Dave without your help.'

'Making comments like that, I'm not surprised.'

She turned away, concentrating on the phone. 'Are you going to stop taking the piss and do it or what? Thank you.' She broke the connection and looked sideways at Pete. 'It should save a bit of time, at least.'

'So does thinking before you open your trap, sometimes.'

'Yeah but where's the fun in that?'

Pete hit the brakes, stopping the big car abruptly as realisation hit him like a punch to the head.

'Jesus! What was that for?' Jane demanded.

'Cameras. Ben's getting the footage from the airport parking place. Mine didn't get anything useful, but I just realised: to get to my place, the person who set that device under here must have gone past the Co-op on Chatsworth. They'd have security cameras. I don't know if they'd cover the road out front, but it's got to be worth a try.'

'You might be right, but there was no need to give me whiplash when you figured it out.'

'Got to wake you up somehow,' Pete replied, unrepentant as he checked the mirrors and set off again with a new determination. 'Dave would confirm that after the conversation you just had with him.'

*

'Right. What have we all got, then?' Pete asked, looking around the team as he put the disc from his local corner shop on his desk and settled into his chair.

'Well, there's no sign of any necrophilliacs in the vic's emails,' Dave said, nudging Jane so that she almost missed her seat as she sank onto it.

She yelped and slapped him.

'Unless she's deleted those ones. Nothing overtly romantic or flirty, either,' Dave continued, ignoring the blow to the back of his head.

'Do what?' Ben looked confused.

'Don't bother,' Pete told him.

Ben shrugged. 'So I've got the footage from the airport parking. They emailed it. But we'll have to wait until tomorrow for the antique place. The bloke who runs it's not in today and the one who is doesn't know how to work the system.'

'So get yourself out there and do it for him,' Pete urged. 'Just get him to call the owner and get permission before you go, and send me the file from the parking place. I'll check that while you're out.'

'Right. Oh, and Claire's computer security was installed in January.'

Pete glanced at Jane. She tipped her head. Grayson had been telling at least part of the truth.

'You weren't joking when you said it would be a big job looking into the solicitor, Shpetim Boshnjaku,' Dick said.

'Bless you,' said Jane.

'Thank you. The two brothers, Aleksander and Defrim, who run ADB Imports, seem to be clean. There's nothing on record against them, at least. The youngest brother, Liridon's going to have a hell of a lot of potential contacts to choose from, though. And the sister – the pub she's running with her husband isn't one of the most salubrious you'd ever want to visit, so there's potential there, too, with the clientele. And that's before you even think about Shpetim's own clients.'

'OK, check with the Met,' Pete said. 'See if they've got anything on the pub or the youngest brother's known associates. As far as the legal clients, we'll need to draw up a list, including locations, and get the local forces to pitch in. We can use the PNC, but there's nothing like local knowledge. Plus, we haven't got time to plough through it all ourselves.'

'Do you really want to put Fast-track's nose that far out of joint?' Dick asked seriously. 'Liaising with all those other forces without him being involved?'

'Is he in?' Pete asked.

'Not that I know of.'

'Well, there's your answer, then. We haven't got time for niceties.'

Dick shrugged. 'Just thought I ought to point it out, in the circumstances.'

'If I worried about staying in his good books, I'd have jacked it in months ago, Dick.'

'Staying?' Dave queried. 'To stay suggests you've been in them in the first place, doesn't it?'

'I never took you for a pedant, Dave.'

'Me? I don't walk anywhere I can ride; you know that.'

'He said pedant, not pedestrian,' Jane said with a jab of the elbow towards his ribs.

Dave looked at her, big-eyed. 'I don't understand, then.'

Dick laughed. 'Why do you even bother, Red?'

'I don't know, really.'

Smiling, Pete inserted the security DVD into his computer drive and waited for it to load while Ben picked up his phone and dialled. The store manager had given him the footage from midnight to 6.00 am. It seemed like a lot but it paid to be thorough and, on the plus side, there shouldn't be a lot of traffic on a basically residential street during those hours. He could use the fast-forward button to spin through most of it, he guessed.

Fortunately, from Pete's point of view, the shop was actually on a bend in the road, which meant that any vehicle passing by would show both its profile and either its front or rear to the camera mounted discretely over the shop doorway.

Once the whir of the loading disc had settled to a soft hum and the window opened up on the screen, he pressed play and filled the screen with the image that came up. Streetlights lit the scene sodium yellow as a cat walked resolutely past the doorway, having triggered the motion sensor.

Ah, Pete thought. *Even better. No need to speed through a load of nothing with the chance of missing something. If the camera only triggers when something moves, that's perfect.* The cat walked out of shot and nothing more happened for about thirty seconds.

Then the time readout in the bottom right of the screen jumped. A car passed, coming from the direction of Pete's house. It rounded the left-hand bend and continued away from the shop. Thirty seconds of nothing. Then the time jumped again to 1:20 am. A car coming into the estate; a large, pale 4x4. Pete recognised the shape of an expensive German brand. It was followed seconds later by another, smaller vehicle. Then one going out towards the main road before, again, the screen rested, nothing happening.

'Right, I'm off out then,' Ben announced. 'The antique shop owner's with his in-laws in Lyme Regis, but he's given permission for me to go and have a look.'

Pete pressed pause on the screen and looked up. 'Right-o. Don't forget to burn us a copy while you're at it.'

Ben gave him a look. 'Of course. I'll see you later,' he said as he headed for the door.

Pete returned to the footage he'd already got. He pressed play and, almost immediately, the screen jumped forward to show a fox trotting past. The animal looked up at the camera as if it knew it was being observed but didn't care. It was followed by three small cubs, gambolling and play-fighting as they went. *Late April*, he thought. *They must live close by. This must be pretty much their first trip out.* There was a small park less than two hundred yards from the shops. The vixen must have her den somewhere there, he guessed as she turned around the side of the building and went from site towards the delivery area at the rear where, no doubt, they kept the bins. Next door but one to the shop, he remembered, was a Chinese takeaway. *Special fried rice and wontons for breakfast. Or supper.*

It wasn't a completely unappetising thought, although it was only just approaching lunch time.

He focussed on the screen again. The time in the bottom right now read 2:12 as a man cycled past, heading out of the estate. Pete was surprised at how busy the place was in the small hours of the night. Three more cars passed before the vixen returned across the screen, cubs in tow, heading back the way they'd come. He checked the time readout. They'd been out of sight for almost an hour. They must have been having a field day back there. No wonder they looked well-fed and healthy.

More comings and goings followed. Cars, vans, a couple more cyclists, the odd cat. Even, at one point, a hedgehog. All taking him closer and closer to the time period he was looking for. It was a cyclist heading out of the estate that finally took the time reading to 3.53 am. By now Pete's mouth was dry. He wasn't sure if it was genuine thirst or anticipation, but he forced himself to hit the pause button again and sat back.

'Got anything?' Jane asked, looking up from her own screen at the movement.

'Yes. A mouth like an old sock. Who fancies a coffee?'

'I'll get them,' Dick offered. He'd been on the phone, off and on, all the while Pete had been viewing the footage. 'I need to wet my whistle.'

'OK,' he said as both Jane and Dave accepted the offer.

'What was Jill's problem today?' Dave asked as Dick headed for the door.

'It's her daughter's birthday,' Jane reminded him.

'Yeah, but…'

'She's five. She's not old enough to understand if her mum can't be there on her birthday. Especially when it's on a weekend.'

'Sooner she learns the better, I'd have thought.'

'Spoken like a true non-father,' Pete grinned.

'Well, we could have used her help in here, couldn't we?'

Pete tipped his head. 'True. But Jane's right. It's Sunday. This is unofficial overtime that we're doing. And it is the kid's birthday.'

Dave grunted and went back to his screen.

'So, that's why they call you Batchelor!' Jane said, wide-eyed. 'There's no woman who'd live with you and no kid that would want you as a dad.'

'I'll have you know, I'm very good with kids, as it happens.'

'To quote Jimmy Saville,' Jane retorted.

'Ouch,' said Dave. 'Harsh.'

'You know what I mean.'

'Yes,' said Pete.

'There, you see. Someone understands.'

'What?' Pete looked up from his computer. 'Not you lot. This.' He jabbed a finger at the screen in front of him.

'You got something?' Dave asked.

'I'll run it on a bit further to make sure, but the time fits.'

'What is it?' Dick leaned across to see Pete's screen, where he'd frozen the image on the shadowy form of a car sideways on to the camera. Its shape was distinctive and it had been moving right to left across the screen – towards Pete's home. The timestamp read 4:06.

'A dark coloured VW Golf. It might be dark blue, but it's a job to tell under the streetlights. And it's coming past in the right direction, at the right time to be our man.'

'So the next twenty minutes of tape will tell you for sure,' Dick said.

'Yep.'

'It's about time something started working our way. Did you get a number plate?'

'No, it was coming towards the camera. But I will when it comes back the other way.'

Dave looked up at that but managed somehow to stay quiet.

'Something to say, Dave?' Jane asked.

'If I had, I'd have said it.'

'You were thinking something, though, weren't you? I could hear the steam building.'

'What, you never keep your thoughts to yourself?'

'I do. *You* don't.'

'I'll have you know I can be very tactful when I need to.'

He hadn't even finished speaking when Dick snorted with laughter. 'Jeez! Can't you control him? I'm at serious risk of a bloody heart-attack here.'

'There's a pill for that,' Dave told him. 'A big, fat white one. You put one in each ear, push them in as far as you can and…'

'Shut up, Dave,' Pete interrupted him.

Dave threw him a salute but stayed quiet as Pete concentrated once more on the screen in front of him and Dick Feeney stood up and headed for the kitchen.

*

Dick had yet to return with the coffees when Pete spotted a dark Golf speeding past the camera from left to right, leaning as it went around the bend.

He hit the pause button, peering at the screen. He couldn't be certain it was the same car, of course, but the colour looked right. Its speed made the image of the number plate on the back blurry, but he had to try. He took a screenshot, saved it and opened a photo-editing program. Dumping the video still into it, he started by simply zooming in, but the image just got blurrier. He tried increasing the pixel count, but that didn't help either. Sharpening the image made it actually worse, so he undid that and tried sharpening the edges. That helped a little, as did boosting the contrast, but there was a lot of glare in the picture from the car's back lights. He cropped them out then made some more adjustments. Sharpening edges and boosting contrast again gave him the best image he was going to get. It was still blurred, but maybe a print would help. He saved the enhanced image as a new file and printed it. The default settings would make it a full A4 size.

The printer had just started whirring and clanking into life when Dick returned with the drinks expertly clutched in his hands. He never did bother with a tray.

'There's no way you developed that skill outside of a pub,' Pete said. 'And I'm guessing it took a hell of a lot of practice.'

'If a thing's worth doing,' Dick said as he set the mugs carefully on his desk before handing Jane's across to her. 'Christ, that's horrible,' he added as he saw the picture on Pete's computer screen. 'How are we supposed to read that?'

'A man of your age, Dick, I'd have thought you'd know that already.' Pete stood up, retrieved the picture from the printer and went over to stick it on the white board. 'There. Now squint.'

Dick grunted.

'Well, the numbers are pretty easy,' Dave said. 'Six four.'

'Yeah, there's limited options there, aren't there,' Dick scoffed.

'There is on the letters, too,' Dave retorted. 'There's only twenty-six to choose from. And the first one's a W.'

'Like ninety percent of them around here.'

'Yeah. The second one looks like a C, a D or an O.'

'It looks like it ends with a T,' Jane added. 'And there's a U or a J next to that. That would be enough to work with, surely?'

'Go for it,' Pete told her. He could pick out no more than they had from the image. The first letter of the three random ones was too blurred to pick out. It could have been B, D, O, R or even a G.

'Oh,' she said. 'If we assume – which is dodgy, I know, but we've got to start somewhere – that the number plate actually belongs to the vehicle it's on, then there's twenty-nine choices in the system.'

'Well, it's a start,' Pete said. 'See if any of them have been nicked.'

Jane tapped at her keyboard again while Pete closed the photo editing program and ejected the DVD from his computer. Then he logged into the Police National Computer system and began helping Dick with the task of ploughing through the family ties and known associates of Petrosyan's solicitor.

After several minutes, Jane reached for her coffee and took a sip then laid her hands on her desk as she looked across at Pete.

'Nothing.'

CHAPTER TWENTY-ONE

'Who are you?'

'I'm Doctor White. I work at police headquarters. Your dad asked me to see if I could help with this matter of you being transferred to Southampton.'

Tommy leaned back in his chair in the same room he'd last seen Clive Davis in. 'Doesn't the fact that my trial starts on Friday knock that on the head?'

'Only until after your trial. If you're given a custodial sentence, then it would still apply if it hasn't been revoked in the meantime.'

'Yeah, but what's the chance of that? First offence and a minor one at that. Carrying a knife,' he sneered. 'I mean, I wasn't carrying it as a weapon, was I? It was a tool of the job. Plus, I'm a minor.' He spread his arms, putting on an innocent expression. 'Look at me. Who's going to send me down for that?'

'There's just one issue with that argument,' the handsome, dark-haired woman said.

'What?'

'Impulse control. From what I gather from your case notes, you... Shall we say, "struggle with it"?'

'Crap. I don't always use it, but there's a difference between not having it and not using it.'

She tipped her head. 'True. So you're saying that you have perfect control of your actions and emotions? If an adult, for example, starts badgering you about something you'd rather not talk about in a circumstance you can't get out of, you can guarantee that, if you can see the logic behind remaining calm, you'd be able to do that?'

Stupid question. 'Yes,' he said.

'You'd be fully able *not* to bite back.'

'I've got a reputation as a vicious bugger. Someone who's got no boundaries. I know that. I created it.' He spread his arms once more. 'I'm not exactly Arnie Schwarzeneger, am I? So, with no help coming from adults, I had to find a way to stop the bullies on my own, and that was it. Fight fire with firestorm. Make 'em too bloody scared to come anywhere near me.'

'That's perfectly understandable, of course. But it doesn't account for where you were for half of last year and how you came to be there – or, more particularly, what you were doing during that time.'

'Yeah, but that's a different case, isn't it? And taking opportunities that you're given doesn't mean you've got no impulse control.'

'No, but rape tends to. As does murder.'

'What are you here for? To help me or stitch me up?'

'As I said at the start, I'm here to help you, Thomas. And part of that is finding out where your boundaries lie.'

'I told you: I haven't got any. I buried them years ago. But that's not the same as having no control.'

'Indeed. But you need to understand how a jury's likely to see things. Any competent prosecutor is going to raise these issues and use them against you. You need to be able to demonstrate that they're not relevant. Which means more than just saying so. It means, effectively, proving it.'

Tommy frowned. 'How the hell can you prove something like that?'

She took a breath. 'What the prosecution is going to try to demonstrate is that you're suffering from a personality disorder. A psychopathy, if you like. A lack of impulse control, combined with a lack of boundaries and a lack of empathy. An absence of the ability to appreciate and understand other people's feelings. Essentially, they're going to argue that you're mentally ill and therefore in need of custodial treatment in a secure facility.'

'Well, I'm in one of them now. That's not so bad.'

She shook her head. 'Not this kind, Thomas. A mental hospital. A place with bars on the windows and warders instead of nurses that's not dedicated to, or even organised around, the care of young people. There'll be both sexes and all ages in there. You've heard of Broadmoor?'

'Yes.' This was sounding far less good.

'Well, somewhere like that. And you'd be in there until the staff decide that you're definitely fit for release. And that's *definitely*, not maybe. Depending on your attitude and their whims, it could mean life. Full life, not fifteen to twenty years.'

A flutter of fear quivered in Tommy's gut for the first time in a long, long time. He tried to push it down, to bury it, but... 'For carrying a knife? Are you serious?'

The psychiatrist tipped her head. 'Deadly, Thomas.'

'That's ridiculous. Kids get let off with cautions all the time for stuff like that.'

'Yes, they do – kids who haven't been on the run for the better part of a year, having been involved in multiple murder and child-rape. Kids who have a stable home background. Who...'

'I've got that,' Tommy butted in. 'My dad's a copper, my mum's a nurse. How much more stable do you want?'

'Impulse control, Thomas.'

'What?'

'As I was saying before you interrupted me, demonstrating a lack of that very thing, we're talking about kids who have a significant prospect of rehabilitation. Who can see the error of their ways, appreciate the benefit of changing them and show the ability to do that.'

'If that was true, reoffending would be zero,' Tommy argued. 'Which it isn't. Not by a long way.'

'True. But that is the aim of the system. It's what people are working towards. So, if they see a case that they think is unlikely to follow that path, they'll react accordingly. *That's* what I'm trying to get across to you.'

'So, I'm fu... Screwed,' he corrected quickly.

She gave him a brief flash of a smile. 'I'm not saying that. But they will have their own people assess you before the case. If I hadn't known your father, I'd probably have been one of them. And their aim will be to show that you have a poor chance of rehabilitation. That you're mentally unfit to be released into the community.'

'And what do you think about that?'

'I think there's a lot more to be done before that concept can be reliably refuted.'

Tommy's eyes narrowed suspiciously. 'What the... Hell does that mean?'

*

'So, are we looking for a cloned plate?' Dave suggested.

'What, take the number from a dark blue Golf and stick it on another one that you've nicked? That's a bit complex, isn't it?' Dick retorted.

'Convoluted, yes,' Pete agreed. 'But good practice if you want to stay hidden. It means we've got to trace all the Golfs of the right colour range that have been stolen recently, regardless of where from. And what are the chances of that?'

'Bugger all,' Dave said bluntly.

'Back to the data slog, then,' Pete said. 'If we can't get him one way, we'll get him another.'

Dick's phone rang and he picked it up as the others returned to their computer screens.

'DC Feeney. Yes. Oh, hello. Thanks.' A pause as the person on the other end explained something. 'OK. Thanks for trying anyway.' He put the phone down and turned to Pete.

'Essex. Of their four possibles, one's in jail and not a fan of our man because of it, one's since died of an overdose and the other two are accounted for.'

Pete nodded. 'Well, that narrows it down a bit, at least.' As he turned back to his screen, though, what he was thinking was, *Shit, when are we going to get a bloody break here? We've only got today because Fast-track's going to take us off it as soon as he hears what's happened tomorrow, me being the target.*

Two more disappointing phone calls came in the next twenty minutes or so, however. Their man was not from Hertfordshire or Buckinghamshire, either. Then Pete's own phone rang. He picked it up. 'Gayle. CID.'

'Boss, its Ben. I just called to let you know I'm heading back. And I've got something.'

A spark of interest ran through Pete. 'What kind of something?'

'Footage of them arriving and leaving.'

Now the excitement was running high. 'Tell me it gives us something good, Ben.'

'It does. I'll see you soon.' He cut the connection before Pete could ask any more.

'Shit.'

'What?' Jane asked, looking up at him.

'Ben. He's got something but he's playing the tease.'

'There, you see?' Dave said. 'He's been spending too much time around you, Red.' He gave Jane a nudge.

'How am I a tease?'

'You're not,' Pete said, ending the argument before it started. 'He's winding you up.'

'Well, it bloody worked. I am not a...'

Dave laughed. 'Some people never learn.'

'Yeah, and some never grow up,' she shot back.

He shook his head. 'No intention of it. I'm just going to grow old as disgracefully as I can get away with.'

Pete's phone rang again. 'Jesus! What is this, the Exeter telephone exchange?' He picked it up. 'DS Gayle.'

'Peter, it's Doctor White.'

'Hello. How's it going?'

'I've just been talking to Tommy,' she said.

'Oh, right. Thanks for that.' *On a Sunday?* 'And what's your assessment?'

'It's early days yet,' she cautioned. 'I haven't made a full one. There appear to be two choices. Either Dr Letterman's correct or Tommy's just a very mixed-up young man who hasn't learned how to express himself conventionally as well as he might have.'

'Well, yes. I could have told *you* that. In fact, I think I did.'

'Indeed. I was repeating it in order to emphasise that there is no easy, quick answer. There isn't a chemistry test that we can do, or an IQ test. And without knowing and understanding the subject's motivations or knowledge base, we can't make any assumptions about their reactions. I mean if, for example, he'd read up about the field and knew what we'd expect from certain conditions, he'd be able to tailor his responses accordingly. It takes time to break through that. You must know this from interviewing suspects.'

'Of course, but there are still certain tells that you can look for.'

'Unless, once again, he's been reading your study material at home.'

Pete grunted. 'Fair point. But we're talking about a child. How sophisticated could he be in that respect?'

'You'd be surprised, Peter. One thing the brain has in common with the rest of the body is that it develops faster in some than in others. Genetics and circumstances both play a role in that, of course. If you have a harsh life, you learn to adapt more quickly than a person who has everything they want.'

'And he was bullied.'

'Exactly.'

'So what are you saying?'

'I'm saying there isn't time to form a proper assessment of Tommy's condition before his court date on Friday. Even if I wasn't fully occupied at Middlemoor during the week. And with the types of deficiencies we're looking at, one can't rely on instinct, even if the courts would accept such things. Which, of course, they won't. Even from a professional.'

'So we're too late. There's nothing you can do.'

'I'm sorry, Peter. I really am. But the courts deal in facts, as you know, and we don't have time to discover them reliably.'

'On the other hand, the opposition don't either,' he said, trying to cling to any positive aspect of the situation.

'True. And the burden of proof is supposed to lie with them. But juries are fickle. Emotional responses do come into play, even though they shouldn't. It's up in the air, I'm afraid.'

'Hmm. Well thanks for trying anyway, doc.'

'Don't give up, Peter,' she said quickly. 'All you need is reasonable doubt, remember.'

'Yeah. Trouble is, even as his dad, I've got plenty of that, much as I hate to admit it.'

'You're a good man, Peter, and a good policeman. You need to cling to the positives in this situation, and one thing I've learned about you is that you're good at doing that.'

All very fine, Pete thought. *But is good, good enough?* 'Right,' he said. 'Thanks again, doc.'

When he put the phone down he found that, although Dave and Dick were studiously concentrating on their computers, Jane was watching him closely, an expression of concern on her face.

'Second opinion,' he said. 'Didn't work. Not enough time.'

Jane's face pinched into a frown. 'Shit. So what does that mean?'

'Don't know. It leaves things up to the jury on Friday.'

'So his brief has just got to keep things focussed on the case in hand – not allow any mention of Burton and so on.'

'Or, if he can't do that, be prepared to call Rosie Whitlock.'

She nodded.

'Still,' Pete said firmly. 'No time to sit here speculating on what hasn't happened yet. We've got a bomber to catch.'

*

Ben walked into the squad room with a grin twitching the corners of his lips.

'Don't ever play poker, Spike,' Dave told him before he got to his desk. 'You wouldn't stand a chance.'

'What have you brought us, Ben?' Pete asked.

'A DVD.' He drew it out of his coat pocket and put it on his desk. 'A photo.' He pulled a rolled sheet of A4 paper from inside his jacket and laid it beside the disc. 'And the name and address the registration belongs to.'

Finally, he sat down and pulled up his chair.

'You know they say pride comes before a fall, Spike,' Dick said. 'Especially when Dave's in the room.'

Ben laughed. 'He can't reach from over there.'

Dick leaned down, his hand whipping across under Ben's chair to the elevation lever. 'No, but I can,' he said as Ben sunk abruptly downwards.

Ben's hands slapped flat on the desk in front of him, almost at the level of his shoulders as the others all joined in the laughter.

'Who does it belong to?' Pete asked.

'Terence Alan Davidson of Bridgewater, boss.'

Ben reached under his chair and readjusted its height. 'I already contacted him. His car's sitting on his drive. With both of its number plates intact.'

'So it has been cloned,' Dave confirmed.

'But the driver hasn't,' Ben retorted. 'And I've got a nice, clear picture of him.'

'What?' Pete spun his chair, hand slapping his desk as he faced Ben across Dick's back. 'Why didn't you tell us that before?'

'I got interrupted, didn't I?' He kicked Dick's chair.

'Is that it?' Pete asked, nodding to the rolled-up print on Ben's desk.

'Yes.' He pushed it across to Dick, who passed it on to Pete.

He unrolled and flattened it on his desk. A night shot like the video images he'd been watching from the corner shop near his home. This, though, was a lot clearer. It showed a VW Golf, front-on in the gateway of the compound that enclosed the antique barn and several other businesses. Lit up by the taillights of another vehicle that was out of shot, the driver was looking straight ahead through the windscreen, his features picked out in sharp contrast.

Pete could tell immediately this was not the man he'd chased down the road from outside the station a couple of days ago. His build was completely different. 'Gotcha. Right, get that disc loaded up and get this image onto the PNC. Preferably five minutes ago. And Dick – send a copy to the contacts you've been making up East, see if anyone recognises him. I want to know who he is and I want to know ASAP.'

CHAPTER TWENTY-TWO

The search of the Police National Computer system gave them nothing on the face of the driver of the dark blue Golf but it took longer than Dick spent on the phone to his newly made contacts in London and the surrounding counties – which produced exactly the same result. Dick, however, did have the chance of getting a call back if someone came in after the weekend and recognised the man, which didn't help immediately, but did hold out some hope.

For now, though, he was another dead end. They would circulate his picture as widely as possible – as a person of interest, as far as the public were concerned, but as a suspect within the force. But results from that could take days to come in: days they didn't have. Pete needed results and he needed them today.

'Put an alert out on the car,' he said when the PNC finally spat out its negative result. 'If we can find that parked up somewhere it might lead to the driver. And check the ANPR system for it. That could give us a direction, at least. It might point to where they're staying if they're from out of town, or where they live if not. I'll get onto Press Liaison, get his picture out there.'

He picked up the phone and dialled through to headquarters at Middlemoor, on the edge of the city.

'Press Office, how can I help?'

'Hello. It's DS Gayle, Heavitree Road CID. I've got a photograph that I need you to get out to the papers and the TV. It's a man who was seen driving a dark blue VW Golf in the vicinity when a vehicle theft was committed near the airport parking facility three weeks ago. We need to speak to him urgently.'

'So a witness request.'

'As far as the public's concerned at this stage. The truth is, we know he was involved in the vehicle theft but we don't want to spook him if we can help it.'

'Fair enough. Send us over the picture and we'll draw something up.'

'Thanks. I'll send it now.'

Pete sent the photo as an attachment with a short explanatory note by email.

'Boss?' Ben looked up from his screen.

'Ben?'

'I just thought: we know the van's got false plates. And the Golf had them, too – with a local number that matches a similar car. So they must have been made locally. I know we broke up a local gang last year but if we could figure out who might be making them again now, they might give us something.'

'Good thought. Last year's lot were down on Marsh Barton weren't they?'

'Yeah. A garage down there.'

'Any intelligence on anything similar lately?'

'Not that I know of, but...'

'Yeah, come to think of it,' Dave said suddenly. 'I heard something a week or two ago. I don't know where or who. It was an out-of-town set-up, I think. Mark Bridgman's team were looking into it.'

Pete didn't need to turn around towards Mark's team station to know that none of his crew were in the squad room this afternoon. 'OK, I'll ask him.' He picked up the phone again, opened his personal phone book to the right page and dialled Bridgman's mobile number.

It rang several times. Pete thought it was about to go to voicemail when the lanky dark-haired DS finally picked up. 'Hello?'

'Mark, its Pete. Sorry to trouble you on a Sunday but I've just got a quick question you might be able to answer for me.'

'What's that?'

'Dave tells me you're looking into another false number plate scam. Is that right?'

'Yes. We think they're coming out of Tavistock but we haven't got enough to make any arrests yet.'

'But you've got a suspect?'

'Yes, why?'

'We've got two vehicles with false plates that must have been made locally. One's a clone of a local car. We're trying to identify and trace the drivers.'

He heard Bridgman suck air across his teeth. He could understand the man's hesitation. Approaching their lead now could jeopardise his case. 'What are they wanted for?'

'Attempted murder.'

'A… Are we talking about that Transit in front of the station?'

'Yes.'

Mark was a good copper but Pete wasn't certain which way he would swing on this as he waited, phone to his ear, for what seemed like an age. Then, finally, he spoke. 'Attacking a copper's got to trump number plate fraud. We think he's working out of a lock-up on the edge of the town. One of a row of garages that belong to the houses just up the road from them. He lives in number twelve. Terry Black, his name is. Works in a plastics factory in Taunton during the day.' Pete wrote down the details as Mark gave them to him then thanked the man and put the phone down.

Dave was looking at him expectantly.

'Might be our man, might not,' Pete said. 'Mark hasn't got enough on him for a solid case yet but he's given me the details.'

Dave nodded appreciatively. 'Do we go for him, then?'

'Check with uniform first. See if they've got anything on anyone else, maybe more local.' It was unlikely, but better than putting another officer's case in jeopardy for nothing.

'OK.' Dave picked up his phone and dialled as Pete returned his attention to his computer, logging into the Devon and Cornwall force database.

'Sarge? Have you heard anything about anyone making false number plates around here lately? No? OK, thanks anyway.' Dave put down the phone with a shake of the head.

Pete hit return on his search. 'OK. We'll just try this.'

His screen changed as the result came back. He sucked air across his teeth and reached for his phone again.

'Something?' Dave asked.

'One case. Plymouth.'

'Devon and Cornwall police. How can I help?'

'Hello. This is DS Gayle in Exeter. I see you've got an outstanding case of number plate falsification over there. Can I speak to the SIO?'

'He's not on duty at the moment. Can I do anything?'

'Are you familiar with the case?'

'Yes. I'm arranging the arrests.'

'Excellent. I've got a case over here of attempted murder where two false plates are involved – one of them copied from a local vehicle. The only other possible source for the plates that I know of is in Tavistock but the suspects are from out East, London way, so that seems less likely than a place like Plymouth. Can you tell me anything about your suspects?'

'They're a mix of locals and a sight further east than London. Baltic, Balkans – something like that.'

'And my main suspect is Armenian.' Pete felt a flicker of interest springing to life. 'When are you bringing them in?'

'Tomorrow morning, bright and early. Well, not so bright at this time of year, I suppose. 3.30 am.'

Shit. Just a few short hours before DCI Silverstone would be in his office, looking over the weekend's caseload and calling him in to inform him that he would no longer be working his own case. 'If I send you the licence plate details from our case, could you check them against what you find, sooner rather than later?'

'Why the urgency?'

'Because the target was one of ours.'

'Oh. OK, I'll see it gets done.'

'Thanks.'

Pete put the phone down with a sense of impending doom settling over him. If he couldn't close the case today, he'd be in for a lot more than the usual ignorable bollocking from DCI Adam Silverstone, especially after recent events.

*

Ben's fist slammed abruptly on his desk, jarring the rest of the team out of their concentration. They'd been working in silence for over twenty minutes, each focussed on their own task.

'Dammit, boy,' Dick complained. 'Do you have to?'

'What is it, Ben?' Pete asked.

'I reckon I know where they've been staying.'

'Tell us.'

'The only ANPR hit we've got that wasn't the real Golf is on the Exmouth Road, right?' He'd announced that discovery twenty minutes ago. 'We've got both vehicles coming up past the Fire Service training centre before the attack on you out the front here. Only the Golf goes back again afterwards, as you'd expect. But it doesn't get as far as the camera in front of the pub at Lympstone, and what's between them, apart from a few farms?'

He looked from one to another of them expectantly.

'And you woke the old man out of his Sunday afternoon nap to ask that?' Dave teased.

'It's the Clyst River Holiday Park, isn't it? Out of the way. Mobile homes. Anonymity. Still on the quiet side, this time of year. It'd be perfect for them.'

'There's also the B&B a couple of hundred yards before the pub,' Dick cautioned.

'Yeah, right on the main road. Less likely, surely? And with daily interaction with the owners. The risk of being recognised when their faces get in the papers, as they will tomorrow. One of them, at least.'

'It's worth checking,' Pete agreed, opening a new Internet window on his screen to look up the camp site and its contact details. It took seconds to bring up the web site, hit the contact button and find a phone number. He picked up his phone and dialled.

'Clyst River Holiday Park, how can I help?' came the response after just three rings.

'Hello. This is DS Gayle with Exeter CID,' he said. 'I'm hoping you can help me with some information. We're trying to trace two vehicles – a white van and a dark blue VW Golf. They'd have been travelling together, although we know the white van's not around anymore.'

'I don't know... Do you mean a little van or a transit type or what?'

'A Transit exactly.'

'A white transit and a blue Golf... No, I don't...'

Pete heard a voice in the background. Then: 'Oh, yes. That's right. Never thought of them. Yes, Officer, we've got a couple of guys staying here on the park driving vehicles just like that. They said they were touring the local auctions for furniture to do up and re-sell, but last we knew, the van was still empty. And you're right – we haven't seen it for a day or so. The Golf's still around, though.'

Pete could barely contain his excitement. He tried to keep his voice calm as he asked, 'Is it there on the park now?'

'I don't know. I saw them go out in it this morning but I've been in the office since. Mandy?' The man took the phone away from his mouth as he spoke to the woman in the background again. Then he was back. 'No, my wife hasn't seen it today. We can check, if you like.'

'No, no,' Pete said quickly. The last thing he wanted was a couple of innocents getting on the wrong side of these guys. They'd proved themselves to be both dangerous and completely uncaring towards those around them already. 'That's OK. We'll take it from here, thanks.'

'What have they done? I must admit, I wondered about them. Nothing in the van. Coming and going at odd hours. Picking a home that's further away from the facilities than necessary.'

'We just need to question them in relation to a traffic incident in the city the other day,' Pete told him. 'Thanks for your help.'

He put the phone down before the man could ask any more.

'A traffic incident in the city?' said Dave. 'That's a good one. Are they there?'

'Don't know, but they have been. You can come and find out if you want,' he added as he stood up, switching off his computer screen. 'But don't forget your truncheon.'

'Sounds like a plan.'

'Just the two of you?' asked Jane.

'We'll take some uniforms with us,' Pete replied. 'If you three are staying, you could follow up some of Claire Muir's friends and family, see what they can tell us about her social life, contacts and so on.'

*

The Clyst River mobile home holiday park covered seven acres of land overlooking the confluence of the Clyst and Exe rivers. It was accessed along a narrow lane off the Exeter to Exmouth road through the village of Lympstone. Pete was hopeful as he drove between the high, dense hedges that led towards the park that it would be one of those that were covered by a thorough set of security cameras that would give him the precise comings and goings of the two vehicles and their drivers but, when he reached the wide gates, he was disappointed to find no signs warning of such a system.

He shrugged inwardly.

That was probably one of the reasons the men had chosen the place. They'd proved themselves to be anything but stupid over the past few days, after all.

He drove into the site with two marked Range Rovers behind him, each carrying four uniformed officers, all but one of them male. The exception was Nikki French, who Pete had worked with more than once before and, as small as she might be, she'd proved herself to be more than fierce enough to take down any man he'd ever met.

There was a high-fenced set of grass tennis courts to his right as he drove in and a crazy golf course to his left. Beyond the golf, the mobile homes were set at an angle to the concrete roadway, plenty of parking room between them, the grass neatly mown. Past the tennis courts a large building housed the camp shop, office and reception. Pete pulled up there, held a cautionary hand up to the vehicles behind him and went in.

A large man stood behind the shop counter, straggly hair hanging over his collar at the back and at least a couple of stones more than he needed bulging his faded pink polo-shirt and green shorts.

'Afternoon,' he said when Pete walked in. 'How can I help?'

Pete held up his warrant card. 'DS Gayle, Exeter CID. I spoke to someone on the phone a little while ago about two of the guests here.'

'White van and a blue Golf. Yes, that was me. Martin Daniels. The owner.' He stuck out a large hand which Pete shook. The man's grip was surprisingly lax though the hand was roughened by work. 'My wife Mandy's in the office.' He indicated another door over to the left.

Pete nodded. 'Which caravan are the subjects occupying?'

Daniels glanced through the window at the three brightly painted police vehicles parked outside. 'Looks like we're being raided,' he said. 'That won't be good for customer impressions.' He grinned, offsetting the comment. 'They're in number forty-three, over towards the back. River view, although not the best one on the site. Nice spot. About as far as you can get from here on the site without getting your feet wet.'

'OK.' Pete had noticed a plan of the site up on a board outside. He would check it out with the team before they went any further. 'Are any of the surrounding caravans occupied?'

'No. It's early in the season yet. Not many in at all, and most of them want to stay close to the shop and the entrance. More convenient for coming and going.'

'Understandable. Can I take a master key, just in case? Save doing any damage.'

'Just a sec.'

He went into the office and returned moments later with a key.

Pete exchanged it for a business card. 'In case they're not in and you happen to see them coming into the site behind us, would you give me a quick heads-up? My mobile's on there.'

'Sure, no problem.'

Back outside, Pete crossed to the board with the site plan painted neatly on it and waved the team over. He waited for them to congregate around him. 'Right. We're not sure if they're in or not at this moment but they're occupying number forty-three.' He pointed to it on the plan. He outlined a plan of approach. 'We do it quietly and smoothly. Hopefully, we can avoid any undue trouble if they see they've got nowhere to go. But I need to emphasise, they're clearly skilled in the use of IEDs so it's possible they could be armed, too, so we need to exercise due caution. I haven't got armed response here because, with the best will in the world, I want at least one of them to talk to me and they can't do that from a mortuary table. That's why we've all got Tasers. They're for use, not ornament. And I've got a trained negotiator on standby in case it comes to that. I don't want anyone hurt – us or them. The first sign of a firearm, we back off, is that clear?'

He looked around the assembled officers, accepting their responses, vocal or nods.

'Nikki and Mick, you're with me. Any questions?'

Shaking heads and blank looks were the only replies.

'Right. Let's do it.'

They piled into the vehicles and, as they set off, Pete saw Daniels watching from the shop window, a small blonde woman standing beside him.

Two hundred yards further on, the two Range Rovers turned off to the left. Pete carried on past the next row of mobile homes and turned onto the next side-road. The target home was the fifth one along. As he made the turn, he counted along the row and spotted the one they were aiming for. Each of the homes was painted differently. Some had different base colours, others just different coloured bands along the side. The one they were aiming for was pale yellow with two dark blue lines along the centre line. He couldn't see if there was a vehicle parked alongside it but, if so, judging by the others, it would be on this side.

With three marked cars, there was no point in trying to stay hidden so he drove straight up to the target. The roadways, with the grassed areas to either side, were far too wide to block with a single vehicle, but he parked at an angle to block as much as he could, despite seeing that the Golf was absent.

A physical barrier was sometimes enough to make a fleeing person hesitate, if only for a moment. And that moment could make the difference between an escape and an arrest.

'No car, but that doesn't mean they're both out,' he said as he switched off the engine and took out the key. 'Give me plenty of room in case one of them's in and tries to make a run for it. We'll try the conventional approach first and if there's no response I'll use the key.' He picked up the radio handset and keyed the mike. 'The car's absent so I need two people from car one to cover the rear of the home in case of an escape attempt.'

'Roger.'

'And be prepared. He is violent and he will be desperate.'

'Sarge.'

He saw two men step out of the Range Rover blocking the roadway at the far side of the target and move out of sight between it and the next one in the row. He gave them a count of five and stepped out of the car to approach the mobile home with Nikki and Mick a few paces behind and spread out to either side of him.

A wooden platform about three feet square was approached by a ramp on one side and two steps on the other, protected by a wooden handrail across the doorway of the home. Pete went up the ramp. With his senses tuned for any sound or movement from inside, he knocked firmly.

'Police. Open up.'

Nothing.

He knocked again. 'Police. Come out now or we come in.'

Still no response.

Pete slid the key gently into the lock. With his free hand on the handle, he waited for a count of three then twisted the key and turned the handle in one movement. His pressure on the door pushed it inwards as soon as the catch released and he stepped forward and in.

Bang.

The impact knocked him back against the wooden railing behind him. It caught him across the lower back, tipping him painfully backwards, his feet almost leaving the small deck.

He wasn't sure what had happened for a moment. Had he been shot? He looked down as he regained his feet, both hands on the railing to either side of him, but there was no blood on his shirt and no damage to the door. It must have been kicked. Then the crash of breaking glass came from the back of the structure.

'Go,' Pete gasped.

A heavy thud came from behind the mobile home.

A shout: 'Police. Stop.'

Wincing, Pete straightened up and turned towards the two steps that led down to the grass. A grunt sounded. Then a voice shouting, 'Spread out. He's running.'

'Dammit,' Pete swore as he jumped to the ground, jarring his back painfully, and set off after Nikki and Mick.

Rounding the end of the mobile home, Pete saw Mike Douglas helping another uniformed constable to his feet. Beyond them, the fifteen-yard-wide strip of mown grass was empty. Pete glanced to his right. Beyond the picket fence and the shrubs and bushes growing behind and through it, the wide expanse of mud flats that was the tidal river junction was similarly empty.

Pete hesitated, at a loss. 'Where'd they go?'

Mike looked up, pointing. 'Down behind the next van.'

Pete ran on, swinging wide so that he wouldn't need to slow at the corner. Rounding it, he once more saw no-one.

'Nikki,' he shouted as he ran between the mobile homes, cursing himself for not picking up his radio as he got out of the car. 'Nikki!'

'Sarge.'

'Where are you?' He reached the far end of the homes and the roadway where his own vehicle and one of the Range Rovers were parked. Her voice had come from ahead and to the right, he thought, but sound echoing off the mobile homes as he ran between them could have been misleading.

'Next row down and... Shit!'

Pete crossed the roadway, still running hard. 'What?'

He started between the mobile homes in the next row.

'Lost him.'

'Everyone spread out and move back towards the entrance,' Pete bellowed. 'Now! Nikki, get on the radio for those who didn't hear.'

He reached the next roadway and saw her, two vans along to his right. Signalled to her to keep going, making sure to look under the vans that weren't covered in beneath. She nodded, lifting her radio as she moved off parallel to him.

Most of the mobile homes had access hatches to the spaces beneath them. Pete checked the one on his right but it was shut and bolted. He moved quickly on. Checked the door but it was also locked. He ran to the far end, checked to either side and crossed the roadway but not before glimpsing a red car parked at the far side of the home on his left. Again, the one on his right was locked up tight. He decided to loop back around.

The red car turned out to be a small Ford. He knocked on the door of the home it was parked in front of. A man in his forties opened it, dressed in a long-sleeved polo shirt and jeans.

'Hello?'

'Police.' Pete showed him his warrant card. 'Have you seen anyone go past here in the last couple of minutes or so?'

The man shook his head. 'No. Why?'

'We're pursu...'

A crash sounded from inside to his left. Rather than the expected curse, there was a strangled whimper, cut off almost as soon as it began.

'Everything all right in there?' Pete asked, immediately suspicious.

'Yes, of course. Why wouldn't it be?'

'Because the man we're pursuing is known to be highly dangerous. If you do see him, avoid him if you can or do not provoke him, OK?'

'Right.'

'Have a good day, then.' Pete stepped back, knowing in his gut that something was wrong within the mobile home, but not able to do anything about it at that moment.

He moved to the back end of the home, checked left and right and saw a uniformed officer crossing the roadway to his left.

'Hey.' The man stopped and looked around. Pete approached him quickly. 'Do not look at it but the van I've just come from with the red Focus outside – I need it put under surveillance immediately and covertly. I'd set it up myself, but I left my radio in the car.'

'Right, Sarge. Will do.'

Pete clapped him on the back and used the hand to guide him across the roadway and out of sight, behind the next mobile home. 'There we go. As I said – covertly. I think our man might be in there. With at least two hostages.'

'Sarge.' He lifted his radio and spoke into it. 'Row eleven, van three. Red Ford Focus outside. Surveillance needed immediately, without letting the occupants know about it. Suspected hostage situation. Over.'

CHAPTER TWENTY-THREE

A uniformed constable's wet and muddy right shoe was pressing hard into Pete's hands, which were cupped on his thigh as he helped lift the man up onto the roof of a mobile home in the next row down from the one with the red Ford outside when an engine roared into life behind him and to his right.

The car clanged into gear and the engine note changed as it was set in motion.

Pete thought instantly of the two men he'd left to discretely guard the entrance to the holiday park. They weren't equipped to stop a fleeing car. The gates were solid enough, but only if they got them closed in time. If not…

'Sarge!'

Pete felt the man's weight shift above him and looked up. The constable was crouching towards him.

'I see him. The target. Let me down, quick.'

'Where?' Pete demanded as he and the other constable – the one who he'd had put out the order to set up a watch on the home with the red car – complied and lowered the man to the ground.

'Two vans back and three across.' He pointed to the south-west. 'He's laid flat on the roof.'

'Did he see you?'

'I don't think so.'

'Radio. Quick.' Pete held his hand out to the other man again. The handset was passed across and Pete keyed the mike.

'Urgent call. Cancel the surveillance on the van with the red Ford. Do not go up on the roof of the next van down. Repeat: do not climb up. Received?'

'All received, Sarge. What's up?'

'Mobile home number eight, third row back from the river. Our man's hiding on top of it. We need to surround him. Radio silence from now. Over.'

'Received. Out.'

Pete handed the constable his radio. 'Let's go.'

They ran back the way they'd come, other officers converging on the same point from every direction except the river. Staying on the grass to mask the sound of footsteps, they closed in, spreading out around the mobile home. Pete looked up as he approached but, from below, there was no sign of the man on the roof. Was he still there? Had he overheard someone's radio and slipped away before they got here?

The next mobile home to the north had a sturdy-looking handrail around a small platform outside the door. Pete climbed up onto it and hauled himself up until he could see over the roof.

His eyes met those of the man who he'd chased away from the police station less than forty-eight hours ago. Shock registered on the stocky figure's face. Pete stood up so that he was head and shoulders above the roof line. He smiled.

'Look over the sides. You're surrounded and every officer here is armed with a Taser. Are you coming down or are we coming up to get you? I can't guarantee your safety if it's the latter, mind.'

The man's round face twisted into a sneer. He said nothing. Stayed put for what seemed like several long seconds. Pete was about to say more when he finally got to his knees and stood up, moving towards the near edge of the roof.

'Wise move,' Pete said and dropped back to the decking boards. He went down the two steps to the ground and started around the end of the big caravan towards where he expected his man to be climbing down in a similar fashion. He'd only taken the first step when there was a shout from the far side of the home.

'No!'

Shit. 'Stop him,' he yelled, sure the man was making a break for it.

In two steps he was rounding the end of the caravan. A uniformed officer was down on his back, coughing hard as his colleagues streamed across the roadway after the fleeing suspect.

'Spread out,' Pete shouted after them as he went to the downed man. 'Are you all right?'

The constable nodded as he turned over onto his hands and knees, choking and wheezing.

'Yeah,' he gasped. 'Go.' He waved a hand vaguely in the direction the suspect had fled.

'Good man.' Pete gave him a quick touch on the shoulder and ran – not towards the entrance of the holiday park but in the opposite direction, back towards the river.

Two rows back, he hopped quickly into his car, gunned the engine and swung it around to try and cut the fleeing man off. As he hit the main roadway towards the entrance and jammed his foot down on the throttle, he keyed the radio. 'Close the gates. Repeat, close the gates. Suspect approaching on foot. Be alert. Tasers to be used if necessary. No warning needed.'

They were all trained in the use of the Taser and it was drummed into them from the outset that it was a weapon of last resort and one that you needed to warn the subject you were going to use, to give them chance to give up beforehand. This man was not going to give up and Pete had already told him his officers were armed with them. The man gave no quarter, would expect none in return and had to be stopped.

As he raced down the concrete roadway, he kept an eye over to the right, where his officers were chasing the suspect through the maze of mobile homes, trying to spot some sign of the pursuit. He glimpsed a couple of running constables. Then more. Splitting his attention between the chase and his own driving was not ideal, especially at this speed, but he had no choice.

He rounded the last curve in the road, saw the shop on the left, the tennis courts beyond it. And the closed metal gates, two men standing alert in front of them. Instantly, his body reacted, relaxing slightly. They had the man hemmed in. Then he saw him. He emerged from behind a mobile home and darted across the road just fifteen yards ahead, angling towards the shop and office.

Where the owner and his wife were ready-made hostage victims along with any members of the public who happened to be in there.

Pete pressed his foot down hard on the accelerator. The big patrol car surged forward. Fifteen yards became ten. Pete angled the car across to the left, aiming to cut the running man off from his target.

Twenty feet.

He wasn't going to make it. He'd hit the front of the building or mow down his suspect, either of which would end his career.

With a snarl of frustration, he wrenched the wheel across to the right. An instant later, he yanked up the handbrake. The big car slewed around, tyres squealing. Pete tapped the accelerator once more then stood on the foot brake, his body leaning into the spin. He felt the jolt of impact as the rear passenger door hit his man, knocking him clear of the shop doorway. The car stopped. A glance at the door mirror. Suspect down. With the clutch down, Pete rammed the big car into reverse and let it nudge backwards no more than a foot and a half. He killed the engine and had the door open, turning out of the car when the shop door opened. The owner of the place looked stunned.

'Shut the door and lock it,' Pete barked. 'Now.'

The man blinked owlishly.

'Do it!' Pete yelled as he moved fast towards him.

Finally, as Pete approached the boot of the car which was just a couple of inches from the door frame, the man woke up and complied. Pete put a hand to the back window of the car and swung himself over it, sliding across the shiny white boot as his suspect shook his head and turned over onto his hands and knees. Pete's feet hit the ground on the far side of the car and he lunged forward.

His man made a clumsy attempt at a sprint start but staggered off balance.

Pete hit the stocky figure from behind with his full body weight. The suspect collapsed under him and Pete grabbed his wrist and twisted hard. With his free hand, he snatched his cuffs off the clip on his belt and snapped them onto the captive wrist. The man twisted and bucked beneath him, desperate to avoid capture, but Pete's weight was fully on his back and he only had one hand free for leverage. Then Pete grabbed that arm and dragged it back.

The man was incredibly strong. Pete struggled to haul his arm around. A battle of wills and muscle power began, the stocky figure holding his arm rigid as Pete fought to bring it down and back without lifting his own weight off the man's back and giving him that chance to fight back. Then a shadow loomed over him.

A pair of dark-clad knees dropped into view, one of them landing directly on the suspect's head while the other drove down into the muscles at the junction of his neck and shoulder.

'Oops.'

The stocky man grunted, the fight gone abruptly out of him.

Pete hauled his arm back and clamped his wrists together behind him, arms bent at the elbows with the rigid cuffs keeping his wrists a hand span apart.

He looked up at the constable from the gate. A similar build to the suspect, he was a good fifteen years older, hair greying at the temples. 'Thanks, mate.'

The man nodded. 'Sarge. Leg strap?'

'Might be a plan. Just in case.'

The constable unrolled a black Velcro strip and wrapped it around the suspects ankles, using its full length to go at least three times around and secure the man's lower legs together firmly while Pete stayed on his back, holding him down. 'There. That should keep him under control.'

Pete gave the suspect a playful tap on the head. 'I don't know your name yet, buddy, but you're well and truly nicked.'

'Fuck you, dead man.' The man's voice was gravelly and harsh, his accent strongly east-European.

'Hold him there,' Pete said, standing up off him and going to the car. He picked up his radio. 'Suspect in custody. Repeat: suspect in custody. Wind it up, guys. One of the Range Rovers can transport him back to the nick. In the boot, roast chicken style.'

Returning to the man, who Constable Nigel Rowlands was still holding flat on the ground, Pete crouched in front of him. 'You're under arrest, matey. You do not have to say anything. But it may harm your defence if you do not mention when questioned something which you later rely on in Court. Anything you do say may be given in evidence. Do you understand?'

The man tried to spit at him in response but failed and said nothing.

'Do you understand?' Pete repeated, still gaining no response. He glanced at Rowlands. 'Well, you heard him speak English, Nige. Let's assume he's just playing hard to get, shall we?'

'Bit late for that, isn't it?' Rowlands looked down at the man he was holding.

'Yeah, but you know how it goes. Resistance is everything. Awkward to the last and all that.'

'For all the good it does 'em.'

'Ego, Nige. It's all about ego. Being the big man. Not giving in.'

Rowlands grunted. 'Till we shove the Paxo up his arse and stick him in the oven.'

'Oh,' Pete complained. 'I was hanging onto that as a surprise for him.'

'Sorry, Sarge.'

*

Minutes later the suspect was bundled into the back of one of the Range Rovers, Pete had selected a volunteer to stay behind – with strict orders only to observe and report as opposed to putting himself in any danger – and they were ready to go. Pete called the squad room.

'Who's still there, Dave?' he asked when the call was picked up.

'All of us.'

'I need someone out here with unmarked transport ASAP. We've got one of the suspects in custody but the other's still at large – with the Golf.'

'I can nip down on the bike.'

'If you've got a spare helmet. I'm leaving a constable here until you arrive.'

'Fair enough. I'll send Dick, then, with the car.'

'He might be here a while, mind. Best ask him first.'

'Nah. He'll be fine,' Dave said with a laugh.

Pete heard a comment in the background. Then Dave saying, 'The boss wants an unmarked out to the camp site. Sentry duty until the second suspect reappears. You up for it?'

'He'll do it.'

'OK. We're on the way, then.'

*

'Where did your friend go?'

Pete stared at the man across the table from him in interview room two on the ground floor of the Heavitree Road nick, but still the heavy-set figure offered no response. He simply stared back at Pete as if he were a piece of dirt.

He hadn't said a word to the custody sergeant when he was booked in. Hadn't even nodded or shaken his head in response to the simplest and most innocuous of questions. With no identification, they had simply booked him in as John Doe and brought him along to the interview room where Pete had set up the recording equipment in preparation.

The voice and DVD recorder whirred softly on the desk between them, the only sound in the room as Pete waited for an answer.

'It's not a difficult question, surely? He went off somewhere. Took the car. Left you behind at the caravan. How long had he been gone when we got there? Minutes? Hours? Are you certain he hadn't abandoned you there? Left you for us to find? After all, you've had what – three tries at me between you? And where's that got you, eh?' He leaned back, spreading his hands expressively. 'Stuck here on your own in my house, that's where.' He laid his hands flat on the table as he stared the man down. 'On your way to a nice, safe prison cell. Attempted murder of a police officer. That's you out of the dating game for a good fifteen to twenty, I'd say. While your mate waltzes off, as free as a bird. How's that fair?'

The man's lip curled into a sneer.

Pete would have been starting to wonder if he understood English, despite his one comment back at the holiday park, until then. But that confirmed it. He understood what Pete was saying perfectly well. He was just trying to play the hard man.

'You know we don't actually need you to confess, don't you? We've got you on camera. Plus, there's witnesses. We don't need a peep out of you. This interview is for your benefit. For you to help yourself. The only thing you can possibly tell us that we'd be interested in, apart from where your friend went off to, is why? Who put you up to it? Because I don't know you from Adam so you don't know me, either.'

The man folded his arms, leaning back in his chair, still saying nothing.

Pete shrugged. 'Oh, well. Your loss. We'll see what your fingerprints throw up. They must be on record somewhere. We can get yours and your mate's from the caravan you were staying in. DNA, too. It'll take some time, but you won't be going anywhere. Except the old jail.' He shivered. 'Cold old places, them. Didn't bother about comforts in Victorian times, when that was built. You were there to be punished, not pampered. Oh, well. No point wasting any more time on you, so interview terminated. I'll leave you to stew.' He reached for the recorder, switched it off and took out the disc, slipping it into a plastic case as he stood up.

Pushing his chair back under the table, he stepped out of the room.

'Any joy?' Bob asked from behind the high-topped desk.

Pete shook his head. 'No. Stick him in a cell for the night, we can transfer him to North Road in the morning.'

'Right-o.'

Pete headed upstairs, interview disc in hand for all the good it would do him. Walking into the squad room, he was faced with three pairs of eyes staring expectantly at him.

'Any good?' asked Dave.

Pete shook his head. 'How about you lot?'

'SOCO are still at the holiday park,' Dave told him. 'Harry Pointer wasn't happy with you. Disturbing his Sunday. He reckons he's going to apply for a transfer to Midsomer for a quieter life.'

'Did you point out that Midsomer isn't real?'

'Yes it is,' Ben piped up. 'It's near Bath. There's Causton, a couple of Midsomer villages and everything.'

Pete looked patiently from Ben to Jane as he approached his desk. 'Put the boy out of his misery will you?' He turned back to Dave. 'So, what have they found?'

'Two sets of male DNA and finger prints. It'll take time to run them, of course.' He shrugged. 'Plus bomb-making equipment, traces of a C4-like substance, one semi-automatic pistol and two knives. Bowie-style as opposed to cutlery.'

He'd tried and failed at the distant approach. He was planning to get more up close and personal. Pete suppressed a shudder.

'Any joy on the other end of the job? Who's behind it all?'

'I've been running down what leads I could find amongst the solicitor's contacts,' Ben said. 'I prioritised them first – the most likely at the top of the list. But nothing so far.'

'And we're sure Petrosyan's only getting the two visitors – the solicitor and the taxi driver?'

'Yes,' said Jane. 'I've been onto the prison again to check. And they monitor his calls, of course. Not that he's made any. The only thing they can't say for certain is if he's used a mobile. They're banned in there, but they still get in. All they can say on that is, he hasn't got one himself. But he might have used someone else's.' She spread her hands in a shrug.

'Well, if it isn't him, who the hell is it?' Pete demanded. 'Ben, give me a copy of that list. You've started at one end: I'll start at the other.' He held out a hand for Ben to pass him a sheaf of paper that was depressingly thick. 'Really?'

'That's your half, boss. He's a busy bloke.'

'Bloody right he is.'

Pete would run down the known associates of the less likely culprits on the list. Boshnjaku was a clever man with a knowledge of police procedure. He'd want to stay as far away from something like this as possible and one way to do that was to put several steps between himself and the men doing the dirty work. He wouldn't ask anyone to do it themselves. Instead, he'd ask them to find someone else to do it and then act as middleman. He'd ask a thief if he knew a thug who knew a killer.

All Pete had to do was pick out the right thief then find him, arrest him and get him to talk. And all that before the man who was still out there in the dark blue Golf got to him or his family.

He stacked the sheaf of papers neatly and laid them on his desk as the printer behind him whirred into action.

'I thought we'd both best have the whole list,' Ben said as Pete glimpsed the time in the bottom corner of his computer screen.

4.15pm.

'Shit, I told Louise I'd only be here a few hours today.'

'Time flies when you're having fun,' Dave quoted.

'Yeah, and it drags when you're out of a job. We need to crack this before Fast-track gets hold of it in the morning.'

'Good luck with that,' Dave grunted. 'The only way we're going to do that is by getting matey-boy downstairs to talk or with a whole lot of luck.'

Pete's phone rang. He stared at it. Was this Louise, wanting to know when he'd be home? But no. It was an internal call. He picked it up. 'Gayle.'

'Hey, Sarge. That blue Golf you were looking for. Are you still?' It was Peggy in the CCTV room.

'Yes, why?'

'It's just passed the traffic observation camera outside the golf club, west-bound.'

Pete stared across at Dave. *A whole lot of luck, eh?* 'Thanks, Peg.'

CHAPTER TWENTY-FOUR

He was out of his seat before his phone hit the cradle. The chair tipped over with a clatter as he ran for the door. He snatched it open and lunged through, hit the stairs running. Two big leaps to the half-landing, two more to the ground floor. He bounced off the wall with an outstretched hand and slammed through the door into the back corridor. Running towards the custody suite, he yelled, 'Get the back door open.'

He glimpsed movement ahead. A dark uniform. Reaching the wide area in front of the custody desk, he bounced off the high counter, then the wall that faced him as he rounded the corner towards the back door. A constable stood holding it open.

'Thanks, mate,' Pete yelled as he went through. 'Emergency.'

'I guessed.'

He had the key in his hand before he got close to the big patrol car. His thumb pressed the fob button. The car bleeped, indicators flashing from fifteen paces. Pete barely slowed as he grabbed the door handle almost in passing, yanked it open and used the movement to drag himself back and in. He hit the start button and gunned the engine, didn't bother with the seat belt as he snatched the door shut and rammed the car into gear, engine roaring as it surged forward.

He was halfway down the side of the station before the alarm bleeped at the lack of a closed seatbelt. He ignored it. Used the radio instead. 'Peg, has that Golf passed the station yet?'

'Not yet. He's going steady. Mustn't want to attract attention.'

'I bet he doesn't. Thanks.' He slowed the car even as he hit the blues and twos. Turned left out of the station entrance, all too aware that he was heading towards home. Flicking the lights and sirens off again, he finally pulled his safety belt across and clipped it in. Eyes peeled, he focussed on the on-coming traffic as he drove steadily, watching for the first glimpse of his target.

Traffic was light in the middle of a Sunday afternoon. There was nothing behind him, only a couple of cars in the distance ahead, going out of town. In the other direction, there was a significant break in the traffic until he spotted a bunch of brightly dressed cyclists coming towards him, two and three abreast. Behind them was a supermarket delivery van and a line of other vehicles. As they drew closer, he wound down the window, tempted to shout across at them: single file. But, going in the opposite direction, chances were they'd ignore him.

He let them pass, the truck still following close behind them. He could see the frustration on the driver's face, but there was little he could effectively do.

Then he caught a flash of dark blue in the line of on-coming traffic. He focussed in on the dark car. It was a Golf. Right in the middle of the close-packed line of moving vehicles.

'Damn it.'

There was no way he was going to be able to stop the car in those circumstances. Unless... He spotted an entrance on the left: part of the old Children's Hospital, now abandoned. Checking his mirror, he stopped, reversed in and pulled out again in the opposite direction, blue lights flashing as he accelerated past the slow-moving queue. Then swore again as the VW turned without warning into the end of Devonshire Road, where he knew Rosie Whitlock was once more attending Risingbrook School, having recovered from her ordeal towards the end of last year enough to be able to go out again, if only in adult company.

Pete hit the brakes hard, signalling and forcing his way into the moving line of traffic. He made the turn moments after the Golf, but the German car had already accelerated down the short stretch of high-hedged road almost to the dogleg bend a couple of hundred yards away. Pete hit the sirens and went after him but barely two seconds later the Golf was gone from sight. Accelerating hard, Pete made the bend in seconds, swung the car hard right and left around it. A hundred yards ahead was the junction where the road ended. No sign of the Golf. He kept going. Hit the brakes hard as he came to the end of the road, the bonnet of the patrol car dipping. He looked left and right.

Nothing.

Instinct pulled him right. He went with it. Keyed the radio as he pulled out onto the crossroads. 'DS Gayle in pursuit of blue Golf whiskey papa six four five delta Romeo foxtrot. Known to be a false plate. Heading south towards the Topsham Road through St Leonards. Any possible intercept appreciated.'

He passed the junction on the left with the road leading down to where the Whitlocks lived, glanced down it but saw no sign of his target. On his right was a row of shops, most of which had been converted into cafés, bistros and coffee shops frequented by the mothers who lived in this affluent suburb. Then a junction led back up towards Heavitree Road. Pete glanced up there. He knew that a driver with local knowledge could easily lose any pursuit in the side-roads and loop-backs off there, but the significant part of that fact was the local knowledge. He doubted the man in the VW had that.

He was more likely to head for familiar territory, Pete guessed. Whether or not he planned to pick up his companion from the holiday park, he would head down towards Topsham Road. It was just a question of which junction he'd have taken.

But did it matter?

If Pete was right about his destination, it would make no difference who got there first.

If

Two little letters. A huge significance.

If he was right... If not, he'd lose his man completely. Having been spotted, he'd ditch the car and steal another as soon as he could. And more than likely, leave his companion to fend for himself, perhaps with the courtesy of a phone call to warn him, though they'd found no phone on the man they'd arrested or in the mobile home.

But this was getting him nowhere.

He took the next left, committed to a gamble that he prayed would pay off. If not, it could cost him his career and maybe more.

The road ahead was straight and empty. Pete used the hands-free system to call Dick Feeney.

'Boss? What's up?'

'Our man's probably on his way towards you. I'm in pursuit but I've lost sight of him. I'm going to chance it and take the direct route. I've already put out an alert on him.'

'OK. We'll box him in if he turns up here.'

'Right. How's SOCO getting on?'

'Done and gone. They said they'd report on the prints and DNA ASAP.'

'OK. Keep your eyes peeled and be careful. He's likely to be armed and desperate.'

'Should we call HQ?'

He was referring to the armed response unit, Pete knew. 'Yes, but don't expect them to get there in time.'

Feeney gave a short laugh. 'I meant for the sake of form. One less thing for Fast-track to whinge about.'

Pete slowed the car as he approached a junction. Again, he looked left and right and again, he saw no sign of the dark blue Golf.

'Yeah, he'll have more than plenty if we don't catch this bugger today. See you soon, Dick.'

He ended the call and concentrated on driving.

But moments later another thought popped into his head. Where had the man been and what had he been doing? He'd been coming into town from the direction of Pete's home when Peggy spotted him.

Pete used speed-dial to make another call.

It was picked up on the fifth ring. 'Hello?'

'Lou, it's me,' he said as he reached another junction and turned right towards the main road, just fifty yards ahead. 'Is everything OK there?'

'Except for the fact that there's only two of us here, why? What's up?'

'Just checking. Peggy spotted our night-time visitor on the cameras. He was coming into town from your direction. I wanted to make sure he hadn't been back there.'

'*You think he's been here?* To do what?' she demanded as he reached the end of the road and turned left towards Topsham and the holiday park beyond.

'I don't think he has. I'm just checking he hasn't. If you haven't noticed anything, that's fine.'

'We haven't, but I can go out and…'

'No, that's all right,' he said quickly. 'Leave it till I get there. I'll be home soon, hopefully. We've got his mate in custody already, not that he's saying anything. We just need to run him down and we'll have the full package tied up in a bow ready for Fast-track in the morning.'

'You're going to come unstuck one day, calling him that, you know.'

He nodded. 'I know. I try not to, but it isn't always easy. Are you two all packed up, ready to go?'

'Annie's not happy. I explained the reasoning behind it, but she's worried. You knew she would be.'

'Yeah, but she's ready to go, right?'

'Reluctantly, yes.'

'And you?'

'I'm... Even at the lowest point after Tommy went, we stuck together, Pete.'

'I know, but this is different. You know that. It's not about emotional or psychological problems. It's about actual physical danger and until we can get our mitts on this second suspect, that danger's still there. So, much as I don't want you to, I need to know you're going to your mum and dad's, Lou. I need to be able to focus fully on catching this guy without worrying about your safety or Annie's.'

She sighed heavily. 'I know. And I've packed. I just don't want to go until you're back, that's all. I thought you were only going in for a short spell today?'

'I was. But then we got a break. Like I said, we've got one of the two blokes who were after me and we're on the trail of the other one, but it took time.'

She paused. 'OK. I'll see you soon.'

'Before you go, I need to ask you to use your contacts at the RDE. We need another assessment on Tommy and we need it fast. Doc White from Middlemoor's seen him but she's too tied up to be able to do what's needed in time. Is there anyone whose arm you can twist?'

'I don't know. I'll try again - of course I will – but I can't guarantee anything.'

'I know. We need someone who can give evidence, if it's needed, that he's not an unstable character. I mean, it's going to be a tricky thing for the prosecution to find a way of bringing up all that happened with him last year without compromising the Burton case, but if there is a way, they'll find it. So we need to be able to refute it, not just try to block it.'

'Yeah. Once something's been mentioned, a jury's not going to ignore it, even if they're told to, are they? Especially something like that. But... I know there are psychological tests like the Rorschach inkblots and so forth, but I don't know if they're admissible in court.'

'They are, but how long does it take to use them reliably?'

'No idea. But I know a man who has. I don't know if he's on duty today, but I can try.'

'OK. You do that. I'll try to get hold of this bloke before he can do any more harm.'

He ended the call and focussed on driving, concentrating on trying to spot the dark blue VW before its driver saw the big, brightly painted patrol car and took flight, potentially abandoning his companion and jeopardising any chance Pete had of tracking him down.

*

He was barely a mile up the road, blue lights flashing though the sirens remained silent, approaching the junction that led up towards Claire Muir's house when his phone rang, jarring his concentration.

He hit the green icon on the car's comms system. 'Gayle.'

'Boss, it's Ben. I've heard back from SOCO. The DNA will take a couple of days but they've run the fingerprints. There's nothing on file at all so I had them send them over and I've passed them on to Interpol, bearing in mind what you said about his accent and that. We won't hear back today, of course, but at least it means when we call them tomorrow it can be a chase-up rather than a cold call.'

Pete was nodding. 'Good thinking, Ben.' Interpol was basically a nine-to-five operation, despite the impressions given in popular fiction. They wouldn't even pick up Ben's email until tomorrow morning.

'I spoke to Bob downstairs, too,' Ben said. 'He said our man's been muttering to himself in the cell, but in a foreign language. It sounded east European, he said. Are we sure he speaks English?'

'"Fuck you, dead man," seems fairly fluent to me.'

'Fair enough. But that's the only thing we've heard him say in English, isn't it?'

Pete hesitated, thinking back. 'Not quite. I heard him yell, "Move," when he went through the queue at the fish and chip shop the other day.'

'It's weird that we haven't got anything at all on him, though. I mean, you don't go from nothing to paid hitman overnight, do you? He'd have some sort of record somewhere, you'd think. Suggests he might have been brought in from abroad, doesn't it? It's a shame Bob didn't recognise the language he was talking to himself in: we could have gone straight to the source. But as it is, we're kind of stuck with him.'

'Well, at least one of them's got to speak English. They couldn't get very far otherwise. So we need to catch this bugger in the Golf, wherever he's disappeared to. In the meantime, pass our boy's picture on to Immigration. See if they can find him coming in anywhere. Again, it'll take time, but it could give us a clue.'

The police radio broke in over the call. 'CCTV room for DS Gayle, over.'

'DS Gayle.'

'We've picked up your man again. The blue Golf.'

'Where?'

'Where he was before, but going in the opposite direction.'

Heavitree Road, going out of town. Towards home, Pete thought. *Shit.* Fear swept like a chill tidal wave through his mind and body. His jaw clamped tight, hands gripped the steering wheel.

The suspect knew he'd been spotted. If he was heading out there to make good on his contract while he had the chance...

'Thanks, Peggy.' He checked the mirror, hit the brakes and swung left into a junction. Flipping on the sirens, he accelerated up the residential street and re-keyed the mike. 'This is DS Gayle. All available units, urgent call to Wesley Drive, Whipton. Suspect approaching, possibly armed and dangerous, in blue VW Golf, whiskey papa six four five delta Romeo foxtrot.'

Switching back to the phone connection, he got nothing but the dead tone. Ben had rung off. No doubt he'd be getting on with what Pete had asked him to do.

The radio cut in again. 'What number Wesley Drive?'

'Seven,' Pete said quickly. 'My place.'

'On route, Sarge.'

'Thanks. I'll be there in three minutes.' *Less if he could.*

Grateful for the quiet roads, he pushed the big Vauxhall hard, using all of his training, eyes peeled for any risk of endangering the public as he sped between the rows of houses. He'd never forgive himself if he hurt someone else's kid on the way to save his own, but he had to get there, to make sure Annie and Louise were safe.

The man he was chasing wouldn't have had time to recognise him, passing as they had. He just knew he'd been spotted and recognised himself. He would be expecting his target to be at home and would waste no time on finesse in the circumstances. Which made him more dangerous than ever.

He saw the Give Way sign ahead that signified the end of the road. Slowing the car, he checked right as he turned left onto the main road. This was a busier route, even now. Cars and a couple of vans eased over and slowed to let him pass. He made the right turn into Polsloe, towards the estate where he lived. He'd yet to see another patrol car or the target vehicle. He had long enough before the bend by the Co-op to use the radio.

'Anyone on site at Wesley Drive yet?'

'Yes, Sarge. No sign of the suspect yet. Hang on. Just turned into the road, saw us and hit reverse. Must be him. Didn't care what was behind him. He's heading east. In pursuit.'

'Roger.' Pete's mind flicked through alternative routes through and around the estate. His first instinct was to protect his family but, ultimately, the best way to do that was to catch the man in the Golf. He was yards away from home, from protecting his wife and daughter in the most direct way possible, yet at the same time, he saw another way to achieve the same end.

The man had been here before. He must have scouted the area beforehand, sussed out possible escape routes. There were limited options from where he was, but if he picked the right one...

The radio hissed to life. 'Target turning left, left, left.'

East.

'Shit.'

Having eased off the throttle until he found out which way to go, Pete gunned the engine, sirens wailing, and turned left past the end of his own short dead-end street.

His phone rang abruptly. He glanced down and hit the button to accept the call.

'Pete.' It was Louise. 'I can hear sirens. What's going on?'

'I told you: we're chasing the second suspect down.'

'What, round here?'

'He was never going to get near you, Lou. We had a car waiting for him. He saw it and took off.'

'But he was coming here. Were we bait?'

'Never. *I'm* his target. But he knows where I live. We knew that from before so I sent protection just in case, seeing as I wasn't there.'

'Without bothering to tell us.'

Pete didn't need this while he was trying to concentrate on driving. 'What, and scare you for no reason? If you hadn't been covered, yes, but you were. I've got to go. I'll see you soon.'

He ended the call and returned both hands to the wheel. His man was heading out towards the Hill Barton Road. From there he could go anywhere – north towards the Pinhoe Road, where he could cut back towards the city centre; south towards Heavitree and down past the force headquarters; east towards the motorway or even west, back into the estate where he could get lost amongst the maze of small, winding streets.

Pete thought he could discount two of those options, but which of the others would he take? There was no way of knowing for sure without knowing the man himself but the fact that he was still here and not already on his way back to London said something.

Pete prayed he was right as he slowed the car for a junction and turned left – northward towards the Pinhoe Road. If he could get there in time to cut the man off...

If he was wrong, he just had to hope there were others in place to continue the pursuit.

The radio crackled briefly once more.

'Suspect vehicle turning left, left, left onto Hill Barton Road.'

'*Yes,*' Pete breathed. Now he just had to get there in time, through these twisty little streets with cars parked up either side of them and the potential of kids running absolutely anywhere without paying attention to their surroundings.

He rounded a bend and slammed on the brakes as he saw a car reversing out of a driveway on the left, the driver oblivious to everything around him. Pete hit the horn, adding it to the cacophony of the sirens. The car stopped and for what seemed like an age, sat there, blocking the road completely between other cars, parallel parked along either side of the road.

'Come on, idiot,' Pete cursed. 'Wake up and move.' He killed the sirens then restarted them immediately, changing their tone and finally the car eased forward, back into the drive it had emerged from. 'Thank you,' Pete muttered as he accelerated away at last.

Two hundred yards to the end of the street. He slowed once more, indicator blinking. Turned right onto a larger, less residential road and accelerated hard, desperate to make up the time he'd lost. Soon, he'd have to cut the sirens or risk warning the suspect of his presence, but he had to make up some ground first.

The radio cut in again.

'Suspect vehicle approaching the junction with Pinhoe Road.'

So am I, Pete thought. *Just at a different junction.*

Which way would the man go? Left or right? Into town or out to the north? Pete hoped he'd cut back left. They'd have him boxed.

A wide strip of grass lined the road on his left now, backed by 1950s brick-built houses, while on the right a hedge closed the road in as it narrowed suddenly, dipping down towards the railway bridge that arched over the top. An approaching car stopped at the far side to let him through and on up the slope.

Hiss.

'Left, left, left onto Pinhoe Road,' came the report.

'Yes!' Pete was tempted to punch the air. He was seconds away. More brick houses on both sides now. One or two cars parked on either side, tens of yards between them. An industrial area was closed in by tall metal fencing, a high-rise block of flats beyond it on his left, the hedge high and dense on his right, bright green with the new leaves of Spring. Now he could see the end of the road ahead. A car turned in, coming from the left. Pete reached the junction, signalling right, aiming to meet the blue Golf head-on.

Ahead, a dark shape, a bright orange flash.

Hiss.

'Right, right, right into Thackeray Road.'

'Bugger,' Pete muttered. The suspect could loop back around on the short parallel road and head north again. 'Follow him. I'll stay on the main road, try to cut him off.'

'Roger.'

Pete saw a patrol car follow the dark shape into the side-road on his left as he approached. By the time he sped past the junction both vehicles were gone from sight. Would their man come straight back out from the far end of Thackeray or try to lose them around by the trading estate up towards the showground?

He killed his siren, hoping it would fool the suspect into the first choice. Left the blue lights going for the sake of other road users as he sped along the main road. The small side-turning came back in from the left opposite the end of Barton Hill Road, where the suspect had just come from. Traffic lights governed the junction but there was little on the roads at this time on a Sunday afternoon. Just a couple of cars between Pete and the junction. One of them signalled right towards the filter into Hill Barton Lane and the supermarket just off the junction. Then the dark blue Golf darted out of the side road to the left, ignoring all risks, not slowing at all. Tyres squealed as it wove dangerously between the two other cars, dipping and swaying like a drunk on a hillside. Ignoring the red lights, it cut around the nose of the other car and across into Hill Barton. Pete hit the sirens and pushed the car hard as he followed, unwilling to lose his man now he had him in sight at last.

High, loose hedges stood to either side of the wide four-lane road, the one on the left giving glimpses of the supermarket car park while on the right more houses stood back from the road behind low walls and neatly manicured gardens. A hundred yards ahead, the footbridge arched high over the road, painted white and glowing in the sun. The Golf was about halfway between Pete and the bridge when it suddenly swung left, smoke billowing from its squealing tyres as the driver pulled it into the back-angled junction with a narrow straight road.

It went briefly from Pete's sight as he stood on the brakes, dipping the nose of the big Vauxhall. The dull crash of an impact sounded even over the sirens, followed by another and another. He reached the junction, still going much too fast, pulled the car around on the hand brake as, ahead, he saw the Golf once more. It had almost made the turn but not quite. A wheel rim spun lazily near where it must have been knocked off when the car hit the kerb in a sideways slide. Beyond it, the Golf was on its side, up against the solid metal fencing that protected the walkway up to the footbridge. Its undercarriage faced Pete, one back wheel revolving lazily as he hauled the big patrol car to a stop no more than twenty feet from the back of the bright yellow tractor that had been moving slowly along the left side of the lane, trimming the verge, but was now stationary, its driver staring dumbly across at the crashed car.

Pete reversed quickly and swung the big car sideways across the entrance to the lane, blocking it visibly from the main road for safety, then keyed the radio.

'DS Gayle. All units. Target vehicle, dark blue Golf, crashed at the junction of Hill Barton Road and Harts Lane. Ambulance and fire service needed. The car is on its side, driver inside.'

He stepped out of the car and ran across to the crashed Golf, peering in through the back window. The driver was still in his seat, his door now resting on the ground. Pete could see grass and weeds poking through the shattered glass of the side window that the man's shoulder was resting on. He was slumped, motionless. Pete couldn't tell from here how badly he was hurt. He could have been stunned, unconscious or worse. Pete ran around to the other end of the car, pushed his way into the shrubbery and weeds to peer in through the somehow still intact windscreen.

The man was slumped motionless, eyes closed. Pete knocked on the glass. 'Sir? Can you hear me? Sir? Open your eyes if you can.'

Nothing.

Pete was watching the man carefully when he heard movement in the grass at his side and noticed for the first time that the tractor's engine was silent behind him.

'Is he OK?'

Pete looked over his shoulder. The tractor driver was standing just three feet away. In his fifties, he was dressed in dark green overalls and a filthy white cotton cap. He looked way beyond worried.

'Can't tell,' Pete told him. 'But if not, it wasn't your fault.'

'Should we tip the car back and get him out of there?'

Pete shook his head. 'If he's hurt, we could make it worse. I've got an ambulance and fire engine on the way. They can get him out without risking any more harm to him in the process.'

The tractor driver nodded slowly.

'You'd best go and have a sit down,' Pete told him. 'Must be nearly knocking-off time anyway, isn't it?'

'What time is it?' the man asked dully.

Pete checked his watch. 'Ten to four. And it is Sunday.'

His head started bobbing slowly again, reminding Pete of one of those nodding dogs that used to sit in the back of cars, years ago. 'Yeah. I'll...' He looked around. 'I'll go and sit in the cab for a minute. You... You need a statement or anything?'

'Just your contact details,' Pete told him. 'I pretty much saw what happened. Technically, I'm as guilty as you here. Which is to say, neither of us are guilty of anything.' He nodded towards the man in the car. 'He's guilty of dangerous driving, trying to evade arrest and reckless endangerment, apart from anything else.' *Like attempted murder,* he thought but didn't bother to say.

The tractor driver was still nodding. 'Right. OK then. I'll go and sit down. Have a cup of tea.'

'You do that. I'll be over in a minute.'

As the man wandered off, Pete focussed once more on the driver. He still hadn't moved or shown any response. In fact, Pete saw as he watched carefully, he wasn't moving at all.

Pete's eyes closed briefly then concentrated on the slumped figure once more. His day had just gone from bad to worse. His one hope of identifying the source of the attacks on him, if Ben was right and the man in the cells back at the station was a foreign national who didn't speak English, was now dead.

CHAPTER TWENTY-FIVE

'Stand down, the pair of you.'

He was surrounded by brightly coloured vehicles, blue lights flashing on most of them, orange on the rest. A fire truck, an ambulance and a vehicle recovery van had joined Pete's own patrol car. The tractor had gone. Pete had taken the driver's contact details although, as he explained to the man, he was unlikely to need them. The windscreen had been removed from the Golf and the driver lifted carefully out, but he'd been beyond saving long before that. The last vehicle to arrive on scene had been the black VW estate car of the pathologist who was now working on the victim.

'You sure, boss?' Dick sounded far from it.

'You've searched the caravan. And SOCO are done and gone?' he asked, long habit bringing out the old term for the scenes of crime team although they had long since been privatised so were no longer actually police officers.

'Yes.'

'So there's no need for you to stay. The man you're waiting for isn't coming. I know that for certain because I'm looking at him and he's not going anywhere except the mortuary.'

'Oh, right. How come?'

'He wasn't as good a driver as he thought. He tried a move that didn't work out too well for him. Nobody else was hurt, thankfully, but there's a tractor-mower driver who's not going to sleep too well for a while.'

'Right. We'll head back then.'

Doc Chambers looked up from the body which was laid out on the grass behind a white windbreak that had been erected to shield it from the view of any passers-by, though the end of the lane had been closed off for now.

'Cheers, Dick,' Pete said, ending the call. 'What can you tell me, doc?'

'That seat belts save lives, for one thing. If our man here had been wearing his, he wouldn't have broken his neck when he rolled the car.'

Pete nodded. 'Anything else? Has he got a wallet or a phone on him? I checked the car: they're not in there.'

'Indeed. One of each, left and right trouser pockets.' Chambers handed them up to Pete.

'Finally! We might actually find out who these guys are.' He flipped open the wallet.

What he guessed at a glance to be around two hundred in cash was backed with a single card. He fished it out. It was black with a silver and white logo, a Mastercard mark on the bottom right. His shoulders slumped as he stared at it.

It was a cash card. The type that was designed to be topped up with cash so that you could spend just what was on it. No need for credit checks, no more than a cursory check of identification. The provider had nothing to lose so no need to put in the effort apart from the nominal chance of being reviewed by the authorities in the effort to stop money laundering.

He looked at the name printed in silver across the bottom.

Juan Perez.

The Spanish equivalent of John Smith.

Pete didn't need to look back at the dead man to know that his swarthy complexion gave him a Mediterranean appearance but

Juan Perez was no more likely to be his name than John Smith or Fred Bloggs.

He searched through the wallet but it was empty apart from the cash.

Damn! How much harder could the guy have tried to conceal his identity? A stolen car on cloned plates, a remote place to stay that was paid for in cash, a cash card with no account tied to it... Where the hell did he go from there? Then a thought struck him. He checked his watch. It was just turned 4.00 on a Sunday afternoon. It was probably a faint chance, but...

He took out his phone and hit a speed dial number.

'Exeter CID, PC Myers speaking.'

'Ben. I've got a cash card in my hand. False name on it. But if I give you the details, can you try and get onto the provider, see where, when and how it was set up?'

'They might have knocked off, this time on a Sunday, but I'll give it a go.'

'Right.' Pete read out the details.

'I'll do it now.' Ben ended the call and Pete slipped the card back into the wallet, dropped it into an evidence bag and sealed and labelled it.

Next, the phone.

It was a small, inexpensive older model, but still a smartphone. When you could easily get hold of the older types that just made and received calls and texts on a pay-as-you-go account, it was incredible to Pete that anyone with a criminal background would even contemplate having something like this. But it was equally amazing how much people relied on modern technology these days.

He switched it on.

"Hello," came up briefly on the screen. So it was a British one, at least. The screen switched to an array of icons and Pete began to search.

The contacts list was, predictably, empty. The messages list too. The last number dialled came up as zero. The photos file held a number of shots of the Heavitree Road police station, Pete's home and his car plus the black Focus he'd borrowed from the carpool after they'd wrecked the Mondeo out at Ashclyst Forest.

The question occurred to him again: had they killed Claire Muir to draw him out? The horror of that possibility had not diminished over the intervening days. But it made no sense, thinking about it now. They couldn't guarantee that he'd be called to the scene. He hadn't even been on duty at the time, after all. It shouldn't have been his case. So they must have been watching him, waiting for an opportunity. And there were two ways back from the site of the body dump. So this guy must have been waiting on the other road with the Golf. It was mere chance that he'd run across the second man in the Land Rover instead.

He concentrated on the phone again as Doc Chambers wound up his examination and waved the two men in with the trolley to transfer the body into their vehicle for transport to the mortuary.

The Internet search history had been cleared, as he expected. There was nothing else he could bring up on it that would give him any leads. Except one thing.

The credit remaining in the phone's account was twenty-seven pounds and fifteen pence. And there in front of him was the name of the provider.

He was reaching for his own phone when it rang in his pocket. He took it out and answered it. 'Ben? What can you tell me?'

'Hey, boss. The card was opened online but then topped up with cash at a PayPoint. There's been no credit transfer onto it.'

'Is there any way of tracing who set it up or where from?'

'I asked that. They say no, but they would, wouldn't they? Bloody lot of records to plough through, all to find a single IP address that we'd then have to track to its physical location. It could be done, but they'd insist on a warrant and it would take a few days.'

'Which we haven't got. OK, thanks, Ben. While you're on, could you or someone else there get hold of the records on the mobile phone I've got in my other hand? It's on Virgin. Let me find the number...' He flipped screens quickly to find it and read it out.

'Got it. I'll do that now.'

'I'll be on my way back there in a minute or two.' He ended the call and waved to the departing pathologist. One more call to make. Bringing up the speed-dial list, he hit the first name on it and waited.

'Hello?'

'Lou. Me again. If you and Annie are as unhappy as you said about going to Okehampton, then you'll be happy to know there's no need anymore.'

'What? You got him? Jesus!'

'There's no need to sound so shocked.'

'Not shocked – pleased,' she said, then realised he'd been joking. 'You bugger. How'd you manage it so quick?'

'Well, technically, I didn't. Get him, that is. He got himself. He tried to out-run a patrol car, which happened to be mine, and he wasn't up to the job. He flipped it turning into Harts Lane.'

'So...?'

'Broke his neck.'

'Oh, God.'

Pete shook his head in wonder that she could sound so concerned for the life of a man she'd never met, but who had tried to kill him, if not both of them. 'Yeah. It'll save us a trial, I suppose, but it doesn't help me find out who was paying him.'

'You've got the other one, though.'

'Except he doesn't speak English, as far as we can tell. Apart from the odd movie quote.'

'Well, what does he speak?'

'At this point, your guess is as good as mine.'

She sighed. 'So we're safe again for now, but only until either you get him talking and find out who's paying him or the mystery man finds out his crew's out of commission.'

'That's about the size of it. I thought you'd like to know, though.'

'Yeah. Thanks.'

Pete grinned at her tone. 'Look on the bright side. At least it's bought us a day or two.'

She grunted. 'Right. Talking of time constraints, I got hold of the psychologist I was talking about earlier. He's not all that keen on going to Archways, but he said he'd do it for us. Are you on your way home?'

'Brilliant! I've got to pop back to the station for a few minutes but then I will be.'

'OK, bye. Thanks for letting us know.'

*

'Hey, boss.' Jane looked up from her screen as Pete walked into the squad room a few minutes later. 'That mobile phone that I assume you've got in an evidence bag somewhere… We don't know where it was bought from, but the SIM inside it came from Membury Service Station on the M4. Paid for in cash ten days ago. The good news is that they keep their CCTV for two weeks.'

That made Pete feel a lot brighter, all of a sudden. 'So...'

'They're used to maintaining a good relationship with the police, for obvious reasons.'

'Yes.' Pete nodded, revolving his arm to urge her on. 'So...'

'So they sent the footage from the relevant day and time-period by email. I was just going through it.'

'OK.' He sat down at last. 'Anyone else got any news?'

'Yes,' Ben said. 'They might have cleared the call log, but that doesn't remove the records from the service provider. They've got the full list. As you know, we need a warrant to get those records from some providers. And they're one, sadly. I explained the circumstances, why we need the information, but it didn't help. I added the fact that the user's deceased. Gave them Doc Chambers' number to confirm it.'

Ben's explanation was going on far longer than normal. Either it was a long-winded wind-up and he'd got the data or, knowing the significance of the time factor in the case, he was struggling to apologise for not having it. Pete wasn't sure which, but he wished the lad would get to the point. 'So the upshot of all this is what, Ben?'

'Well, they went away and called the hospital, confirmed what I'd told them. Which I suppose is fair enough. After all, I called them, not the other way around. I could have been anyone, couldn't I?'

'Get to the point, Ben,' Pete said, his patience wearing thinner by the second.

Ben winced. 'There's good news and bad news.' He held up a hand defensively. 'The good news is that I've got the records. They saw the sense in using a bit of common sense. The bad news is there's no link on there to the solicitor, Boshin' thingamy.'

'Yaku,' Pete reminded him.

'Bless you,' Dick said quickly.

Pete ignored him. 'So, who does it give us links to?'

'His mate in the cells downstairs, a suspected member of the Albanian mob in London and an address in Harlow, Essex.'

'Whose address?'

Ben grimaced. 'I was afraid you might ask that. It's residential and it's a foreigner. I tried calling, but all I got was a woman who clearly doesn't speak English. She sounded a bit German or Russian or something.'

'Dick have you got any contacts in Essex?'

'Yes, but not Harlow.'

'Shame. OK, Ben, get onto the Harlow nick and get them to send someone round there, see who this woman is and if she knows our deceased driver. Or his mate downstairs.'

'Right.'

'I'm going downstairs, see if I can figure out what language our guest in the cells does speak, if not English.'

'How are you going to do that?' Jane asked.

Pete met her green eyes. 'I'm going to start with the basics and work out from there.'

*

'You realise nobody's coming for you? You're on your own.'

The man might not speak English, but he had shown enough understanding of it, from whatever source, to use the odd word or phrase in the correct context. Pete had had Bob bring him back to the interview room, where he'd set the digital recording equipment going to capture any response.

'I'm guessing your friend was the primary contractor here. You were just hired muscle, right? So you think he's going to come for you. Get you out of here.' He shook his head. 'Not going to happen, mate.' He opened the Manilla folder on the desk in front of him and slid out a large photograph. Slapped it down face-up on the desk in front of the stoic figure sitting opposite him. 'Recognise that car? The one you came down here in.'

These were pictures from Pete's phone that he'd had Bob print out in the custody suite before coming in here. There was no response from the man across the table. He slid out another picture and slapped it down over the first. 'There's the number plate. The one you had made once you got here.'

Still nothing, apart from a slight tightening of the lips.

'Thought he was a good driver, didn't he? Been watching too many action movies is my guess.' Time for the main event. Pete slid out the third and final picture, turned it over and slapped it down. 'That's him an hour ago. Dead.'

The stocky man's eyebrows scrunched into a frown. He looked up from the photo to Pete and the hate emanating from his dark eyes was like a physical force.

This was more than a casual colleague or even a friend. This was family. 'Who was he?' Pete demanded. 'What's his name?'

A sneer curled the man's lip, but he said nothing.

Pete half rose out of his chair, jabbing a finger at the photo on the table. 'You can see that, can't you? He's dead. He broke his neck because he was stupid enough to try and get away from me. So, you want to think I killed him, that's fine with me. All I want's a name for his gravestone. Otherwise, it'll be unmarked. You want him buried here, in a city he didn't know, in a grave with no name on it?'

He said something rapidly in a thick foreign language, his voice coarse and gravelly like it had suffered a life-time's smoke and hard drinking.

Pete sat down, both hands still on the table. 'Do what? Say that again, more slowly?'

Nothing.

He shrugged. 'OK. He gets an unmarked grave and you get twenty-five to life for the attempted murder of a police officer. Alone in a prison full of people who don't speak your language.' He shook his head. 'Twenty-five years being utterly alone in a crowd. That'd be enough to drive a man crazy, I'd have thought. If he survived. And that's a big if in a place like that. They'd pretty soon beat the language into you, I should think. You speak or you die. Another unmarked grave in a foreign city. In your case, in the city jail.'

The man sneered a brief response, shoving the photos away as he sat back in his chair.

'Whatever,' Pete said. 'I didn't understand a word of that, so it's not going to help you. You speak English or it gets you nowhere.'

The man folded his arms, lip curling derisively.

'Sure?' Pete asked.

Nothing.

'OK.' He reached over and switched off the recorder. 'Interview terminated.' Checking his watch, he added. 'Sixteen thirty-nine. I'll be off home then. I'll see you tomorrow, before you go off to jail.' He stood up, retrieved the disc from the voice and video recorder and left the room.

Back at the custody desk, he leaned on the high counter. 'Send him back to his cell, Bob. And shove this in the computer, see what you make of it.'

Bob sent a constable to return the stocky man to his cell while they replayed the brief interview. Reaching the suspect's eventual response, Bob paused and replayed it.

'What do you reckon?' Pete asked.

Bob shook his head. 'No idea, mate. Nothing like I've ever heard of. East European of some sort would be my guess.'

'Have we got anybody on the translator list?'

Bob grimaced. 'Don't know. Never had the need before. Let's see.' He closed the image from the interview room on his computer and brought up another program. A list of names and details filled the screen. Bob scrolled down slowly. Seconds later, he stopped. 'There's one. Polish, German, Czech and Slovak.'

'Might be worth a try. Any others?'

Bob continued his search of the database.

'Here's one. A bit further south. Albanian, Bulgarian and Greek.

Pete nodded. 'That's another possible. Keep going.'

Moments later, Bob's finger paused again. 'How about Croat, Serbian and Romanian?'

'Between those three, I reckon we've got a pretty good chance.'

'Which do we try first?'

'Whoever you've got there on the screen, I suppose.'

Bob grunted and reached for the phone. He dialled the number on the screen and waited. 'Hello? Miss Jankovich? It's Sergeant Struthers from Heavitree Road police station. Have you got a couple of minutes to help us out with something?'

'No, that's OK. I can play it over the phone. I just need to know if you recognise the language and, if so, what the subject's saying.'

She obviously agreed, from Bob's response. 'Great. Thanks.' He glanced up at Pete and nodded. 'It's a male suspect in a potential murder plot here in Exeter. We've no idea what he's saying or what language it's in so any help you can give would be extremely useful. Right. Here we go.' He brought up the interview recording on the screen again and hit play, holding the phone near to the computer to capture the sound from the speakers.

'Anything? OK. That's fine.' He paused. 'I see. How about this?' He skipped the footage forward to the prisoner's second response and played it. Listened again. 'Right. Thank you very much, Miss Jankovich. That's very helpful.'

He put the phone down and looked up at Pete. Finally broke into a grin. 'Hole in one, matey. He's speaking Albanian. Although she's not listed as a translator in that language, she knows enough of it to get by. He wasn't complimentary about your parentage and proclivities, but then he said – and I quote – "His name was Aziz Krasniqi. He was from Bubq." Apparently, it's in the north-west of the country.'

'OK. And was that it?'

'All that'll stand translation in polite company.'

Pete gave a brief chuckle. 'I bet.' *At last we're getting somewhere.* 'Well, maybe we can call her in – or the other one, who's actually listed for the language – in the morning and give our man another try. For now, I've got a wife and kid to get back to while they still remember who I am. Thanks, Bob. You're a gem. Has anyone ever told you that?'

Bob laughed. 'That's not what I generally get called down here.'

CHAPTER TWENTY-SIX

Tommy set down the last of the forks on the top table and picked up a handful of knives from the cutler cart. He was on table setting duty this afternoon - probably the least onerous of the tasks he could have been allotted. He'd placed only five knives on the first table when muscle-bound staff member Gavin came into the room.

'Gayle. Put them down and come with me.'

'What? Why?'

'Looks like you've wriggled out of another chore. You've got a visitor.'

'Another one?' Tommy replaced the remainder of the knives he was holding in the cart. 'Jeez! I thought Sunday was supposed to be a day of rest. Who is it this time?'

'Somebody who's clearly got your best interests at heart for some unaccountable reason.'

'Well, thanks for telling me nothing except you don't like me. Which I knew anyway.'

'Ah. Poor boy. Never mind.'

'I'll get over it. It's entirely mutual anyway,' Tommy retorted, stepping forward. 'So, are you going to tell me who it is or what?'

'He says he's part of your legal team. With reference to the Burton case.'

Tommy felt a slump of disappointment. He'd hoped for a brief moment that it was his mother. He'd barely seen her since he drove Annie away in tears, and Annie herself hadn't been back at all. Which had been the whole point of the exercise, of course, but he'd hoped that his mother would still come and see him.

'Come on. He's in the interview room.'

Gavin stepped back to allow Tommy to lead the way back to the room next to the manager's office where he'd met his solicitor several times as well as Doctor White just a few hours ago.

He pictured the dark-haired psychologist as he walked down the corridor. Slightly older than his parents but still fit and attractive in her white blouse and jeans, hair down around her shoulders. He might have hoped that, if Mr Davis wasn't going to turn up in person, he'd sent someone like her, but Gavin had said, "He," so no such luck.

They crossed the reception area. The woman Tommy always thought of as 'Matron,' was sitting at the desk, working on something in a large book. She didn't look up. He went through into the other part of the building, stopped at the second door on the left and waited for Gavin to open it.

When he did, Tommy stepped forward and Gavin shut the door behind him. Tommy was left facing the back of a broad-shouldered man in a suit who was seated at the table in the centre of the sparse room, a briefcase on the floor by his feet.

'I hope you're getting overtime for being here on a Sunday,' Tommy commented as he stepped forward.

The man turned in his chair and Tommy's stride faltered as cold fear flowed like water through his veins. He felt the hairs on the back of his neck stand up and his face tingle. He'd know this man anywhere. The wide build might have given it away, but he'd never seen him in a suit before. But still the crew-cut blond hair might have been a clue if it weren't for the context. It ran seamlessly into the trimmed beard. In his more usual attire of T-shirt and jeans, it made him look even more like a football hooligan or a neo-Nazi than the tattoos on his neck and arms, but they were covered up now, along with another fact that Tommy knew all too well: his bulk was not made up of fat, but of solid muscle.

The visitor was grinning broadly, but the smile didn't get anywhere near his glittering ice-blue eyes. 'Hello, kiddo. How's tricks? Fucked any pretty young girls lately?' His accent was similar to Tommy's own, but coarser, broader, from north and east of here: rural Wiltshire.

Even as he stepped forward with all the swagger he could muster, Tommy knew it was too late. The man had seen the truth. He had a snake-like sense for fear or vulnerability. But he had to try.

'Mr Southam.' He didn't know the man's first name. Mel had never used it in all the time Tommy had been with him. 'I'm working on one,' he replied. 'What are you doing here?'

'*What are you doing here?* Is that any way to greet a visitor in a place like this? I've come to see to your welfare, of course. What else would I be doing here?'

'Scouting for talent?' Tommy suggested, only half-joking. He'd have put nothing past the man at the table. Nothing at all. If Tommy claimed to have no boundaries, this man didn't even know such things existed. If his dad reckoned Mel Burton was a bad bugger, he had nothing on the man Tommy was facing now. He was in a completely different league of evil.

Southam nodded appreciatively. 'Now, there's an idea. Do you reckon the boss in here would be open to it? Or any of the staff, on the sly?'

Tommy shrugged. 'The boss has only just arrived. Old one got suspended. A couple of the staff might be willing, for the right incentive. Including the one who just brought me here. But that's not why you've come, is it?' He reached the chair on the far side of the table and slumped onto it.

Southam shook his head. 'I'm here to make sure you understand the gravity of the situation you're in, Tommy boy. See, I've visited my little brother in Morpeth since he got sent there. It's not pretty. That's why I helped him get out a few weeks back. And I know that if Mel Burton gets convicted – or even gets close to it – he hasn't got the bottle to keep his mouth shut in a place like that. Now, there's a cure for that, of course, but no good shutting the stable door after the horse has bolted is it? So the way I see it, there's two ways I can deal with the situation. The most obvious is also the most difficult to arrange, me not being local. Not so easy but still do-able, understand. The second way, you and Mel both get to stay alive but you need to convince me that you'll do what's needed.'

Tommy's eyes widened. 'What do you mean, we both get to stay alive? We're both in prison. You kill him, someone's going to notice before you get out of there.'

Southam's grin returned. He licked his lips as his head shook from side to side. 'You ain't that daft, son.' He lifted his meaty hands off the table and turned them, displaying them to Tommy. 'Do these look like they get dirty too often?'

Tommy knew perfectly well how much Southam enjoyed getting his hands dirty, but he also knew the man was no fool. 'No more often than's good for you, I expect.'

'That's right. Like I said: you ain't that daft.'

He'd find a way. And he'd enjoy that almost as much as he would enjoy doing it himself. 'So, what's the second choice entail? Doing what's needed?'

'Staying schtum. You don't testify. Against him or anyone else. You stay quiet and do your time.' He looked around. 'Place like this, a couple of years or so with good behaviour if you can manage that, can't be that hard. Not like a real prison, is it? Home from home by the look of it. And what you said before, you were never that happy at home anyway.'

The "before" he was referring to was their previous meetings, Tommy knew, though he didn't recall ever discussing his personal life with the man in front of him. Other personal matters, yes... 'Sounds logical,' he said. 'But how do I know you wouldn't come after me anyway, after? I mean, once he gets off so he's no longer a problem, that'd leave me as a loose end, wouldn't it?'

'Except you're already tried and convicted, he's already tried and acquitted, so no more trials, no more testimony. And once you're out we can pick right up where we left off. Back in business. With or without Mel Burton.'

Tommy wasn't convinced. Not in the least. Now Southam had found him and demonstrated his ability to get to him, he was as good as dead, whatever he did at Mel Burton's trial. The only thing he could do was delay the inevitable. He nodded. 'OK. I can see that.'

'Thought you might.' He slapped his hands on the desk and stood up.

Tommy fought to suppress the jolt of fear that ran through him.

'That's us, then,' Southam announced. 'See you at the trial.'

Tommy's eyes widened. 'Really?'

'I'm a legitimate businessman, not like our Steve. I've got every right to be there.'

Tommy blinked. 'I'll see you there, then.'

He stayed in his seat as Gavin led the big man away towards reception, his brain whirling. What the hell was he going to do? Testifying against Mel would get him out of this place, back home to a new start with Annie and his mum, maybe even with his dad. Not testifying would get him sent back here, or to a worse place, as a convicted kiddy-fucker with all the risks to his personal safety that entailed.

He knew what happened to paedophiles in prison. And he didn't expect kiddie-prisons like this one to be any different in that respect. Even if you were the same age as the girl, it was still rape, according to the law.

And yet, if he testified – if he could testify with Southam sitting there watching him – he'd be as good as dead before he even got out of the dock. And knowing Southam, the same would probably apply to Annie, his mum and even his dad, too.

Talk about a rock and a hard place. He felt like he was sliding down a greased ramp towards a couple of huge, spinning millstones.

CHAPTER TWENTY-SEVEN

Pete slid his briefcase under the hall table and shrugged out of his jacket. He was in the act of tossing it over the newel post at the bottom of the stairs when he heard rapid, heavy footsteps behind him. He turned just in time. Staggered under the impact. His neck was compressed in the iron grip of a strangle hold, his back hit the wall, almost knocking the breath out of him as he barely missed the narrow table.

'Jesus, Button, you're getting too bloody big for moves like that,' he gasped as her knees gripped his lower ribs and her face buried itself in his neck.

'I'm not even a teenager yet.'

'And thank God for that.' He got his feet under him and pushed away from the wall, carrying her through to the lounge, where Louise sat on the sofa, the TV on. Some sort of fancy go-kart racing, he noticed. 'Look what I caught.'

'It sounded like you struggled. All done?'

'Yeah. Till it hits the fan in the morning.'

Annie pulled her head back to look at him. 'Why? What's wrong?'

'Well, I might be home early tomorrow, Button.'

She frowned, confused.

'If I get fired for disobeying protocol again and investigating my own case.'

'Well, who else was going to do it?' she demanded.

'Technically, I should have called Uncle Colin and handed it off to him.'

'So you're going to be in trouble?'

He grinned. 'What's new, Pussycat? We did what we needed to at the time. I'll stand by it, whether the DCI likes it or not. And at the end of the day, its results that count.'

'And you got both of them?'

'Yep.'

She was beginning to slip but, rather than hop down, she clung on tighter and hotched herself up. Pete locked his hands under her skinny backside.

'So we're safe.'

'We're safe, Button.'

She squeezed his neck harder than ever, burying her head in his shoulder again. 'I was so worried.'

'I know, love. We all were. That's why I had to spend all weekend catching the bad guys. But now I've done it, you can stay at home for another week, until half-term, and everything can go back to normal.'

'Unless you get the sack. Then it'll be even better because you'll be at home all day.'

Pete couldn't help but laugh. 'Yeah, except we've got bills to pay so I need to go to work or else we'll be turned out on the street like a bunch of tramps.'

Finally, she hopped down and returned to the sofa with her mother, taking her hand as she nestled in beside her. 'At least we'll be together.'

'Yeah, I suppose that's true,' he admitted.

'So, who were they? The bad guys. And why were they after you?'

'They're brothers. Come from Albania, but they live in Essex now. As to why they were coming after me, I don't know exactly. Not yet. We've got a few things to sort out tomorrow, but at least now we know where they're from, we can actually talk to them.'

'So, it's not over.' She stared up at him, big-eyed.

'All but the shouting, love. We've just got to identify the man who sent them – and the wife of one of them's helping with that already – and that'll be it.'

'Why's the wife helping? Why not her husband?'

Pete drew a breath. 'She's helping because she wants to stay here in England. He isn't because he can't. He's at the hospital. With Doctor Chambers.'

'He's dead?'

'He is. And his brother's in the cells at the station.'

'The poor wife...'

An overwhelming surge of love for her welled up inside Pete. He stepped forward, dropped to his knees in front of them and gathered both his wife and daughter into his arms.

*

'Hey, boss.' Ben was putting the phone down as Pete walked into the squad room at a little after eight-thirty in the morning. 'That was Essex police. They sent someone to talk to the dead guy's wife. Widow,' he corrected himself quickly. 'She said a mate came round just under a fortnight ago, offered him and his brother some work down here. She didn't catch the details. But she did name the mate.' He glanced at his notepad. 'I wrote it down. Another one of those mouthful-of-marbles names. He's not on any of our lists, but he has got a record. Essex suggested I look him up on the PNC.'

'And have you?'

'I was just about to when you walked in, boss.'

'So, what else is happening?'

Dick and Jill were watching the exchange from their desks, the other two members of the team notable by their absence.

'Dave and Jane have gone to Claire Muir's workplace,' Dick told him. 'Get an early start on interviewing her colleagues, see if there's any chatter around the office about her personal life, seeing as her sister didn't seem to know about anything untoward.'

Pete nodded. 'Coffee time?'

'Sounds like a plan,' Dick replied. 'Mind you remember to turn left off the corridor, not right, though. The shit's been hitting the fan already, from the sound of it. Fast-track and the guvnor have been having serious words. Don't know what about, but I can guess.'

Pete grimaced. 'Where's Dave with his padded book when I need it? I'll be back in a minute.' He headed out to the small kitchenette along the corridor, its door almost opposite that of the DCI's office. He could guess what the "discussion" had been about, too. He'd made sure to type up his daily notes for the weekend before he left last night and place a copy on Colin's desk. He hoped that Colin had had time to read it before Silverstone caught onto what had been happening and started on him.

Two peaceful minutes later that had felt like the calm before the storm, he returned to the squad room with four steaming mugs in his hands to find Ben at the case board, writing carefully.

He put the mugs down and handed Dick and Jill theirs before returning his attention to what Ben was doing.

He'd stuck up a photo of a swarthy male with greased-back dark hair who looked to be in his late thirties or early forties, stubble darkening his lower face and neck. Under it, Ben had written the name Fatun Gradzinski. And beneath that: "Born 1978, Albania.

Resident legally in UK since 2013. Markers for drugs, procurement, offensive weapons – knives and firearms. No convictions."

'Who's he?' Pete asked as Ben put down the marker pen and returned to his seat.

'A mate of our dead driver's, boss. But the more pertinent question is, who does he know?'

'All right. Who does he know?'

'Well, among others and besides your car-flipper, one Lucy Forrester. Or, to be more exact, her husband, Matthew.'

'Again – who's he?'

'Well, as far as we know, he's a legitimate local businessman. Got fingers in two or three different pies here in Exeter, including a taxi firm, a courier and an airport transport company. Posh taxis. But *she* runs said taxi firm. Which also happens to be the one that our friend and Gagik Petrosyan's, Davit Achabaihan, works for.'

'Finally!' Pete said loudly. 'A link.'

'Yep. Firm as you like.'

'Well done, Ben. Drink your coffee. All that talking, you must be parched.'

'Nice one, Spike,' Dick said, slapping him on the back. 'So all we need to do now is talk to Matthew Forrester, his Mrs and Achabaihan and we should be able to tie it up and get back to normal.'

'Them and our pal in the cells, now we know what language he speaks,' Pete added. 'But before that, I'm off to give Jane and Dave a hand. The faster we get through those colleague interviews, the sooner we'll have a chance of finding out who killed Claire Muir.'

*

There were a lot of people to interview at Portside Insurance but not a lot of questions to ask each of them. By the time Pete got there, Jane and Dave had already got through a third of Claire's team. Jane was installed in her office while Dave had taken over the conference room at the end of the corridor. It had taken just moments for Jane to wave him across and bring him up to speed when Pete walked into the large open-plan office space that the victim had been in charge of. He turned to the company's customer service manager and asked if there was anywhere that he could use to help speed things up.

Dunne thought for a moment. 'How long is it likely to take, roughly?'

'Depends what we discover but, potentially, if we can keep up the pace that my two DCs have set, no more than the rest of the morning between the three of us.'

'OK. I've got a meeting at ten that's likely to take until lunchtime so if I can get a few things out of there first, you can use my office.'

'Great. Thank you.' Pete nodded appreciatively.

'This way.' Dunne led the way back across the open plan space and down the corridor. Pete was about to follow him in when the door to the conference room opened a few feet away and a small blonde woman stepped out. She hesitated when she saw him then walked resolutely past, back towards where Pete had just come from.

Inside the medium-sized office, Pete waited while Dunne collected some papers from his desk and the filing cabinets behind it, picked up his briefcase and stepped towards the door.

'Right. I'll leave you to it, Detective Sergeant.'

'Thanks again. We won't take any more of your staff's time than we absolutely have to.'

'As long as it helps catch whoever killed Claire, it's fine.' He opened the door and stepped out. 'Make yourself at home.'

Pete settled himself behind the big, modern desk, notebook and pen at his elbow and called Jane.

'Boss?'

'You can start sending them along to me, Jane. I'm in Richard Dunne's office.'

'Right. Will do.'

Moments later, there was a knock on the door.

'Come in,' Pete called.

The door opened to admit a tall, thin man in his forties. 'Your colleague sent me along.'

'Yes, come in. Have a seat.' Pete indicated the chair across the desk from him. 'This shouldn't take long.'

The man settled himself, crossing his long legs at the knee. 'So, how can I help?'

'We're here to find out all we can about Claire Muir. Her habits, her friends, any boyfriends, office relationships. Whatever anyone can tell us to give us an insight into her life. Help us build a picture so we can figure out where she might have encountered her killer.'

The man was nodding like the parcel shelf bulldog that one of the company's competitors was famous for. 'Yes, I see. I'm not sure I know of anything useful. Claire was a nice woman. Friendly, helpful, supportive, but I don't know any gossip about her.'

'We're not looking for gossip, Mr...?'

'Davidson. Andrew Davidson. No, quite,' he said as Pete made a note. 'Facts are what you need, of course. I'm just saying, I've not seen or heard anything around the office about her seeing anyone or anything like that. I know she goes out with friends in town on a Friday or Saturday quite often, but I imagine Chris

Thackeray would know more about that side of her life. They were quite pally.'

Pete noted the change from present to past tense as the thin man spoke, but it was quite natural, he knew. Part of the adjustment process. 'Yes, we've spoke to Miss Thackeray at some length already. We need to get a handle on what anyone else in the office might know at this stage.'

'Well, in my case the answer to that is remarkably little, I'm afraid, for someone I've worked with for nearly two years.' He looked contemplative. 'It's amazing, isn't it? How you can see someone and speak to them every day, yet know next to nothing about their lives outside the workplace.'

'The pace of modern life, I suppose,' Pete said. 'All right. Thanks for your time, Mr Davidson. If you'd send one of your colleagues along who hasn't already been spoken to…?'

'Of course. The best of luck with it all, officer.'

He stood up, back straight and head pulled back, and left the office.

He hadn't been gone for more than a few seconds when Pete's phone rang. He checked the screen expecting it to be Jane or maybe Dave, but it was neither. He tapped the button to answer.

'Dick? What have you got?'

'A negative on Lucy Forrester, boss. She doesn't know anything about the brothers. Never even heard of them, she says. And I believe her. So does Jill. So we're off to the airport, to see her husband, see what he's got to say for himself.'

'OK. Keep me posted.'

A knock sounded on the door in front of Pete. 'Come in,' he called. Then said more quietly, 'Cheers, Dick.'

He put his phone down on the desk as a woman in her mid to late twenties stepped in, blonde hair pulled back in a ponytail though her deep fringe was swept sideways across her brow in a style that Pete always thought was foolishly and unsustainably gravity-defying. With the ultra-short skirt and dark tights, it made her look half her real age. But maybe that was the point?

'Have a seat,' he offered and waited while she complied, crossing her legs neatly, her blue eyes never leaving his, like she was daring him to drop his gaze and see what she knew she was showing him.

Pete allowed a slight smile to show on his face, letting her know that he understood exactly what her game was. 'And you are…?'

'Abby Harper.'

Pete made a quick note.

'OK. How well did you know Claire Muir, Abby? I mean, beyond work?'

'I wasn't one of her inner circle, if that's what you mean.'

'But you're obviously a bright girl. Aware of what's going on around you, how people interact with each other and so on. What can you tell me in that capacity about her?'

'I said I wasn't in her inner circle. That doesn't mean I didn't like her. I haven't been here long. I started in January. She was nice. And she made a nice boss. Approachable, you know?'

Pete nodded. When she didn't carry on, he asked, 'Did anyone approach her more than work strictly justified?'

One narrow, arched eyebrow rose, going out of sight behind the deep fringe. 'I don't know what you've been told, but I never saw her being anything other than professional with anyone here. Friendly, yes, but…' She shook her head. 'She could be a good laugh but she wasn't a flirt or anything.'

'I'm not suggesting she encouraged it,' Pete said. 'What I'm asking is if anyone appeared to perhaps want a closer relationship with her than was professionally necessary.'

'Did anyone have the hots for her?'

'Exactly.'

She drew a long breath. 'No.' Her tone was dismissive.

'But…?'

'Well, no. Definitely. There's one guy who struggles a bit with the job. He's had some personal issues lately that Claire helped him through. But there's never been any hint of anything between them like that.'

'Fair enough. What kind of issues are we talking about?' Pete used the collective term deliberately, drawing her into a team scenario with him, encouraging her to say more.

'I think he's had some problems at home. I don't know the details, apart from the fact that he's recently had a baby and I think he's in the process of moving house.'

Two of the most stressful events in the average person's life, right on top of each other, Pete thought. 'OK. Is there anything else you can tell me?'

She shook her head, the fringe staying put as if it had been glued in place.

'So, what's this chap's name?'

'Henry. Henry Marston.'

Pete nodded. 'Thank you. You've been very helpful. I'll let you get back to work. We promised not to disrupt things any more than necessary round here.'

'Right.' She stood up much more quickly than she'd sat. As she turned away, Pete saw that the tight skirt had ridden up almost to the point of indecency, but she didn't do anything about it as she reached for the door.

Maybe that was his reward for not looking earlier, he thought as he picked up his phone and tapped into the speed dial list. He found the number he wanted and pressed call.

'Boss?'

'Henry Marston, Jane. Have we talked to him yet?'

'No. He's not in today. Got a new baby at home, apparently. Wife's not too well. Why?'

'Just something blondie with the legs was saying. It might be worth asking the others about him while we've got the chance: see what comes up, if anything.'

'Yeah?'

'He's also moving house. New baby. Sick wife. That's a lot of stress all at once.'

'True. But what's any of it got to do with Claire Muir, apart from the fact she's his boss?'

'Well, that's what I don't know yet, Jane.'

'OK. Want me to let Dave know or will you?'

'You can. I'll get onto Dick, get him and Jill to go see Mr and Mrs Marston and sprog, see what's up with them.'

He ended the call and redialled.

'Give us a chance. We haven't got there yet,' Dick said when he picked up.

'I know. Turn round. I need you to find an address for Henry Marston, a colleague of Claire Muir's, and go pay him a visit. He's on the sick today. Or so he says.'

'You don't think it's genuine?'

A knock sounded on the door in front of him. 'Two seconds,' he called. 'I don't know,' he said to Dick. 'Timing's a bit dodgy though, isn't it?' He quickly brought Dick up to speed and ended the call. He really needed someone to go and talk to Matthew Forrester before his wife warned him they were coming, but he was out of options. They had to concentrate on finding Claire Muir's killer or it would only add fuel to the fire of DCI Silverstone's wrath.

Pete needed to focus.

'Come in,' he called.

CHAPTER TWENTY-EIGHT

Pete had interviewed three more people and was part-way through talking to a fourth when his phone rang again. He glanced at the screen and looked up at the middle-aged woman sitting across from him.

'I need to get this, if you don't mind...'

'Of course. I'll be outside.' She stood up and left the room.

Pete answered the call. 'Hello, Dave.'

'Boss. I've just been speaking to a Charlene Dougherty who tells me that Henry Marston was after the job when Nathan Hollingsworth left. The one that Claire Muir got although he'd been here two years longer than she had.'

'Well, *there's* an interesting fact to add to the mix. Thanks, Dave.' *Another stresser for Henry Marston. And, this time, one linked to our victim.* This guy was rapidly heading for a full house. 'Dick and Jill are already on the way to speak to him and his wife if they're not already there. I'll let you be the one to pass that little gem on to them, as you were the one to dig it up.'

'Just hope it turns out to be more than a little gem,' Dave said. 'I don't know but I think I can feel the sparkle.'

'Yeah, the question is, how do we get from a feeling to solid evidence? We can't get a search warrant on the strength of your gut, Dave. Or mine.'

'You agree, then?'

'At this stage, yes. So does Jane. But like I said, it's evidence that counts.'

'We need to catch him in a lie.'

Pete nodded to himself. 'Give Ben a ring. Get him to find out what Henry drives and where it was on the afternoon and evening in question. CCTV, ANPR – whatever it takes. Track his every move from noon onwards that day. We know where Claire left her Toyota. Maybe there was an overlap. Or maybe he parked in the same place she did that morning and we can pick him up walking back to it. Did they meet up by arrangement and go somewhere together? Was he stalking her? We need something beyond suspicion. Once we've got it, we can take the next step. Search warrants, phone warrants, the works. Or we eliminate him and move on. Either way, the sooner the better.'

'Right. I might suggest getting Graham to help him too. It might speed things up a bit.'

'Good idea. I just… I've got to go, Dave. Nice work.'

He rang off and quickly dialled another number.

'Exeter police, Major Enquiries.'

'Hello, guv. It's Pete. Can I ask you a favour?'

'Not sure at this point,' Colin Underhill replied. 'My ears are still sore from the bashing the DCI gave them this morning. What is it?'

'Well, I've got interviews going on here, there and everywhere as well as CCTV to check and I've got one more interview that needs doing urgently, before the subject hears we want to talk to him and potentially does a runner.'

'Who?'

'Matthew Forrester. Owner of the taxi firm that Davit Achabaihan drives for. He and the two brothers from Essex have got a mutual friend who sent them down here to do a job. Which we both know the exact nature of but that's supposedly all the elder brother's wife knew until Essex police enlightened her after they'd notified her of her husband's demise.'

'And why might he know we're coming?'

'Because Dick and Jill have already spoken to his wife. She's the dispatcher for that same taxi firm.'

'When?'

Pete checked his watch. 'About twenty-five minutes ago, guv.'

The DI barely missed a beat. 'Where will he be?'

'He also owns the Airlink executive transport service. Apparently, he's there this morning. It's based at the airport.'

'Right. We'll talk later.'

There was a click on the line before Pete had a chance to respond. He put the phone down on the desk and stood up, heading for the door. The woman he'd been interviewing before Dave called him was standing patiently a few steps away down the corridor. 'Mrs Anderson? Sorry about that. Can we continue now?'

He held the door, closed it behind her and returned to his seat on the far side of the desk. 'Right, where were we?' He glanced at his notes. 'Oh, yes. I was about to ask you what you know about Claire's relationships with her male colleagues. Is there any particular one that stands out for any reason at all?'

*

The first call back he got was from Dick Feeney.

Along with Jane and Dave, he'd finished the interviews of Claire's team members and spread out through the building, asking other team leaders and managers about Claire. Did they know her? Was there any association between her and any of their staff?

Pete was on the first floor of the building, walking along the main corridor from the lifts when his phone rang. He checked the screen and answered it, stopping at the side of the long, pale green walkway with its rich wood doors and bland landscape pictures.

'Dick?'

'Henry Marston's got an alibi, boss. Supported by his wife. Claims he worked on the new house until dinner time then came home and spent the rest of the evening with her.'

'OK. We need to see if we can get corroboration from the neighbours on that. At either address. Ben's already looking at camera footage to try and track his vehicle. And the guvnor's taken over the Matthew Forrester interview, just so you know.'

Dick grunted. 'Glad of a trip out, I expect, is he?'

'He did mention something about earache.'

'I'm not surprised. We could hear it at our desks first thing. Fast-track was not a happy bunny. Not happy at all.'

'All the more reason, if it were needed, to make sure if Henry Marston's telling the truth.'

'We're on it.'

'Good man.' Pete ended the call and continued along the corridor. He was about to turn into another open plan office space with the label *Customer Complaints* on the door when his phone rang again. He took it out. His eyebrows rose at the name on the screen. That hadn't taken long.

'Guv?'

'Looks like you should have called me sooner. Matthew Forrester's done a runner. I spoke to his receptionist. She said he got a call from his wife and legged it like his arse was on fire. End quote.'

Shit. 'Did she say what he was driving, guv?'

'Yes. His own vehicle rather than a company one. A BMW SUV. I've put an alert out on it but, with the number of cars we've got out there these days, it's more likely to get picked up on camera than seen in person. Except you've got Graham tied up on tracking a suspect in the Claire Muir killing, I gather.'

'Yeah, well. Got to keep the DCI happy, haven't I? We'll just have to hope he goes past an ANPR camera instead and gets an automated ping.'

'You're presuming the DCI's happy in the first place. Let me tell you: he's not. If you'd got in before me this morning, you'd have already been to the benefits office by now, to sign on.'

'Given the circumstances, what was I supposed to do different? I was there. The situation needed an instant response. And yes, they were after me but, that being the case, who'd have been better placed to figure out who they were?'

'I didn't say you did anything wrong. I just said the DCI thought so. You know what he's like for rules and regs. And you know one of the cardinal ones is, you can't investigate your own or your family's case. Which is why I took over Tommy's.'

'Yes, I know all that, guv. But like I said: I was there. Where's the logic in stopping to call someone else in and bring them up to speed while the suspect's busy doing a runner? You get your trainers on and go after him, don't you?'

'It's not me you need to convince, Pete.'

'I know. Sorry, guv.'

'Let's finish the job while you've still got your warrant card. See if we can persuade his lordship to let you keep it.'

'Right.'

Underhill ended the call. Pete put his phone away and took out the warrant card they'd just been discussing as he went into the open-plan office space and glanced around, seeking the person in charge. There were about twenty people in there, male and female, all busy on the phones. At the far side of the room was a glass cubicle similar to Claire Muir's. He headed for it. A stern-looking woman in her forties sat behind a desk, tapping at a computer keyboard. He knocked and opened the door as she looked up.

'Hello. Are you the team leader?'

'I am. Who are you?'

He held up his badge. 'DS Gayle, Exeter CID. Could I have a word?'

She frowned. 'What about?'

Pete stepped in, letting the door close behind him. Taking a photo from his inside pocket, he held it up. 'Do you recognise this woman?'

'Yes. She's upstairs. Customer Services. You need to…'

'I'm aware of who she is,' Pete interrupted. 'I needed to know if you are.'

'Well, yes. As I said… I don't know her personally. I see her coming in and out now and then, say hello and goodbye, that's all. I don't think she's been working here that long.'

'OK. Are you aware of any relationship, of any kind at all, between her and any of your staff? Does anyone down here know her?'

'Not that I know of. Why? What's going on?'

'You're not aware of the body found in Ashclyst Forest a few nights ago?'

'No. Are you…? You mean she's dead?'

'I'm afraid so, yes.'

Her eyes widened as she blew the air out of her lungs. 'God, you never think these things will happen so close to home, do you?'

'That's right. OK, thanks for your help.'

Pete put the photo away and turned to leave.

He was reaching for the door when she said, 'If you email me the photo, I can put it up on the main company screen and see if we get any response that way.'

He turned back. 'You can do that?'

'Of course. It's a system we use quite frequently for staff notifications and so on.'

'Great. What's your email address?'

He keyed the address into his phone as she read it out, typed a short message and attached the photo of Claire Muir before hitting send. 'There you go. It's on its way. You can put my address on the bottom of it for any responses if you like. Save you the trouble of passing them on. Thank you.'

'No problem.'

Pete left her office feeling a lot more positive than he had when he'd entered. If the woman could get that photo out to every member of staff in the company with a request for information, then their job here was done. They could move on to other things – like finding out more about Henry Marston and Matthew Forrester, for a start.

Crossing her open plan domain, he keyed in a speed dial number and waited for it to be answered. It took only a couple of seconds.

'Boss?'

'I've just managed to get Claire Muir's picture put up on the company's digital noticeboard with a request for any information on her, Jane. I'm heading back to the office to get a data search started on Henry Marston among other things.'

'Right. Do you want Dave and me to stay here, keep going with the face-to-face questions or should we head back, too?'

'No, you two stay on. The digital version might pick up anyone that's not in today, but it's always best to look a person in the eyes when you question them. That way you get to gauge their reactions.'

*

'You going for a new record yesterday, were you? The most different visitors in one day?'

Tabitha was seated with Tommy, legs curled up under her in one of the easy chairs in the far corner of the common room from where the bulk of the kids were playing games and chatting in their mid-morning break. It was the first chance they'd had to talk since yesterday afternoon when he got pulled out of the canteen before dinner and she was brimming with curiosity.

'That was a visit I could have well done without,' he said sourly.

'Why? I thought Gavin said it was your solicitor.'

'No. I think he said it was a member of my legal team, whatever that's supposed to mean. But it wasn't.'

'So, who was it?'

Tommy drew a deep breath, not really sure if he ought to discuss the matter though he wanted to. 'No-one that you ever want to know anything about. He used to deal with Mel Burton sometimes. He's the bloke that taught the Devil how to be evil, but he kept three quarters of what he knew about it to himself.'

'Eh?'

'I've heard him called a stone-cold killer but he isn't. Stone-cold, that is. He enjoys it. He's the sort of bloke you stay the hell away from at all costs and don't ever cross him. His brother's a paedo, a thug and, from what I've heard, probably a killer too, but he's a pussy compared to this bloke. I don't know how true it is, but I heard a story about him once. His brother was jailed for molesting young girls. After the trial, he tracked down one of the key witnesses, tied him down, picked up an axe and asked him which limb he was most willing to lose. Said, "You choose or I will." Apparently, the bloke wasn't quick enough choosing. He dumped the body outside the courthouse.'

Tabitha had gone distinctly pale. Her skin had a light sheen of sweat as if she was feeling nauseous. 'You're winding me up.'

'I wish,' Tommy replied. 'I swear, I kid you not one speck. And he wants me not to testify against Mel Burton.'

'But that'll get you a jail sentence, won't it?'

Tommy tilted his head. 'So, what do I do? Keep my mouth shut, go to jail and he might or might not believe I'll stay quiet, so let me live if the other inmates don't get me anyway; or testify regardless, and he'll come after me with that bloody axe of his? Guaranteed.'

'Jesus! That's twisted. You need to talk to someone other than me about this, Tom. Really. I mean I have no clue.'

'Yeah, me neither. But who the hell am I supposed to talk to? I pick the wrong person, I'm dead anyway. Literally.'

CHAPTER TWENTY-NINE

Pete had only just finished one call when his phone rang again in his hand as he was walking along the corridor of the Portside Insurance building towards the main reception.

He lifted it to his ear as his thumb hit the answer button.

'Hello?'

'Boss, it's Ben. Mrs Forrester's just gone off out. Don't know if she normally does, of course, but she looked like she was in a hurry.'

They must have picked her up on camera. 'Which way's she headed?'

'She nipped round to the back of the building, came out a few seconds later in her little white Beamer, headed north towards the Black Boy roundabout.'

And they lived in Foxhayes so she'd be heading west from there if they were intending to grab a bag and go on the run. 'OK. Get a car out to their place in Foxhayes, see if they can pick either of them up. And check for family connections. They might be planning to stop off on the way to wherever they're headed.'

'I don't know about family, but I do know they've got a boat. One of those big, posh yachts, costs more than the average house. They keep it moored down at Exmouth harbour.'

'Get someone down there as well, then, in case they don't go home first.' Pete walked into the expansive reception area and crossed quickly towards the outer doors.

'Already have, boss.'

'Good. Although they might just use both those options as decoys and go by road, so we need an alert out on both vehicles. They could use either.' He went through the revolving doors and into the bright, fresh late morning sun. 'In fact, make it a general one. All airports and seaports, too. I'm on the way back now so I'll see you in a bit. Nothing on Henry Marston's car yet?'

'*Yes!*'

Pete recognised the voice in the background. 'What's Graham found?'

'Don't know, boss. Two secs.'

Pete was almost back to his car when Ben came back on the line.

'Marston and the victim walking together, boss. He didn't park in the same place she did that morning. They've met up somewhere other than work and they're headed through Cathedral Yard towards Fore Street.'

There was more muttering in the background as Pete climbed into the patrol car and started the engine.

'They went down Fore Street and turned into South Street.'

Pete switched to the hands-free system and laid the phone on the passenger seat. 'OK. While Graham tracks them, you get that alert out and get Exmouth station to send someone down to the harbour. When you've done that, call the harbour master too, see if he can stop them leaving on the yacht if they try to. I'll see you soon.'

He ended the call, slipped the car into gear and, as he drove out of the company car park, used the hands-free to call the transport police.

*

He'd been in the queue up to the Heavitree Road roundabout for little more than fifteen seconds when the in-car ANPR system pinged for the second time since he left the Portside Insurance building. Pete checked the screen. Lucy Forrester's white BMW sports car had just passed a camera, heading west towards Foxhayes.

Here we go, he thought and brought up the Bluetooth system to call Dave Miles.

'Hello, boss. We're almost done here…'

'Get yourselves out of there now,' Pete interrupted. 'Each take your own vehicles. I need everyone available out towards Foxhayes. The Forresters are both on the way home. We don't want them leaving there if we can help it.'

'You'll be lucky. There's got to be half a dozen ways in and out of there.'

'At least. That's why I said each take your own vehicle. We need to cover them all.'

He ended the call, hit the blues and twos and pulled out of the queue to power up the opposite lane and cut across the traffic to turn left up the hill towards the city centre as he keyed the radio mike. 'All available units to Exwick Lane, Foxhayes. Suspects in conspiracy to murder a police officer about to flee. We need to approach from every direction. He gave the vehicle details as he turned right at a crossroads where the road in front of him was one-way – towards him. 'I'll be approaching from the city centre.' He brought up the hands-free phone system again. When his call was answered, he said, 'Ben, get out of that chair and into your car. I need every available body out to Foxhayes now.'

'Right, boss.' There was a click as Ben put the phone down.

Sirens far louder than the narrow street required, Pete drove fast up to the roundabout at the far end and straight across into the first exit. From here his route would loop west towards the suspects' home. He was using the same route as Lucy Forrester had, moments before.

His phone rang. He tapped the screen.

'Boss, it's Dick. We're over by the rugby ground so we're heading up from there.'

'Thanks, Dick.' That was the southern approach covered, then. Dick and Jill on the far side of the river, Dave and Jane on the near side.

His radio crackled briefly. 'Car four two six leaving scene of accident, Cowley Bridge. We'll head down St Andrews.'

Pete pictured the narrow, twisting country lane that ran down the north-western edge of the city. It was only a few short weeks since he'd chased a suspect down there himself, only to lose him in the maze-like residential streets of Exwick, just north of Foxhayes. He keyed the mike. 'Are you sure you can, four two six?'

'There's two other crews there, sarge. The only casualty was a dog.'

'Can you get one of the others to come down Cowley Bridge Road when they're done, then?'

'Will do.'

Another voice came over the airwaves. 'Car four one niner. That'll be us. One minute.'

'Thanks, guys.'

That covered every way but west. He keyed the mike once more. 'DC Bennett, DC Feeney, head to the subjects' address. We could do with catching them there, if possible. In case that doesn't work out, though, DC Miles, assuming you're on the bike, go straight through and take the Crediton Road. I'll take the Okehampton road. Be safe, everyone.'

The response came almost immediately. 'Dave Miles for DS Gayle. Confirming I am on the bike. I'll shoot through to the Crediton Road.'

'Received, Dave.'

He concentrated on driving, pushing the big car hard through the streets towards Okehampton Street, no longer trying to follow the little sports car as he realised where she was headed and that she was going around in a large circle. Pete doubled back and headed directly down the Western Way inner ring road towards the Alphington Street gyratory over the river, trying to save time and gain whatever ground he could.

He made it back down to the dual carriageway, turned right and gunned the engine, driving hard, lights and sirens warning the other road users of his approach so they slowed and pulled over to let him pass. Still, he kept his eyes peeled, his attention focussed. It was surprising how often some idiot would try to take advantage or not be paying attention.

Jane came over the radio as he hit the Alphington Street junction, taking the easy route to maintain his speed.

'I'm at the Forresters' address, boss. There's one vehicle on the drive. Correction: two vehicles. Didn't see the little one behind the 4x4. No sign of movement.'

'OK. Are there gates across the drive?'

'Affirmative. A single field-type gate.'

'Close it then, Jane, and park across it so it can't be opened. Then go in and give them a knock. At this stage, treat them as witnesses.'

'Will do, boss.'

'Back-up's on the way.'

'Received.'

He made it round the gyratory and turned onto Okehampton Street. He'd only made another few hundred yards when Dick Feeney's voice came over the radio.

'Arrived at the subjects' address, boss. Going in with Jane.'

'Split up,' he responded. 'Cover the back door, just in case.'

'Received.'

That was Jane.

He was driving more slowly now, the potential danger to pedestrians urging caution over speed. He didn't want to hit a careless kid or a deaf old fogey by accident. And he was now less than a minute away from where Jane and Dick were approaching the Forresters' house, hopefully with every means of escape covered.

A bus indicated as if it was going to pull out in front of him, then he saw the brake lights flare as the driver realised his mistake. Pete raised a hand as he passed, eyes peeled for anyone stepping out from behind the big vehicle. But no-one did and the bus pulled out behind him, taking full advantage of the brief lull in traffic in his wake.

'No response at the Forresters', boss,' Jane said over the radio. 'Do you want us to force entry?'

'Both cars are there so yes, with due warning. I'm about a minute away.'

'Is that your siren I can hear in the distance?'

'Probably.'

'Do you want us to wait?'

'No, do it.'

'Received.'

'PC Evans on location,' Jill reported.

In moments, Pete reached the end of the narrow lane and slowed, indicating. He killed the sirens and lights.

The properties along here were large, widely spaced and set well back from the road in lush private grounds.

'Access gained,' Dick reported. 'Still no response from the owners so we're commencing a search.'

'Go ahead,' Pete replied as he drew up in front of Jane's distinctive little green Vauxhall. 'I'm right behind you.'

Stepping out of the big patrol car, he climbed over the five-bar gate and jogged up the gravel drive between dense glossy-leaved shrubbery that opened out abruptly to an expansive lawn with the house and detached double garage set well back from the road.

The Forresters had to be raking in some money to be able to afford a place like this, Pete thought.

The large, solid wood front door stood ajar. He could see a figure standing in the shadows beyond as his feet crunched across the pale gravel. He went up the two wide steps and pushed the door open.

'Jill.'

'Hey, boss. They're upstairs.'

'Who, the subjects?'

'No, Jane and Dick. No sign of the Forresters yet.'

Pete felt the slump of disappointment then heard footsteps from above. Jane came down the grand oak stairs.

'Hi, boss. No sign of them, I'm afraid. We've missed them.'

'And yet...' Jill stopped as Pete cut in.

'They used a bloody taxi, didn't they? Slipped away in a car they knew we wouldn't look twice at.'

'Fuck.'

As bound up in his own disappointment as Pete was, he was still shocked at Jane's rare use of the word.

'Sorry,' she added, seeing the look on his face. 'It just slipped out.'

'As the bishop said to the actress,' Dick added from a few steps behind and above her. 'There's no-one up here, boss.'

'I'm with Jane,' Pete replied. 'Her first response.'

'If you're right, they could be anywhere.'

Pete sighed. 'Yeah, thanks for that. Not.'

CHAPTER THIRTY

Pete turned back to the others. 'Before we make any assumptions, is there a loft in this place?'

'Yes,' said Dick. 'I checked it. It's clear.'

'A cellar?'

'Not that we've been able to find.'

'Right. You and Jill can double-check for that, then, while Jane and I have a look in the garage and any other out-buildings. Nowhere goes unchecked, OK? Let's go.' Pete picked up the two sets of car keys from the side table in the hall and tossed one of them to Jane. Each included an extra remote control for the garage doors. As they stepped outside, heading for the detached double garage, Pete reached for his radio. 'Cars four one niner and four two six, stand down. Suspects believed to have left the scene in a taxi. No clue as to which one.'

A short crackling hiss preceded the response. 'Four two six. Received, sarge.'

'Four one nine. Received.'

'PC Myers. I just passed a taxi. A light blue... It was Achabaihan's or one just like it, heading towards the city centre.'

'When you say just, Ben...?'

'A few seconds ago, boss.'

'Any chance of catching up with him?'

'I'm just turning round to give it a try.'

'Keep me informed. And get some back-up.'

'Will do.'

A few steps in front of him, Jane pressed the remote on the keyring he'd given her. The left side garage door started to rise. Pete followed suit, urging the other door into motion. As he stepped into the shadowy interior, he heard Ben over the radio, requesting all available vehicles to look out for Davit Achabaihan's light blue Skoda and giving both the registration and PSV licence numbers.

The two roll-up doors gave onto a single large space, the front section evidently given over to vehicle storage while the rear doubled as garden shed, tool store and workshop. A quick glance told Pete that Matthew Forrester was into both gardening and woodwork. But it also told him that the couple were not in the building. There was, however, a solid-looking wooden door leading out through the back to the garden beyond. He crossed the concrete floor quickly and reached for the handle. It was locked. He looked around. Could see no other exits.

'Let's try the garden.'

Back outside, they went between the garage and the house into a large garden. A stone flagged patio stretched across the rear of the house, another smaller one in the back right corner of the plot, shaded by an arbour covered with jasmine and honeysuckle and fronted by a large pond that was fed by a stream that ran across from the left, behind the veranda-fronted summer house. Next to the summer house, reached by a bridge and a stepping-stone path, was a wooden-framed greenhouse that, from the lush and brightly coloured flowers it was filled with, Pete guessed had to be heated.

There was not a sign of a tomato plant in there and nor were there any vegetable beds in sight. Matthew Forrester might like his garden but it was purely for decoration. Shrub and flower beds provided a mass of colour, even this early in the season.

'Check the arbour and down the far side of the house,' he said to Jane.

White metal garden furniture showed in the shaded arbour while bulkier wooden chairs and table stood on the patio by the house. As Jane stepped round it, Pete approached the wooden summerhouse. When he got close enough to see there was no-one in there, he changed direction, back across towards the greenhouse. The floor and shelves were filled with a mass of planting but his angle of approach let him glimpse something else, beyond the double-glazed structure. His eyes narrowed.

'Jane?'

She turned at the sound of his voice. Saw his raised eyebrow and gave a quick shake of the head to indicate she could see nothing at the far side of the house.

Pete jerked his own head to beckon her over.

She shrugged and headed across as he continued towards the greenhouse, concentrating once more on what he'd seen.

Behind it was a dark-stained wooden gate let into the tall hedge, the shrubbery arching over it. The greenhouse itself stood three or four feet from the hedge, allowing access to the gate while at the same time concealing it from the casual observer.

Pete waved Jane around the eastern end of the greenhouse while he approached from the west.

The gate had a simple black iron latch and a loop and hasp for a padlock which currently hung open. Jane saw it too and tipped her head. Reaching for the latch, Pete turned it and snatched the gate open.

A tree-lined footpath ran along the back of the property, up into the hills to the left or down towards the main road through the village to the right. Beyond another hedge on the far side of the path was an open field dotted with sheep and lambs.

There was no-one in sight.

'Which way?' asked Jane.

Pete checked the soft, black earth. It showed a prevalence of footprints, large and small, angled to the left. He nodded that way and set off. It looked like they used the gate and the path fairly frequently and this was their usual direction. Whether it was the one they'd taken this time, if they'd come out this way at all, remained to be seen, but a choice had to be made so he'd made it.

They walked quickly, Jane keeping up despite the unsuitable nature of her shoes. For the most part, the path was firm, in some places grassed over despite the early season, but in others it was wide, pitted and puddled. They couldn't avoid getting their shoes filthy as they hurried along, focussed on the hunt.

Pete had turned the volume down on his hand-held radio but he still picked up the phrase, 'Target in sight. Repeat, target in sight.'

Ben.

'Heading south on Bonhay Road.'

The path took a turn to the right, around the top corner of the sheep field then turned left again to continue uphill towards the woods, now going between two fields. High dense hedges bordered either side for several yards, the one on the left thick with Old Man's Beard, its feathery seed heads still like a covering of cotton wool even this late in the season. Beyond it, Hawthorn was bright green with new Spring leaves, then the path darkened as it went through a high, unkempt stand of Blackthorn, the last of the early blossom clinging ragged and filthy to its outer branches. The ground under it was soft but without any standing water. Sunlight beckoned them on through the tunnel of dark, tangled branches as Pete jogged forward, trying to gain a little ground on the fleeing couple, Jane a couple of steps behind him.

Beyond the Blackthorn, the path curved left. A few yards further on, a stile on the right gave access to the corner of a field with a green wooden sign for a public footpath cutting back towards Exwick.

Which way now?

Pete stopped, examining the stile plank and the long, straggly grass and weeds around it. There was no sign of disturbance. He shook his head to Jane and nodded towards the continuation of the path they were on.

'They didn't go over here.'

They ran on. Soon, the path opened out on the left, the hedge trimmed low to reveal a view down across the slope of the hill towards the now distant Okehampton Road. Pete glimpsed a flash of red from a lorry heading out of the city. Other traffic showed but he paid it no attention as he quickly examined the fields between. There were no human figures out there.

He kept going.

The path curved this way and that. They passed an old tumble-down stone barn, its roof timbers long ago collapsed over a heap of rubble at one end while the other end stood stark against the sky, one large door still hanging by both hinges though the accumulation of weeds at its base and the mounded rubble at its inner side meant it couldn't swing in either direction.

The hedge on their right grew taller now, untrimmed for a number of years, Pete guessed. Then dark woodland loomed ahead. Pete kept going. The ground to either side was now dense with budding bluebells. Here and there a few had broken into flower. Splashes of white showed where stitchwort and wood anemones grew amongst the bulbs. Another path crossed the one they were on.

Pete stopped again.

Now what?

The ground was firm, the plants around them low and undisturbed. There was no way of knowing which way the Forresters would have gone. He looked at Jane but she was as clueless as he was. Then her attention was drawn past him. He heard the snap of a twig and turned. A couple were walking hand-in-hand towards them along the path from the left. The man was tall, slim, curly dark hair neatly cut. She was smaller, blonde. Both in their late thirties, at a guess.

Pete stepped forward. 'Excuse me…' Then he recognised her. 'Mrs Forrester. Fancy meeting you out here.'

He reached surreptitiously under his jacket and switched off the radio that was hooked to the right side of his belt.

'And Mr…?'

'That's right.' The man spoke for himself as they drew closer.

'You don't remember me?' Pete focussed on the woman.

She shook her head. 'Sorry. I see an awful lot of faces every day, I'm afraid, Mr…?'

'Gayle.' He was close enough now. 'Detective Sergeant Gayle. We met a few months ago. I was looking into a case that remotely involved one of your drivers. Albanian chap. Achabaihan.' He shrugged. 'He was a friend of a suspect, that was all, but we needed to speak to him.'

'Ah.' She was nodding. 'I remember now. So what's this? A day off? Out for a walk with the wife? Like us.' She glanced at her husband.

Pete shook his head. 'This is a colleague of mine. Detective Constable Bennett, meet Lucy Forrester and her husband Matthew. We're working, I'm afraid. Looking for you two, actually.'

She frowned. 'Why? What for?'

'We need a word.'

'Really?'

'Perhaps we should head back to your house?' Pete stepped to the side to allow them past.

'Or there's a seat a few yards down, at the edge of the wood,' she countered with a jerk of her head back the way she and her husband had just come from. 'Lovely view over the valley. We come up here and sit sometimes.'

'Sounds wonderful but it'd probably be more appropriate to talk somewhere more formal in the circumstances.'

'I see. So, what do you need to talk to us about? You never said.'

'Ah. No. It's about a death that occurred in the city, yesterday. A car accident. A man was killed on Harts Lane.'

She frowned. 'How can we help?'

'It turns out the man who died was a friend of your husband's, Mrs Forrester.' Pete focussed now on the man at her side. 'A chap from up East: Essex, I believe. Aziz Krasniqi.'

A blink was deliberately blocked, but the man's eyes still narrowed.

'He was down here with his brother, Gjergi. Is there anything you can tell us about that, Mr Forrester?'

The tall man's lips tightened. 'Not that I can think of.'

'Well, it turns out they were sent down here to do a job. A friend of theirs in Essex had got a call from here in Exeter. You know how it goes. Thing is, that job that they came down here for was the murder of a police officer. It didn't work out, but you can see how we'd be concerned by that.'

'Murdering a police officer?' the blonde woman exclaimed. 'How d'you... What's going on here?' She looked from Pete to her husband and back.

'Quiet, Lucy.' His voice was quiet but firm.

'What? Never mind quiet, what's going on, Matt?'

'We've done nothing wrong,' he said.

'Nevertheless,' Pete interjected. 'Matthew Forrester, I'm placing you under arrest for conspiracy to murder and aiding and abetting a felon in the commission of a criminal act.'

*

'Again?'

Tommy looked up from his exercise book and put down his pen. 'Who is it this time?'

Gavin, standing half-in the classroom doorway, just jerked his head in a beckoning motion.

Tommy sighed. 'OK. Sorry,' he added to the teacher at the front of the class. 'Not under my control.'

'Very well,' the woman said.

Tommy stood up and headed for the door where Gavin stepped back to allow him through. It wasn't until he'd closed the door behind Tommy and was following him along the corridor that Gavin answered his question. 'The policeman. DI Underhill.'

Shit. Tommy felt something slump heavily inside, almost like one of his organs had slipped under gravity. It left him with a faint, weird fluttering in his guts as he walked on resolutely, determined not to show Gavin any sign of weakness.

'What's the matter? Cat got your tongue?' Gavin probed.

Tommy was thankful that the muscle-bound staff member was behind him, so couldn't see his face. 'What do you want me to say? Whoopie-do, my favourite visitor?'

'I could have told him he'd have to wait for the end of your lesson.'

'Yeah, but that would put *you* on the wrong side of a copper, not me for a change, wouldn't it? I didn't ask him to come here, after all.'

'I could go back and tell him you refused to see him,' Gavin suggested.

'And my trial's coming up at the end of the week. That'd go down really well, wouldn't it?'

'True. Maybe I should do just that.'

'What, you love me that much you want me to stay?'

'You're not my type, sonny. I like some competition in a tussle.'

Tommy grimaced. He'd never understand how a guy could be sexually attracted to other men. It was just... Wrong. Biologically wrong, he qualified to himself, aware of the irony of calling anything "wrong" with his history.

Gavin let him lead the way to the meeting room – the police would have called it an interview room, he knew – next to the manager's office. When they reached the door, Tommy stopped and waited. Gavin stepped around him and opened the door. Colin Underhill was seated with his back to the door, his tweed-clad bulk dwarfing the chairs and table that were the only furniture in the room as he waited, his stillness almost meditative.

Tommy stepped in. He waited for Gavin to close the door before speaking as he headed for the seat at the far side of the table.

'Uncle Colin. What's up?'

'I was out this way, thought I'd call in, see how you're doing.'

'Out this way? I thought you were pretty much office-based these days?'

'That what your dad told you, is it?'

Tommy grimaced. When had his dad last told him anything, never mind talked about work? 'It's just what I gathered.'

'Well, mostly, you're right. But this morning, he hadn't got enough pairs of hands to cover everything he needed to, so I offered to help. I went to interview a murder suspect.'

'Did you arrest him?'

Colin shook his big head. 'He had an alibi. Supported by his wife and a friend.'

'Back to the drawing board then, eh?'

'Looks like it. But in the meantime, I thought it might be useful to go over some of the things that can happen in a court room. For when you testify.'

Tommy sat back in his chair. 'Yeah, about that… I'm sorry, Uncle Colin. I really am. But there's only one way I'm going to testify against Mel Burton. You've got another couple of arrests to make. And they've got to stick better than superglue.'

Colin frowned. 'Why? What's happened?'

Tommy felt the physical need to squirm in his chair but held himself still by force of will. He met Colin's gaze and forced himself to hold it. 'I had a visitor last night. In here. Bold as brass and twice as shiny, like he could just waltz in anywhere he wanted and any time he wanted. Warned me that, if I testify against Mel, he'll kill me and my family. And I know him. He'd not only do it, he'd enjoy it.'

Colin leaned forward, leather-patched elbows on the table, big hands clasped together. 'Who was it, Tommy?'

'I don't know his first name. Surname's Southam. He's got a brother who was in clink up north somewhere. Said he helped him escape. *His* name's Steve. Used to be into karate and that. Mel told me about him once. Likes to play the hard nut but, compared to his brother, he's nothing. Like comparing a playground bully to Adolf Hitler.'

'Adolf Hitler was a playground bully,' Colin said. 'He just never grew out of it.'

'Well, this Southam bloke grew further into it. I don't know how you'd find him but I can't go anywhere near that court until you have – found him, nicked him and got him banged up tighter than that bloke in the Silence Of The Lambs.'

Colin frowned. 'How do you know about what's in an 18-certificate movie?'

Really? Tommy thought. *Wake up to the real world.* 'It's been on telly. Loads of times.'

Colin grunted. 'Anything useful you can tell me about him?'

'He's a big bugger. Over six foot and pretty much that far around. Crew cut hair. Likes to wear a suit as if he's some sort of businessman. Pretended to be working for my brief when he come in here. But he looks more like a nightclub bouncer. All it would want is a black suit instead of the grey one he was wearing. He said he'd be staying around for Mel's trial.'

'OK. I'll see what we can do. He's one man against an entire police force. You don't need to worry about him, son.'

'Yeah, right,' Tommy snorted. 'Nothing against you, Uncle Colin, but until you've got him locked up solid, that's just words. And he deals in actions. I know Mel Burton was terrified of him. Wished he'd never started dealing with him.'

Colin straightened in his chair. 'Dealing with him how, exactly?'

'Sent him videos to start with. Then he came down and… Took part in them a couple of times.'

'Took part how?'

'When the girls weren't compliant enough... Once, he...' Tommy felt queasy at the memory but he knew he couldn't stop now. 'There was a girl. She was fighting and wriggling and all sorts. Mel couldn't do anything, camera-wise. Southam picked her up by the ankles, lifted her right up and...' He swallowed. 'He did her. I... I never saw her again.'

'And where had she come from?'

'Dunno. He brought her with him.'

'Tell me about her. What she looked like. How old she was. What accent she had. What she was wearing. Anything that stood out.'

Tommy pulled in a breath. 'She was probably about eleven or twelve. She was tallish - five three, maybe - but she hadn't started to... You know. Develop.' He shrugged. 'She didn't have much of an accent. Well spoken, I suppose, but not posh. She had a white blouse and socks. Her skirt and jacket were like a yellow and black tartan kind of thing. The skirt was on the long side. Below the knee. I remember thinking how unusual that was, these days. And she wasn't... She didn't look English although she sounded it. Not black or Indian but a bit darker than your typical white girl. Her hair was black and curly and she had a couple of moles. There was one on her cheek about an inch from her nostril. Almost black. And another right by her left nipple. Almost like a third one, you know? Like that bloke in that James Bond film.'

'A mole or a birth mark?' Colin asked as if it was the most normal thing in the world for Tommy to have seen her bare chest.

Tommy shrugged. 'Like a birth mark, I suppose. Bigger than a mole, generally.'

'And the one on her face. Which cheek?'

'Right.'

'Eye colour?'

'I don't remember. Brown, I suppose. She had a chipped tooth, though: I remember that. Not the front two, but the next one on the left.'

'All right.' Colin sat back and took out his phone. Tapped at the screen for a few moments then leaned forward and held the instrument out for Tommy to see. 'Is that him?'

The little screen was filled with a full-face portrait of a heavy-set man in front of a white wall, the flash directly in front of him.

A mug-shot.

'Yes, that's him.'

Colin nodded. 'Adrian Southam. OK. Thanks, Tommy. I'll let you get back to your class.'

'What was he in for?'

Colin put the phone away and looked up, meeting Tommy's gaze. 'Murder. He crushed a young girl to death. Jumped on her ribcage.'

Tommy blinked. 'Well, then, you know what I'm dealing with. How's he back out on the streets?'

'Same as his brother – he escaped. Four months before his brother and from a different prison.'

'And now he's here. With his eyes on me.'

Colin reached across the table to pat Tommy's hand. 'I know he's scary, Tom, but he's one man. Your dad and me – we've got an entire police force behind us.'

'Yeah, but you stick to the rules. He doesn't even know there are any. To him, anything goes and the nastier the better.'

Colin chuckled. Tommy couldn't believe his ears. He pulled back, drawing his hand away from the comforting bulk of Colin's big paw.

'If you only knew, son. Our station commander came in this morning, found out what your dad's been up to over the weekend and bloody near had a stroke. It took me twenty minutes to talk him down from firing him on the spot. So, he might not be Dirty Harry, but your dad'll do just about whatever it takes when it comes to family. And he's not the only one.'

Tommy was far from convinced. 'You've got to find him first.'

Colin spread his hands. 'We're coppers, Tommy. That's what we do. And Exeter isn't that big a place. We know he's here. We know he plans to stay around for a while. How hard can it be? He's not exactly going to blend in, in a university town like this.'

'Yeah, well... Come back to me with a date-stamped photo of him in custody and a copy of the charge sheet that says he's not going anywhere out of handcuffs for the next twenty years and we can talk. Until then, I'm sorry, Uncle Colin, but I don't want him even thinking about our Annie. It's bad enough he's in the same city as she is. And if that means Mel Burton getting off then so be it. Whoever first said, "lesser of two evils," invented it for this situation.' He pushed his chair back and stood up. 'I need to get back to class. I'll see you around.'

CHAPTER THIRTY-ONE

Pete walked into the squad room with a tray of six coffees and set them on the corner of his desk.

'Matt Forrester's lawyered up,' he said to the assembled team. 'And the brief won't be here for forty minutes.' He began passing out the steaming mugs. 'I think he's stretching it deliberately, but what can you do? Meantime, I need you lot to be getting busy again. Jane and Dave, I want you to interview Lucy Forrester. She may or may not be involved. Her reactions out in the woods suggested not, so build a rapport with her. Treat her as a witness, not a suspect until we know different. Dick, take Jill with you and go see this friend of Henry Marston's that he told you about. Make sure she's confident of the dates and times in her statement. We know his alibi's false so get the truth out of her. If you need to, remind her that perjury can pull jail time and will certainly give her a criminal record, with all the problems that brings. Ben...' His phone rang, interrupting his flow. He picked it up. 'DS Gayle, Exeter CID.'

'It's Colin. We've got a problem.'

Pete felt his brow pull into a frown. 'What kind of problem?'

'It's Tommy. He's had a visitor. The unwelcome kind. He's no longer willing to testify against Malcolm Burton.'

'What! Why?'

'Because he's bloody terrified, that's why. This bloke's scared the shit out of him.'

'So, who is he? Let's fetch him in for tampering.'

'Well, that's one option. He's also wanted for two prison breaks including his own. But it's not enough. We need him on a murder charge. At least. That's the only way Tommy'll get on the stand.'

'So give me the details and we'll get after the bugger.'

'Uh-uh. I can't give you this one.'

'Well, who is going to take it, then? Simon?' He snorted.

'I'll keep it myself. I'll use Mark's team for legwork. I was just letting you know because it's Tommy. You might want to call Louise before she goes to see him, if she's planning to, today.'

Pete grunted. He knew the Detective Inspector was right. It still didn't sit well, though. 'Yes. I'll do that. Thanks, guv.'

He put the phone down and looked up to find his whole team staring at him. They didn't need to ask the question. It was written all over their faces. 'There's a new player in the Malcolm Burton case,' he told them. 'Sounds like a real bad bastard. He's got to Tommy. Scared him into not testifying. Now, where was I?'

'Never mind where you were,' Jane said. 'Where are we now?'

'*We're* OK without Tommy's testimony. *He's* up shit creek without a paddle, though. And I know there's those who think that's where he belongs but the reason he's there is because we've got another killer on the streets, from what the guvnor said.'

'And we're not taking the case?' Dave checked.

'That's right. The guvnor's going to deal with it himself. With Mark's help.'

'Did I hear my name?' DS Mark Bridgman asked from the next group of desks.

Pete turned in his seat. 'Talking about you, not to you, Mark,' he said as the other man's phone began to ring. 'That'll be for you.'

'You don't say.' He picked it up. 'DS Bridgman. How can I help?'

Pete turned back to his team. 'Right, so... Ben. I was going to go see Graham myself but I'll need you to do that now. See if he's found anything useful. By the time I've warned Louise about Tommy's situation it'll be nearly time Forrester's brief was here.'

*

'Right. Everybody comfy? Then we'll begin, shall we?' Pete reached over and started the digital recorder. 'Present in the room, DS Peter Gayle of Heavitree Road police station, Mr Matthew Forrester and Mr Forrester's solicitor, Mr Nigel Humphries. So, Mr Forrester, you fully understand the implications of your presence here today, yes?'

Forrester nodded. One of those implications was the effect that criminal charges would have on his ability to retain a taxicab licence. He could lose a major portion of his business.

'My client would like to make it perfectly clear that he's here in a spirit of co-operation, Detective Sergeant.'

'Your client's here because he was arrested for conspiracy to murder, Mr Humphries,' Pete told the little man in his expensive grey three-piece. 'Any spirit of co-operation is purely for his own benefit. Just so we're perfectly clear. Now, do you have any contacts in the county of Essex, Mr Forrester?'

The thin man blinked. 'Not currently.'

'So you did, but not now, is that correct?'

Forrester nodded.

'Do you know Aziz or Gjergi Krasniqi?'

'I knew Aziz. You told me he's dead.'

Pete nodded. 'He is.' So Forrester was going to try being pedantic. 'How about Fatun Gradzinski? Do you know him?'

Forrester glanced at his solicitor then returned his gaze to Pete. 'No comment.'

'No comment on Fatun Gradzinski. If I were to tell you that the mobile phone we found in your BMW contained his number and that you'd called him from it more than once in the past couple of weeks, would that help?'

Forrester pulled in a long breath but said nothing.

Pete waited a few seconds but still got no response. 'OK, so let me tell you what we already know, Mr Forrester. Maybe that'll help your memory. What we know is that the Krasniqi brothers got a call from Gradzinski and came down here to Exeter on the strength of that call to, "Do a job," as it was described to us by a witness. And we know that, immediately before Gradzinski made that call, he received one from you. Which suggests he was acting as a middleman between you and them, doesn't it?'

'Suggestions are like statistics, Detective Sergeant,' the solicitor said smugly. 'They mean very little in the real world.'

Pete smiled briefly. 'But you and I both know how far removed the real world is from the court room and the minds of a jury, Mr Humphries. They see two and two, they automatically add them together. Like it or not, it's human nature. And once Essex get hold of Mr Gradzinski – which is only a matter of time – then we'll have his testimony to add weight to the suggestion.'

Humphries smiled. 'You really think so, Detective Sergeant?'

'Well, the thing is this, Mr Humphries,' Pete said. 'When it's a choice between testifying against someone accused of murder or going down for it yourself, then logic dictates you testify. Am I right?'

'But when it's a matter of personal safety, Detective Sergeant...' He lifted his hands in an open gesture.

'Are you suggesting your client's frightened of Fatun Gradzinski?'

Forrester snorted derisively.

'Who then, if not Gradzinski?'

'He's a middle-man. A ferret.'

'Then who does he work for?' Pete demanded. 'Petrosyan?'

A grunt.

Pete couldn't tell if it was a positive or a negative one but it was all he'd got. 'You're frightened of Gagik Petrosyan, Mr Forrester? Well, let me tell you, there's no need to be. He's locked up firmly in the city jail for now and the only place he'll be going from there is another prison.'

'But you and I both know, Detective Sergeant, that an intelligent criminal's reach can stretch through prison walls,' Humphries pointed out. 'You can't guarantee my client's safety, no matter where the threat comes from. This isn't America with its witness protection program. This country isn't big enough for such things.'

A line from an old song from the 1970's popped into Pete's mind *This town ain't big enough for the both of us...* He smiled.

'Or maybe it's not Petrosyan that you're scared of, Mr Forrester?' he suggested. 'Maybe it's someone else?'

Forrester frowned, but his eyes now held a definite hint of fear. Pete was onto something, he sensed. But what? Or more accurately, who?

'Who is it, Mr Forrester? Who are you really scared of? If it's not Gradzinski and it's not Petrosyan – and it can't be the Krasniqi brothers because one of them's dead and we've got the other one locked up – then who is the real threat?'

Forrester held his silence.

'If you don't tell me, then we can't do anything about it,' he said. 'Do you really want to live under that kind of threat? Especially in prison, once you're convicted. You know the kinds of things that go on in places like that, these days. You're seen as a threat, you don't come out of it well, if you even come out alive. And then there's the threat to your wife. I take it you love your wife, Mr Forrester? You don't want to risk any harm coming to her?'

Even as he said it, Pete's mind pictured Louise. What would he not to, to keep her safe? There wasn't much, if anything.

'You really think we'd be safe after we helped you put him away, Sergeant? You must be out of your tiny mind.'

Pete nodded. 'You'd be a lot safer afterwards than you are now, with him knowing that you could tell us what you know at any time. Despite Mr Humphries' lack of confidence – based, I might add, on lack of knowledge – we can protect you. Once we know who we need to protect you from. *Now* – while he's out there suspicious and worried and we don't have the knowledge to do anything about him – is when you're most at risk. Once you tell us everything, then we can whisk you away to safety and deal with the threat directly.' He shrugged and spread his hands flat on the table. 'There is the fact that, going along with Mr Humphries' analogy, you won't be able to go back to your current home or maintain any of your current friendships and so forth, but you will be safe and comfortable. As long as you maintain basic security measures, you won't be traceable. Even from within the police force. There are multi-step processes that allow complete separation from one life to the next. I won't be able to find you and nor will Mr Humphries, here. Or anyone else.'

He sat back in his chair.

'Maybe we ought to suspend this interview and let you mull that over, Mr Forrester.'

*

'Boss?' Dick picked up his phone on the second ring.

'How've you got on?'

'We found Beth Harrison at home, boss. She's a pleasant, honest woman by all appearances. If she gave a false alibi it was by mistake. She did admit to having spoken to Henry Marston last night. He called round for a chat, she said. During the course of which, he put it into her mind that she was at his and his wife's place last Tuesday evening when in fact, she's sure now it was Monday. She thought she must have got confused. He's always seemed like a nice bloke, apparently, and she's known his wife since they were kids. But, thinking about it now, she realised that she was at home to watch Phil and Kirsty on Tuesday. It's one of her favourite programs.'

'Which leaves his wife as his only alibi,' Pete said. 'And, being his wife, she would support him, wouldn't she? Unless she thought he was being unfaithful.'

'Was he?'

'We don't know. It's possible. And we do know that he met up with our victim outside of work that day. We've got that on CCTV. Any idea where the wife would be around now?'

'I'm guessing at work. She's a nurse.'

'Where?' *Did Louise know the woman?*

'She's with the renal unit at Heavitree Hospital.'

That would be a no, then. Shame. 'OK. Get over there, see what she has to say for herself when he's not around to influence her. Especially when she knows he's going out and about with one of his co-workers.'

He heard the suck of air over the line and Jill's voice came from a distance. 'That's a bit harsh if he turns out not to be guilty.'

'We haven't got time to play nice, Jill.'

'I'll pass that on, boss,' Dick said.

'No need. I heard.'

'You go see her, I'll see you later. I'd best get back to Matt Forrester, see if he's sufficiently marinaded.' He hung up and headed back to the custody suite. He'd almost reached the door to Graham's bolt-hole when it opened and Ben stepped out.

'Hey, boss. I was just coming to find you.'

'Why? What have you got?'

'Henry Marston and Claire Muir, still on foot, going up Holloway towards his new place on Bull Meadow. You know that camera down by the bus stop? Caught them nicely.'

'When?'

'A few minutes after that last sighting of them on South Street.'

'So they were headed to his new place on foot. Her car was in Princesshay, as usual. His wasn't. Was it at the house?'

'Don't know, but we can check.'

Do that, Ben. Good work.'

Pete clapped him on the shoulder and continued down the corridor towards the custody suite.

Back in the interview room with Matthew Forrester and his solicitor, he sat down, switched the recorder back on and reintroduced everyone for the sake of the discs. 'So, Mr Forrester, have you had time to think about what we were discussing a few minutes ago?'

'Mm-hmm.'

He sounded reluctant, but at least it was an answer of sorts.

'And have you decided to co-operate?'

'The way you put it, what choice do I have?'

'I wasn't trying to pressurise you in any way, Matthew. I was just pointing out the facts of the situation.' The intimacy of switching to his first name was quite deliberate at this stage. Pete wanted him on-side, saying as much as he could. 'So, my last question to you was about who it is that you're so scared of. Who it is that's really in charge of things. Who called for this contract to be put out on a police officer here in Exeter.' He still didn't mention that that police officer was himself. It would put him in a position of vulnerability that wouldn't suit his purpose at all. He needed to appear in control. And he didn't know if Forrester was actually aware of who the target was intended to be. That was a question he was saving for later, towards the end of the interview. 'If it's not Gagik Petrosyan with his reputation for ruthlessness and violence, then who is it, Matthew? Do you prefer Matthew or Matt, by the way? I noticed your wife called you Matt.'

Keep him on his toes, his mind whirling in different directions. Easier to control that way.

'Either's fine. Petrosyan's just muscle. A front. A hard man to keep the plebs in order. The brains is one of our drivers, except he's a lot more than that. Look into the company paperwork, you'll find he owns half of it, through a front company.'

Pete waited.

'It's Davit. Davit Achabaihan.'

CHAPTER THIRTY-TWO

Pete sat very still, fighting to keep his expression neutral. 'You're saying that Davit Achabaihan is the man behind the Armenian? The real boss of the city's biggest drug gang?'

'That's right. You didn't think it was Petrosyan, did you? He hasn't got the brains for something as complex as that.'

'Complex how? What do you know about the setup?' Pete leaned forward, elbows on the table.

Forrester shook his head. 'Not much. I don't have anything to do with it. Never have. I'm just a... *Was* just an ordinary businessman. Until a few months after I took Achabaihan on as a driver. Then he came to me with a proposition. More like one of those "Offers you can't refuse," actually. He has the stuff brought in by a firm based up near Heathrow. East Europeans, like him. They bring it in from the far East. Hong Kong, Cambodia – I don't know. Ship it over this way to wherever he has it processed. Somewhere remote. Off the grid. Literally. He uses power from a solar array; he told me that once. No tracing it, that way. And his distributors take it on from there. He doesn't get his hands dirty. He's just the CEO. The man behind the scenes. A silent partner, like he is with me. He uses our companies to launder the proceeds.'

Pete concentrated completely on Forrester as he spoke, barely even aware of the solicitor sitting beside him. 'Have you got evidence to back any of this up?'

'I told you: the company documents. Other than that, I dare say there's some way a forensic accountant could figure out what's going on as far as the money laundering side of it. I don't know. I'm not one. And as for tying Davit into it directly, like I said, he stays at least one step back from it all – two or three steps if he can. Pay as you go phones that he buys second-hand. Meetings in his car, pretending to be taking them somewhere. He even makes them pay the fare, to keep it above suspicion.'

He was Petrosyan's taxi driver of choice, Pete recalled. *If this is true, there's got to be some way of tying him into it.* 'What does he do with the proceeds? He doesn't live lavish.' He remembered the nineteen-thirties semi he'd visited once during the investigation that led to Petrosyan's arrest, the year before.

'I don't know. Swiss bank account, strong-room under his mum's house in Albania...' Forrester shrugged. 'No idea. And frankly, the less I know, the better I like it. The less I know, the safer I feel.'

'Well, obviously I'm not going to just take your word for all this. It's going to take some investigation to confirm or not.'

'So, I suggest you bail my client while you conduct those investigations, Detective Sergeant. They won't be swift, I don't suppose.'

Pete shook his head, the solicitor coming back into his sphere of awareness. 'Bail him? On a charge of conspiracy to murder a police officer? I'll give you one thing, Mr Humphries: you've got a very rich and very dry sense of humour. Either that or no grasp whatsoever on reality. Your client's staying with us here until my investigations are completed. And that's a concession to the fact that Gagik Petrosyan and most of his gang are already in the city jail, so your client might be at risk of harm if he went there.'

*

'OK, Jill. Well done. Thanks for that.' Pete put the phone down and referred to his notebook as he picked it straight up again and dialled.

'Customer Services, Christine speaking. How can I help?'

'Christine, its DS Gayle. Do you know if your boss is out of his meeting yet?'

'He should be. They normally end in time for lunch. Do you want me to check?'

'If you could, please.'

'OK, hold on.' There was a click, followed by some bland muzak. Then another click. 'DS Gayle?'

'Hello.'

'He's in his office. Do you want me to transfer you?'

'No need,' Pete said quickly. 'I just wanted to make sure you're both there and available. I need to come round there for a quick chat. It won't take many minutes, but it is important and fairly urgent.'

'OK.' She sounded dubious.

'Nothing to worry about, it's just something I need to check with you both about Claire. I'll be there in a few minutes.'

'OK, I'll tell him.'

Pete put the phone down and left his seat, slipping his jacket on and checking that his radio and his mobile phone were in the pockets as he went.

It was approaching mid-afternoon. The school pick-up run would be in its early stages. Traffic would be heavier than it would have been half an hour ago but it still wouldn't take him long to get down to the insurance company offices, especially in the big, brightly liveried patrol car. People tended to get out of the way if they could, whether or not the blue lights were spinning on the roof. Nobody wanted to attract the undue attention of the police.

It took him just under ten minutes to make the short drive, most of the time spent in the queue down Heavitree Road to the roundabout on Western Avenue. Once he turned left into the redbrick canyon of the inner ring road, he was there in less than two minutes. He parked in front of the main doors of the high-rise and walked in, ignoring the receptionist as he headed for the lifts and pressed the button for the third floor.

When the lift doors opened he stepped out and headed along the wide corridor towards what had been Claire Muir's department.

As he stepped in, he saw that her office at the back was unoccupied, but Christine Thackeray was at a desk just outside it in the large open plan area. Her short blonde ponytail was waving quickly as she spoke into her phone. She looked up at the opening door and seeing him, waved him over. By the time he'd reached her desk, she'd finished the call she was on, hung up and removed the headset she'd been speaking into.

'Hello,' she said. 'I spoke to Richard. He's expecting us.'

'Thanks.' Pete shook her hand. It was small and delicate, but her grip was sure as she used his hand to help her to her feet.

'Shall we?'

He nodded, appreciating both her efficiency and her sense of humour, playing the part of the lady while making it clear that's exactly what she was doing – playing a part. 'Delighted, ma'am.'

She giggled then stopped as she released his hand. 'Sorry. It feels almost wrong to laugh in the circumstances.'

'It's not. Trust me. It's part of the way we cope.'

'Hmm. Still doesn't feel right.' She led the way across the open plan space and along the corridor, past the lifts to where Richard Dunne's office, at the front of the building, overlooked the river and the twin bridges of the Alphington Road gyratory with their tall and graceful superstructure standing stark white against the bright blue sky.

The high window at the end of the corridor in front of them gave the same view. From the third floor it wasn't a panoramic view, but it was elevated enough to see across the heavily trafficked roads towards the estate where, a few months ago, Pete had visited the

Armenian drug dealer Gagik Petrosyan in his home after the sudden death of one of his lieutenants in a road accident that was far from accidental.

And now he was being told that Petrosyan was no more than a front for the real boss of the drug gang. The taxi driver, Davit Achabaihan. He was still struggling to get his head around the idea but, in some ways, it made an ironic kind of sense. It went against every cliché that Petrosyan represented. It was the perfect cover.

Christine knocked on Dunne's door and went in, Pete consciously clicking his mind back into focus as he followed her. Dunne stood up from behind his desk and extended a firm, dry hand. 'Please, sit.' He indicated the two chairs that had been set in front of his desk, in preparation for the meeting. 'How can we help?' he asked when Pete and Christine had complied.

Pete drew a breath and plunged straight in. 'What can either of you tell me about Henry Marston and how he got on with Claire?'

Dunne blinked. 'Henry? He's had his issues, but I think they got on OK, in the main?' he turned the statement into a question as he referred to Christine.

'They got on fine as colleagues – as equals - but not so much after she got the promotion. For one thing, he'd been great pals with Nathan and for another, he went for the job too. And he'd been with the company longer, so he thought he ought to get it. When he didn't, he didn't take it very well. There was some tension. She tried to be as supportive as she could with him, but it came to a head a few weeks ago. It seemed to have calmed down recently, though.'

Pete was nodding. 'I see. How long ago did things flare up between them?'

'About four or five weeks, I suppose.'

'And they'd improved again, as of when?'

She grimaced. 'Maybe a fortnight. It took him a while to calm down.'

'So, what happened? Other than the promotion.'

'As I said, he's had some problems, the last several months and, well, I suppose he made one too many mistakes. Claire took him to task over it. She had to. She wasn't blatant about it or anything, took him off for a private talk, but he... Well, as I say, he didn't take it well.'

'But until then...?'

She shrugged. 'They'd been OK for some time. He seemed to have got over the situation with the promotion. They were back to the old banter and so on. I know he'd had some pressures at home and lately he'd bought a new house; been doing it up every minute of his spare time. I think he'd even invited Claire to see it.'

Pete's eyebrows rose. 'When was that?'

'I don't know. She mentioned it in the pub. That would have been... Friday, maybe? The Friday before she was killed.'

'And do you know if she agreed to go?'

'No.' She shook her head, ponytail swinging. 'She was friendly, helpful and all that, but she knew where to draw the line. She told him maybe after they'd moved in.'

Pete's lips pressed together as he nodded. 'OK. Thanks for that.'

'You think Henry was... You think he killed her?'

Pete shook his head. 'We're just eliminating possibilities, Miss Thackeray. We don't think anything until the evidence leads us to.'

*

As soon as he was out of the building, though, Pete was on the phone to the squad room.

'Have you got the address of Henry Marston's new house?'

'Of course. It's number seven, Temple Road. Why?'

'Get a warrant to search it and meet me there, Dick. I know Ben and Jill are working on the Forresters' company books and Dave was taking her home, but bring whoever's available so we can speed the job up.'

'A warrant? On what grounds?'

'That our main suspect was seen approaching the place on foot with the victim just a short time before she was killed, Dick. What more do you need?'

'OK. I'll talk to the guvnor. Dave called a couple of minutes ago. He's on the way back.'

'Did she do as we suggested and pack a bag, go off somewhere untraceable for a few days?'

'Yes. I don't know where. Dave didn't ask.'

'Good. Be prepared when you get to the address. Our man's probably on-site despite the fact he's supposed to be at work.'

'Right. Mob-handed then.'

'And quick about it.'

Pete hung up and climbed into the car. He started the engine and drove out of the car park and across to the junction that led up onto the Topsham Road. He wouldn't go in alone, but it would be foolish to sit here when he could be making sure from the end of the street that their suspect didn't go anywhere before they were ready for him.

CHAPTER THIRTY-THREE

The Marstons' new home was without doubt the oldest on the narrow dead-end lane that overlooked the expanse of Bull Meadow Park. The houses were all large, old and widely spaced but all the others were of Victorian brick whereas theirs was stone. The other main visual difference was the state of the hedges and the gardens behind them. All the rest were neatly trimmed and manicured. Henry Marston – and, it seemed, the owner before him – had clearly not had the time to follow suit.

The lane itself was just one car wide. It felt rural and remote as Pete drove slowly and quietly along it, despite being just a few minutes' walk from the cathedral on one side and the hospital where his wife worked on the other.

It was pretty much the perfect location for them. Pete wondered how long they'd had to wait for the old boy who'd lived here since the 1940's to die so they could buy it at auction for little more than half what it would be worth once done up to modern standards. Or had they waited…? He made a mental note to check on the old man's cause of death when he got back to the station.

Pete was in the middle one of three cars with a van following behind. The space here was much more confined than it had been out at the caravan park so he thought ten of them ought to be plenty to take one man into custody. And although he'd never met the man, he didn't imagine he was even remotely similar to the Krasniqi brothers in any way whatsoever. He was a thirty-something telephone operator with no police record, not a thug of any kind.

He stopped himself as they pulled up just inside the end of the lane. 'Don't make assumptions, Pete,' he muttered aloud, switching off the engine. 'They are the mother of all fuck-ups.'

Once again, he mentally thanked Steven Seagal for making the movie that quote came from. As thoroughly over the top and wildly implausible as the rest of the film was, that line had always stuck with him.

He stepped out of the car and waved the rest of the crew over. Dick and Dave had ridden in the car in front of Pete, Jane in the one that had come up the lane behind him. With them were several uniformed officers including, for this event, Sergeant Andy Fairweather himself.

'So, what are we dealing with?' Fairweather asked, his grizzled features even more crinkled and lined than ever, out here in the bright sunshine.

'Single suspect. Male. Mid-thirties. No criminal record. No history of violence that we know of. Except that what he's suspected of is killing his boss with a hammer and dumping her body in Ashclyst woods last Tuesday night with a fire burning between her legs.' Pete looked around the assembled officers. 'I recognise a couple of you from the scene, so you know what that was like. He's been under a lot of pressure for the past several months, both at work and at home, so he may be unpredictable. We don't want to risk his putting any innocent bystanders in harm's way, hence the mob-handed approach. Initially, I'll go in. I'll take Jane with me. A female presence can have a calming effect, although it's not guaranteed, of course. We'll knock on the front door, see if he responds. Dave, you can take a couple of the guys around the back quietly before we do that. Make sure he doesn't do a runner out that way. We need all the vehicles manned in case he manages to get past us out the front. We'll use all three cars to block the entrance to his place. Andy, if you watch us through his hedge, you can call them up. Get them into position as soon as Jane and I go out of sight. Also at that point – or faster if he makes a break for it – I need his car covered. It's parked in the front garden. We don't want him getting in it. We can break the glass to get him out of course, but there's no telling what he's got in there. There could be a weapon. So we need at least one other officer with Andy to deal with that. We want nothing left to chance, OK? Questions?'

He looked around the assembled faces again but saw no response. 'Right, let's do it.

He tossed the keys of the patrol car he'd been using to one of the PC's and set off on foot up the narrow lane with Jane, Dave, Andy Fairweather and three uniformed constables. They parted at the gate to the old stone house that Henry Marston and his wife had bought to do up and make into their home.

So much for that plan, if Henry really did murder Claire Muir. Pete looked around his now smaller team. 'Everybody ready?'

He was answered with a series of nods.

'Here we go, then.' He stepped up to the gate for the second time in fifteen minutes but this time he opened it and went through, followed by Jane, Dave and two of the constables while Andy and the other constable stayed outside, crouched behind the tall, unkempt hedge having found a point where they could peer through the greenery.

The front garden was a mass of weeds and straggly, unmown grass, brightened in patches by Spring flowers peeking through the mess. Parked on the moss and weed-choked gravel in front of the house, the tumble-down detached garage ignored, was Henry Marston's black Nissan car. The front door of the house was closed but a couple of the upstairs windows were partially open, Pete saw as he heard the sound of a power tool from within.

He nodded to Dave, who led his two companions at a run up to the side of the house and out of sight around it as Pete and Jane strolled up to the front door, giving them time to get into position while at the same time giving their suspect, if he happened to glance out of a window, the impression that all was well in the world. Just two visitors approaching his front door.

Reaching the heavy old brown-painted door, Pete knocked loudly. The sound of the drill or sander or whatever it was continued for a few moments longer. Had he not heard? Then the noise stopped and Pete took the opportunity to knock again, to make sure.

'Hold on,' came the call from within. Moments later, the door in front of them opened and Pete saw Henry Marston for the first time in any other form than his staff ID photo. He was pretty much covered in plaster dust from head to toe, apart from areas around his mouth, nose and eyes which were clean but damp with sweat. Even his hair was pink.

He looked from Pete to Jane and back again. 'What can I do for you?'

'You could answer a couple of questions,' Pete suggested, holding up his warrant card. 'I'm DS Gayle. This is DC Bennett.'

'Questions?' He swallowed. Went to knock some of the dust off but stopped himself just in time. 'Sorry. About what?'

'About your colleague. Claire Muir.'

'Claire? What about her? I gather she hasn't been in for a few days but I don't know why.'

Pete nodded, noting the expansive nature of his response. 'Well, it's about that, actually. Would you mind coming down to the station and talking to us there?'

He stepped back, turning slightly and Pete tensed, ready to follow if he ran for it. 'Well, I'm kind of in the middle of some stuff at the minute. Could it wait an hour or two? I could get cleaned up, at least.' He looked down, spreading his hands to show the mess he was in.

'Well, I'm sure our cleaners would prefer that option,' Pete admitted. 'But it's not that kind of mess that concerns us at the minute. It's the one that Claire was left in, the other night and what we think you might be able to tell us about that.'

'But I already spoke to your colleague, earlier. Big fellow. DI, I think.'

Was he trying to pull rank? Pete wasn't sure but it wasn't going to do him any good, either way. 'DI Underhill, yes. We're aware of that but some further information's come to light since then so we really do need to speak to you more formally at this stage.

And we also have a warrant to search these premises.' Pete pulled the document out of his jacket and unfolded it.

'A warrant? Why? On what grounds?'

He was starting to show signs of agitation now. As well he might, Pete thought, but it would make no difference to what was about to happen. 'On the grounds that we suspect this is the location where Claire Muir was killed last Tuesday afternoon or evening,' he said firmly. 'Now, you can come with us willingly or we can arrest you. Your choice. The only significant difference is whether you're wearing cuffs when you walk out of here.'

'No. No way.' He stepped back quickly and reached for the door to slam it in their faces but Jane was too quick for him. She stepped forward and slipped through the space he'd left as Pete's arm came up to stop the door's movement, his foot stamping down on the filthy but ornately tiled floor at its base.

'Henry Marston, I'm arresting you for hindering a police investigation and for the murder of Claire Muir. You do not…'

'No!' he repeated more loudly, drowning Pete out. 'No, no, no, no, no!'

Pete pushed back on the door. Marston struggled with him until Jane forced his head forward against the heavy wood and dragged one arm up behind his back. A knee to the back of his leg brought him hard down to his knees. He cried out again, this time at the pain as his knees hit the hard floor and Pete slipped inside to help her. Handed over a pair of cuffs that she snapped onto his captive wrist before pulling his other arm behind him.

Marston slumped, head hanging as he repeated over and over, his tone bereft, 'No, no, no, no, no.'

Pete finished quoting the caution and asked if he understood but Marston was beyond the penetration of normal conversation or even reason, it appeared. He just kept mumbling, 'No, no, no. No, no, no. No, no, no.'

'We'll help you out to the car,' Pete said and hooked his forearms under Marston's armpits to lift him to his feet.

It wasn't until they got outside and the sun hit his face that Marston seemed to react. He ducked away from the brightness then looked up, turning towards Pete. 'You don't understand. You don't understand.'

'No, we don't,' Jane admitted from his other side. 'But we want to. That's why we're here. So we can get to the truth: understand what happened.'

CHAPTER THIRTY-FOUR

'Jesus!' Pete barely managed not to slam the brakes on and cause a multi-vehicle pileup as realisation suddenly dawned partway up the back street leading back to Heavitree Road and the police station. 'What the hell? Why didn't I think of that before?'

'What?' Dave asked from the passenger seat next to him.

'The bloody solicitor's brothers. The Boshnjakus. They've got an import-export business in Hayes. Which is only just across the M25 from Heathrow. And what did Forrester say? Achabaihan uses an import-export company near Heathrow to pick up his goods from there and bring them over this way to his processing plant. Who got Petrosyan his solicitor, eh? What's the betting it was Achabaihan? And what's the betting he got him that one because of the connection through his brothers?'

'It would make sense,' Dave agreed.

'Wouldn't it? When we get back, I'm going to nip up to the office quick and make a phone call. You can book our buddy in, can't you?'

'Of course.'

Pete reached the end of the narrow side-road and turned left onto Heavitree Road, heading down towards the station.

'What else do we need at this stage?' Dave asked.

'Some good results from Jane and Dick's search of the house back there, preferably with some nice, juicy forensics. Other than that, it depends. If you're right about Lucy knowing nothing about Achabaihan other than he's a part-owner of the company – what was it, he wanted somewhere to invest his spare cash?' He grunted.

'What spare cash would a taxi-driver have, for Christ's sake? Then, once we get the first nugget of information on him, we'll need search warrants for his house and any other property he might own. Including his car, phone and bank accounts. And we'll need to serve them double-quick. But first, we need that initial break because, without it, we've got nothing. Let's hope Ben and Jill have come up with something good. If not, we'll need to locate him and set up surveillance.'

'Oh, great. Another night on the tiles with Jane.'

'I'm sure she'll be equally keen.' Pete turned into the station and drove up to the car park at the rear. Locking the car remotely as they crossed towards the back door, he went in, followed by the others, and headed quickly upstairs.

Jill looked up as he entered. 'Hey, boss. Did you get him?'

'We did. Surprisingly easily. Dave's booking him in downstairs. How've you two got on?'

Ben took his hands off his keyboard and looked up. 'We started with the taxi firm's books. It's true – Davit Achabaihan does own a fifty percent share of the company and of their delivery company. Beyond that, though, we were out of our depth. I sent everything on to the specialists at Middlemoor and we moved on with stuff we could make head or tail of. We know he's got no police record. He wouldn't have a taxi licence if he had, of course, but we did check again, just in case. Also, on the basis that if he was dealing in drugs on that sort of scale, he'd want somewhere to do it away from his home, we did a land registry search.' He pressed his lips together briefly. 'That's where the bad news comes in.'

'Which is?' Pete hung his jacket on the back of his chair and sat down.

'He has got another place, but it's out of our bailiwick. In Avon and Somerset's, actually. Out in the levels. A place called Wedmore.'

'Really? What sort of a place are we looking at?'

'Well, that's what I was just doing, boss – looking at it via Google Maps. It's out on the edge of the village, remote but not too remote, up a dead-end road. An old farm with some big buildings and a great big solar panel array taking up an entire field.'

'So, off the beaten and off-grid. Ideal.' Pete smiled. 'Good work.' He opened his notebook, picked up the phone and dialled.

'ADB Imports. How can I help?' The voice on the line was young, female and very definitely English. Cockney, even.

'Hello. This is Pete Gayle. I'm down here in Exeter, in Devon. I'm wondering if your blokes come down this way much?' Pete emphasised his natural accent, making himself sound like a yokel.

'Devon? Don't think so, no. Bit off our patch. We've got one client in Somerset, but that's as close as we get, why?'

'Well, I've got a little job needs doing, I thought maybe it could piggy-back on one of your deliveries but, if you don't come this far… Somerset's only next-door, though. Whereabouts in Somerset? It might be practical.'

'A little out-of-the-way place called Wedmore.'

'Blimey, that's a bit remote, isn't it? How'd you land a job out there, from where you are?'

'Oh, the bloke who owns the place is an old friend of the family up here.'

'Ah. Well, I'll tell you what, love. It's only a one-off job but it is probably half a load so, if it's too much to add onto a delivery, that's fine. I'll see what else I can come up with. Don't want to mess a regular customer around, do you?'

'If you gimme a number I can ask the bosses and get back to you,' she offered.

'That's fair.' Pete gave her his mobile number. 'You can get me on that anytime, love. Nice to talk to you.'

'Bye.'

He hung up and immediately redialled, this time from memory. Again, it was picked up within three rings.

'Avon and Somerset police. How can I help?'

'This is DS Pete Gayle of Devon and Cornwall police. Can you put me through to your drugs squad?'

'One moment, sir.' The line clicked, was silent for a beat then started ringing again.

'Hello? DC Washbourne speaking.'

Pete introduced himself again. 'I need to speak to your department chief.'

'I'm sorry, sir. He's in a meeting at the moment.'

'Then I'm sorry, but you'll need to get him out of it. This is a matter of urgency. We suspect there's a major drugs processing and distribution hub on your patch and the owner may suspect that we're onto him.'

'Well, that'll be news to us, if it's true.'

Pete stopped himself from saying what popped into his mind. 'Have you heard of a place called Wedmore, Constable?'

'No.'

Pete sighed. 'Right. As I said, I need to speak to your squad chief, ASAP.'

'He's not going to be happy about it.'

'He'll be a damn site happier if he can take the credit for closing down a distribution hub that covers your patch along with large parts of ours and Dorset's, among others, before the gang running it get wind of the fact we're onto them and do a disappearing act.'

'Hold on.'

The phone clattered onto Washbourne's desk before Pete could respond. Pete shook his head. 'And they have the cheek to call us bloody yokels! Jesus!'

He waited for the Bristol detective constable to do what he'd been asked. It seemed to take an age. Pete began to wonder if he'd been cut off, but the dial tone hadn't returned so he must still be connected. Was Washbourne leaving him hanging deliberately, just to piss him off? Then, after what seemed like several minutes, there was another scraping noise and the DC's voice was back, if only briefly.

'Hold on.'

A click sounded, a buzz followed by another receiver being picked up. A deep, masculine voice said, 'This is DCI Haverhill.'

'DS Gayle from Exeter, sir. A witness has given us some intel on a significant drug operation that's based partly here in Exeter and partly in your neck of the woods. We believe the drugs are being imported and shipped to a location in Wedmore, Somerset, for processing. There's an isolated farm on the edge of the village, up a dead-end road called Windmill Lane. It's owned by our chief suspect and it has significant outbuildings and a solar farm so it could be operated off-grid to reduce the chances of detection. I've also just learned that it receives regular deliveries from the Heathrow area. The trouble is that the suspect, one Davit Achabaihan, may have already learned that we're onto him so time is of the essence. Otherwise I wouldn't have had your meeting interrupted, sir.'

'I see. Thank you, Detective Sergeant. Who's your guvnor?'

Pete winced at the thought of this man contacting DCI Silverstone. 'DI Colin Underhill, sir.'

'Underhill? I met him the other week, didn't I? On a course here in Bristol.'

'Quite possibly, sir. He did go on one there.'

'Right. OK. I'll get some eyes on the place. Windmill Lane, Wedmore, you say?'

'That's right, sir. Should I send you over a picture of our man Achabaihan so your men can ask anyone there if they recognise him?'

'Excellent idea, Detective Sergeant. Do that, would you?'

Pete picked up his mobile phone with his free hand and called up a photo of the taxi driver. 'What's your email address, sir?'

The Bristol man quoted a police email address and Pete typed it in as he spoke. 'Got it. Picture's on the way, sir. Thanks for your help.'

'And thank you for yours, DS Gayle. We'll let you know what we find.'

Pete ended the call, put his mobile phone away too and sat back. 'Right, that's out of our hands now,' he said. 'I'll go and see if Dave's booked Henry Marston into the cells.' He was in the act of standing up when his mobile rang. He took it out of his pocket and sat back down when he saw the name on the screen.

'Guv?'

'Just to let you know, I've finally persuaded Malcolm Burton to tell us what he knows about Adrian Southam. There isn't much. What there is, I'll pass onto Mark in a minute, but I thought you should be the first to know.'

'Thanks, guv. When you say, "Not much," what exactly does that mean?'

'The name of one of his victims. The location of another. We'll have to wait and see if there's any forensics to link him to her.'

'Yes. You might get a call shortly. I was just talking to a mate of yours from Bristol. DCI Haverhill.'

While Pete briefly updated the DI the rest of his team came into the squad room and took their seats. He hung up and looked around the assembled faces. 'Any bad news to ruin my mood before I go and see what Marston's got to say for himself?'

Heads were shaken.

'Any good news for me to take downstairs to him?' He focussed on Jane and Dick as he asked the question.

'Yes,' said Jane. 'From our point of view. Not so much from his. We found blood. Initial typing matches it to Claire Muir. It was on the skirting board inside one of the bedrooms upstairs and on the neck of a hammer in the kitchen. Also, forensics say the carpet on the stairs and landing is a visual match to the fibres found on her coat and in her hair. They've taken samples to make sure.'

'Excellent.' He stood up again as, behind him, Mark Bridgman's desk phone rang and was picked up. He went along to the kitchenette and made coffee for everyone, took them back and set them on his desk. 'Enjoy,' he said. 'You deserve it. And when you've finished yours, Dave, get out there on that bike and find Davit Achabaihan. Don't arrest him. Just find him and keep an eye on him so we can grab him up as soon as we hear back from the boys in Bristol.'

He took his coffee with him as he headed for the stairs. In the custody suite, he asked the female duty sergeant, 'Which interview room's free, Karen?'

'You can have one or two.'

'I'll take two for a change. And Henry Marston.'

Two minutes later, he was seated in the room, his half-empty mug on the desk in front of him and the digital recorder set up ready to go when there was a knock on the door and Marston was shown in by a uniformed constable. Pete showed the man to a seat, took a sip of his drink and said, 'Do you want anything, Henry? A drink?'

Marston shook his head.

'OK. You know why you're here, don't you?'

A nod.

'And you're willing to talk to me about it?'

Marston's lips pressed together for a moment but then he nodded.

'All right, then.' Pete reached for the recorder and started it rolling. 'Interview with Henry Marston of... Should I record the house you now own or the one you're currently renting, Henry?'

Marston frowned as if he didn't imagine it made any difference.

'Number seven Temple Road, Exeter, then,' Pete said for the recording. 'With myself, Detective Sergeant Peter Gayle of Heavitree Road police station, Major Crimes Unit.' He rarely used the squad's official title. People still understood CID much more readily. But for the sake of officialdom, he felt obliged to in interviews. 'Henry, you've been arrested with regard to the death of Claire Muir, your late team leader at Portside Insurance Ltd, where you're both employed. You've said you're willing to talk about that here. I should remind you that if, at any time, that ceases to be the case, you're perfectly entitled to the presence of a solicitor, OK?'

Again, he was merely trying to draw a response from the man across the table and again, all he got was a nod.

'Henry, I'm not here to try to get you to admit anything. There really isn't any need. We've got all the evidence we need of *what* happened. There's CCTV footage of you and Claire walking towards your house a short time before she died, forensics proving that's where she was killed. All that side of it is established fact. The only thing I want to ask you about is why it happened.'

Henry raised his eyes from the tabletop and looked him in the eyes at last but still didn't speak. His eyes were haunted, grief-stricken and moist, his breathing so faint it was almost non-existent. This was no longer a man in panic mode. He clearly and obviously regretted what he'd done but he was fully aware of it. The only thing he didn't know was how to explain it – at least, how best to put the reasons behind it into words.

'Why now?' Pete asked, still trying to provoke a reaction. 'Why throw away everything you've achieved in life – your wife, your career, your new house – on a moment's... What? Madness? Rage? Frustration? Revenge? What was it that made this the only way forward, Henry?'

Marston's eyes had tightened as Pete spoke, his lips pressing together then curling into a sneer. No, a snarl, Pete decided. A sneer.

'What was it that made you so angry with her?'

'Career?' Henry said at last. 'I never had a career. My only chance at that was when Nathan left. And she took that away. Claire. We'd been friends. She knew how much it meant to me, to get that promotion, but she went after it anyway. Some friend! She was always going to get it over me. Equality and all that shit. So-called equality. Bloody farce, that is. Just making the numbers match, whether it's justified or not. So, yes, there was frustration. Anger. Resentment. Especially when she showed her true colours afterwards. Condescending bitch. It took me months – months! – to reach the point of being able to have a civil conversation with her after that. And then one mistake. One mistake!' He waggled a finger at Pete. 'And it's not even as if it was my fault. Bloody woman just wouldn't listen when I was trying to explain to her. Then she put in a complaint about me, and Claire-bloody-bitch Muir hauled me into her office in front of everyone, ranting and moaning as if I was a ten-year old in the headmaster's office. What gave her the right, eh? Tell me that, if you can. She hadn't even been with the company as long as me. Five years, I've been there. Five years! And she comes in, Miss Jenny-come-lately, tearing me off a strip as if I don't know how to do the job. Hell, yes, I was angry. Who wouldn't be?'

Pete had been nodding encouragingly, letting him rant, letting him get it all out, off his chest, into the open, hoping for what he appeared to be building up to. But now he seemed to expect an answer. 'You're right, Henry. Anyone would be.'

'That's right. Anyone would. Anyone would. And I was. So bloody angry! It was like I was right back at the beginning again, all that effort wasted. I was going to have to start all over again. I couldn't face that. I just thought, to hell with it. Let's try a different approach. One step instead of hundreds. Show her I wasn't completely useless. Show her what I'd achieved with the house. In my spare time. In just a few weeks. It's not like I'm a builder or anything. She knew that. I thought she'd be impressed. How wrong can you be, eh? I could see it in her face. She wasn't impressed. Not at all. And then she said it.' His forearms slammed down on the table, his eyes wild. 'Said maybe this was why my work was suffering. *My work was suffering!* How could she? I snapped. I just... Snapped. I'd been putting up a picture rail in the room we were in. It's an old house. They'd have had them in those days. The hammer and nails were still there on the floor. I just picked it up and lashed out. And then...' He shook his head. 'She was... She was still breathing. So I hit her again. I don't know how many times. But then she wasn't breathing any more, but I was! God, I was panting like a dog on a hot day! And it reminded me. It reminded me of how I'd often fantasised about... About having sex with her. Rough sex. Rougher than she'd have wanted it. Putting her in her place: that kind of sex. So I... I didn't actually do it. She was dead already.' The horror on his face seemed genuine to Pete, but he was on a roll, in the flow, so he let him ramble on. 'I just made her look like that's what might have happened. Like the tart she really was. Then I... I rolled her up in some polythene that one of the doors for the house had come wrapped in and waited for dark to take her out and put her somewhere to be found.'

Having said it all, he simply stopped, perfectly calm now as he met Pete's gaze like there was nothing wrong in the world. Like all he'd just said was perfectly normal and acceptable.

'OK, Henry,' Pete said. 'Thank you for that. Are you sure you don't want that drink now?'

'Yes, I think I will, thank you. A tea, please. Two sugars.'

'No problem. Interview concluded at...' He checked his watch. 'Good grief. It's ten past three. Where's the time gone, eh?' He switched off the recorder. 'Right. Teatime it is.'

CHAPTER THIRTY-FIVE

The call came in an hour after Henry Marston had been returned to his cell.

When Pete got back upstairs to the squad room, DS Mark Bridgman and his whole team were gone. All they'd said to anyone before they left was that they were following up on a lead. Pete could guess what lead, in what case. But even if he was right – even if they found the body they were looking for – there was no guarantee that it would hold any forensic evidence of who the killer was. It could be Adrian Southam. It could equally be Malcolm Burton, trying to pass the buck, to drop the other man in it and thereby save his own skin.

Dave, Jane reported, had found Achabaihan in his blue Skoda hatchback within fifteen minutes of leaving the station and was following him discretely, as ordered. 'Don't know how long he's going to manage to be discreet, though,' she added. 'It's a bit too close to subtle for Dave.'

Pete smiled. 'It's a stretch, I know, but the bike gives him a degree of flexibility that a car would lack. And I only asked him to watch the bloke. What could go wrong with that?' He grimaced. 'On second thoughts, don't answer that.'

They were typing up their case reports when Pete's phone rang. An external call. He picked it up. 'DS Gayle.'

'Haverhill here. I said I'd call back.'

'Yes, sir. Thank you. What happened at the farm?'

'A lot more than we expected, Detective Sergeant. We were greeted with semi-automatic gunfire. A couple of assault rifles.'

'Blimey,' Pete blurted.

'Thankfully, we'd taken an armed unit, considering the possibilities you'd outlined, and no-one got hurt. At least on our side. The opposition suffered a casualty and one wounding. He's now under police guard in the BRI, handcuffed to a bed while he recovers from surgery enough to be arrested. A highly sophisticated set-up they'd got there. As you suggested, they were running it off-grid. They'd got ten of the solar panels connected to a battery array to power the place independently. Importing clothes soaked in drug solution, believe it or not. They had a team of fifteen illegal immigrants from east Asia dissolving the drugs out of the clothing, re-concentrating and processing them. The irony is, they were all working naked – presumably to prevent them secreting any of the product away for themselves. And the best they could do for accommodation was a couple of rooms off the side of the processing shed with multiple mattresses on the floor and an electric heater in each. Talk about a fire-risk!'

'They must have been getting through a hell of an inventory, to need fifteen of them,' Pete commented.

'It doesn't bear thinking about,' Haverhill agreed. 'It's going to take a week or two to process the place, never mind getting interpreters in and interviewing the victims – because that's what they were. Slave labour.'

'I don't doubt it, sir. Which gives us yet another charge for our man Achabaihan. Assuming anyone recognised him?'

'They recognised him all right. And they're bloody terrified of him. We didn't need an interpreter to see that.'

'We'll get a warrant signed off then and sweep him up. Thank you for that, sir. Thank you very much.'

'No, thank you, detective. You've helped to wipe out the biggest drug ring I've come across in twenty-two years of policing.'

'Might even get a smile out of my DCI then, sir.'

'If not, he doesn't deserve to be one. But then, from what I've heard…'

'I'm saying nothing, sir. I'll let you know when we've made the arrest.'

'Good man.' Haverhill rang off and Pete allowed himself a smile across the desks at Jane and a high-five to Dick, sitting beside him.

'Jill, take the paperwork through to our lord and master, would you? One arrest warrant for Davit Achabaihan on charges of drug smuggling and distribution. We'll let Avon and Somerset do him for human trafficking and slave labour, seeing as those offences were carried out in their jurisdiction.'

'Right, boss.'

As Jill headed for the DCI's office, Pete took out his mobile phone and used the speed dial function. It was answered almost before the first ring was completed.

'Boss?'

'Call in the cavalry and bring him in, Dave.'

'We've got him?'

'We've got him.'

'Yes! Will do.'

'See you soon.' Pete hung up and dialled a number he'd used once already that day.

'Hello? British Transport Police.'

'Hello. DS Pete Gayle again, Exeter CID. I have reason to believe it might be beneficial to send an officer with a drugs dog to the premises of ADB Imports in Hayes, Middlesex. They seem to have been transporting drug-laden items from Heathrow to an address in Wedmore, Somerset on a regular basis. And if I send you a photograph of our main suspect in the processing and distribution of those drugs, maybe you can check if anyone there recognises him?'

'Of course.'

'Perfect. I'll send it now.'

*

'Gayle. What is this? What's going on?'

Pete sat down beside Dave Miles in interview room one, opposite Davit Achabaihan, who had asked the questions, and his solicitor. The same solicitor as Gagik Petrosyan was using, Pete noted.

'Mr Boshnjaku,' he said, ignoring Achabaihan for now. 'This is something of a conflict of interest, isn't it? Working for Mr Achabaihan at the same time as Mr Petrosyan?'

'How so, detective?'

'Well, the charges against your new client put him in direct conflict with your existing one. I mean, what's his argument going to be? It wasn't me, officer, it was that nasty Armenian gentleman. You can't argue that and, at the same time, argue on behalf of that same gentleman. It wouldn't be ethical.'

'Nor is arresting my client with no evidence linking him to any crimes, detective.'

'Oh, we've got plenty of evidence, Mr Boshnjaku. Against both men. Now, it's time you made a choice. Which one are you representing? Because you can't work for both.'

He glanced at his client. Pete knew that he'd been working for the man beside him all along. It was his duty as well as his pleasure to force the issue.

'I am working for Mr Achabaihan.'

'Then, shall we pause for a moment while you contact Mr Petrosyan and resign as his council?'

'I will do that later.'

Pete shook his head slowly. 'No, Mr Boshnjaku. I can't accept your presence here until it's done. And our twenty-four hours with your client do not commence until he has proper legal representation, having requested it. In the meantime, our investigations will continue. Have you heard from your brothers in Hayes yet? If not, I'm sure you will very soon. Their vehicles and premises are being searched with the help of sniffer dogs as we speak. So, if you want to represent them, I'm afraid you'll have to forego the pleasure of Mr Achabaihan's clientship as well. Because we know exactly what they've been transporting and where to.'

'You...' He stopped, turning his frowning face to Achabaihan and back to Pete. Back and forth. 'You...' Pushing his chair back abruptly, he stood up. 'I quit,' he announced. 'I'm out of here.'

'Sit down,' Achabaihan barked.

'Family comes first,' the solicitor said firmly.

'No. Safety comes first.'

'You threaten me? Here, in a police station with two police to witness?'

'Sit.' Achabaihan's voice was flat and cold.

'No.' The suited man stepped around the table and towards the door. Pete stood up to open it for him.

Returning to his seat, he folded his hands on the table. 'And then there were three,' he said. 'We all know you can afford a solicitor. For now. So I won't offer to provide one.'

'What you mean?' Achabaihan frowned. 'For now.'

'Well, once we seize all your assets as proceeds of crime...' Pete smiled, spreading his hands apart on the desk and sitting back in his chair.

'You have nothing on me. I am innocent bystander.'

'You keep telling yourself that, Davit. We've closed down the place in Wedmore. The transport company in Middlesex is being searched as we speak. We've got the Forresters' company papers and their testimony. At this point, we've even got enough to offer Gagik a deal. I wonder if he'll take it, eh? What do you think? A nice reduction in his sentence in exchange for your arse in a sling? I think he will. No honour among thieves anymore. Especially not among drug dealers and human traffickers. They shoot and stab each other all the time. We both know that. It's all over the news every night, these days.'

'Gloat while you can, Gayle. It won't last.'

Pete chuckled. 'I'm not the type, am I Dave? A quick glow of satisfaction and move on, that's me. Another day, another criminal to drag in off the streets. Or some days, its several criminals. But no doubt you'll want to make a phone call.' He stood up again and they took the Albanian back to the custody desk.

'Mr Achabaihan needs to use the phone, Karen. Needs a new solicitor.'

*

While he was close to the back door, Pete went out and drove to the nearest supermarket, where he bought a box of fancy doughnuts. He took them back for his team to share in celebration of closing not one but two cases and spent the rest of the afternoon typing up case notes, sending the others home promptly at five.

Mark Bridgman's team had been trickling back in from around four onwards but hadn't responded to questions about the case they were working. They were subdued and reticent, keeping to themselves until Mark himself came in some time after Pete's team had gone. Pete was taking little notice. There wasn't much that was going to dampen his mood this afternoon. He was winding up his paperwork, putting the finishing touches to the case files on his computer, aiming to leave in another ten minutes or so when Colin stuck his head out of his office and called him.

Pete turned. Was about to say, "Give me a minute," when Colin jerked his head in a beckoning motion that could have only one meaning. *Now.*

With a quick frown, Pete stood up and walked the length of the squad room towards Colin's door, which had been left open for him.

He stepped in and found Mark Bridgman already there, Colin seated behind his desk, his big hands spread on its top. A single file lay closed near his right hand.

'Shut the door,' Colin said.

Pete complied. 'What's going on?'

Colin nodded to Mark, who pushed himself away from the side wall of the small room.

'We've been out to the location Malcolm Burton gave us for one of the bodies he claimed to know Adrian Southam had left behind.'

'You remember I told you he said he knew the name of one, the location of another,' Colin interjected.

'Yes.'

'Well, we found her,' Mark continued.

'Brilliant. That's what we needed, wasn't it?'

'That's right.'

So why weren't they as jubilant as they ought to be?

'We can't positively identify her yet. She's been dead too long. But initial indications – height, build, hair colour, approximate age, clothing and a birth-mark on her leg – point towards a girl who went missing last June from Chippenham, Wiltshire. Mandy Raines. She was just turned eleven. Had her birthday a week before she vanished. She'd been buried in a ditch between the railway line and a service road that runs alongside it out by Mosshayne.'

Pete was familiar with the name. It was a tiny place on the other side of the M5, out to the east of the city. Completely rural and surprisingly isolated, given that it was only a few minutes' drive from where he stood. 'Well, if it is Mandy Raines, that would support Southams' involvement. But to put her there would take some local knowledge. Which goes along with Burton's involvement. So why aren't we in the pub, toasting a successful outcome?'

Colin drew a deep breath and let it out. 'Well, that's where the bad news comes in,' he said. 'Obviously, we haven't got DNA yet. SOCO tell us they should have results on Thursday for that. So again, it's only initial results, but there's evidence of two perpetrators. One of them might well be Southam. The hand size would match. Certainly bigger than Burton's. The other one, though, appears to have been a juvenile. A boy.'

Pete felt the strength drain from his body as if a plug had been pulled. He reached for Colin's spare chair and sat down. *Tommy.* For the second time, his son was implicated in the death of a young girl.

'Shit,' he murmured. Was this nightmare rollercoaster ever going to end? He looked up at Colin, from him to Mark and back again. 'Are we sure?'

'It's not her own. The angle's wrong,' Colin said. 'Not physically possible. Beyond that, at this stage, as I said, nothing's certain yet, but...' He shrugged.

'Who else would it be?' Pete finished for him with a sick feeling boiling up in his gut. 'Jesus.'

'Sorry, mate.'

'Yeah.' Pete leaned forward to rest his face in his hands.

THE END

NOTE FROM THE AUTHOR

This particular episode of Pete Gayle's ongoing story ends here but he will be back in the next book of the series. I wish I could say what is going to happen, but there are two very good reasons not to. Firstly, it would be inappropriate to give a spoiler at this stage and secondly, I don't yet know myself. All I know is that it won't be another cliff-hanger ending. I know there are many readers who don't like them, just as there are many, including myself, who don't like the device of jumping in at an action scene three quarters of the way through a story and then flipping back to the beginning to lead back up to where you started, but this ending seemed appropriate on this occasion.

I hope, as a reader, you will forgive me for it just this once.

If so, and if you enjoyed reading the book anywhere near as much as I enjoyed writing it, then please do go back to where you purchased it and leave a review, if only a word or two. It is always good to get feedback on what readers like or don't like, what they want or don't want. Authors are, ultimately, here to entertain and are always striving to improve that entertainment. A review is our form of applause or the lack of it – our way of telling if we're getting it right as well as a way for other readers to tell if they might like the book.

I hope you're looking forward as much as I am to Pete's return. All things being equal, it should be later this year. But for now, thank you for reading this book.

Jack Slater. April 2018.

The following links can be used to leave reviews:

https://www.amazon.co.uk/JackSlater/e/B003X8IMEC/ref=dp_byline_cont_ebooks_1

https://www.kobo.com/gb/en/search?query=jack%20slater&fcsearchfield=Author

https://www.barnesandnoble.com/s/jack%20slater/_/N-8qa

You can also contact the author directly by email at jackslaterauthor@mail.com through the website: https://jackslaterauthor.site123.me or on Facebook: https://www.facebook.com/crimewriter2016 where you will find the latest updates on his writing and lots of other relevant content.

DS Pete Gayle returns in **No Middle Ground (DS Peter Gayle thrillers, Book 5).**

A missing father. A desperate daughter. A terrible discovery.

A new case is the last thing DS Pete Gayle needs right now, but when it falls right into his lap, he has no choice. Justice is crying out to be served. With a career-making trial about to begin and his son in imminent danger from a pair of psychopathic brothers, Pete goes on the hunt in what could turn out to be the biggest case of his life.

No Going Back by Jack Slater

Other books by the same author:

Nowhere to Run (DS Peter Gayle thrillers, Book 1)

A missing child. A dead body. A killer on the loose.
Returning to Exeter CID after his son's unsolved disappearance Detective Sergeant Peter Gayle's first day back was supposed to be gentle. Until a young girl is reported missing and the clock begins to tick.

Rosie Whitlock has been abducted from outside her school that morning. There are no clues, but Peter isn't letting another child disappear.

When the body of another young victim appears, the hunt escalates. Someone is abducting young girls and now they have a murderer on their hands. Time is running out for Rosie, but when evidence in the case relating to his own son's disappearance is discovered the stakes are even higher…

No Place to Hide (DS Peter Gayle thrillers, Book 2)

A house fire. A suspicious death. A serial killer to catch.
When a body is found in a house fire DS Peter Gayle is called to the scene. It looks like an accidental death, but the evidence just doesn't add up.

With only one murder victim they can't make any calls, but it looks like a serial killer is operating in Exeter and it's up to Pete to track him down.

But with his wife still desperate for news on their missing son and his boss watching his every move, the pressure is on for Pete to bring the murderer to justice before it is too late.

No Way Home (DS Peter Gayle thrillers, Book 3)

A dead body. A mysterious murder. A serial killer on the loose. A taxi driver is found murdered in a remote part of Exeter. He is a family man, no enemies to be found. There is no physical evidence, except for dozens of fingerprints inside the cab. How will DS Peter Gayle ever track down his killer?

Then another cab driver is found dead. Now this isn't just a case of one murder but a serial killer on the loose, once again…

Nowhere to Run: The Dark Side

The other side of the mirror from DS Pete Gayle's investigation in Book One of the series, Nowhere to Run – this is The Dark Side. A young girl is snatched from right outside her school.
While she fights to survive in the clutches of her abductors, her family is ripped apart by guilt and recriminations. And, with no demand or even a message to go on, they are forced to rely on the police to find her. But not even the officer in charge of the case is aware until it's too late of just how close he is to the kidnappers.

The Venus Flaw

Murder and corruption in the Maltese government combine with the concealment of a horrific secret in a minefield of intrigue and violence.

When Dan and Wendy Griffin find a cave full of prehistoric artwork on the coast of Malta they are plunged into a living nightmare. Someone is trying to keep something hidden, but who? And what? Unable to trust the police or the British Embassy and with no clues other than the cave itself and the fact that one of the men trying to keep them from it works for the National Security Service, they must try to figure out what is going on before one or both of them are killed.

Made in the USA
Columbia, SC
09 June 2025